DEAD
HAPPY

DEAD HAPPY

JOSH SILVER

DELACORTE PRESS

All rights reserved. Published in the United States by Delacorte Press, an imprint of Random House Children's Books, a division of Penguin Random House LLC, New York. Originally published in paperback in the United Kingdom by Rock the Boat, an imprint of Oneworld Publications, London, in 2024.

Delacorte Press is a registered trademark and the colophon is a trademark of Penguin Random House LLC.

Visit us on the Web! GetUnderlined.com

Educators and librarians, for a variety of teaching tools, visit us at RHTeachersLibrarians.com

Library of Congress Cataloging-in-Publication Data is available upon request.
ISBN 978-0-593-81206-8 (hardcover) — ISBN 978-0-593-81206-8 (ebook)

The text of this book is set in 11.5-point Adobe Garamond Pro.

Editor: Kelsey Horton
Cover Designer: Sylvia Bi
Interior Designer: Michelle Canoni
Production Editor: Colleen Fellingham
Managing Editor: Tamar Schwartz
Production Manager: Natalia Dextre

Printed in the United States of America
10 9 8 7 6 5 4 3 2 1
First American Edition

The Ten

hotmuthafker14

I used to like video games.

Dad bought me a PlayStation when I was fourteen. It was secondhand, but I didn't tell anyone that.

All the other boys in my year played *Fortnite*. They would join these "squads" and play together. At first, I thought they all went to each other's houses and sat around the TV in a group, which sounded horrific. But then I found out they *didn't* do that. They were doing it in their own bedrooms. Separately.

And I remember thinking I could probably make friends if I could sit in my room, alone. That sounded . . . much easier than making friends in real life. So I told Dad that and he got me the PlayStation.

I practiced doing the solo games. Then, after weeks of practice, I was ready to join a squad. I thought I was good enough. I also thought, *I can be someone else.*

I opened the box with the headset that you talk to the other players through. It had lights that flashed and was covered in camouflage graphics like I was about to crawl into combat in the jungle. As I stood in my bedroom and put it on, readying myself for battle, Mum waved at me from the landing, beaming with hope, *pride.*

Have fun making friends, Seb, she mouthed.

I shut the door and loaded up the game. I chose this banana guy as my avatar. It seemed more robust than the others, what with its thicker skin and all. And it looked so *cool.*

I chose the player name new-on-here!234.

Then I had this weird giddy moment and I changed it. I changed the player name to hotmuthafker14.

My hands were shaking as I gripped the controller. My banana stood waiting in the load-up lobby, doing a strange little dance with its backpack full of weapons, and my whole body fizzed with the thrill of the unknown.

One by one, other people joined the squad and started talking to me through the headset. They said, "Hey, hot motherfucker fourteen, nice to meet you."

I said "Nice to meet you" back. And they laughed.

As the voices of these random fourteen-year-olds (I mean, I assume that's what they were) called me "dude" and "bro" and said things like "Let's go pow pow some bitches," something happened.

I felt happy.

It was a little odd at first, sure. Joining a group of (apparent) fourteen-year-olds to try and kill other groups of (apparent) fourteen-year-olds, while disguised as cats and superheroes and bananas with faces, was definitely within the realm of anxiety-inducing. It was us, but not us. And we were killing each other. But not.

The whole thing was so far removed from everyday life. It was so much *easier*. Because it was all allowed. It was OK for me to be hotmuthafker14. In fact, it was pretty normal.

Normalized Banana Killing.

My parents didn't mind. My sister, Lily, didn't mind. My friend Shelly minded, but that's Shelly for you. She said I'd turn into a brain-dead zombie with no personality. But I thought the complete opposite was true.

Hotmuthafker14 had a great personality. People liked him. They liked me.

And I got good at it. Really good. At both the game and being liked. After one game, I was named the Ultimate Sniper King by some angry Scottish person called anonymousbadboi46 for my skill with the bolt-action rifle. I could do head shots and kill in one, which he really appreciated.

I lived in that world for months and months. I made friends through my camo headset and said things like "bro" and "Wow, your building skills are sick" to complete strangers. Well, not *complete* strangers. But people I'd never met and probably never would.

I was able to hear people laugh at what I had to say. To hear them tell me I was "cool as shit" and that without me they would've lost the game. That I was the Most Valuable Player. And I agreed with them. I had built myself an armor. An armor of strength, attitude, and confidence, all while sitting cross-legged on my bedroom rug at two a.m. in my paisley briefs. On a school night too.

Then one day the PlayStation broke. I didn't want Dad to pay for another one, so I lied and told him I didn't like it, and that the other players could be rude and swore a lot. But I really missed it. I missed being in that world where things were different. Weird and potentially very *bad*, but different all the same.

Once it was gone, I understood something. I realized that I didn't like reality very much. It was the first time I could articulate such a thing. That it can be real to not like reality. To not feel comfortable in it. To not feel safe in it. Because in the game, I did.

The game showed me how else I could feel. Powerful and strong and . . . *other.* Which was all so new. So exciting. So freeing.

And the comparison made reality so much worse. Because I saw that in reality there are much scarier things than sniper-shooting avatars. There are real people with their opinions. Their ability to look at me, really look at me. Look into my soul and see me. See the truth and then think with their real brains and talk with their real words about what I really am. Or what I'm not.

So what I guess I'm saying is the whole PlayStation experience amounted to a mini existential crisis. When I really thought about what all of this meant, the core of the matter was this:

I, Sebastian Harry Seaton, would prefer to be a cartoon banana.

ONE

Dead Fish

I can smell dead fish. And blood. Putrid. Metallic. Mingled with salty air.

"Seb! *Move.*"

Fragments of memory begin to circle. The HappyHead building. Sterile and white. A video playing in the assembly hall. The coach. A bitter pill. A blindfold pulled over my eyes.

The ground lurches beneath me. A hand on my shoulder. *"Come on . . ."*

I'm sitting on the floor. Something is moving around me in the darkness. Something wet. Seeping into the fabric of my clothes, my shoes, weighing me down.

"What's the matter with you, Seb? Get up!"

The voice is loud and comes from right next to me. I open my eyes, but the darkness remains. The elastic of the blindfold cuts into the tops of my ears.

The memories keep coming. A boy. Blistered hands. A bee tattoo.

Suddenly the blindfold is pulled from my head.

Light flickers. On and off. Blazing white. Then back to pitch-black.

"I—" My voice tears against my throat. "I can't—"

Creaking. More shouting. Crying.

Hands push my chest, forcing me back. My arms twist, searing with pain.

I'm tied to a pipe jutting out from the wall.

The hands pull at the rope around my wrists. Fingers fumble with a knot. Shaking. Bloody.

"Guys! It's getting deeper!"

Blazing white. Pitch-black.

"Seb, you need to help me here, for God's sake!" I focus on a pair of eyes—bloodshot and filled with terror. A trickle of red runs down the side of the girl's face, over her dirty cheek. I hardly recognize her. Blond hair sodden and filthy. Green hoodie torn.

Eleanor?

She bites down on the rope and pulls with her teeth like an animal. The knot begins to loosen. As it does, I wriggle my arms, pulling them down to free them. My hands slide out, red raw.

"What the . . ."

She turns to me, eyes wild. "Focus, Seb. *Focus.*"

In the flickering light I see snapshots of rusty walls. A long metal room. Figures steadying themselves, hunched over, half submerged.

Water. Water everywhere. Knee-deep now.

"It's filling up," she says, breathing heavily. "Here." She holds out her hand, and I take it. "We need to help the—"

The ground rocks again, and she's thrown into me, slamming us both into the wall. The air is knocked from my lungs, and I buckle forward. As the room tilts, the water swells and crashes over us. The weight of it forces me down, the burning cold tearing into my brain. For a moment, I'm suspended, floating, weightless.

Move. I twist my body and feel for the floor with my feet. *There.*

I push myself up, breaking through the surface, inhaling gulps of freezing air.

"Help! Please! Help me!" someone screams. I spin around to see two people crouched by the opposite wall. *I remember them from before. From the facility. The twins.*

Li is pulling at the arms of her sister, whose head is below the waterline, her dyed-blue hair floating above her.

"The knots are too tight!" Li screams. "Get up, Jing, *please!*"

I thrash toward them. "Let me try!" I plunge underwater and fumble in the murkiness to find the end of the rope that's tied around her waist. I follow it with my hands and locate the knot, somewhere near her back. Then I dig in my nails and pull until it feels as if they might snap off.

Come on, come on.

The rope loosens, and she begins to wriggle free. My lungs pound in my rib cage. *My inhaler. Where is it?*

When I break through the surface, my body doesn't feel like it's my own.

Jing pulls herself up, gasping, and leans back against the wall.

"You're OK. *Breathe.*" Li pushes the hair out of her sister's eyes.

"What the hell is happening?" Jing splutters.

I look behind me, and for a moment, the light holds for long enough for me to see nine other teenagers cowering against the metal walls.

The Ten.

"Is everyone free?" a voice booms out. Man-Bun Boy—Sam. His eyes dart around the group, counting. Then he nods.

My brain throbs. Voices enter it from around me, words struggling to find meaning.

"How do we get out?"

"Everyone, just take a second. This is clearly a challenge. We need to think."

"Search the walls—there must be a door."

I run my fingers over the coarse rust, fumbling for something, *anything.* . . .

Someone joins me, breathing in shallow sobs.

Lucy. *Lucy. She was always so nice.* . . .

"Seb," she whispers. "There's nothing—"

A bang. More screams. The light above us explodes and sparks fly, showering down over the water.

Darkness. I feel the water swirling around my waist.

"What now?" Matthew Parry-Brokingstock. His voice is strained with panic.

Something catches my eye from above. As my eyes adjust, I see the outline of a square of light.

"Look! Up there!"

"It's a hatch," I hear Raheem say from somewhere close by.

"How do we get to it?" Jing asks.

"Lift me," Ayahuasca Girl—Rachel—shouts, and I can just make out her outline wading into the center of the room.

A hulking figure joins her. Fridge Boy—Jamie. He picks her up, places her on his shoulders, and maneuvers himself under the hatch. "This had better work. . . ."

Rachel runs her hands over the ceiling.

"There! You've got it!" Raheem yells.

She can just about reach. She pushes.

"Hurry up!"

"All right! It's really heavy. . . ."

She struggles, nearly toppling back down into the water. Then, all of a sudden, the hatch creaks open and a shard of light pours in. She slides it to the side, revealing a square of sky. A gust of wind blows down, whistling around us.

"Easy now, Rachel." Jamie steadies himself as the room tilts again.

"Give me a push," she calls down to him.

He lifts her legs so her head rises up through the square hole.

"Holy shit!" Rachel's voice echoes down to us.

"What is it?"

Her head reappears. "A boat. We're on a fucking boat."

TWO
Bad, Bad, Bad

Rain whips into my cheeks, and the harsh tang of petrol fills my nostrils. As I try to pull myself up through the hatch, my legs dangling beneath me, the muscles in my arms shudder uncontrollably. The weight of my body is about to drag me back down, when Jamie gives my feet a shove.

I jolt forward. My hands slip.

Crack. My chin slams against the deck.

"Get him up."

Feet scurry into my vision; then I'm heaved upward and dragged across the deck, sliding along the grimy wooden panels until I'm dumped down onto a heap of fishing nets.

I spit. Blood.

Someone sits me upright. Raheem. "Arms up, mate. Quickly."

He pulls something over my head, clipping it around my waist.

A yellow life jacket. My name written on the front. Below it, a smiling HappyHead face.

My stomach drops.

"You OK?" Raheem says. "You good?"

I nod.

I watch the chaos happening around me. Panicked faces and flailing limbs, obscured by lashing rain. One by one the rest of the group is lifted up through the hatch and scrambles to get the life jackets scattered across the deck. Matthew and Sam then lean down and pull Jamie out.

Move. I drag myself up.

A captain's shelter stands at the boat's top end. I crawl toward it, hoping there might be some instructions, some*one*, inside. When I reach it, I steady myself on the window ledge, paint flaking loose in my hands. Through the single pane of glass I can just make out a large steering wheel in the gloom. A dashboard. A stool.

Empty.

The deck creaks, sending tremors up into my legs. The window frame vibrates.

I realize two things in quick succession. One: we are alone on this boat. Two: it is sinking. Sinking into the water, the actual *sea*. The reality of it makes my brain feel thin, stretched. Like it might snap.

How did we get here? I don't remember getting here. . . .

I notice my reflection in the cloudy glass. Gray. Half dead. A crack appears, creeping its way across my face, cutting me in two.

"Seb!" Eleanor shrieks. "Get away from that!"

I edge toward the side of the boat and reach for the metal handrail, but my fingers struggle to grip. They're swollen. Unnaturally white.

I peer down into the water. Black. Foaming. Alive.

Shit. This is bad.

Bad, bad, bad.

I turn my back to the churning sea and scan my eyes across the deck. They're all here. The Ten. Clinging to the railings, blinking the rain out of their eyes. The HappyHead face smiling at me from their chests.

"What now?" Lucy looks to me for an answer.

"It's sinking." I hear how emotionless my voice is.

"We need to work together," Sam yells. "A team. That's what they'll want to see. Everyone just think for a second. . . ."

"Yeah, let's take our time. Great plan," Matthew says. I can see his lip trembling.

"What's *your* idea?" Sam snaps.

"Surely someone's coming?"

"Let's look for some kind of distress signal!"

"The life jackets have whistles. . . ."

Whistles shriek through the air. The noise makes my head spin. I try to block it out, to think like HappyHead wants us to, but I can't pull my thoughts together.

"They're not coming! We need to figure out what they—" I start to say, but no one listens.

Water begins to bubble up from the hole in the deck, spilling out around our feet. I raise my head up to the sky and watch the vapor escaping my lips, merging with the swirling clouds above. I want to disappear. To evaporate into them. To be carried off in their vastness and taken somewhere far away. Anywhere.

No. Not just anywhere. *To him.*

A pain ignites in my chest, clawing at my throat.

Where are you? I need you.

And then I see something yellow in the periphery of my vision. A flag. High on a pole jutting from the back of the boat, streaking out in the wind. Words painted on it in big black letters.

FIND THE FIRE
FIRST COUPLE WINS
☺

I gesture to Eleanor across the deck. *Look up.* She spots it and stares.

Eleanor. My match. Oh, God. I'd almost forgotten. . . .

She then looks straight at me. Widens her eyes. *Don't tell them. . . .*

I ignore her.

"Guys. Stop. Stop!" I scream, waving my arms. "Look! The flag!" I feel Eleanor glaring at me as everyone turns their head. The words slowly register on their faces.

"The *fire*?" Matthew says. "What the hell does that mean?"

For a moment, no one speaks. We look around as if flames might burst from the deck.

"Over there!" Jing's voice rings out. She points across the waves toward a mass of land, shrouded in the gray haze. *Land.* On the shoreline, a bonfire flickers in the wind.

And I remember. They said we were going to an island. *Elmhallow.*

I hear an almighty crash. The window in the cabin has shattered, shards of glass now litter the deck.

"Come on!" Jamie yells, grabbing Rachel by the arm.

Suddenly Eleanor's face in mine. "What are you doing? Don't just stand there!" She grabs my hand and pulls, but my feet don't move. "What's wrong with you, Seb? Don't you want to *win*?"

I blink.

She cocks her head, then leans forward and whispers into my ear, "Remember what I did for you. *I saved you.* I gave you your chance back. Don't you dare ruin this."

My chance for what? Happiness?

I blink again. "You're bleeding."

She touches her head. "I'm fine." As she looks at the red on the tip of her finger, the faintest shadow of fear crosses her face. She snaps her head up. "We're wasting time." And the shadow is gone.

Then she's pulling me to the side of the boat and we're climbing up onto the handrail. I wobble, looking down into the inky black.

"Ready?" she yells, taking my hand. "Now!"

Together we plunge into the water. The cold explodes into me, smashing the oxygen from every cell of my body. The life jacket pulls me up, and my head surfaces.

Breathe.

In. Out. In. Out. *Come on.*

There's a loud splash next to me, then another, as the couples begin to launch themselves into the water.

I see Eleanor up ahead of me, fighting through the waves.

"Move, Seb!" she gasps.

I start to swim. Away from the others, toward her.

I kick and kick and kick. My shoes and clothes dragging at me, pulling me down. I swallow mouthful after mouthful of water. My body numbs. The cold fizzles away.

My muscles burn and a ringing in my ears takes over, but I

keep my eyes on the fire. As it slowly grows closer, it reminds me of something. The end of someone's cigarette, burning.

His cigarette.

Finn's.

My mind locks onto this image. His hair, his smell. His ice-blue eyes. Rough fingers, gentle on my skin.

What have they done to you?

Breathe.

There is a way to get out. To stop all this. To stop Professor Manning and her Never Plan. To get Finn back. She took him away at the facility, but we have Dr. Stone. She'll know the answer. He will be OK.

I have to believe that.

Stay strong, Stone said on the pager she gave me. *See you at Elmhallow.* I can try to message her. . . .

A rush of panic surges inside my skull.

The pager. I stop dead in the water and feel for my pockets.

No. *No.*

"What are you *doing*?" Eleanor treads water a few yards ahead.

I dunk my head beneath the surface and scream into the blackness.

THREE
Dancing Queen

When I reach the shore, I dig my hands into the rough shingle and pull myself forward out of the water. My body thumps down hard onto the beach. I focus on the bonfire up ahead, feeling its heat as it pumps black smoke into the gray sky.

Warmth.

Eleanor is already there, silhouetted by the flames. She's the first to have made it.

"*Hurry,* Seb!"

I push myself up and take a moment to stand and inhale the cold air. More memories start to emerge, becoming less like a series of snapshots and more like . . .

Reality.

I am here. This is real. And this is awful.

How could I be so stupid? The pager was our only way out of this. Our only chance to escape.

Finn. Where are you?

"Come on!" Eleanor screams.

I want to scream back that I heard her the first time.

Suddenly there's a piercing yell from behind me. I whip my head around. The noise has come from Raheem. He's pulling Lucy out of the water, dragging her onto the beach.

She looks strange. Unnaturally limp. No life jacket.

Behind them, the other couples are beginning to emerge. Drenched and spluttering, they wade their way up onto the rocky shore.

The boat is nearly fully submerged now. The yellow flag and the top of the cabin the only things visible above the waves.

"Why are you stopping, Seb?"

Jesus, Eleanor.

"Someone help!" I watch as Raheem lays Lucy flat on her back. Her limbs flop around like she's broken. Something's not right. *She doesn't seem right.*

Matthew pulls Jing past them, grabbing at her arm. "We did it!" he yells as they reach the fire.

Jing yanks her arm free.

"What are you doing?" he barks.

"I think Lucy's in trouble," Jing replies, turning back. "She needs help. Come on!"

Jing and I run over. We drop down next to her.

"What happened?"

"I don't think she clipped her life jacket on correctly. . . ." Raheem's voice trembles. "It came off." He takes Lucy's face in his hands and begins to shake it. "Lucy!" he cries. "Lucy!"

"She needs rescue breaths," Jing says.

"What?"

"Mouth-to-mouth. She's not breathing!"

Lucy's skin is paper white, the edges of her lips blue, like she's sucked on the end of a ballpoint pen.

Not good. Not good at all.

Jing leans forward over Lucy's face, tilts her chin back, and begins to blow into her mouth. I feel the others gathering around us.

Jing blows again, but nothing happens. She lifts her head and looks at me. "Chest compressions, Seb. Now!"

I fumble my hands forward to the middle of Lucy's chest, pretending I know what I'm doing. I begin to pump them up and down.

"Harder!"

I put one hand on top of the other and push, leaning my weight right into Lucy. I can feel her ribs springing beneath my hands.

Is she going to die?

"Jing, how many?"

"Keep going!"

"Come on, Lucy," Raheem whimpers, tears streaming down his face.

"Faster, Seb!"

"I'm trying. . . ."

"You need to do it to a rhythm. Two every second."

"What?"

"Use a song."

"What song?"

" 'Stayin' Alive.' "

"What?"

"Move your hands to the rhythm of the song. You need to be faster, Seb!"

"I don't know it! Does someone else want to—"

" 'Dancing Queen' by ABBA?"

Oh, I know that one. The tune, anyway. I start to hum the chorus in my head, my hands moving to the beat.

Mmm mmm mmm—mmm mmm mmm. Mm mm mm mmm mm mm mmmm . . . Ooo ooo ooo—

"That's better," Jing says.

My arms begin to throb. For a second I leave my body and I'm floating above, watching from the sky. The magnitude of what's happening hits me. A bunch of teenagers on a deserted island, trying to save someone's life to the soundtrack of '70s disco.

Suddenly I feel Lucy's body twitch beneath my fingers and she begins to cough.

"Turn her!" Jing shouts. "Turn her on her side!"

The others bend down to help.

Once she's on her side, Lucy vomits all over the shingle. Jing uses her fingers to scoop the vomit from her mouth. She bangs Lucy on the back and more dislodges, causing chunks to fall out onto her chin.

"That's it, Lucy," Jing says, rubbing her shoulder. "Well done!"

"Oh my God, Lucy. Are you all right?" Li asks.

Lucy pushes herself up on her arms, dribbling yellow and brown. She wipes her mouth. "What the hell?"

She looks up at us, eyes bloodshot.

"You nearly drowned."

"Right. Nice," she says, oddly calm. Then she grasps the sides of her face. "My head."

"You need to get warm," Jing says. "Let's get you to the fire."

I sling one of her arms around my shoulder while Raheem takes the other. We stumble up toward the bonfire—*who lit that?*—where Eleanor and Matthew stand staring. We lay her down in front of it.

"She OK?" Matthew asks, hovering sheepishly.

"Yeah, no thanks to you." I hear the words escape my lips.

"What was that?"

"I said *no thanks to you*. You just ran straight past her."

"I didn't know she'd *drowned*," he says, his hands in the air, relinquishing any responsibility for his shitty choices.

"Guys, just leave it. Is everyone here?" Sam does another head count. "Good. Let's just take a second, OK."

We huddle around Lucy, attempting to keep the wind off her trembling body. The heat from the fire tingles my cheeks as I look around the group, at the faces of the Ten. The top five couples who've been selected to move forward in the program.

Jing with her dyed-blue hair, her sister, Li—hers green— standing next to each other, poised, focused. Behind Jing is her match Matthew, sulking stupidly. Sam stands tall, protective behind Li. Jamie has his barrel arm around Rachel, who is leaning her head into it. Raheem is kneeling beside Lucy. He takes her hands and rubs them in his.

I look over to Eleanor. My match. She stands slightly away from the rest of us, her arms folded. Like she's *annoyed*. I can see she's fighting the instinct to speak. Then it overtakes her. "So . . . who won?"

It's confirmed. She's a complete, raging psychopath.

"I don't think it matters now," Rachel says.

"Just wondered. Since it was a challenge . . ."

"Yeah," Matthew chimes in. "Didn't the flag say the first couple to find the fire would win? Who was first?"

"I was," Eleanor says.

"We were the first *couple*," Matthew argues.

"Please just stop talking," Jing says.

Silence falls. I can't tell if the others are thinking what I'm thinking. That this still feels like a very bad situation and we should probably get Lucy to a hospital because she looks like she just died.

Technically, she did.

I turn to Jing. "Where did you learn all that?"

"We used to be lifeguards. Kids' classes," she says, her eyes still fixed on Lucy.

"Oh, right. Well, you were amazing."

"Thanks."

"Will she be OK?"

"She needs to go to the hospital," Li says quietly. Jing nods.

"Yeah," I say. "I thought that. . . ."

I look around, as if trying my best to find one, and I see the beach clearly for the first time. Long and bleak. Jagged rocks stick up everywhere, spiky tufts of grass poking out from between them. They congregate, creating a slope that leads up to the top of a low cliff that juts out above our heads, shrouded in mist.

"Is someone coming, do you think?" Jamie asks, sounding less sure of himself than usual.

"Maybe we should go look for help," Raheem says.

Then I hear something. It sounds like *music.*

"Guys, can anyone else hear that?" My eyes follow the line of the grassy slope.

There are two people standing there. Staring down at us. A girl and a boy. Probably a little older than we are. Both dressed in yellow cloaks that billow around them in the wind, hoods up over their heads.

They are holding lamps. But that's not the weirdest thing. The weirdest thing is that they are *singing.* Their voices sound thin on the wind, but I can see their lips moving in unison. I can hear them harmonizing, and it's not English. It sounds old, like Celtic or something.

"Hey!" I shout, waving my arms. "We need help down here! Someone's hurt!"

The others notice them too.

"Hey! Help us!"

"We have an emergency down here!"

"Who are *they*?" Eleanor says, eyes wide.

Together, the two figures turn, ignoring us, and walk away over the grassy mounds, back into the mist.

OK. That was . . . *What was that?*

I look at the others, all staring up with their mouths wide open.

"So what do we do now?" Jamie asks.

Don't say "follow them." This is literally how the worst kind of horror films begin.

"It's obvious," Sam says. "We follow them."

FOUR
A Higher Purpose

Two lanterns drift ahead in the swirling mist as we make our way across the island. I'm still out of breath from scrambling up the rock face to follow them. From here, the Couple look like phantoms floating above the uneven ground. They remind me of those twins from *The Shining*. The dead ones.

There's something unsettling about the way they move. Delicate but purposeful, like they have somewhere important to be but will just casually float their way there and probably murder someone along the way.

They're still singing.

The lanterns grow dimmer as we lag behind, and we have to pick up our pace in order not to lose them entirely. The wind whips against me, pushing me back. My clothes are sodden. Everything hurts.

I close my eyes and picture a log fire, his arms wrapped around me. . . .

"Seb! Keep up!"

The ground is peaty, an endless bog. I lose one of my Vans and have to stop to search and dig it out, fighting against the gurgling mud. It feels alive beneath my feet, desperate to drag me down into its depths.

Finally I catch up to the group, and we shuffle forward, taking turns supporting Lucy.

Now and then Sam runs on ahead, returning to tell us the direction the spirits have taken. It's almost as if he's enjoying this. He spurs everyone on, saying things like "Yes, team" and "We got this."

As we continue, I can only make out brown earth and mist in every direction. Nothing like the video at HappyHead. I remember the aerial shots of the island—all crystal waters and lush green grass. . . .

This is the complete opposite. *Liars.*

The two lanterns suddenly stop moving.

"What's going on?"

"They've stopped."

"No shit."

"So . . . do *we* stop?"

"Let's just keep going."

"They're so *weird.* . . ."

"Shh, they'll hear you."

A gust of wind momentarily clears the mist around them, and I realize they're standing beneath a huge tree. Its broad trunk slants over their heads as if it's spent years resisting the battering winds that have tried to topple it.

A wooden sign is nailed to the trunk, a single word carved into it.

Twisted branches, black as death, hang above the Couple, creating a dark, webbed canopy. Directly beneath the branches a ring of lanterns rests on the ground, lighting up a circle of five large white stones. In the center is a firepit full of unlit logs.

A little farther out, I see two long wooden huts, like cattle sheds, with tiny windows and low doors. And farther away still, cloaked in the mist, is a small brick shed without any windows. Just one big iron door, padlocked shut.

That *definitely* wasn't on the video.

The singing stops. I almost preferred it before—the silence is horrible.

"Let's go," Sam says, a little more cautiously.

We support Lucy as we make our way toward the Couple. They stand watching us, holding their lamps.

"Hey!" Raheem calls. "Are you going to help us?"

"Lay her down here." The girl points to the ground beside the firepit. She lowers her hood, and her face shines like porcelain, her green eyes gleaming. Two long auburn plaits fall in front of her robes. There's a hippie vibe about her—a little dreamy, a little disheveled, but sort of . . . model-like. Like she's just been to Glastonbury with her famous mates.

But this isn't Glastonbury. And she doesn't appear to have any mates. Just him.

When the boy lowers his hood, I see his face is all chiseled, with stubble and shoulder-length brown hair. He reminds me of someone. Either the picture of Jesus on Mum's dressing table or that serial killer Charles Manson. I can't decide.

They're like some freakishly beautiful rural power couple.

As we head toward them, into the middle of the stone circle, the Couple dart their eyes over us, studying our every move. We lay Lucy down gently beside the firepit.

OK, what now?

"Sit in your pairs," Jesus Boy says.

Jing looks at him. "Don't we need to—"

Glasto Girl holds up her hand. "Sit with your partner." There's an edge to her voice that sends a chill through me. It doesn't quite fit with the softness of her face.

Eleanor grabs my arm. "Come on, Seb. Let's take this one." She pulls me down onto the nearest stone, then shuffles over so the side of her body is pressed firmly into mine. "God, I hope Lucy's OK."

Do you? Do you *really*, Eleanor? You were willing to let her die on the beach earlier.

I turn to her. She still has a faint trace of blood in her hair from the boat. "They're both so . . . *interesting*," she says. "Isn't this *exciting*?"

That's not the correct word for this, Eleanor, no.

I watch as the other pairs take their places on the stones around the firepit.

Rachel and Jamie.

Li and Sam.

Matthew and Jing.

Raheem on his own, looking down at Lucy.

"Baffling" is the word I would use. "Concerning."

Silence. More silence.

Perhaps they'll sing again. Why are they just staring?

"Sorry, but aren't you going to say something?" Raheem finally asks. He has a point.

"Hello?" Jamie waves his hands at them like they're stupid.

I'm pretty sure these people are not stupid. Not stupid at all.

They don't respond. Instead they turn and glide toward the base of the tree, where there's a stack of wooden crates. Taking them one by one, they set them down on the ground beside Lucy. Jesus Boy opens one to reveal pots of dried leaves and colored powders and seeds. He begins to mix them together with a couple of drops of oil, using his hands to churn them into a browny-green paste.

He scoops the gunk up with his fingers and holds it in front of Lucy's face.

"Eat," he says. "It will help."

Right. Sure. Lifesaving care in the form of crushed bark.

Raheem shuffles on his stone. "Are you . . . ?" He doesn't finish his sentence.

I could. Trained? Capable? Normal?

Lucy falters for a moment, then opens her mouth. God, she's brave. Jesus Boy pushes the paste into it. She gags. Her face is ash gray.

The others look on with a mixture of unease and complete bewilderment.

"I think she needs a hospital . . . ," Jing says.

"Please, do not speak."

Jesus Boy feeds Lucy more of the gloop, then shifts her closer to the firepit. Glasto Girl pulls out a large woolen blanket from another of the crates, wrapping it neatly around her shivering body. She then bends over the firepit, grinding together two pieces of slate to create a spark and blowing on some dry moss beneath the logs. Flames lap up like tongues, reaching into the air. She is ethereal. Otherworldly. But there's also something disturbing about her movements. Exact and made with complete conviction, like she's been doing this for years.

"She's so cool," Eleanor whispers.

We watch and wait as the color starts to return to Lucy's skin. Slowly she sits herself upright. "I'm OK," she says quietly. "I think I'm OK."

"Thank God!" Raheem bolts from his stone. He crouches down beside Lucy, putting his arms around her. Everyone starts to clap.

"Wow!" Eleanor gazes at the Couple. "Aren't they *amazing*?"

Again, not the word I'd choose.

Raheem looks up at them. "Thank you so much."

Jesus Boy nods, the creases between his eyebrows deep with thought. "She will be well, Raheem. The island will heal her. Now go to your seat."

Raheem puts Lucy's arm over his shoulder, and she hobbles to their stone.

I wonder if now is a good time to ask for a blanket. I can't feel my toes.

Sam raises his hand. "Sorry, but *who are you*?"

They turn to him, their movements completely aligned.

"I am Ares," Jesus Boy says.

"I am Artemis." Glasto Girl clasps her hands in front of her. "You must trust us more than you've ever trusted anyone before."

Ares and Artemis? Who comes up with this shit? Manning, no doubt.

"You are the chosen Ten." Artemis's eyes move over us all. "You are the Elite. And your journey here will be more important than anything you have done in your lives up to this point."

"You have been chosen for a higher purpose," Ares adds. Eyes meet around the circle. "The island will be your friend, if you let it. If you embrace it and all its power. That is what it wants." Why is he acting like these are ordinary things to say? "If you do not, it will turn against you." Oh, right. "You must show it the utmost respect."

Artemis steps forward, taking over again. *Have they rehearsed this?* "The very stones you sit on once formed the foundation of a monastery here on this island. *Elmhallow.* Named after this ancient tree that hangs over us, protecting us." She raises her hand. "Hundreds of years ago, a handful of devotees lived here in this incredible place and became as one. They found a way to exist in a place free from the restraints of the outside world, within the elements." It can't have been that incredible if it's now rubble. Just saying. "Together, they found the utmost contentment. They learned the art of benevolence. True, untainted goodness. From this stemmed great strength, real happiness, and pure love. You will learn that here. And then your love will become sacred, like ours."

They turn to each other.

And they kiss.

And it's really, really long. Uncomfortably long. Don't-know-where-to-look long.

When they eventually part, Ares smiles at Artemis and whispers something into her ear. He then looks back at us and his face darkens. "The island has some rules it wants you to adhere to."

Of course it does.

"Firstly, you must never leave the camp at night without one of us. This is imperative for your safety. Do you understand?"

Everyone nods.

"Secondly, you must put everything you have into your upcoming betterment trials and rituals."

Rituals?

Li raises her hand.

"Yes, Li?"

How do they know our names?

"What are those?"

"The trials will help you grow, like the one you have just done." More a near-death experience than a trial, but sure. "The rituals will help you *prove* to us that you are learning." Oh, cryptic. *Fun.* "The third and final rule: you will fall in love. That is what the island wants from you. Needs from you."

Love. My throat tightens. *Where are you, Finn?*

People look at their partners. Eyes flash with anticipation. Cheeks blush. Eleanor touches my hand.

Fuck my life.

"Each pair will now be given a gift." Artemis reaches into one of the crates and lifts out a wooden dish. "A vessel."

Vessel? It's a fruit bowl, Artemis. I've seen them in IKEA.

"These vessels will represent your partnership. They are made from the fallen branches of the tree above us." Or in a factory in Sweden. Mum has the same one on our dining table where she leaves apples to rot and mail she doesn't want to open. "You must fill it."

Artemis walks around the circle, placing a bowl at each couple's feet.

I look at ours. Something is etched into the side.

Eleanor nudges me. "So cute, isn't it?"

No. No, it is not.

"Fill it with *what*?" Jamie asks.

Ares holds up a stone. Green-black, flecked with deep red, about the size of a snooker ball. It looks *heavy*. "These." He turns it in his hand so it glints in the firelight. "Sacred bloodstones."

"Wow!" Eleanor gasps. "It's so pretty."

"They are incredibly rare, mined on this very island. Each of them represents core traits we want to see from you. Courage. Compassion. Faith." So no longer commitment, growth, gratitude, and obedience? OK . . . "You shall be rewarded sacred bloodstones for showing these traits as you undertake your trials and rituals."

Eleanor raises her hand. "So the first to fill their vessel . . . *wins*?"

Jesus, she can't help herself.

Ares looks at her. "When it is full, it means you have proven yourself to be ready. And you will leave."

Leave? What?

Is that the only way off this island? To find Finn . . .

Do they even know where he is? *Who* he is? Should I ask them? *No. Not a good idea.*

"You said ready?" Matthew asks. "Ready for *what*?"

"A life unlike any you could have dreamed of," Artemis says.

That's not *really* answering the question, is it?

"Cool," Matthew says, eyes wide.

"Game on, guys!" Sam chimes in.

I raise my hand.

"Yes, Seb?"

"Um. Hi. Yeah. So what happens if we *don't* fill it?"

Artemis smiles weirdly at me. *Why is she smiling like that? Why isn't she answering?*

Then Ares turns to face Jing and Matthew. Sacred snooker ball in hand, he walks toward them. "Jing and Matthew." He stops right in front of them and they lean back slightly. *Please don't bash their brains out with it.* "You were the first couple to reach the fire," he says. "And so the first sacred bloodstone is yours." He places the stone into their bowl.

Eleanor tenses. "I got there first," she protests, letting go of my hand.

"But more than that," Ares continues, "Jing, you showed great kindness with Lucy. Courage. Leadership. This strength is what we're looking for. You showed no fear." He places another stone in their bowl.

"Are you kidding me?" Eleanor mutters.

Jing smiles. "Wow, thanks!"

"You showed benevolence." Why am I starting to hate that word? People begin to clap.

Matthew puts his arm around her. "You did amazing."

"You deserve it," Lucy says.

I look at Li. Her face tenses for a moment. Fighting something. Jealousy? She forces a smile. "Well done, sis."

Eleanor suddenly leaps up. "Go, Jing! You're an inspiration!" she whoops, keeping her eyes on the Couple. Then she hisses out of the side of her mouth, "If you hadn't been so slow, that would have been us right now."

Artemis puts her hand in the air, silencing us. "Now for the welcoming ritual." Ritual. *Already?* "Put these on."

She hands us each a yellow cloak like the ones they're both wearing. We pull them around our bodies, and I glance around the circle. It's like a scene from one of those films where witches get burned at the stake. So that's encouraging.

I look at the Couple. Her, with her plaits. Him, with his jawline.

There's something in his hand. About the size of a pen. Its wooden handle engraved with swirls and markings, strange symbols that I don't recognize. A dagger.

Oh, God.

The blade gives off a sickening glint.

"The world we have come from is broken." Ares pauses, taking us all in, his eyes burning red in the firelight. "It ruined us. And it continues to ruin our young people. The pressures. The comparisons. The fears. On Elmhallow, it will be different. There are no distractions. No technology. No one else. Here, you can thrive. You are the first. You are so very, very special. You have what it takes; we know you do. It's why you were chosen." He lifts the dagger up in front of him. "We will now enact the Commitment Ceremony."

The *what?*

"You must now release yourselves from everything you have ever known. Let us commit to a new life." He turns to Artemis. She holds out her hand to him, and the blade hovers over her palm. "With this cut, we kill our old selves."

I watch the knife flash as he slices. She doesn't make a noise.

Doesn't flinch. Blood begins to trickle from her palm, down over her fingers, and onto the ground. Ares wipes the blade on his cloak, marking a streak of red across the yellow. Then he cuts his own hand.

They both stand with their bloody palms, facing each other.

"Artemis," Ares says softly. "I commit myself to this island. And to you."

She smiles. "And I, you."

FIVE
Blind Faith

The Couple faces each other, an inch apart. Chests heaving, eyes staring. We sit in our circle, shivering in our yellow cloaks over damp clothes, watching them.

And then something strange happens. They lift their hands up to each other's foreheads, and they begin to draw. With the blood.

"What are they doing?" Rachel whispers.

"Shh," Eleanor hisses.

When they turn back to us, I see two smiley faces. On their faces. Their foreheads.

The HappyHead smile. In thick, dripping red blood.

"All of you, now hold out your hands."

No one moves.

"Physical pain is nothing compared to the pain of being trapped in the old world," Ares says, his apparent girlfriend's blood now trickling into his eyebrows. "Of being unhappy. We must show ourselves, show each other, that we truly understand what this means."

I truly *don't* understand what this means. Any of this.

"Are you ready to show that you are willing to put the pain of your past lives behind you?"

Nope, nope, nope.

I look around the circle. Blank expressions. Fixed stares.

Eleanor shifts next to me. "We are," she says.

Before I realize what is happening, she's standing up with her hand stretched out in front of her, rolling up her sleeve.

"Wonderful," Artemis says. "We see your passion, Eleanor." Eleanor's cheeks flush pink as Artemis steps toward her. "You are showing something to be valued highly. Blind faith."

Artemis takes a strand of hair that has come loose from Eleanor's ponytail and tucks it behind her ear. "You are very special," she whispers.

"Yes," Eleanor says.

Yes?

Artemis takes her hand. Ares joins her and raises the blade above Eleanor's palm.

Isn't he going to clean that? No? "Are you ready, Eleanor?" OK, no he's not.

She nods.

He slices.

I watch the blood seep out of the cut in her hand. She closes her eyes. "Thank you."

Why is she thanking them?

They turn to me. "Seb? Will you unite with Eleanor?"

No. I absolutely will not.

"Seb?"

"Yeah? Hi."

"Are you afraid?"

I look at the dagger in Ares's hand pointing directly toward my chest. "Nope."

"This is no place for fear."

"I'm not scared."

"Then please stand."

Eleanor turns to me. She looks possessed. I hate it when she looks possessed. It's like she's trying to move me up off the stone with her eyes.

"Seb, we are waiting."

"Right, yeah." As I slowly stand, my legs feel weak. Shaky. Like they're hollow.

"Hand," Ares says.

I hold it out to him.

He grabs it, squeezing my wrist a little too hard. "Are you ready?"

"He's ready," Eleanor chimes in. "Aren't you, *sweetheart?*"

Ares keeps his grip firm. I stare into his eyes. They are open very wide. "We need to see that you care."

That I *care*? Of course I care. About my hand.

I hear Stone's voice in my head. Remember her message on the pager. *Stay strong.*

"OK."

The knife flashes. Slices.

It doesn't hurt. That's strange. . . . Oh, wait. Yes, it does. Holy hell. I clench my jaw. *Don't let them see you flinch.*

As I watch the blood spill out from the gash, I'm reminded of Misty back at the HappyHead facility. *Why are these people obsessed with cutting us open?*

"Well done, Seb. You are very special."

Just copy Eleanor. "Yes."

"Please, now commence the commitment. Mark each other as a sign of your commitment."

Eleanor turns to me. "I'm so excited to do this with you, Sebby. I give myself to this island and to you."

Is this a nightmare? There is no other explanation.

"Great," I say. Eleanor nods eagerly at me. "Oh, right. Yeah. And I, you."

Finn, where are you where are you where are you.

Eleanor lifts her hand up to my forehead and presses her finger into my skin. I gag. It's sticky. Like syrup.

Oh, God. I can feel the sick at the back of my throat.

Her finger moves slowly around my forehead, tracing a circle. Two dots for eyes. The swipe of a smile.

"Done!" She steps back, then closes her eyes and leans her head forward. "Your turn."

I flick my eyes to Artemis and Ares.

"Go on, Sebastian," one of them says. Right now I can't tell the difference. They're both the same. Both total nutjobs.

I look down at my trembling hand. I dip my finger into the blood on my palm, then lift it up. As I touch her forehead, she makes a noise. A gasp. Like she's experiencing some sort of *pleasure.*

I quickly draw the eyes, the smile. "Done," I say flatly.

Artemis speaks. "Seb and Eleanor, you are now bonded. United here." God, what is this? "Commitment, growth, gratitude, and obedience lead to a happy head."

Hearing the phrase again triggers a strange reaction in my body. It *warms* me, the familiarity of it making me somehow feel *safe*. Well, saf*er*. Like there's someone in charge of all this madness. Like there's a plan.

No. I push the feeling far down inside me. I drag the images of Finn and Stone back into my mind.

Artemis holds out a bandage. "We don't want it getting infected."

How kind. How thoughtful.

She begins to wrap our hands. As she does, I smell a sweetness on her that reminds me of someone. Citrus.

Manning. *I can feel her everywhere.*

The blood from my palm seeps into the bandage like a red cloud.

"We'll go next." Rachel and Jamie rise to their feet.

As the Couple makes their way around the Ten, slicing each of them in turn, I watch the others' faces. No one else gags. No one else nearly vomits. Ares wipes the knife after each cut, until his cloak looks like he's been in some horrific traffic accident.

Everyone does it. Everyone allows themselves to be cut. Red foreheads. Drippy smiles. Bandaged hands.

"And I, you."

"And I, you."

"And I, you."

"And I, you."

"Good," Ares says after each slice. "Well done."

When it's over, Artemis and Ares stand beside the fire and bow to us. We bow back.

"Beautiful!" Ares begins to laugh. "You are all so beautiful."

We begin to laugh along with him. The nervousness, the ridiculousness, the fear exploding out of us.

"Let it out!" Artemis shouts. "Be free. Be joyful!"

The laughter rises to a hysterical pitch.

"Goodbye, old me!" Ares yells. "Say it with me!"

"Goodbye, old me!" we all scream.

"I kill you!" *Huh?* "Say it! To your past self!"

"I kill you!" we all yell to our past selves.

"Good!" Ares shouts. "I'm impressed. Professor Manning chose well."

Manning.

"Now we shall enter our dwelling houses," Artemis says. *Dwelling houses?* These two seriously think they're from some ancient poem. "We shall be keeping you separate from your partners for now. Until the time is right."

The time is right? Right for *what?*

I see the others whispering. Turning to their partners. Flirtatious nudges.

"Don't worry, it *will* happen. But you must be patient. You will earn it."

It? What is it? What will happen? Is *it* sex? Because if it is, I'm—

"Seb," Eleanor says. "Can you imagine?"

Not even nearly, Eleanor.

"Um . . ." I'm starting to panic.

"Now, boys, follow me. Girls, follow Artemis. Say your good nights. We will meet again in the morning."

"What do we do with our bowls? *Vessels,*" Eleanor asks.

"Leave them in front of your stone."

Eleanor fixes her eyes on Jing and Matthew's bowl with its two greeny-black stones flecked with red glinting inside.

"You'd better up your game," she whispers, standing up. "We need those stones." She then turns and heads toward the line of girls following Artemis into their dwelling house, my blood dripping down her cheek.

As Ares leads us to our dwelling house, I watch them trying to talk to him.

"It didn't hurt me at all, you know."

"Will I get a scar? I think that's kind of cool."

"What happens tomorrow?"

"Will we all get a knife?"

Ares doesn't answer. When he gets to the door, Matthew holds it open for him.

"Thank you, Matthew."

Matthew does a little bow as Ares passes him. But when it's my turn to walk past, he puts his foot out so I trip.

"Oops," Matthew says, overtaking me.

As I step inside, I have to duck under the wooden rafters. The walls are made of thick brick. Six single beds run down the length of one wall, covered with patchwork blankets. There are small lights positioned above each one and each has a bedside table. A fireplace nestles in the wall opposite, giving off a warm glow.

"The washing facilities are through there." Ares points to a door at the end of the room. He then assigns us our beds. Ares has the one closest to the door, and I'm nearest the bathroom, with the others in between. They each have our names carved into their wooden headboards like something from a weird boarding school.

I'm told I can use the washing facilities first. As I enter, I try to lock the door behind me, but there isn't a lock, which is weird. I'm met with a small, dark room with a grate in the floor. A window with murky glass panels rattles in the wind. A toilet. A tap in the wall. Beneath it, a single bucket. Six rusty hooks.

On the hooks are fresh clothes. Not green this time. Red.

Red hoodies. Red pants. Six towels neatly folded on the floor beneath them. Six bars of soap. Six toothbrushes.

I go to the tap and turn it on. Freezing water spurts out. I take my cloak off, placing it on top of my mucky Vans. I remove my sodden greens.

I let the tap run to see if it will go warm. It doesn't.

I stand, naked, in the middle of the room and splash water over myself, using one of the bars of soap to scrub at the smile on my forehead.

I scrub and scrub and scrub. The water runs red. When I feel clean enough, I rub myself dry with the coarse towel and pull the new clothes on. *Reds.* I hang my cloak on the hook.

Back in the bedroom, I perch on the end of my bed while the others take their turn. On the bedside table, I see an inhaler and a medication box. My pills.

I open the box and take one.

I look at Ares across the room. He smiles at me. I smile back.

Then he slides his dagger under his pillow. I notice his strong brow and how his eyes beneath it don't change. They have that constant, fixed look. Doleful, like he's feeling something very deeply at all times and he wants everyone to know but won't talk about it.

Like it's too precious.

When everyone has finished using the Bucket Room, we sit at the end of our beds. Ares stands by the fireplace, facing us.

Matthew is the first to speak. "Ares, may I ask a question?"

"Of course, Matthew."

"Is Manning coming?"

"She will," Ares replies. "But we must make sure you are ready."

That word again. Ready. *Ready for what?*

"I will be," Matthew says.

"Good. And the rest of you? Brothers?"

We all nod.

"Good. Now to sleep." He flicks a switch, and the lights go out.

"Good night, brothers," Matthew says.

I lie back on the bed, pulling my blanket over my chest. I stare up at the wooden beam above, lit by the orange glow of the fire, and I follow the traces of the grain that run along it with my eyes.

I wait until I can hear everyone is asleep. Then I let myself think about him. Every part of him. I allow the memories to flood into me, to consume me. The image of him, of us. On the balcony, his wet hair, his tattoos—the bee, the lightning bolt. The smell of cigarettes. The glow of embers as he inhales.

In the fields on our way to find Stone. His face as I make him smile, laugh. The single sleeping bag. His touch on my body. His teeth showing between his lips when he smiles. The blisters on his hands. His eyes as he told me about his parents. Ice Eyes.

The way he dropped the shard of glass in the stairwell when I told him not to run. When I told him to trust me. The look on his face as they dragged him off the beach. Eleanor telling me how he has done things, terrible things. That he's bad.

Where is he? Is he even alive?

My cheeks are wet. My breathing becomes juddery and my chest heaves.

Stop. They'll hear you.

I push his image back down into the depths of myself, to the place where I've been keeping him. I focus again on the grain of the wooden beam, tracing the swirls, the irregular patterns. Then my eyes stop. There's something on the beam, directly above my head. A small, dark patch. *Ashy.* Like the end of a match has scratched it.

I lift myself up onto my elbows and squint. *What is that?*

My stomach jolts. Etched in the beam is the outline of a *bee.* A worker bee. The same shape as the one Finn has tattooed on his arm.

SIX

How to Be Good

There was this weird thing that happened at my church once, but no one ever talked about it. It was like this unspoken secret that had sunk into the walls—a stain that had been scrubbed away, but that everyone knew was once there.

There were four "core" families at the church. The inner circle. All the other families were desperate to be a part of the inner circle because they made important decisions, like what meat would be on the Christmas lunch menu and how the collection money would be spent. No one really knew what the collection money went on and the church was always freezing, so it wasn't on the heating like they said it was. There was an element of secrecy to the inner circle. Very *holy Illuminati* vibes.

Mum baked cakes for the core families in an attempt to get them to consider us worthy to join. Apparently you had to be asked. We were never asked.

The vicar was a man named Johnny. Pastor Johnny. He was young and trendy and very good-looking, which was unheard of when it came to the church leadership, so everyone absolutely loved him. He had this passionate way of delivering his sermons, gesticulating wildly, so his intentionally messy hair bounced enthusiastically on his head. He wore sneakers and had a tattoo.

He was a deeply holy man, but he was also *relatable*. He introduced a guitar and keyboard to the worship group, and he waved his hands in the air with his eyes closed when he was singing the songs. Before long, other people started to do the same. Mum said he had charisma. She had a massive crush on him.

So did I, to be fair.

I remember the day the thing happened. It was a typical Sunday, and the church congregation was full, fuller than it had ever been. People said that it was because of Pastor Johnny and his wife, Cara. Together they were a shining example, and the community was really responding to their new direction. It was current. Uplifting. These were the words I kept hearing.

Johnny did his sermon. It was about being faithful. Faithful to God, faithful to each other. People had taken to saying "Amen" and "Yes, Johnny" from the pews whenever he said something particularly inspiring. I actually tried it once, and Mum beamed at me like I'd done a wonderful thing. Like I'd evolved into someone more devout. Like a spiritual Pokémon upgrading.

Johnny was talking about the importance of a man loving his wife, when suddenly from the back of the pews a woman shouted, "That's rich."

Everyone went completely silent. I turned my head to see a young woman standing with her arms folded. I'd never seen her before.

"Can I help you?" Johnny asked.

"Are you for real?" the woman said. "You think you can stand up there and talk like that after what you've done?"

"Can someone help this lady outside, please?" Pastor Johnny finally said. There was shuffling in the pews, and some of the dads from the core families began to approach the woman. "I'll happily talk to you after the service. You are very welcome here," he said calmly.

The woman laughed. "Does Cara know?" I watched the back of Cara's head. She didn't turn around.

The men tried to usher the woman out of the church, and she began swearing and cursing and taking the Lord's name very much in vain until she was eventually removed.

"We need to pray for this woman," Johnny said. "If you would all join me. Cara?"

Cara got up and joined him at the front. The two of them stood behind the pulpit, and she held his hand. "Lord, we pray that this lady will come to know your grace and forgiveness. . . ."

And everyone *umm*ed and said "Yes, Johnny" and "Amen."

A rumor circulated that the woman had come from one of the hospitals and that she wasn't well. People felt sorry for Johnny, that this had happened to him. Cara was his biggest defender. She carried on supporting her husband, even more so than before. But after that, I noticed she never was the same. She looked . . . lost. Vacant.

But no one said anything.

I spoke to Shelly about it.

"That's the thing about cults," she started.

"My parents' church isn't a cult, Shelly."

"The followers will never accept that anything bad is happening. The leaders will blind them to the truth." She chewed intently on a Refreshers bar. "It's how they function. How they grow. How they keep people in line. I watched a documentary about it."

"Right."

"The leaders will try to break people. Like, break their *souls*. Their confidence. Destroy their sense of self."

"Jesus, Shelly."

"And when they are broken, that's when the followers start to really trust those in power. They have no choice. To them, there is no alternative. And that's when it gets *really* crazy. They'll try to seek the cult leaders' approval. To impress them. *Protect* them. Because by that point, they don't know who they are anymore. They've lost themselves completely."

Pastor Johnny still does the sermons at my parents' church. He still tells people how to be faithful. How to be good. People still love Pastor Johnny.

I told Shelly that there's something about him—the way he talks, the way he offers hope. Something that made his congregation forget the incident with the young woman in the pews. Or at least pretend to forget it.

"People are so sad," she said. "About their lives, about the state of the world, that when they're promised a fantasy version of reality, they'll keep believing it could come true. Sure, it makes them do weird and stupid things. But all they want is to feel something new." Then she looked up at me, still chewing her Refreshers bar. "And I guess, who can blame them?"

SEVEN
Ken Doll

I don't think I slept much, but I can't be sure. I haven't seen a clock since we left the HappyHead facility. Outside the window opposite my bed, the sky is turning pale violet. Nearly morning, I think.

At some point in the middle of the night, I heard noises outside.

Scratching. Banging. Like foxes rummaging.

Do remote Scottish islands have foxes?

Stop thinking, Seb.

But I have been thinking. I've been thinking a lot.

Even if it is a bee, it doesn't mean it's Finn. It could be some pagan symbol that just happens to be the same as the bee tattooed on Finn's arm. Or a nice design flourish to make the place feel cozy. It could be that the wood was imported from Manchester, where the worker bee symbol originates. I could be hallucinating. Wishing. Hoping for a sign.

I did think of one more explanation. That it's a trap. *Eleanor.*

She's the only one who knows about us. *Isn't she?*

She wouldn't tell. *Would she?*

After she saw us together in the basement corridor at the facility, she said that she wouldn't because she needs me. But she hates Finn. She was the one who told Manning it was him who broke into her office and tried to escape. She's the reason he's gone. And she's Manning's niece. What else has she told her aunt?

Enough.

I notice something on the floor by the fireplace that wasn't here last night. Newly chopped wood and a wicker basket with a loaf of bread and a bottle of milk poking out of the top.

Where did that come from?

Maybe Ares unwinds by preparing breakfast baskets in the dark. That does seem like the kind of thing he'd be into. He's harmless. Homey. Him and his little dagger.

I glance down the row of beds to where he is sleeping, and I see something else.

Black. Metal. Angular. Leaning against the wall next to his bed. A sheath full of arrows beside it. Bright yellow feathers at the end of each one.

A crossbow.

OK . . . Don't know what that's for. I don't have much of a reference point when it comes to lethal bows other than The Lord of the Rings. But in those books (OK, films, I pretend I read the books), things don't end well for people.

Why the hell is there a *crossbow*?

It's probably to defend us. Yes. Ares is going to defend us. *Protect* us. From all the threats of this island. Like the . . . foxes and stuff.

I should take a closer look, just to make sure. It could be a toy.

I can make out Ares's perfect face. Eyes closed, torso slowly rising and falling under his patchwork quilt.

I swing my legs over the side of the bed. As I stand, my head goes weird and everything around me swims. I suddenly realize I haven't eaten anything since we got here. I tiptoe over to the crossbow. It glints in the pale morning light. Its angles and edges make me feel sick. I turn my head. Ares is stirring.

Quick, make it look like you're doing something normal.

I creep as fast as I can back to the door of the Bucket Room and unlatch it. But when I go to lock it behind me, I remember that there's no lock. Still weird.

OK. Now what?

Using the bathroom is normal. *Just use the bathroom.*

I look around. It's been tidied. New bars of soap have been laid out, along with clean towels. On the floor underneath each hook I see freshly folded underwear and socks. I stick my head under the tap and drink as much water as my body will allow me to. When my brain goes numb, I gasp and pull my head up. I take a towel, dry my face, and pick up the clean boxers.

They have yellow HappyHead smiles repeating across them. I'd . . . *buy* these. If you remove all the context, they're actually pretty cool.

I change into them and ball up my old ones, but I'm not sure what to do with them, as there doesn't seem to be a laundry basket. I catch my reflection in the window. My pale torso, splotchy from the cold. The boxers are a tad short, revealing the eczema at the top of my thighs.

"Good morning, Sebastian."

Jesus Christ. I spin around, hiding my old boxers behind my back. "Sorry, Ares. Did I wake you? I needed to . . . take a piss."

He stares at me, eyes all wistful like he's just woken from a deep and significant dream. "You're allowed to use the bathroom, Sebastian."

"Great."

"You look nervous."

"Me? No."

His eyes trace my face. He doesn't speak. It appears he's attempting to have this conversation through eye contact alone.

"OK, cool." I become very aware that I'm only wearing the HappyHead underwear. "What time is it?"

"Time is not important here."

"Of course."

He puts his hand on his chin like he's thinking deeply. "What are you hiding, Sebastian?"

Shit. He knows. He knows everything. The bee. Finn.

"Hmm?"

"I said, what are you hiding?"

"Nothing."

"You're lying."

"I'm . . ." This whole thing is over. He's going to shoot me with his crossbow.

"I saw something in your hand."

"Oh, right!" Phew. "It's just these." I whip out my old boxers from behind my back. "My dirty—"

"I see."

I can feel the goose bumps spreading across my pale chest. "Um . . . so what should I do with them?"

"Just leave them in the corner. They will be dealt with."

Dealt with? They're not that bad. "OK, great." I throw them in the direction of the corner, but they land on the floor between us, all splayed out. "Thanks, Ares."

More staring. "Your leg."

My leg? I look down. I'm still wearing Stone's bandage from where I fell down the cliff, some crusty blood on its ragged edges. "Oh, that. It was from one of the assessments."

"Which one?"

"The Hide."

He nods. "Is there anything else you wish to tell me, Sebastian?"

"Nope! Loving this place. It's really, like, *earthy*. And I *love* these new boxer shorts." That part is true.

"How is your relationship with Eleanor?"

"Um . . . Yeah, I . . ."

"I have been told it is pure. Is it?" God. What kind of a question is that? Maybe I can answer with my eyes.

I open them wider. Nope. Not working. "I . . . Yes . . . Pure. Yep . . . but . . ." Stop talking.

"But what, Sebastian?"

Come on. "She's the first girl I've ever had these kinds of feelings for, and I'm trying to process them." He looks at me skeptically. "It's quite overwhelming to meet someone that makes you consider sort of . . . everything. Your place on this earth, you know? It scares me a little, I guess."

He waits. He stares. He knows I'm living a lie. I'm doomed. The island will kill me if this crippling eye contact doesn't do it first. He is without a doubt the most intense person I've ever met, and that includes me.

Finally he sighs. "I understand. You must *lean into it*. Show her you care. Show *us*."

"Right. Of course. Lean in."

He turns to leave.

I exhale. Goodbye, Intense Jesus.

Then he stops. "You saw the crossbow."

Oh, shit. "What? No. What do you mean?"

"I was going to move it before you all woke."

"It's nothing. Not a big deal."

"You look worried."

"Do I?"

"All will become clear. You are safe here, Sebastian."

"Brilliant."

"I see it." A pause.

"See what?"

"How much you have feared yourself in the past. How much you disliked yourself." Um. Too early for this. "So much trauma."

"Right."

"Promise me you won't slip back. This is the right path for you. I *know* it is. Prove it to us, and to yourself."

What the hell? "I'll try."

"Here, you will be free and your love with Eleanor will be truly unstoppable." Another pause. "You remind me a lot of my former self. I see you, Sebastian."

"I see you too." I do a silly little wave.

"No, Sebastian. I see *all* of you." I hope this isn't about my new boxer shorts being a little too tight. I cross my hands in front of them. When he speaks again, tears glisten in his eyes. "I see you for who you were. And for who you can be."

Just agree. He might leave. "I agree."

He stares. This is unbearable. For me, anyway. He seems to be loving it. He practically vibrates with unspoken emotion.

Change the subject. "Thank you for doing all of this."

"All of what?"

"The tidying. The breakfast. It looks lovely, thank you."

He smiles. "All will become clear." Again, so cryptic. "Go back to sleep, Sebastian. I will see you when you rise, for breakfast."

I decide to try something. "But you *already* see me! All of me!" Jokes are always good.

"Excuse me?"

"Um, nothing."

He then leaves. Finally. I wait for a while, trying to understand what just happened. When I go back into the bedroom, Ares is asleep and the crossbow is gone.

I'm woken by a rhythmic beat. A drum.

"What *is* that?" I hear Jamie say. I lower the blanket from over my head to see the boys gathered around the window.

"What are they doing?"

They run to the door, pulling on their Reds.

By the time I join them, the girls are all standing in the door-way of their dwelling house, whispering to each other. Lucy is there. She looks better, which is good.

Like them, I'm drawn to the sight of the Couple, who are by the firepit, bathed in sunlight. Artemis is sitting cross-legged in a white dress, flower wreath on her head, banging a little drum. In front of her is Ares. With his top off. *Fully* off. Wearing only a pair of white shorts, standing completely still, legs apart in a massive lunge. Arms in the air. Eyes closed.

Artemis puts a finger to her lips. "Shh. He is welcoming in the morning."

Ares bends forward, touching his toes. If by "welcoming in the morning," she means trying to split his shorts open, then I understand exactly what she means.

"Gather around," she says.

As we do, I trace my eyes over the outline of Ares's torso. His abs. His pectoral muscles, glistening with sweat. He reminds me of a Ken doll Mum once gave me as a compromise after I put Malibu Barbie on my Christmas list four years in a row. The only difference is Ares has nipples.

"Well, hello," Rachel murmurs, biting her lip.

"He's *ripped*," Sam says.

"Boys," Artemis says, her fingers still tapping away on her drum. "It is your duty to welcome in the morning with Ares. Join him."

Um. *What?*

"Like, *now*?" Matthew asks.

"Go on, lads," Rachel says. "Welcome in the morning." The girls all giggle.

Please, God, no.

Sam begins to pull off his hoodie. "I'll do it," he says. He drops it on the floor next to him. "I don't care."

The girls all stare. Well, of course *you* don't care. You look like you're on an Olympic swimming team.

"Me neither." Jamie takes his hoodie off too. His chest is like a barrel. His arms are wider than my head.

What is happening?

Then Raheem does the same.

Can people stop doing that?

He winks at Lucy. She blushes. She definitely doesn't look sick now.

The three of them join Ares, copying his movements as he turns and stretches, their muscles flexing in the morning sun.

"Well, this is fun," Rachel whispers as the girls sit cross-legged next to Artemis.

I stand with Matthew. Pretending this isn't happening.

"Come on, you two," Artemis says.

Matthew pulls his hoodie off. "I don't care either." He puffs out his little, shivering chest. He looks at Jing.

She smiles awkwardly at him, and his eyes widen in glee. He joins the boys. He looks so tiny next to them.

"Sebastian?" Artemis smiles at me. "Embrace this moment of liberation."

Oh, I'm sorry, I didn't realize I had woken up in hell. If hell had frozen over. It's so cold I can see my breath.

"On the island, we are free."

"Yeah," I say. "Free. Got you."

I look at Eleanor. She pouts at me. *Ugh.* I slowly lift my hoodie over my head and step forward, trying to stop my body from spasming with the cold.

"Seb?" Eleanor calls.

"Yep?"

"Are you leaving your tank top on?"

"Um . . ." I hear someone laugh. Oh, God. Flashbacks. PE changing-room flashbacks. "Yeah, I think I will. . . ."

"Aw . . ." She makes a sad face.

As I join the boys, I feel the girls' eyes on us. I can hear them saying things. Laughing.

Block it out. Just block it out.

I follow Ares's movements, circling my arms around my head to the rhythm of the drum like a stalling windmill.

"That's it," Ares says. "Really *feel* the energy moving around your body." He starts to hum.

"Join me, brothers," he says. "Hum with me."

I hear them all doing it. *Why are they doing it?*

"Mmmmmmm," I begin. My lips tingle.

"Good, Sebastian." He looks at me. "Do you *feel* the vibrations?"

I *feel* like a tit. I nod enthusiastically.

Eventually the drumming stops.

Ares bows, his hands pressed together in front of him like he's praying. "Good morning, Elmhallow."

"Good morning, Elmhallow," we repeat.

Ares smiles. "That was really peaceful."

I agree, if by "peaceful" he means "horrific."

"Is this going to be a regular thing?" Rachel asks hopefully.

Please, no.

"Yes. We will welcome the morning every day," Ares says. "It is a blessed time on the island. Now take your seats."

I sit on my and Eleanor's stone, pulling my hoodie back on as quickly as is humanly possible. Some of the boys stay shirtless, which I find deeply confusing.

Eleanor sits down next to me. "Why didn't you take your top off? You're not embarrassed, are you? You've got a great body," she says loudly. She is such a good liar.

"Just chilly," I say.

The Couple wait for us to settle. "We must now show gratitude," Artemis says. "Lucy is well. The island has healed her." She begins a round of applause. "Is there anything you'd like to say, Lucy?"

"The girls were all amazing last night. Helping me stay warm and hydrated. And Artemis." She looks up at her. "Thank you for staying up by my side. Honestly. You were so kind."

Artemis smiles back. "Now, let us eat. We have a big day ahead. Your second trial."

Artemis hands out backpacks, each with our name on, while Ares pulls on his fleece. He then heads to the base of the tree, where there is a larger backpack. As he slings it over his shoulder, I see a bright yellow feather sticking out of the zip.

EIGHT
Little Suckers

We walk down the hill. I'm already sweating profusely as I pick my way carefully through the heather and gorse brightening the muddy ground with purples and yellows and whites.

At one point, I see a lone seagull. The sight of it transports me back to a vacation in Cornwall where a massive one stole my ice cream. Lily found it hilarious. It feels strange that this bird can find its way here, to wherever we are, and then just . . . leave. I watch as it opens its wings, glides up into the air, and disappears into the blue sky.

We reach the edge of a wood, which slopes down toward the coastline. I can make out the gray sea lapping on a pebble shore in the distance.

"Packs off," Ares says. "Time to hydrate and give yourselves some energy before we begin."

The others sit down in their pairs and open their backpacks.

"What's this?" Matthew unpeels the tinfoil from a huge home-made oatmeal cookie thing and takes a bite. "It's *so* good."

Ares nods. "If you like them, I will make a request for more."

"Great!" Matthew puts his thumbs up like a toddler.

I watch as Artemis and Ares sit down slightly apart from the rest of us. She nuzzles into his neck as he strokes her hair.

Raheem has his arm around Lucy, and they keep pecking each other on the lips. Rachel and Jamie are laughing about something to do with their apples, while Li and Sam are deep in conversation. Jing sits a little way apart from Matthew. When she sees Artemis looking, she quickly takes his hand.

I keep myself outside of the love-in on a wet patch of grass.

Eleanor plonks down next to me. "Are you not eating?"

"Not hungry."

She lowers her voice. "You should look at me more, Seb."

"But I'm always looking at you." With loathing.

She smiles. "You need to up your game, or we're going to fail," she says through gritted teeth. "They need to think we love each other. Artemis told me she is yet to see our chemistry." She strokes my cheek, glancing over at the Couple to check they're watching. "You were really brave helping Lucy yesterday," she says, louder. "I'm so attracted to your generous spirit." She's nearly shouting now. "You're so *fit* when you're saving someone's life."

She should see me in my new underwear. "Thanks," I mumble.

She then kisses me. I detach myself from my body until it's over.

"Your lips are so soft, Sebby."

I don't know when it became OK for everyone to just kiss each other willy-nilly.

"However much we enjoy seeing you connect, we must continue," Artemis announces, pulling her pack on. "These trees are ancient and have a powerful energy. We will pass through them in silence, to pay our respects."

OK, Gwyneth Paltrow.

When we enter the woods, it's eerily quiet. I can smell pine, and the ground is littered with needles, so it's spongy underfoot.

I suddenly feel lightheaded. I pull my pack off my back and reach inside for the cookie thing. I peel back the tinfoil and take a bite.

"Ow!" I cry.

"Shh," Artemis hisses from up ahead. "Show your respect, Sebastian."

"Sorry," I splutter, crumbs spraying from my mouth. "Bit my tongue."

I look down at the cookie in my hand. Between the layer of tinfoil and the oaty-raisin thing is a shard of wood. That's weird. I pull it out slowly. Flip it over.

There's something written on it in handwriting I recognize. Scratched with what looks like the burnt end of a match.

WOODS. Tonight

A lightning bolt. The same as the one tattooed on his arm. The Bowie bolt.

It's him. Finn. It has to be. No one else would know about—

"What's up, Seb?"

I jump. Eleanor. "Hmm?" Stay cool. "Oh, just a piece of wood. It was in my cookie."

"Show me."

I lift up the shard, keeping the side with the writing facing me.

"You should tell them. That could've choked you." She says this like it wouldn't have been such a bad thing.

As she heads off to join the rest of the group, I put the shard in my pocket. I slow my breath, gathering my thoughts.

Is it definitely him?

I feel the warm buzz of hope sparking inside me.

But if it is . . .

I search in the depths of my memory for Stone's explanation of the Never Plan. What it said about the fate of the Bottom Percentile, those most resistant to change.

Manning had discussed the idea of the Bottom Percentile being used to serve the Elite. To give them a new purpose. Are the others here too?

But there was something else too.

The most hopeless cases, those who pose a threat to the development of the superior percentile, they'd look to remove them entirely.

Terror and guilt flood into me, extinguishing the hope.

I remember Finn's face as he read from the pages of the Never Plan. How desperate he was. How scared. I fight against the prickle of tears in the corner of my eyes, the weight of one single word threatening to pull me under.

Ended.

I'm the last to emerge from the forest.

I see the sea. Dark and endless. Then I spot the five targets lined up along the pebbles. They're about my height, maybe taller. Round wooden boards on metal legs, with blue and white lines repeating inward and a yellow circular bull's-eye in the center.

"Welcome to target practice," Artemis says, ushering us toward her.

"No shit," Jamie says. "This is *so cool.*"

Ares and Artemis stand in front of a blue rope that's been laid out along the width of the shore, facing the targets roughly ten yards away. Placed along it are five plastic bows. Bright yellow. Like you might see in the kids' section of a department store.

"Line up in your pairs behind the rope," Ares says.

We make our way along the pebbles until each pair is standing behind one of the archery sets.

I scan my eyes along the tree line. *Where is he?* I feel for the shard of wood in my pocket. It makes my fingers tingle to know he has touched it.

"Seb?" Eleanor nudges me.

"Yep," I say. "All good."

I look down at the sheath with its long plastic darts. Rubber suckers on the end of them.

Ares walks up and down the line, his hair blowing into his eyes. "You must work together to perfect your aim. Take your *time*. This is about teamwork. Trust."

Artemis joins him. "Each of you has proven your ability to learn quickly, and we encourage you to lean into that here." They both like leaning into things, don't they? "This is the ultimate test of precision, clear thinking, and your ability to act under pressure. These are all qualities you should aspire to while on the island. Now, choose who will go first."

Eleanor snatches up the bow. She takes one of the arrows and attaches it to the string.

Matthew already has his bow held up, Jing standing just behind him.

Sam hands his to Li.

Lucy takes the one at her and Raheem's feet.

Rachel lets Jamie go first.

"On my count," Artemis says.

Those holding the bows step forward until their toes touch the rope. I watch as they fiddle with the arrows, trying to attach them to the string, then raise the bows to their chests.

"Three, two, one . . . Shoot."

The arrows fly off in different directions.

Eleanor's lands about three yards in front of us, which surprises me. "Argh!" she shouts, so loudly that it almost makes me like her.

Lucy's makes it a little farther. Li's actually hits the target but ricochets off. Jamie overshoots. Matthew's sticks on to one of the white circles.

"GET IN!" he yells. He starts dancing around, pointing to himself and shouting his own name like a nob. "Give me another bloodstone. Woo-hoo!" He begins trying to chest-bump the other boys but stops when the force of Jamie's torso sends him flying to the ground.

"Good attempt, Matthew," Artemis says. "Now, pass your bows to your partners."

As Eleanor hands me the bow, I can see she's fuming. I lean down and pick up an arrow. I look at the little sucker and lick the end of it.

I shouldn't have. Tastes disgusting.

I lift the bow to my shoulder. My eyes begin to dart around the trees. Then I notice something. Right at the bottom of the shoreline, tucked into the trees. A dilapidated old shack. At least, I think it is.

Focus, Seb.

I look at the target. And I picture Manning's face, the yellow bull's-eye the point right between her eyes. I feel a heat rise within me, a mixture of anger and what I can only assume is some sort of . . . *power.*

OK, that's new.

"Ready? Three, two, one . . ."

Screw you, Manning.

"Shoot!"

I let go of the string. The sucker of the dart smacks the board, about an inch and a half beneath the bull's-eye.

That felt . . . great. I realize I'm smiling.

"Oh," Eleanor says, her eyes wide with disbelief. She sees Ares coming over. "God, you're sexy."

For a fleeting moment, I believe it. "I have been called the Ultimate Sniper King before, so . . ."

"What?"

"In *Fortnite.*"

"You play *Fortnite*? What are you, *twelve*?"

"I was actually really good at—"

"Well done, Sebastian." Ares slaps me on the back. "Beginner's luck? Let's see."

Over the next few hours—I assume it's hours, I can't be sure because time doesn't exist here—we take it in turns to perfect our aim. I mostly manage to hit the target.

Why am I good at this? Every time I hit, I picture Manning. *That's why.*

When I miss, it's because I'm looking for Finn in the trees.

Woods. Tonight. Is he really here?

Eleanor keeps missing. At one point she hits Li and Sam's target on our left.

Sam laughs. "Finally, something you're not good at, Eleanor."

Her cheeks go pink.

"You're holding your breath," I say. "Try to inhale through your nose."

"That's right, Eleanor," Artemis says, and I realize she's standing right behind us. "Listen to Sebastian."

Eleanor looks at me like she wishes my head was the target. She exhales and turns. She lifts the bow. This time, the sucker hits our board. She lets out a squeal of glee.

"Much better!" Artemis pats me on the back like Ares did, and it makes me feel really *good*. Eleanor looks hurt, like she's just caught me cheating.

Isn't this what she wants from me?

The sky begins to darken.

"Right!" Ares calls. He holds up a bloodstone and then walks over to me and Eleanor. "Congratulations. Your first bloodstone."

People begin to clap. Eleanor squeals.

"Thanks!" I take the stone, smooth in my hand.

Ares scans his eyes over us all. "It's encouraging to see you listening to each other. Trusting each other. Working together. We have time for one more shot before we lose the light. This time, it's Artemis's turn."

There is a united *"ooooh"* from the group.

Ares picks up his bag and hands it to her. Then he begins to walk toward the central target. Artemis opens the bag and takes out the crossbow.

People gasp.

"No shit," Matthew says. "That thing is awesome!"

"Um . . . ," Jing starts. "What's happening?"

"Silence, please." Artemis carefully takes out one of the arrows. Long, with bright yellow feathers at one end and a sharp metal tip at the other in the shape of a serrated triangle. Not quite the same as our little plastic suckers.

Ares reaches the central target and stands in front of it. He turns.

"Oh my God," Jing murmurs.

Artemis places the arrow into the wire on the bow. "This is the bolt," she says evenly, pulling it back until it clicks. She lifts it to her eye and looks through the black metal cylinder on its top. "This is called the scope." She then aims it directly at Ares. "And *this* is where we would like you to get to," she says. "*This* level of trust."

She breathes through her nose. Her eyes narrow. Then she presses the trigger.

Thwack.

My head turns with everyone else's.

Ares doesn't flinch. The bolt juts out about an inch above his head, right in the center of the bull's-eye. I feel sick. My hands begin to shake.

"Now, *that* was fucking cool," Jamie whispers.

The others erupt into applause.

"No way!"

"How did you learn that?"

"That's amazing, Artemis!"

"I have a question!" Li says, in complete awe. "When can *we* use one of those?"

68

"In time, Li. In time. You must prove yourself first."

Artemis lowers the crossbow, her hands steady, eyes fixed intently on her partner.

The knot in my stomach tightens. I also have a question.

Who the hell are these people?

NINE

The Most Benevolent Thing

As we head up the hillside back toward the camp, the sun begins to set behind the sea. The shadows of Artemis and Ares up ahead stretch out in front of them.

Eleanor bumps my shoulder with hers.

"What?" I say.

"Well done."

"Oh, thanks."

"It's nice to see you showing some strength."

"Right."

"Can I see it? Our bloodstone."

"*Sacred* bloodstone."

She frowns. "Yes. Sacred bloodstone."

As I reach to lift it out of my pocket, my fingers brush against the wooden shard.

"Wow, it's gorgeous, isn't it?" She tries to take my arm in hers, but I pull away. "What's wrong?"

You are. You told Manning that Finn should be stopped. We would have got out. It's your fucking fault. "Nothing."

"Seb, you need to be more—"

"What? I need to be *what*, Eleanor?" I snap, louder than I expected.

"Are you two OK over there?" Ares calls, glancing back.

"Yeah, great!" Eleanor says. "We're just being passionate! Aren't we?" She nudges my arm. "We love being passionate together."

"Yeah, we love it," I say.

She lowers her voice. "Please, can you just *try*. . . ."

"I did better than you back there, didn't I?"

"I don't mean that. . . . They need to see you . . . *you know.*"

"What?"

"*Wanting* me."

"But I don't," I say. I don't wait for her response as I move away from her, following the group over the hill. After a while, I see Artemis and Ares stop ahead. The group begins to gather around them.

"What's going on?" Eleanor says, pulling at my sleeve. I yank it away and go to join them as they all stare into the long grass.

"What is it?" Sam asks.

I look down to see a small, trembling white fluffy lump.

"Oh my God, is it a *lamb*?" Li says quietly. It is. Legs twitching. Eyes bloodshot. Making soft bleating noises. It sounds like it's *crying*. "What's wrong with it? It looks so *limp*."

Artemis crouches next to it. "Its mother must have disowned it." She gently strokes its face. "Or it's diseased."

"Can we save it?" Jing asks.

Ares kneels beside Artemis. "It's too far gone." He puts his fingers to the lamb's neck. "Its pulse is faint," he says, his voice solemn.

"Oh, God." Rachel covers her mouth with her hands.

Artemis looks at Ares. "It is suffering."

He nods and begins to take off his fleece. "You should never leave something to suffer," he says. "It is vile. Inhumane." He has tears in his eyes.

"What are you going to do?" Li asks, her voice shaking.

"The most benevolent thing," he says quietly. Then he takes his fleece and holds it over the lamb's face, until the bleating, the crying, the twitching stops.

A horrible silence hangs in the air.

I see Eleanor staring at it, frowning, like the sight of it is making her queasy.

"Let us not dwell on this," Ares says, removing the fleece. The creature's eyes are still open. "The lamb is now at peace."

Li sobs behind me. Artemis puts her arm around her and kisses her on the forehead. "This is a *good thing*," she says. "The suffering is over. We should be happy."

Happy?

"Yeah," Li croaks. "I know. You're right."

"You must be strong. We can take this experience that the island has given us and learn *resilience*. We want you all to show resilience."

"God. Yeah, I'm sorry. Sorry, guys."

"It's only a lamb," Matthew mutters.

Ares stands. "Pay your respects, then we shall not talk of it again. Let us move forward in hope. In love. The island has had its way."

When we're back inside the boys' dwelling house, Ares tells us to change into our cloaks. For what reason, he doesn't say. I sit on the edge of my bed and watch as he brings in a basket full of food. The boys gather around him beside the fireplace.

"We will become brothers on this island," he says earnestly. "We shall form a bond. I want to invite you to join me in that special place of fellowship."

I think of the lamb. Its quivering body. Its glazed eyes.

"Will you?" Ares asks.

The boys nod enthusiastically.

"I am here for you as a source of advice and guidance. Here, you will learn how to just *be,* forever in the moment."

The boys nod some more.

"On this island, my love for Artemis feels . . . *other.* I want this for you and your match."

I listen as the boys try to say meaningful things in response.

"I already feel like I'm falling for Rachel, you know?" Jamie says. "It's deep. Another level."

"It feels different out here with Li," Sam chimes in. "More . . . *free.*"

"Yes," Ares replies. "That's it. Free."

I think of Finn, flicking my eyes up to the etching on the beam above me.

Woods. Tonight.

But as I keep stealing glances at it, it looks less and less like a bee. At least, not the one Finn has on his arm. It's shaped differently and doesn't have the same number of legs, like it was drawn by someone else. I feel for the shard of wood in my pocket.

The lightning bolt. That was clear as day.

I start to think about how he could have got in here. About the fact that someone could be impersonating him. Pretending.

It was his handwriting. Wasn't it?

Someone could have forced him to write it. I think about whether I should wait until I'm sure. . . . *Sure of what?*

"What do you think, Seb?"

I look up to find Ares staring at me.

"Um . . . Yeah, I agree." He doesn't look convinced.

"We were just talking about the complexities of physical attraction."

What and not the fact that you just killed an animal with your bare hands, you maniac?

"Right!" I say brightly, as if this is my favorite subject.

"How are you finding things with Eleanor?"

"It's, um . . . yeah, it's happening!" He waits. He wants more. Quickly. Say something he would say. "Physical attraction should be a blend of both love *and* desire. We should invite those two things . . . to meet. Together. Within us."

Matthew rolls his eyes.

"Yes, it's important they are united." Ares folds his arms. "We can discuss finding this balance together soon."

No thanks. I drop my gaze and pick at my blanket.

"Well, brothers"—Ares turns back to the group—"it is time to meet our matches at the stone circle for this evening's ritual."

Another ritual? The last one we drew blood, so that's promising. And yet the boys chat excitedly as they head for the door. I stand up and shuffle after them.

Before I can make it out, Ares puts his hand across the doorway. "Are you OK, Sebastian? You seem . . . preoccupied."

"Me? I'm fine." Act fine, then.

"Should I be concerned?"

"Not at all. The lamb thing was just a bit—"

"The lamb thing?" He stares at me. "You should be stronger

74

than this, Sebastian. There's nothing to be sad about. You need to move forward."

"OK. Cool. I will." I try to edge past him, but he doesn't let me.

"I can see you resisting. With Eleanor."

Shit. He's onto me. "I think I'm just distracted . . . you know, by the new environ—"

"When you're distracted, mistakes can happen. And we don't want that." He places his hand on my shoulder and squeezes. "Do we?"

"No. We don't." He squeezes harder, until I wince.

"Good." Then he leans forward and whispers into my ear, "Don't want you getting hurt out here, Sebastian."

TEN

Couple Goals

The sky is black like tar, and the wind rustles in the branches of the elm tree above us. The ring of lanterns casts shadows that swirl on the muddy ground beneath our feet. Flower wreaths have been placed in front of each stone.

The girls are already here, dressed in their cloaks, gathered around the roaring fire with Artemis. They all have plaited hair just like her.

Chatter bubbles around me as the matches greet each other. I find our stone and sit, trying to figure out how to get away tonight without being caught by a maniac with a crossbow.

"I love it here," Eleanor says, appearing next to me. I look at her plaits and see bits of straw in them. Her two pink hair clips part her hair so there's a line of scalp right down the center of her head. "Artemis is so cool. She's teaching us to just *be*. Is Ares teaching you how to just *be*?"

"Yeah," I say. "It's great."

"They're literally the perfect couple. They're so *strong.*

Emotionally resilient. Know what I mean?" No. "What's he like with you boys?"

I look over to Ares, and our eyes meet. "The best."

Eleanor pauses, checking if anyone is in earshot. She drops her voice. "You need to stop messing around, Seb. They can sense something isn't right. Artemis told me while she was braiding my hair that she's noticed we don't seem fully *aligned*."

Her eyes are dark, but her smile remains bright.

"What do you expect me to do?" I whisper.

"Do better."

"I—"

"You can and you will. Now *smile*." I force a smile as she begins to run her fingers through my hair. "You need to forget about Finneas." The sound of his name on her lips makes me flinch. "He's *gone*." What does she know? Manning's niece . . . "This is it, Seb. Me, and HappyHead." She leans forward and rubs her nose on my cheek. "You hold my hand, you kiss me, you tell me you love me so they can hear. If you don't, I'll reveal your secret." She clasps the back of my hair in her fingers and twists.

I keep smiling. "You're blackmailing me."

"Yes." She begins to kiss my ear, hissing into it. "You don't know what these two people are capable of, and I wouldn't want us to get on the wrong side of them." For a moment, I think I hear a note of fear in her voice.

"Do you know what they're capable of?" I whisper.

"Start to *play along,* Seb, or things will get very grim for you."

I turn my face to hers so our eyes are less than an inch apart. "Grimmer than this?"

"You have no idea." She flutters her eyelashes. "Kiss my neck."

"What?"

"They're watching. Kiss my neck."

I lean in and put my lips on her neck. She moans and giggles. "I'm not going to let you ruin this for me. I *need* to do well here." She taps my nose with the tip of her finger. "OK?"

"Fine," I mutter.

She throws her head back and laughs like I've said something brilliant, then slaps her hand on my leg. Hard. "Wonderful."

There's a shuffling around us.

"It's starting!" Matthew whispers.

"It is time to begin," Artemis calls out.

Ares leans down into a large basket at his feet. I'm fully preparing myself for him to pull out a shotgun. But it's a guitar. Which is almost as bad.

He starts to strum it softly, his eyes closed.

Artemis steps forward. "At your feet you will see wreaths of flowers. These are your Gratitude Garlands." Please, no. "Whenever we wear them, we should remember to be grateful for each other. Put them on." I lean down and pick up the nearest wreath.

"It suits you," Eleanor says, giggling playfully.

She's scarily good at this. Whatever this is.

Just play along. For now. "Yours does too," I mumble. *I have to believe he's here. That he's alive.*

Artemis holds her hand up to quieten us. "Sebastian won a bloodstone today. Place it in your vessel, Sebastian."

I take it from my pocket and drop it in our bowl. People clap.

"Woo!" Eleanor yells, pointing at me. "That's my man, right there!" She grabs my face and pushes her lips onto mine with so much force our teeth bang together.

78

"Now," Artemis continues, "tonight, *you* shall decide who will be awarded sacred bloodstones."

A chorus of "*oooh*s" from the circle.

I look at her bare feet and spot the faintest trace of purple nail polish. In the corners, where she couldn't get it off. Before. Before all this . . .

"Repeat after me," she says. "Elmhallow. Lead me. Guide me."

We speak in unison. *"Elmhallow. Lead me. Guide me."*

"Give me courage, confidence, and compassion."

"Give me courage, confidence, and compassion."

"So that I may become my most powerful self."

"So that I may become my most powerful self."

"Good. Now turn to face your match." As I face my beloved Eleanor, the smoke stings my eyes and they start to water. "Take their hands. Look at them. What do you see?"

People say things like "beauty" and "wisdom."

"I see a leader," I say, because it's the first thing I think of. Eleanor's eyes widen in delight.

She smiles toothily. "Oh, honey."

Please, God, not "honey."

"Now say to each other: our love is other."

"Our love is other."

"You will now decide which of the other couples you feel is the most compatible."

"No way."

"Plot twist."

"Settle down. You will vote. Each vote will correspond to a sacred bloodstone. Pick truthfully. We will give you a moment to make your choice."

The couples begin to talk quietly between themselves. Eleanor leans so far into me that I feel her breath waft up my nose. It smells like Marmite. "So who do you think?"

I think you need some toothpaste, *honey.* "I dunno. . . . Maybe Raheem and Lucy . . ."

"Why?" she snaps. "Why does everyone think that?"

"Maybe because they seem to actually get along."

"Hmm," she says. "Well, it's definitely not Li and Sam. They're just sort of . . . *meh.*"

She's brutal. So brutal. "Right."

"Maybe Rachel and Jamie. I can tell *they* fancy each other."

I look at Jing. I like Jing. "Maybe Jing and Matthew, then?" I mumble.

She shoots me a look. "Are you *joking*?"

"I don't know. . . ."

"Matthew is a *child.* Everyone thinks so. *And* they already have two stones."

"OK, fine, you decide."

Suddenly her face lights up. "You know what, I think you're right. No one will pick Matthew because he's such a prick." She taps her fingers on her knee, thinking. "It's a gamble, but I think it might work out for us in the end. I don't see them doing very well here. Jing clearly can't stand him." She smiles. "We need to pick the weakest pair. You're *really* good at this, Seb."

What just happened?

"It is time to vote," Artemis announces. "Stand and face the outside of the circle."

We all turn around.

Eleanor grabs my hand. "People better vote for us."

As we stand, holding hands, staring out into the darkness, I hear Artemis moving around the circle. I wonder what she was named before. When she let her nails be purple.

Her face appears in front of ours. "Your choice?" she whispers.

Eleanor leans forward. "Jing and Matthew."

Artemis nods. "And why?"

"Because they are . . . they are *literally* couple goals."

Artemis turns her floating head to me. "Do you agree, Seb?"

"Um—"

"Seb suggested them," Eleanor cuts in.

Artemis nods, and then her face disappears back into the darkness.

When she's finished moving around the circle, she speaks from somewhere behind us. "I will now place the sacred bloodstones into the bowls. Only turn when I say you can. Then you may see how you have fared. How you have inspired others."

Eleanor shoots me a look. *This had better go well.*

Donk.

Donk.

Donk.

Donk.

Donk.

"The votes have been cast. You may turn around."

"Good luck, honey," Eleanor says.

We turn. I look down into our bowl.

One sad, lonely, little stone. My one from earlier.

Eleanor digs her nails into my hand so hard that I might scream. Her eyes dart around the other bowls.

"Raheem and Lucy now have *three*," she whispers frantically.

"Everyone else voted for them, and they must have voted for Jing for saving her. Now she and Matthew have *four*." Huh? "You're an *idiot,* making us choose them."

Sure.

Ares stands, speaking over the whispering couples. "There will be ample opportunity to win bloodstones. Now we must move on in happiness. It is time to celebrate." He strums on his guitar.

Artemis stands on the grass in front of the fire and begins to sway. She moves her hands around her body and twists, occasionally stamping her feet.

I think she's . . . dancing.

As Ares strums faster, Artemis starts to spin. She spins and spins, and I get a head rush watching her. The volume of the music crescendos, and when it stops, she falls down into the mud.

"Come, join me!" she shouts up at us. "Be free!"

And they do. They stand by the fire and wave their hands about and stomp their feet and jump up and down.

It's like watching a weird woodland rave without the uppers.

"Come on, Seb!" Eleanor shouts from the melee, her plaits whipping around her face. She grabs my hand and drags me with her.

I feel Ares watching as she weaves us into the middle of the spinning people. I put my hands up in the air and begin to step from side to side.

"Loosen up, Sebby!" Eleanor takes my hips and twists them in her hands.

What is happening?

I turn and turn and turn.

The fire roars.

Laughing faces with flower crowns float in and out of my vision.

It's like a very strange dream. But this is real. All of it.

Fire. Faces. Fire. Faces.

I spin until I feel like I'll throw up.

I stumble to my stone as the world dips and turns around me. I look at Ares, watching us as he strums. He looks so pleased with what he's witnessing.

His little dancing clones.

He flashes his eyes at me, red with flames. I smile. He smiles back. There's something in the curl of his lip that makes me shudder.

Eleanor appears. "What are you doing?"

"Just needed a second."

She moves her lips. No sound comes out, but I read every word. *Get up or I will tell them everything.*

I stagger to my feet. "Yes, honey."

I'm coming, Finn. *Tonight.*

Because our love is other.

And theirs is *nuts.*

ELEVEN

Number One

I take one final glance over the sleeping bodies and slip out of my blanket. I pick up my shoes and move my feet across the floor, careful to keep them on the sheepskin rugs and not rustle the straw. When I reach the door of the Bucket Room, I put my thumb on the latch.

I turn to check the pillow I've placed under the blanket. In the flickering firelight, it looks enough like a body. I hope.

I push my finger down. *Click.*

I look over at Ares and see the crossbow leaning by his bed. *He's asleep. Just go.*

I pull the door behind me. It squeaks. I freeze. *Why am I so scared of him?*

Because he has a weapon. Because his girlfriend has a deadly aim. Because they're innocent-lamb killers.

I pull on my Reds and my shoes, then shuffle over to the window and twist the handle. The window suddenly swings open, and wind gushes into the room, throwing it outward. I catch it just before it smashes against the walls.

Shit, shit.

I wait a moment, blood pulsing in my ears. When I'm sure no one is coming, I pull myself up onto the ledge and swing my legs over it, perching half in, half out.

Come on.

I drop to the ground. Feel around in the mud until I find a stone big enough to wedge the window open so I can get back in.

I try to find my bearings. Rain whips into my face, blurring my vision. *That way.* It's just one straight line, I think. *Down the hill toward the shore.*

My thoughts race ahead of me as my feet pound into the mud, trying to keep up with them. I think of their faces, Ares and Artemis. His Jesus hair. Her purple nail polish. How good-looking they are. How the others gaze at them with adoration and longing.

The way he looked at me when I hit the target. How it felt. That slap on the back.

I think of what he said to me. *I see you.*

As my chest heaves and the wind stings my skin, my brain begins to blank out. My feet pound and pound, harder and harder. Then I trip. Into the mud.

I blink the rain from my eyes. *Get up.*

As I stand, I see something in the distance.

A figure. Walking my way. Holding a small flashlight pointed at the ground.

"Finn!" I shout through the wind.

The figure stops. Green hoodie. Green sweatpants. Head down.

"Finn!"

The figure turns and begins to walk quickly in the opposite direction.

"Hey, stop!"

I follow the circle of flashlight as fast as I can. Why is he running away?

"It's me!" I close in on him, reach out, and grab his sleeve. "Finn!"

He turns. His hood drops.

But it's not . . . *It's not him.*

"Seb, you need to go back."

"What are you doing here?"

"I can't be seen with you." Betty pulls her hood back up and begins to scurry off in the direction I've just come from.

Betty? From the facility. From the Bottom Percentile.

"Wait!" I cry.

She stops. "I can't talk to you, Seb. You shouldn't be out here." Her breath rasps.

"What's going on?"

"You need to go back."

"Why are you here?" I grab for her sleeve again. "Answer me, Betty. Please."

She yanks her arm away. "Let go, Seb. If they see me with you . . ."

I see how thin she looks. How pale. Her hoodie has a large number one plastered on the front. I notice she's carrying a basket. She looks down at my muddy handprint on her sleeve. "Oh no." She begins to rub at it. *"No . . ."*

"What's happening, Betty?"

"I can't be seen with you, Seb. I told you."

She starts walking away from me again.

"Which way are the woods?" She keeps walking. "Please, Betty! I'm looking for Finn. Where is he?"

Suddenly she stops dead. "This isn't a good idea," she says, her voice trembling.

"Please," I say. *"Please."*

She hesitates, then holds her hand out and points. "That way."

"Thank you, Betty."

And then she's gone. I watch as the flashlight disappears.

Go, Seb. Now.

I turn in the direction she pointed, and I run.

I run and run. Arms thrashing. Feet hammering the mud. Everything burning. Lungs. Muscles.

Why is she here? Where are the rest of the Bottom Percentile?

I see trees ahead.

Keep going.

I run until the canopy of branches is above me and I can no longer see the night sky. I can't see *anything.* . . .

I stop. Wheezing. Head spinning. I drop down onto my knees. Onto the pine needles. I crawl forward until I find a tree trunk and lean against it. I fumble for my inhaler.

In. Hold. Out.

In. Hold. Out.

There's a ringing in my ears and my brain feels like it's unraveling.

I realize I'm crying. Sobbing.

And then I hear the crack of a twig somewhere behind me. A rustling. I sense someone standing over me. See the flash of flashlight on the ground.

"Seb," a voice whispers. I don't dare look up. "It's me." I flinch as a hand touches my sleeve. "Look at me, Seb."

I lift my head.

Ice-blue eyes pierce through the darkness.

Him.

TWELVE
Helpers' High

"We're not safe here. We need to leave. *Now.*" He takes my hand in his.

My mind is blocked. I can't connect it to my body. I try to focus on him, but his face is distorted by my tears. "Seb," he says. His voice doesn't seem real. "I need you to get up, Seb." He wipes my eyes with his sleeve, bringing him into clarity.

Finn.

His face looks . . . not how I remember it. It's . . . *gray.* His hair is matted, thick with dirt. His cheeks hollow, black marks streaking from under his eyes down to his translucent skin. He's *empty.* Like someone's taken a plug out from his body and let all of him drain away.

"Seb. *Now.*" His eyes flash. Wired. Alert. Ready.

I remember *that.*

"O-OK," I stammer. I start to stand.

"That's it," he says. "Come on. We need to go somewhere we can't be seen."

Seen by who?

I let him guide me as we weave through the trees, his fingers never leaving mine. Every now and then he stops, eyes darting through the darkness, checking left, then right. Then we move again. We pick up our pace, and I taste the adrenaline in my throat, feel my heartbeat pulsing in my temples. I feel alive, energized, *free*. Like there's nothing but us.

Then we stop.

"Here," he says.

I look down to see we are standing at the top of a ravine. We descend into it, navigating the dead leaves as they slip beneath our feet. When we reach the bottom, he leads me to a fallen tree, its roots twisting up from the ground, reaching into the sky.

"Sit here," he says, clicking off the flashlight. I can still see his eyes shooting around us through the black. "We should be safe for now."

I crouch down and lean back against the trunk, my ribs heaving. As I slow my breath, I feel him crouch next to me.

He turns to me, and I see a number five printed on his tatty hoodie. I try to speak, but the words catch in my throat. He puts his hand gently on my arm, and I manage to push them out through my trembling lips. "I'm sorry. . . ."

"Seb—"

"Back at HappyHead. We should've tried to run like you said. Shouldn't we?" He doesn't answer. He looks so different. *So broken.* "I messed up. I thought Mark's plan with the boat would work. I honestly thought we'd get out." I can hear my voice getting louder, but I can't control it. "And I lost the pager. The *pager,* Finn. I lost it. I'm so sorry—"

"You need to stay quiet, Seb."

"I just . . . I can't—"

"Quiet."

He pulls me into him. I feel his chest expanding into mine, his breath steady, constant. Slowly I begin to match mine to his. I bury my head in his neck, my lips on his skin. On the wing tattoo that creeps up behind his ear. I inhale. I can taste the salt of my tears mixed with his sweat and dirt.

He's really here.

He leans back and takes my arms in his hands. Holds me in front of him. Wipes the hair out of my eyes. "I found you," he says. He smiles. But it's fragile. Barely there.

Then I hear something.

Suddenly his hand is over my mouth. "Shh." His head turns, eyes flashing as they scan the trees.

I hear it again. *Footsteps.*

"Under there, *now.*" He points to a gap between the ground and the fallen trunk.

I lie flat on my stomach and drag myself into it. It's wide enough for me to be covered by the underside of the trunk, which scrapes my back as I push myself farther beneath it. I turn my face so the side of it is pressed into the dirt.

As the footsteps come closer, I watch the back of Finn's torn shoes, which remain completely still.

"Number Five?" a man's voice barks. Twigs crunch under heavy feet. "Number Five? Is that you?"

"Yes, sir," Finn calls back. But it sounds so unlike him. He sounds *terrified.*

Another pair of feet emerge into my view. Solid black boots.

"Why are you down here?" the man says.

"Looking for firewood, sir."

"You don't seem to have any."

A pause. "No, sir. It's all wet here."

"Then get back to where it's dry."

"Yes, sir."

I flick my eyes up, but I'm only able to see the man's heavyset torso. His thick black jacket with pockets across the front. "Don't go any farther than here, Number Five, or you'll be out of the woods."

"Yes, sir."

"Why are you out of breath?" he asks.

"I fell."

"Fell?"

Another pause. "I'm sorry."

"You should be more careful."

"Yes, sir."

"You know the rules."

"Of course."

"Remind me of them, Number Five." Silence. "I won't ask again."

Finn's voice, almost inaudible. "To serve unseen."

"That's right. And if you *are* seen?"

"I will have to . . . learn."

"Yes. You will." The man steps forward. "What does your tag say?"

Finn leans down. His fingers come into view and lift up the elastic at the bottom of the sweats on his right leg. I'm about to push myself farther under the trunk when I see a strip of metal around his ankle.

Some sort of tag with a small screen.

It flashes. A green light. Words appear.

Gather Firewood

"Firewood," Finn says. He pushes the pants back down over the tag and stands up straight.

"You have a few hours yet. Get back to it."

One of the man's boots lifts as if he is about to go. It hovers off the ground for a moment, so I can see its thick tread; then he places it back down. "And, Number Five?"

"Yes, sir?"

"Remember your gratitude. You're very lucky to be here."

"Yes, sir. I am, sir."

I hold my breath as the man's silhouette—shaved head, built like some kind of army sergeant—moves away from us.

I look back at Finn's feet. All I can hear is his breath and mine. Finally he crouches. His face appears. "This way."

I slide myself out of the gap, careful not to make a sound. I follow him, watching my foot on every twig. We meander our way through the trees, slower this time, until I can smell the sea. As we get to the edge of the wood, just before the beach, he stops.

"We need to find somewhere out of sight. Now." I hear the panic in his voice.

I step out onto the pebbles and look all the way down the length of the bay. I can still see the row of targets, halfway down, that we were shooting at earlier today. Beyond that, catching the moonlight, is the little hut. Low walls, corrugated-iron roof, covered in vines and branches so it's almost invisible.

"I've got an idea," I whisper as he waits in the shadows. "Trust me."

He probably shouldn't. Not anymore. But he nods.

I take his hand this time, and we run along the edge of the pebbles until we reach the hut.

Finn stares up at the crumbling walls. "I didn't know this was here."

I scan my eyes over the hut; then I see it. Wooden, peeling blue paint, faded from the wind and sun. A *door*.

"Quick!" I grab its handle. Pull.

Shit. A padlock. Rusty. Old.

"It's locked."

Finn's face drops.

Fuck this. I lean down and grab a rock from by my feet. I raise it up above my head and am about to smash it down on the lock when he puts his hand on my arm.

"Wait!" he hisses, glancing back toward the trees. "Too loud."

I place it back down on the ground, and we circle around the hut, searching for windows. Another door. Another way in. But there's nothing.

There has to be. . . .

I look up at the iron roof. Just above the vines covering the wall in front of me is what looks like a gap where the metal has corroded. "There." I point.

"Is it big enough?"

I look at him. *What choice do we have?*

We push ourselves against the wall and fumble with the vines until we find some that are sturdy enough to hold our weight. We then clamber up until we're both perched on the edge of the roof. It creaks beneath us as we stand over the hole, looking down at its edges, sharp and flecked with orange rust. It looks just big enough to fit through.

"Go on," Finn says.

I drop through it and hit the concrete floor. Hard.

I scan the room. Empty, except for some old wooden crates, ropes, and dusty glass bottles. It smells stale. It's *freezing*.

"All good?" His voice from above. "I'm coming down."

I crawl out of the way, feeling the grit of dust beneath my hands, and watch as he drops, landing in a cloud of dirt.

"Over here," I call. He scurries next to me. I can feel him breathing fast, his chest moving up and down. The vapor from our lungs mingles in front of us.

I put my hand on his and realize he's trembling. I look down at his fingers, ragged and dirty.

"He shouldn't find us here," Finn says. "But I can't be too long. Or he'll . . ." He doesn't finish.

And I don't ask him to.

We wait. For what, I'm not sure.

I look at him, framed in the moonlight filtering down through the hole. The dust settles around him, lingering on his skin.

He's made for this time of night.

He doesn't look back.

He slowly moves around the edge of the room, skimming his hand along the crumbling brick wall. "I think this used to be some kind of boathouse," he says, leaning down to pick up an old rope. He twists it around his hand.

"Who was he?" I say, but he doesn't answer. "Finn? Who was that man?"

His hands go still. "Our Keeper," he says quietly.

"Your what?"

"Our Keeper. He makes sure we do everything we're supposed to."

"We? The Bottom Percentile?" He flinches as I say the words. "So you're all here?" He begins pushing a crate around with his foot, so it scrapes on the floor. "What's going on, Finn?"

As my question disperses into the dust, it leaves behind something thick and cloying. I feel stupid. I have no idea what's *going on.* I have no idea what he's been through since the moment he was dragged off the beach. I wish I could take it back. "Sorry, that was—"

He goes still. "We're here for you lot, Seb," he says. "We're doing our own program on the island. For you."

He looks down at the floor, shrouded in the silver light.

"What program?"

When he speaks again, his voice is monotone, emotionless, like he's reciting a script that he's read over and over again. "The Helpers' High. It's a program of giving. Of unrequited selflessness. It's been designed to help the most resistant. We work at night so you don't see us. So we don't distract you. You must never know we're here. If you find out, we'll be punished. There are five of us. The Bottom Percentile. The Less Fortunate. The Most Resistant. Whatever the hell they want to call us. The five of us who rowed the boats for you lot back at the facility. Just before . . ." He trails off.

But I know the end of his sentence. *Just before they took him. Just before Mark's plan to get us out failed.*

"We each now have our roles to fill. Our *new purpose.*" He spits these words, shaking his head, but not angrily. More . . . resigned. Hopeless.

"We chop your firewood. Make your food. Clean your clothes. Every log you burn, every meal you eat, every sheet you sleep on. That's us. *The science is steadfast.* That's what Manning said to us before we came. She made it sound so fucking convincing, Seb. All this stuff about selfless acts releasing chemicals into our brains that will make us *feel better.* She said helping you would force us to look outside of ourselves. Cos that's our problem. We're too involved in ourselves. We need to find our place in the world, or we'll never be happy. And Helpers' High will give us that."

He points to the number on his hoodie, his eyes staying fixed on the floor. "I am Number Five. I will serve unseen and I will be grateful."

Serve unseen.

He laughs softly. But it isn't a laugh I've heard before. It's weak. Thin.

"I saw Betty," I say. "On my way down."

His body tenses. "You saw her?"

"Yeah, she showed me which way to—"

"You can't tell anyone, Seb."

"I won't."

"Promise me. Because—"

"Of course I promise, Finn. *Of course* I won't say anything."

Why might he think that I would? Why won't he look at me?

He nods. "She has the hardest job. She carries stuff up to the dwelling houses in your camp after we've prepared it. Those two—the *Couple*—then say it's them. Make you think it's *them* doing it all for you. And we need it to stay that way. We don't need your thanks."

The way he talks makes me feel uneasy, like he's a stranger. "Do you ever go up to the camp?" I ask.

He shakes his head. "I'm not allowed because of what happened before, at the facility. My attempt to escape with Mark." He says this like I had nothing to do with it. But this is what

Manning thinks. And I now can't remember why that is a good thing.

"I nearly went with him when she sent him away. But this is apparently the more benevolent option. Manning said she'd *afford me some grace.* So fucking kind, isn't she? She said I deserved one last chance. I should consider myself *very lucky.*"

"Where did Mark go?"

"I don't know," he says. "Last time I saw him was at the facility. They kept us in these white rooms while they figured out what to do with us. I could hear him screaming through the wall next to me. I think she told people he'd lost it. That he needed help." He taps the side of his head. "Like *proper* help."

"No one will believe her."

"They will."

"What have they told your parents?"

He snorts. "She's clever. I'm sure she's come up with something to convince them that this is all for the best."

My brain begins to hurt. "It's the Never Plan," I say.

"Yeah. This is it. And it's only just beginning. Stone was right about everything."

I pause, considering whether I should tell him. "She was on a video," I say carefully. "Before we came here. With Manning."

He frowns. "What do you mean?"

"They were telling us about this next stage, and she seemed . . . I don't know. Not like the Stone we knew."

He pushes his hands into his hoodie pockets. He stands like this for a long time, a shadow in the middle of the room. "Manning's got to her too?"

I don't know the answer. I don't.

"Finn . . . ," I say. "What did the Keeper mean when he said you have to *learn*?" I watch his body tense again. "You said you'd be punished. . . ." I step toward him, but he puts his hand out.

"Don't. Just . . ."

"We can stop him. Get out of here. Together." He starts shaking his head. "We can overpower him. There's only one of him, and five—*six* of us now."

"No, Seb."

"Why? It's worth a shot. Anything's better than this."

"You don't understand."

"What don't I understand? I want to help."

"Please—"

"What's he doing to you, Finn?"

"Just stop it!" he says, so sharply that his words bounce between the walls. When their echo has subsided, he drops his head. "Please, Seb . . ." He closes his eyes, exhaling as his eyelids flutter like he's going somewhere else. Away from here. Escaping from the pain.

"I'm so sorry," I say quietly. "I am. It's my fault. All of this." *Stay with me. Please.* "Look at me, Finn."

"I . . ."

"Please, just look at me for a moment." He doesn't. "You have every right to blame me."

"I don't blame you. I don't, Seb. I just . . . I wish we'd got out before all this."

"I know. Me too."

"She said I'm diseased."

The word hangs in the air. *Diseased.* Like the lamb.

"Maybe she's right," he says then.

I remember what Eleanor said about him. About the deal he struck to go to HappyHead. To avoid a sentence. "Why would you say that?"

"What is there to go back to? Just more of this never-ending shit." He kicks an empty bottle so it spins. The noise of glass grinding against the concrete floor.

"Loads of things, Finn. Your foster parents. Me . . ."

He shrugs. "Maybe this is right for me now."

"No, Finn—"

"It starts to get to you, you know." He cuts me off. "All the stuff they say. That's the worst thing of all. Fucking gets under your skin, and it's hard not to . . ." He rubs his face with his hand like he's trying to dislodge the thought.

"You can't believe her, Finn. I know you don't actually think that. She's wrong."

"I sometimes wonder if maybe she has a point."

"Stop it."

"Stop what?"

"Giving up."

"It's easy for you to say, Seb."

"Don't . . . start that."

"Start what?"

"Saying it's easy. It's not been easy. It's been *horrible*."

"You didn't listen to me."

"What? I—"

"I said we should run. Why didn't you listen?"

"But—"

"You said the plan would work—you *promised* me." He strains to keep his voice quiet. "You promised. And I believed you."

He shakes his head, and I suddenly feel *angry* at him for not looking at me, for not letting me speak, for not letting me apologize. For being so . . . far away. So distant. So *different*.

"Why did you leave me the note on the shard of wood, then? The bee above my bed? Why, Finn? If it's so dangerous seeing me? If you think Manning's right? If this is what you deserve?" He still doesn't look at me. "Why?" But as I feel my body begin to tremble, I know I'm only really angry with myself.

"Because I wanted to see you," he whispers. He lifts his head, and his bloodshot eyes meet mine for the first time since we dropped through the hole. They're wide with fear and hurt and shame. They ignite an instant heat inside me, a cramping twist so visceral it makes me miss a breath. I weave through the wreckage strewn across the floor toward him. *I missed you so much.*

"I'm glad you did," I say. *I hate this place. I hate it all. But without it, I would never have met you.* "I know you're angry, and so am I. But you're not giving up. No way. We're getting out of here." I stop in front of him and put my hand gently up to his face. As I feel his skin against my fingertips, I laugh.

I laugh. Relief. It's him.

He frowns. "What's so funny?" he says.

I lean into him, pushing my forehead into his. "I thought you were dead."

"Not yet."

I take the collar of his damp hoodie and pull him closer. The sudden feeling of his lips on mine, the taste of him, makes me feel as if I'm dropping at speed through the sky.

THIRTEEN
Somewhere Else

"Those boxer shorts are really something." Finn looks up at me as I stand wearing nothing else, framed in the pool of moonlight.

"I know," I say. "Don't tell anyone, but I kind of *like* them. . . ."

"I can see that. Give us a twirl." I do, then curtsy. He laughs. "Wow."

"Don't ask me how I learned that."

"How did you learn that?"

"*Princess Diaries.*" I do one more spin, then lie back down next to him on the old blanket he found in one of the crates. I place my head next to his on my hoodie, a makeshift pillow, and pull the blanket up around me. I lift my arm, and he shuffles forward until he is under it too, his face inches away from mine.

"Hello," he says. How can hearing him say the word make me feel so *good*?

"Hello, Finneas."

"So formal." He seems fuller now. More *him*. "So polite."

"Oi!" I push his shoulder. "I'm not."

He grins. "You literally just curtsied."

"True." He laughs. "I have a question," I say.

"Go on."

"How did you draw the bee above my bed if you can't go up there?"

"I asked Betty to do it. She didn't want to."

"I wondered if it was someone else. It only had three legs."

"Oh, Betty."

"Better than no legs."

"Were there wings at least?"

I nod. "She did good. Well done, Betty."

"Now I have a question," he says, putting his arm around me.

"Go on."

He smiles. "Has it been horrible without me?"

"*Dead* horrible," I say.

He nudges me with his elbow. "Hey, that was all right, that. You'll fit right in."

"Thanks, proper chuffed." It goes a bit weird. Very Dick Van Dyke in *Mary Poppins*.

"Well, let's see," he says. "Early days." He turns onto his back, looking up at the hole in the roof. His eyes catch the moonlight.

"What would you have, right now? If you could have anything," I say. "No price tag."

"Anything? That's tough." He pauses. "Probably a can of Coke and a fish and chips. Or a pack of cigs."

"Or ice cream."

"Oh, Seb. You're killing me. I *love* ice cream."

"Get all the sprinkles on."

"All the syrup." He scratches his cheek, now peppered with stubble. "My foster parents used to make me watch this show with them on a Sunday night. And they'd always get out the ice pops. I'd give anything for one of those right now." I remember him telling me they adopted him when he was six.

"Which show?"

He turns back to me. "Huh?"

"Sunday night."

"Er, that one where they go to rural places like the Lake District."

"Countryfile."

He raises his eyebrows. "Yeah, that's the one." He smiles. "Go on, then. What about you?"

Right now, I don't really want anything else. "Maybe my phone and some speakers."

"Bowie."

"Yup."

"Not sure we'd get a signal out here, sadly."

"All my music is downloaded. I did that just in case."

"What, in case you got stuck on an island?" I watch the brightness in his eyes suddenly dim, as if he'd forgotten. As if for a moment it was like we weren't here at all. That we were somewhere else entirely.

As he sits up, I trace my eyes over his back, the tattoos rippling on his goose-bumped skin. The dragon's flames look real, *alive*. They warm me. I watch as he picks up his hoodie, pulling it over his head, then reaches for his sweatpants. He slowly stands. I grab my Reds, still damp, crossing my arms around my knees, drawing them into my body.

"I'll tell the others what's happening. I'll expose them. I'm not scared anymore."

"No."

"But—"

"You need to carry on doing what they're asking of you, Seb. You need to gain the Couple's trust so they suspect nothing. Remember, everything on this island is controlled by *her*. Don't let them know anything is wrong. Because then *she* will."

He waits for a moment. Then he speaks very quietly, his eyes shimmering once more. "I might have an idea. A plan."

My stomach jolts. "What idea? What plan?"

"It's risky. It would be dangerous. And I'll need your help."

Beep. Something flashes. He looks down at the tag around his ankle.

"Shit." His face changes, the darkness flooding back in. "Shit."

He scrambles around the room, pulling crates under the hole in the roof.

"What's happening?" I say.

"I need to go. *Now.*" He pulls up the bottom of his pants, revealing the metal tag. I read the words that flash across the screen.

Back to dorm. Immediately.

"What's the dorm?"

"Where they keep us."

"In the woods?"

"More like *under* the woods."

"What?"

"It's a bunker. Quick, help me."

We stack the crates until they are waist-high. He goes to climb onto them, but I grab his arm. "What do you need me to do?"

"Nothing yet. I'll try and leave you a message via Betty. Look out for it. But if they know anything about us . . . *this* . . . I won't see you again, Seb. Do you understand?" I nod. "Don't let them suspect anything, OK?"

"OK."

"Good."

"Wait . . . what about the wood? For the Keeper? Won't he—"

"I stashed a pile just in case. Same time tomorrow, I'll be here." Then he kisses me, and it hurts my stomach.

Because I have to go back. To *that*. To where everything is a lie. But this, *this* is real.

"You're still very handsome." He winks. "I missed you loads, you know."

And then he pulls himself up, back through the hole in the roof.

I stand in the Bucket Room, looking down at my Reds. They're brown. Thick with mud. It's still dark.

I wait, listening for any noise inside the bedroom. Anyone who might have heard me come back in through the window. Ares.

My brain feels as though someone has pumped a weightless gas into it, heightening my senses.

I'm alive. He makes me feel like I'm living.

I wait a little longer, holding on to the memory of him. Preserving it. Taking my time to tie the images together so they don't slip away from me. I trace his body in my mind. The curve of his back under my hands. His lips on my skin.

I go to the bucket and pull my hoodie over my head. I then turn the tap on carefully so it can't be heard and wash the mud from the fabric in the trickle of freezing water.

Finally my eyes begin to droop. I shove the clothes under the dirty pile in the corner and take the fresh ones hung up on the hook.

Betty.

I inhale and step back into the bedroom as quietly as I can. I look over to Ares, breathing heavily.

You don't know me, I mouth to him. *You don't see me at all.*

As I pull my blanket over my body, I realize this is the first thing I've said to him that isn't a lie.

FOURTEEN
Let Go

I open my eyes. It takes me a moment to come around, but then the memory of last night floods back in.

He's alive. He's *here.*

I hear them. All the boys. Snoring. A cacophony of testosterone, mingled with a strong tangy smell like the changing rooms at school.

I look over at Ares's bed. He's sleeping soundly. All . . . beautiful.

I creep over to the fire and crouch down by the basket of logs. I carefully lift each one, searching. Nothing. No note. Not yet.

"You're up early." I turn. Ares stands by his bed, topless, his muscles rippling. I feel tiny, *puny,* in my little white tank top.

Wasn't he just asleep? How does he move so quickly and so silently? I don't like it.

"Yep," I say. "Ready for the day! Just putting another log on the fire." I try to sound bright and effortless. Like there isn't a group of people on this island locked in a *bunker.* Like he doesn't know it's happening.

"Great." His face is so symmetrical.

He heads over to the wicker hamper next to the log basket and takes out a croissant. "Here." He hands it to me. "Eat. It's fresh. You must be hungry."

I am. I really am. He knows *everything*.

"Thanks!" I take it and stuff it into my mouth. His eyes linger on me as I chew.

"Perhaps we could prepare the morning welcome together, since we have both risen early. Sound nice?"

No. "Oh, sure. *Love* to," I say between mouthfuls.

"Get dressed," he says. "Meet me by the firepit in five minutes."

There are no clocks. How the hell do I know when five minutes are up, you hippie weirdo?

He takes the keys and unlocks the door. "You seem different today," he whispers before he leaves. "I wonder why."

When I get to the stone circle, he's already on his knees in a prayer position. His eyes are shut.

Jesus. Quite literally.

I tiptoe forward, the mist swirling around my feet, glimmering as the morning light cuts through it. The tip of each blade of grass sparkles with dew.

"Join me," Ares says.

I kneel beside him.

"Close your eyes."

I do. Suddenly I feel his hand take mine. I flinch, but he grips tighter. Clammy. Strong. I immediately think of my Lysol wipes.

"Um . . . what are we doing?"

"Being present," he says. "Together."

"Oh, great."

"I've noticed your inability to do this. To accept that the present moment exists and that it is all that matters."

"Right." I mean, he's not wrong. I definitely do not want to accept that this present moment exists.

"It's the key to your potential. Stop questioning things, Sebastian. Allow this experience to mold you."

We kneel in silence for what feels like ages. The knees of my pants soak up the dew.

Don't let them know anything is wrong.

"Ares, can I speak?"

"Please."

"I wanted to say, I've been reflecting on what you said . . . about proving myself to Eleanor."

His grip tightens. "Go on."

"I really want to lean into that, you know?"

"Sounds like a good idea. It will set you free."

"I know. And I really want to be set free. I do."

I hear the air going in and out of his nostrils. "How much do you want it, Sebastian?"

"I . . . want it more than anything."

"Do you?" He grips my hand tighter. "Good. She is an incredible girl."

"So incredible."

"She only deserves the best."

"The *absolute* best."

"And we—*Manning*—has such high hopes for you both." *Manning. She controls everything.* "Don't let your mind distract you. Stop listening to it. Listen to me instead."

Um. OK.

"I know what is right for you."

110

OK . . . "Yes."

"The trauma of your past is still in your body. I can feel it. But the way the old world made you perceive yourself is wrong. It weakened you. Stole your potential. It blocks you. You are capable of anything. Be free. Be brave. *Let go.*"

I let go of his hand.

"Not of *me.*" Oh, right. I take it again. "Of the way you think of yourself, Sebastian."

"Right."

"The only thing stopping you is *fear.*"

I know he wants me to speak. Just give him something. Anything.

"I've always been scared. . . ."

"Yes . . ."

"But I don't want that anymore."

"No . . ."

"I want to be the best version of me I can be." God.

"Yes, Sebastian. *Yes.*" His hand is sticky in mine. "And you can. It's the simplest thing. Just release yourself from everything you think and feel about yourself." So simple. "And you shall have the chance to show that version of yourself to Eleanor today."

Oh, joy. "Sounds *exciting.*"

"I think it will be." He pauses. "I can hear a change in you this morning. I'm proud of you, Sebastian. I know how hard this can be. Letting go of our old selves." And finally he releases my hand.

I open my eyes. His are already open. *When did he open them? Were we supposed to open them? Has he just been staring at me?*

He looks weird. But not in the typical way. He actually looks a little . . . *sad.*

He swallows. "I'm so proud of you. In this moment."

"Well! Time to welcome in the morning!" I say, standing up.

He puts his hand on my arm. "Would you like to *lead* it today?"

Dear God. Why? *Why?* "I would *love* that."

"Don't let the fear stop you. Just feel your way through it."

Sure. "I'll let the island guide me."

"Good, Sebastian. That's right. And *lead* the others."

Note to self: just talk bullshit. That's what he responds best to. "I will lead them like they're little lost lambs."

He stares at me. Too far?

We wait for the others to join us.

"Sebastian will be leading us today as we welcome in the morning," Ares says.

I hear them whispering through mouthfuls of croissant. They sound sort of . . . jealous.

We welcome in the morning. I even take my top off.

The girls whoop when I do. "Go on, Seb!"

The boys follow my movements. And I hum like I have never hummed before, nipples shriveling in the wind. I tell the girls to drum harder. Louder. Faster. And they do.

I let go. And it's weird. Because . . . I kind of like it. I move my arms around my body, and I stretch my legs in positions they have never been in before. And the boys copy me.

I know I look stupid. I know all of this is stupid. But I don't care.

He is here. And we will get out somehow. Together. Whatever it takes.

When we finish, Ares nods at me. *That's it. That's better.*

I go to Eleanor. "Hey, honey," I say, kissing her on her forehead.

It's sweaty from all her vigorous drumming. "You look beautiful this morning."

"Oh, thanks, Seb." She blushes. "What's with you today?"

"Just feeling good."

"You *look* good."

"Really?"

"Yes. Confidence can make someone look *different*."

"You're so kind."

"Aw, thanks, babe." *Babe.* Ugh.

In for a penny. "No worries, babe."

She giggles. "We're so *coupley* this morning." She links my arm in hers. "Keep it up," she whispers in my ear.

As we take our seats in the stone circle, everyone looks . . . expectant. Hopeful.

"Today," Artemis says, "we will be testing your faith. In each other. In us. We want to see how far you are willing to go." She reaches down into the crate at her feet and takes out a yellow blindfold with the HappyHead face on the front. "We're going on a little journey."

Artemis pulls my right arm. "Here," she says. "Take her hand." I don't know who she's talking about. I can't see anything.

"It's me," Eleanor whispers.

Oh, right.

Then Artemis begins to tie something around our wrists. It feels plasticky, like one of those bag ties that you can't break, even with your teeth.

"Ow," I say. "It's tight."

"It needs to be."

I hear her step away from us, back into the middle of the circle. "Listen to me, all of you," she says. "You are all bonded to your partner. This could either make things easier, or more difficult. You decide."

"What do we do now?" Matthew says. I don't like him, but it's a good question.

"All you must do is follow the sound of our voices. Trust us. Trust your partner. Work together."

Then the Couple begin to sing. A weird, wailing ballad. All dark and moody.

"is uain thu ni's mò . . ."

Wait.

"feumaidh tu a bhith làidir . . ."

Wait a second. The song. It sounds a lot like one I know from that film. The one Shelly made me watch that was full of blood and death. The one with Russell Crowe.

"Come on, Seb," Eleanor says, her arm pulling at mine.

Gladiator. I mean, it's *not,* but it sounds very similar. It plays after Joaquin Phoenix literally stabs Russell in the back. Then Russell floats across fields all the way to the afterlife. *Elysium.* It's like a death lullaby calling him.

Oh, God.

"Seb!"

"thoir an aire don mhadah-allaidh . . ."

"It's like a lullaby," Lucy says from somewhere nearby. Yeah. *Exactly.* A death one.

"feumaidh tu earbsa a chur annainn . . ."

The song starts to move away from us, and we follow. Our

little blindfolded death march, shuffling forward through the grass.

I can hear the others around me.

"Where are we going?"

"Stop standing on my toe, Matthew."

"Stop putting your toe under my foot, then."

"feumaidh tu a bhith làidir mar am madadh-allaidh . . ."

We walk like this for what feels like . . . I can't be sure—time doesn't exist. Blindly following. Blind faith. My feet moving in time with Eleanor's. Our hands clasped together.

The whole thing is almost *peaceful.*

And then the ground changes. Rubble. Sloping upward.

"It's an incline," Eleanor says.

No shit. We start to ascend, placing one foot in front of the other. I feel unsteady, all slanted, as the wind whips around us. I slip, and my arm wrenches her with me. Suddenly she's on top of me. Her whole body on mine. Our arms twisted together. My mouth in the dirt.

Is this how I'll go to the afterlife? Smothered to death by Eleanor Banks?

Sod it. "Let's just crawl," I say.

We continue, on all fours, arms moving together, up and up. The sharpness of the ground digging into our hands, knees burning. And I wonder what we must look like to someone else. A lonesome bird, hovering above, thinking, *What the hell are they doing down there?*

And then the ground becomes flat. I'm exhausted. Thirsty. *So* thirsty. Dripping in sweat.

The singing stops. I feel the wind raging in my ears. Are we here? Is this Elysium?

"Well done," Ares says. "Now stand up."

We do. Awkwardly twisting around each other, trying not to topple over.

"Take a few steps back," he says. I move my feet slowly, Eleanor right next to me. "That's it. Now stop. No farther."

Why no farther?

I hear him helping the others to their feet, guiding them until they're lined up beside us.

"No sudden movements," Ares says. Oh, fun. "Stay exactly where you are." I hear his feet on the gravel. They stop somewhere in front of us. "You must all keep your eyes forward, on us. You must not, I repeat *must not,* look backward. If you do, you have failed the trial."

What is this?

"Blindfolds off."

I lift my hand up and pull it over my head. The brightness startles me. I blink.

Artemis's face. Then Ares's. All doleful. Pensive. Earnest. The sun cuts through a cloud, a sudden shard of light illuminating them. They look like a pair of angels. Angels of Death.

I fight the urge to look around me. *Why can't we look?*

I feel like we're high up. Very high up.

Artemis smiles. "All we're asking you to do is trust us. That's it. It's that simple." She pauses, her eyes narrowing. "Behind you, there's a drop." Um . . . What? I hear gasps around me. "Do not look."

I instinctively glance down at my feet, at my Vans on the rubble. The heels of them right in front of . . . where the rubble stops. And then . . . nothing.

Holy shit.

I feel Eleanor's hand grip mine. Her eyes are wide. Her mouth gapes open like a dying goldfish.

OK. That's . . . new.

Jing's voice comes from somewhere to my left. "I don't think I'll be able—"

"You must not *think*, Jing," Artemis says. "Thinking has ruined you. All of you. The old world has taught you to live in the anxieties of the past, the fears of the future. Throw all that away. Be *present*. Be here. *This* is happiness." Interesting logic. "There is no logic to it." Oh. "Just *be*."

Jing hesitates. "But . . . is it . . . safe?" I'd also like to know the answer to that question.

Artemis's face softens. "This is the safest you have been in your life, Jing." She scans her eyes over us. "Now all you have to do is fall backward."

I hear a collective intake of breaths.

No way. Nope. Not doing it.

Eleanor tenses up next to me, her breath quickening. "Seb . . . I don't—"

Someone begins to cry. It's Jing.

"Silence!" Ares orders, his voice firm. "This fear must go."

"Fuck's sake, cut it out," I hear Matthew whisper.

"We know you can take it. It's why you were chosen. Who would like the opportunity to go first?"

Opportunity? This isn't some job interview.

Suddenly Finn's voice enters my head. *You need to gain the Couple's trust. So they suspect nothing.*

My mouth opens before I can stop it. "We will."

Eleanor's trembling hand tightens around mine.

"Well done," Ares says. "The rest of you should take note."

He opens his bag and roots inside it. He then holds out his cupped hands. In them are five bloodstones. Our initials are marked on each one in bright red paint. *E&S.*

"These are yours," he says. "If you want them."

"All five, just for them?" Matthew says.

"They chose to go first. This bravery will be rewarded."

And then he throws them over our heads. They fall through the air behind us, but I don't hear them land.

"All you have to do is trust us," he says. "Can you truly let go?" He looks me dead in the eye.

"Yes," I say.

"Good. On my count."

We will get out of here, Finn.

"Three . . ." he says.

Oh, shit.

"Two . . ."

I look at Eleanor. Eyes closed.

Oh, holy shit.

I lean back. I feel her resist. Her hand pulling against mine.

"One."

And then the whole world pauses like we've been sucked into a vacuum.

My hand pulls her. She screams. We tilt together. And I see the whole sky.

I open my mouth, but nothing comes out. It's like someone has stuffed my throat with paper.

Then my feet leave the ground. And my head leads me.

Backward.

Downward.

Bound to Eleanor.
We're plummeting.
Hurtling down.
And there is nothing else.
Just us.

FIFTEEN
The Light

A wax candle. Its antique stand burnished metal, twisted and Gothic. The candle is tall and the flame bright, throwing shadows across the room. That's what I sometimes think of when I'm not with him. When I'm missing him. That's what I picture. I don't know where it came from, but that's how I see him. It's strange, but I like it. It warms me. It's beautiful.

The shadows the candle casts—*he* casts—are all angular, distorted, irregular. They make the room look odd. In fact, it's not a room at all, but a forest of unknown shapes. And I can hide in them. I can stand and be cloaked in their strangeness, their uniqueness. Safe.

But recently I've noticed something else in this forest. And every time I go to it, I'm filled with a new, unwelcome dread.

Someone is there. A figure. Poised. Quiet. Still. Just outside the shadows. I can't see their face. But I know they are waiting. Waiting to turn on the lights. To make all the shadows disappear. And when they do, there will be nowhere for me to hide.

As I hit the water, it feels like my head smashes open. Like a watermelon against a rock.

Darkness engulfs me. It's deafening.

Whuuummmmmmuuuummmmmm.

I'm thrown around a swirling black mess of nothing. If I'm dead, this is far worse than I ever imagined. And I thought I was going to hell.

Jesus. *My arm.*

My elbow twists, then my shoulder, pulled by the force of Eleanor's body as she tumbles, sending me turning through the water with her. We flail together, limbs colliding, like we've been tossed across the floor in a plastic bag. A plastic bag with no oxygen inside.

I need to breathe. Right now.

Which way is up?

My mouth involuntarily opens and my lungs try to draw the water in.

Don't do that.

My throat constricts like I'm choking. I *am* choking.

The taste of salt coats my tongue and floods up into my nose. A sudden pain radiates behind my eyes. I feel the pulse in my neck drumming, ready to explode.

Thud. My back hits something hard. The bottom.

Move, Seb. Look up.

A blurry light.

Go to it. Toward the light. There's a reason people say that.

I push my feet against the bottom, and I move up through the water, pulling Eleanor with me. Her weight threatens to rip my arm off. My legs kick with every ounce of strength I have.

The light. Closer now.

Ripples.

The surface.

Push.

I break through the water, my body spasming as the cold, peaty air enters it.

Thank you. Thank you. Oh, God. Thank you.

Eleanor's head bobs up in front of me. She gasps, her eyes bulging. She gulps in mouthfuls of air and water, making a sound like a rattling bark.

"Slow down, Eleanor!"

She starts thrashing in the water, pulling me with her. She's panicking. Her head dips under and up, her arms clasping for something, *anything.*

"Eleanor!" My voice echoes around us as I try to keep her head—and mine—above the surface. "Stop! Stop moving!" I yank my arm, dragging her body into mine so we're face to face. "Look at me. *Look at me.*" Her eyes flick up to mine, desperate. "Kick your legs and breathe, Eleanor. Just focus on breathing. Nothing else."

"Seb," she rasps. "I can't . . . I can't . . ."

"You can. Just *slowly* . . ." She closes her eyes. Breathes in through her nose. And out. "That's it." Her body starts to calm. "Just keep treading water."

I suddenly realize how cold it is. *Where the hell are we?*

I flash my eyes around us. Shelves of rock, shining black, reach all the way up to a hole above. I can see a circle of sky. Clouds.

Is that what we've just dropped through?

We're in a deep pool of water at the bottom of what appears to be some kind of underground cavity. A cave. Maybe thirty yards tall. The pool is no wider than my bedroom at home, and my bedroom is small. I try not to think about the fact that we could have smashed into the rock walls on our way down, which would have been pretty painful. Pretty fatal, actually.

I squint up, trying to find . . . I'm not sure what. A ledge, something we can use to pull ourselves out of the water. And then I see it. Nailed to the rock face, illuminated in a circle of light, is a wooden board.

YOU HAVE FIVE MINUTES BEFORE
THE NEXT PAIR DROPS.
COLLECT ONLY YOUR MARKED
BLOODSTONES.

THEN COME THIS WAY

I turn to where the arrow is pointing. A low, arched opening in the rock face, rising above the waterline. Just big enough to swim through. A tunnel.

"How long is five minutes?" I ask, but Eleanor doesn't reply. I look around for some sort of clock or sand-timer, but *time does not exist here.*

I glance up to the hole again, fighting my own rising panic. Two silhouettes stand with their backs to us, the heels of their shoes right at its edge. Raheem and Lucy, I think. The next to go. To drop.

They're going to land on us. Right on our heads.

"Ready?" I ask. Eleanor doesn't look ready. She stares blankly at the sign, bobbing in the water. "Listen to me, Eleanor. We need to *move*. The others are going to drop on us." Her face has gone a concerning shade of beige, and her lips are turning a blueish gray. "Eleanor! What don't you understand? We won't get any blood-stones! We will *lose!*"

She blinks. Then her eyes lock on to mine. "We can get all five, if we're quick."

Yes. There she is. Of course she responds more to the threat of losing than the threat of imminent death.

I look at our wrists. The plastic cord. "We'll be quicker without this."

She scans the rock face. "There." She nods in the direction of a jagged rock protruding from the wall.

We push through the water toward it, side by side.

"Ready?" I say.

We clasp our hands together, our fingers interlocking, and place the cord onto the edge of the rock where it's sharpest.

"Now." We scrape our wrists across it. Back and forth. Back and forth. "Keep going." I say through gritted teeth. I watch our skin tear with it, flaky flesh on the shiny black rock. Strangely it doesn't hurt. It's either too cold or I'm in shock, or both.

And then the cord snaps.

"Yes!" Eleanor gasps, breaking away from me.

I look up to see the two shadow figures. Oh, God. How long?

"Seb!" Eleanor cries. "We need to dive. What are you wait-ing for?"

"We don't know how long until—"

"Two minutes and forty-four seconds. Quickly!"

"But . . . how?"

"I've been counting. Stop faffing about!" She takes a huge breath and disappears beneath the surface.

She is . . . just something else.

I dive after her. As I open my eyes beneath the water, they immediately sting, clouded by the dirt. I push my hands out in front of me, searching through the green-brown murkiness, swimming downward until my hands meet the bottom.

I scrabble around. *Come on, come on. Where are you, you little fuckers?*

Then my fingers meet something round, the size of a snooker ball. I clasp it and see it glint. *S&E. Yes. Got you.*

I push my feet against the bottom, and my body cuts through the water, the cold piercing my brain.

When I surface, she's already there.

"Got two," she splutters.

How does she do it?

I hold mine up. "One."

"Two to go." She glances up. "One minute, nine seconds."

I look at the tunnel. "Shouldn't we—"

"Again!" she shouts, then disappears below. She's a machine.

I take a breath and dive down once more. I push my hands along the grit. *Nope. Nope. Come on. . . .*

And then I feel it. Round. Glinting.

When I surface, Eleanor is already at the entrance to the tunnel.

"Twenty seconds!" she cries, her voice bouncing off the black stone. I look up at the hole to see the two figures teetering, leaning backward.

Oh, shit.

"Come on, Seb!" Eleanor ducks through the gap.

I thrash after her. I slip under the arch just as there's the small splash of the next couple's bloodstones and then the whoosh of something heavy falling through air. A blood-curdling scream. The sound of two bodies colliding with the water.

The waves from their impact propel us forward, into the depths of the tunnel.

It's very quiet. We've been treading water for a while.

"Which way?" I say.

But there only seems to be one way. Forward.

I see the outline of the back of Eleanor's head bobbing in the water ahead of me. "Are you OK?" I say. "That was—"

"I'm fine."

"Eleanor—"

"I said I'm *fine*," she snaps. God, OK. "Come on."

"I just need to breathe for a—"

"There's no time." No time to breathe? She really *is* back. "We need to keep moving. Our bodies are in shock, and when it wears off, we'll really feel the cold. And then probably drown." Oh, right. Sure. Now *you're* the one saving lives. "How many did you get?"

"Two."

"Good."

"You?"

"Three. We got them all. Make sure you don't drop them."

"Roger that, Captain."

"What?"

"N-nothing." My teeth are chattering uncontrollably.

I push the stones down into my pants pocket. We seem to be in a low tunnel just wide enough for me to touch the rocks on either side.

"Let's *go*," she says.

My fingertips feel the inhaler in my pocket. I take it out. Put it in my mouth. *Click.*

"What are you doing?"

Jesus. "Stopping my lungs from imploding. You have a problem with that?"

"God, that thing." I thought the cold had maybe numbed the part of her brain that made her a massive asshole. Apparently, I was wrong. "Just . . . hurry up."

I inhale it. *Don't listen to her, my little blue friend.*

She sets off, swimming forward with a perfect breaststroke.

I dog-paddle. Dog-paddle has always served me well.

Clonk. My head bashes into a low rock. "Jesus." She keeps swimming. "I'm fine, by the way."

She doesn't respond. I preferred her mid–panic attack. How does she do it? Just . . . change like that.

I keep my head low, chin in the water. The walls feel like they're closing in on me. Oh, God. "Could we run out of air down here? I saw a documentary once—"

"No, Seb. There will be an exit. Just show some trust. You really think they'd let us get trapped down here?"

I wouldn't put it past them.

I keep following, the glint of her hair clips my guide. I don't think I've ever seen her without those. Even with her new Artemis braids. Maybe she was born wearing them. I suddenly picture her on a swing set, five years old. And someone is pushing her. Her aunt. Manning.

Donk. My head again. "Ow."

Rubble rains down on me.

Panic begins to rise in my chest. *What if it suddenly caves in?* I really don't want to be buried alive under a random Scottish island. If we even are in Scotland. I think I should keep talking. It makes me feel better.

"I like your hair clips."

"Just stop talking."

"OK."

I paddle behind her. Not talking. I watch the back of her head as she dips below the jagged rocks, skillfully dodging them, never once turning back to check on me.

Eventually we round a bend, and the tunnel suddenly opens out into the sea.

The sea.

And there is *sunlight.*

"See." Eleanor stops ahead of me, looking out across the water. "I told you there'd be a way out." But I hear something in her voice. It sounds a lot like relief.

I swim forward until I'm treading water next to her, in the warmth of the orange glow. Oh, God, that feels good.

I laugh. "Well," I say. "That was *awful.*"

I see her eyes are red and puffy, her skin flushed beneath the layer of dirt.

"Are you sure you're OK, Eleanor?"

"I'm fine," she says.

"You seemed pretty scared back there."

"I wasn't scared."

"It's fine if you were."

"I wasn't. I'm just . . ." She smiles, the sunlight bouncing off her face. "I'm fine."

"You did amazing. That was really impressive. You managed to—"

"Don't."

"What?"

"Just don't." She starts to chew her lip. "Please don't tell them."

"What? Who?"

"Ares and Artemis. Just. Please. It's important that you don't."

"Why? What's going on, Eleanor?"

"Nothing." But I can hear the uncertainty, the *fear,* in her voice. "You wouldn't understand."

"Try me."

"Let's just pretend it didn't happen. Right?" She nods. "Good." That empty smile again. "Come on, hon."

She's scared. *What does she know?*

I follow her through the hole in the cliff face. As we swim around the cliff, I see a little sandy cove nestled right into the cliffs ahead of us. If you passed by on a boat, you'd probably miss it.

As I watch Eleanor stumble onto the shore, dripping wet and shivering, I see six yellow tents in a circle around a firepit. Along with another sign, jutting out from the sand.

WELCOME TO THE LOVE BEACH

SIXTEEN
Sweets

"Quick," Eleanor says, pulling me up out of the water. "Let's get the fire lit." As we reach the circle of tents, I notice that in front of each one there's a large wooden crate.

They each have initials on them. I look at ours: *E&S.* And then at the tent directly behind it.

Are we both staying in that? Together? Just us?

How will I get to Finn?

"Aw, it's so cute," Eleanor says, pointing to the tent.

It's not *cute,* Eleanor. It's troubling. Very troubling.

"And that box with our initials!" She runs toward it, her sodden Reds dribbling a line of water across the sand behind her. She opens it and begins to rifle through its contents. "Fresh clothes. Towels. A blanket. Oh my God, Seb. Chocolate. Marshmallows! Strawberries!" She turns, beaming. "Isn't this so cool?" She throws a towel at me.

"Yeah," I say, wiping my face with it.

She stands up, clutching a fresh set of Reds in her hands.

"Use the tent," I say. "I'll change out here."

"Thanks!" She unzips it and disappears inside. I hear her rummaging around as I pull off my wet hoodie.

"The bedding looks so comfortable. . . . It's got hearts all over it!"

Oh, God.

Breathe. I will be with him tonight. *But how?*

Even if I do get out of the tent without Eleanor seeing, I have no idea how to get to Finn. I have no idea where the hell we are. This island can't be that big, can it?

My tank top and my pants slurp and slap as I peel them off, trying to balance on a sock to avoid getting sand on my feet. I towel myself off and pull the new clothes on.

The sun has gone behind a cloud, and I can feel the wind picking up. I can't stop shivering. I need to get warm.

I go to the firepit, where there's a stash of logs. I start to lay smaller pieces of kindling into the base of the pit, my fingers struggling to move, thick like sausages. I then take a flint and some dry mossy stuff and spark it until it lights. I carefully place the logs onto the fire, and it roars into life.

Well, what do you know? HappyHead *has* taught me something.

I suddenly realize how thirsty I am, so I head to the crate. There, right at the top, are two cans of Fanta. Pop. Why didn't she tell me there was Fanta? I pick one up, crack it open, then down it in one. Sweet Jesus Mother of Mary. There's nothing quite like it. Finn was right.

I'm about to put the empty can back into the crate when I see something right at the bottom.

A pack of Jolly Ranchers.

My stomach does a flip. *How did they know?* As I reach for the pack, I feel something hard. *That's weird.* I turn it over. There's a thin piece of wood tied to the pack with a piece of string.

I look at our tent. Still zipped up. I tiptoe back to the fire and undo the string, then turn the piece of wood over.

To get to boathouse follow the coast to your right.

Do __NOT__ cross the beach.

I have a plan.

My heart leaps. *Finn.*

"What's that?"

I jump at the sound of Eleanor's voice. "Oh, just a piece of wood."

I snap it. Then snap it again.

"Is there something on it?"

"Hmm?" I keep snapping. "Oh, no." I throw the wood into the fire.

Move it along. "Where do you think the others are?" I say. "It's been way longer than five minutes."

She shrugs. "Lost. Stuck. Who knows?" She doesn't sound particularly concerned for their welfare. "We got all our bloodstones."

I glance at the burning pieces of wood. His handwriting is still just visible, so I make a face to distract her. I hope it looks like hunger and a little like flirting. Hungry flirting, why not? "Could I have a strawberry please, hon?"

She smiles coyly. "Are you in a *romantic* mood, Seb?"

"Something like that."

As she darts back to the crate, I gaze at the pieces of wood as they disintegrate to ash. Has he been here? When? I scan the surrounding cliffs.

"Look at all this!" She reappears in front of me with her hands full. She places a blanket over my shoulders and sits on the sand next to me.

"Thanks," I say.

"Oh, what have you got there?"

"These? Jolly Ranchers. My favorite." I put them in my pocket. "I'm saving them for later."

"So restrained." I watch her rip open a pack of Love Hearts. "These are *my* favorite."

She's still trembling.

"Do you want to get under?" I hold up the side of the blanket.

"Are you sure?"

"It's freezing, Eleanor. Of course I'm sure."

She shuffles under it with me, and we sit for a moment, warming ourselves in front of the flames.

"I actually wanted to tell you something . . . ," she says quietly.

Uh-oh. "Oh, yeah?"

"I'm . . . *grateful*." Oh, wow. "That you helped me out back there."

"What, by pulling you down into hell with me?"

"Yes."

I smile. She does too. It's not her typical smile. It looks . . . real.

"Well, it was my pleasure."

"And in the cave," she adds. "Thank you . . . for *that*."

"It's all right. You seemed like you were strugg—"

"You did really well. I wasn't *scared* . . . but I might have forgotten myself for a moment. That's all."

"No worries."

"I think you're becoming braver. It's good, It suits you. We're back in the running. And I have to—*we* have to—keep it that way."

I see her face twitch. "What happened back there?"

"The Drop was very—"

"No. Not then. I mean after, in the tunnel. You said something about what they would do if they found out you were scared."

"I wasn't scared."

"Is it Manning?" I say. I watch her blink, mouth half open. She looks like a goldfish again. "I just wondered if—"

"No." She says this so cuttingly that I flinch. Then she smiles broadly, holding up the pack of Love Hearts right in front of my face. "Want one, hon?"

Jesus. I do worry she is partially bionic. But actually . . . "Sure."

I take a sweet from the pink foil wrapper and go to put it in my mouth.

"Wait!" she yells. "What does it *say*?"

"Oh, right." I hold it out in my palm.

FIRST LOVE

She raises her eyebrows. "Interesting."

I put it in my mouth and crunch.

"My turn," she says. She takes one and closes her hand around it without looking.

"Drumroll," I say.

She opens her hand.

ONLY ME

"Oh." Her face flushes, and she looks down at the ground. Then she puts the sweet in her mouth, and I listen to her slowly suck until it's gone.

As the sun moves lower in the sky, the others join us, stumbling up onto the Love Beach.

Raheem and Lucy arrive first, still tied together.

"That was intense," Raheem says.

"What took you so long?" Eleanor asks. "We were worried."

Were you?

"That tunnel." Lucy wipes her wet hair out of her face. "Raheem gets claustrophobic. He nearly had a panic attack."

I glance at Eleanor. She shoots me a look. *Don't you dare.*

"That's horrid," I say. "Sorry, Raheem."

"You both did well." He looks down at our bloodstones. "We got three."

"We got five," Eleanor says smugly.

"That's great, Raheem," I say quickly. I like Raheem. Always have.

"Cheers, mate." I think he likes me too. He isn't really the type of boy that usually likes me because he's, well, *cool,* and I like him even more for that.

"How did you manage to get three without breaking your cord?" I ask. "That must have been hard."

"Wait. Did you *snap* it?"

"It was Seb's idea," Eleanor chimes in, clearly panicking that we've broken all the rules.

"Clever," he says. "Didn't even think to do that."

We help them to break their cord with the flint, and they dress and join us by the fire.

Then Jamie and Rachel arrive.

"That was like some mad Indiana Jones shit!" Jamie says, emerging from the sea with his top off. *When the hell did he take his top off?* "I feel ALIVE!"

"Fuck my life," Rachel says, appearing behind him. I see they've already snapped their cord. "I look like a drowned rat." As she shakes her hair out, I think she looks more like a Bond girl. But what do I know?

"How many did you get?" Eleanor asks.

"One." She holds it up. "Fucking *one*."

"And it's not even yours . . . ," Eleanor says.

"What?" Rachel looks down at it, reading the initials: *R&L.* "Are you *kidding*?"

"Oops," Eleanor says. "That's a shame. I guess it's theirs now."

"I'll take that," Raheem says, snatching it from her hand.

Rachel turns to Jamie. "This is your fault."

"What? I can't help wanting a little snog in a place of natural beauty, with a natural beauty." He winks.

"You're such a knob." She sticks her tongue out at him, then scans the cove. "We nearly got our heads smashed in by Li and . . ." She stops. "Wait a second . . . have we got our *own* tents?"

Jamie picks her up in one swoop and carries her over to the one with their crate outside of it, both laughing hysterically.

Just then Sam and Li splutter up to us from the water, their faces a mix of terror, panic, and relief. Still tied together.

Li looks . . . *upset.*

"You OK, Li?" Lucy asks as they waddle over to us like two sad lost penguins.

"She'll be all right," Sam says. "Won't you?"

She nods, eyes down.

"What happened?" I say.

"It's . . . Jing," Li mutters. "She was really frightened. She didn't want to do it. And then Matthew . . ."

"What?" Raheem asks.

"He's such a prick," Sam says. "He was basically screaming at her. Like, really yelling."

"It's just because he was terrified himself," Raheem says. "It's pretty clear."

"Do you think they'll do it?" Eleanor asks.

Li shrugs.

Sam lifts up his arm, and Li's goes with it. "Right, someone help us snap this stupid thing."

"I don't think they got any bloodstones, Seb," Eleanor whispers into my ear. I can practically hear her brain doing the math. "I think we're now just behind Lucy and Raheem!" I look at her face, now full of barely contained glee. "I'm keeping a tally."

Course she is.

The couples gather around the firepit, eating sweets and chocolate, warming themselves as the sky begins to darken.

"So . . . Since they're not here, what do we all make of those two?" Raheem says, his arm around Lucy. "Artemis and Ares."

"I think they're fucking cool," Rachel says. "And they're so *sexy*, aren't they? Both of them. God."

"He's like a *sculpture*," Lucy says.

"Oi." Raheem nudges her playfully. "I can hear you, you know?"

"Sorry, but it's *true*. It's like they've been created or something. It's almost like they aren't real."

"Couple goals," Eleanor says brightly. Jamie laughs, and not in the way I think she was hoping for. Her cheeks go scarlet.

"I love how tough they are, but also sort of gentle," Sam says. "I want to be like that."

"And they're so free," Rachel says. "When you think about what they're actually saying, it's kind of incredible. Like, how amazing to be given the freedom to just . . . release our brains from the constraints of the world we lived in before all this."

"All right, Big Words," Jamie says. "Check you out. My girlfriend is an *intellectual,* everyone." *Girlfriend.*

"Oh, sod off!" Rachel pushes him so he nearly falls backward into the sand. "It's true, though. Before this I would never have questioned it. The old world." *The old world.* "Just . . . gone along with it. Making myself miserable. HappyHead is showing us a new way of thinking."

Lucy nods. "I've never known anything like this before. School was so *strict*. All the rules and constant worrying you're doing something wrong."

"But here it's different," Raheem puts in.

"Yeah," Lucy says. "It's a little scary sometimes, but Ares and Artemis are here, guiding us, and I do trust them."

"Me too," Eleanor says.

"I just feel like they have it sorted," Sam says. "Like they get it. Like they *know.*"

"Know what?" I say.

He looks at me. "I dunno. The secret to life." He smiles. "It just got me thinking. We're just these . . . *animals,* really, aren't we?

And we were forced under all these conditions, in the old world, but here, we can just . . . be."

Right, Sam is becoming intense, even for me.

Li hasn't said anything. She still looks worried. Distant. "You OK, Li?" I ask.

"Yeah. I was just thinking. . . . I haven't even thought about my parents. Is that bad?" I thought she might still be worried about her sister, but apparently not. "I kind of love it without them." She makes a face like she's revealed a terrible secret.

"It's fucking amazing without them. I feel ALIVE!" Jamie yells, and everyone laughs.

"It all seems really . . . far away. Doesn't it? Home," Raheem says. "Almost like it doesn't exist."

"Which is *why* I love it," Li says.

"Like a fresh start," Rachel agrees.

"They say we're special, guys," Sam says earnestly. "It's a big responsibility."

"Cos we *are* special!" Jamie lifts his can of Fanta. "A toast! To us. To the Ten!"

One by one, the others lift their cans with him. "The Ten!"

Um . . . OK. This is all getting a bit . . .

"Let's embrace it," Sam says.

"Yeah, fuck it. I'm all in," Rachel says.

"Me too," Lucy says. "What's there to lose? I genuinely think they care about us and want us to be happy. Don't they?"

"We do." Holy shit. I turn to see Artemis, standing just outside of the circle of tents. *How long has she been there?* "More than you could know."

She floats toward us, until she's right next to the fire. As the flames illuminate her, she looks like a mythical Greek goddess. "Congratulations, all of you," she says. "You are really showing us your faith. It's very exciting to see."

"What about Jing and Matthew?" Li says quietly.

"They decided not to make the Drop, which is a real shame. They will spend the night back at the camp with Ares."

No Ares. Thank God. That should make things easier.

I go over Finn's instructions in my head. *Follow the coast to your right. Do not cross the beach.*

Artemis floats around the firepit, scanning her eyes over the bloodstones that we've placed on the sand. She stops in front of me and Eleanor. "Well done, Eleanor and Seb. That is truly wonderful work."

"Thanks," Eleanor gushes.

I put my arm around her. "Eleanor did amazing; she got three of them." I feel her squeeze my hand.

Artemis nods, then looks around at us all. "Well, this is your prize. You will enjoy the whole night here."

"In our *own* tents?" Rachel says. "In our couples?"

"That's correct," Artemis says.

"This is so cool," Jamie says, then winks at Rachel. "We can practice our survival skills."

"Ew," Rachel replies, rolling her eyes.

I suddenly remember being with Finn, in our makeshift tent.

Artemis holds up her hand, and something glints, greeny-black, in the light of the fire. "Before we relax, a small ritual, in which there is one more bloodstone on offer." Jesus Christ. Really? What now?

Eleanor stiffens. Can she just chill out? We got five. *Five.*

"What I want you to do is very simple," Artemis continues. "Do not overthink it. In one sentence, I want you to tell your partner how their love makes you feel." The energy between us suddenly changes. "You may not have said those words to each other yet"—I haven't said that word to a single person in my entire life, so saying it to Eleanor Banks is going to be a leap—"but tonight I encourage you to be open to it. We are on the Love Beach, after all." People fidget apprehensively. "We will go around the circle. Li, if you'd like to start? Look at your partner and tell him how his love makes you feel."

Li scratches her head, her green hair dye now washed out. She looks at Sam. "Sam," she says. "Your love feels like a warm hug, a safety blanket."

Aw. Sweet.

Artemis nods, clearly not blown away. "Sam?"

"Li, your love feels like strength in quietness. And it will only grow stronger because together, here, we can push forward, learning to guide each other while being guided by the leadership of such inspiring people."

Really, Sam? That was so full of sh—

"That was beautiful." Artemis smiles. She loves it. Of course she does. Then she moves along. "Lucy. Tell Raheem what his love feels like."

Lucy turns to him. "Raheem. I honestly am just so glad I met you, and your love to me feels . . . enough."

"Raheem?"

"Lucy, your love feels so easy, natural, like it was meant to be."

"Very good," Artemis says.

That *was* good. Can these two please just win so we can be done with all this?

Artemis turns to Rachel and Jamie. "Jamie, would you like to tell Rachel what her love feels like?"

"Sure," he says. "Rachel, your love feels like a huge fire, burning bright." He stops, then adds, "And you're well fit."

Everyone laughs.

"That was two sentences," Eleanor whispers.

"Rachel?"

"Yeah, OK." She looks at Jamie and giggles. "OK. OK." She closes her eyes. "Jamie, your—"

"Open your eyes, Rachel," Artemis says.

"Sorry. OK. Jamie." She stares at him, fighting the urge to laugh again. "Your love makes me feel excited, and a little giddy, and honestly, like anything is possible."

"Thank you, Rachel."

Finally Artemis turns her attention to me and Eleanor. Staring. Why do these two stare so much? "Eleanor. Your turn."

Eleanor shuffles her bum, turning to me. "Seb. Your love feels loud and clear, telling me we can achieve anything and rise up to become an example to others," she says robotically. I almost want the Eleanor from the tunnel back.

"Thanks, Eleanor. That's really kind."

"Seb?"

Oh, God. I hadn't fully computed that I'd have to do this. OK. This is fine. Just . . .

Finn.

I think of his hair. His Ice Eyes.

I wish I could tell you how it feels. . . .

"Go on," Eleanor whispers eagerly.

"Um . . . OK. Your love . . ." I exhale and hold his image in my mind. "Your love makes me feel safe, like I'm in the shadows of your light, your candle. I will hide in them with you, in the shadows, and I won't let anyone take them away because they are the most beautiful thing I've ever known."

Eleanor looks at me. Her expression is hard to read. She has her mouth open. I'll go with confused. Then it shifts slightly and she almost looks *sad*.

No one is speaking. Someone should say something. Shit.

She furrows her brow, then smiles broadly. "Thanks, Seb. That was so sweet and . . . *abstract*."

"Glad you liked it." I can feel my cheeks burning.

"Thank you, everyone," Artemis says. "Those were lovely, impulsive responses. I will now make my choice."

She puts her hand on her chin, turning around the circle, her eyes moving over our faces. She then stops and steps toward Sam. "This is yours, Sam."

He smiles. "No way!"

"You find love in strength. You appreciated that you are here to learn, and that it has served a purpose in the way you and Li are loving each other. I like that."

Of course you do. He basically said he loves you.

Everyone begins to clap.

"It's their first one," Eleanor whispers. "Rachel and Jamie still don't have any." She can barely contain her glee. Artemis sits cross-legged on the sand. "Now, let us relax and enjoy each other's company."

I watch as the couples toast marshmallows, hanging on Artemis's every word as she speaks. And she speaks a lot. I just sit and watch her mouth moving, not really hearing any of it. The warmth of the fire makes my eyes droop.

Shit. Don't fall asleep. Tonight. *Tonight.*

What time is it? It must be getting late now.

Eventually Artemis gets up. "I will leave you to enjoy your evening. You've earned it." She goes to her tent.

Gradually the couples begin to trickle off into their own tents, giggling, arms around each other. The tents light up and glow a warm soothing yellow. They remind me of those paper lanterns that people release into the sky.

And then it's just me and Eleanor. Together by the fire.

She nudges my shoulder. "Is it time?" she says in a funny voice.

Time for what? "Um, all right, yeah. OK."

She takes my hand and leads me to our tent. She unzips it, then switches on a small flashlight hanging from a hook in its roof. I see rose petals, scattered across the cushioned floor. It's like one big mattress. On top of it are two sleeping bags, covered in yellow hearts. One with an "S" and one with an "E."

"Cute, isn't it?" Eleanor says.

I crawl onto mine. Oh, it is so comfortable. I lie my head back. My body sinks into it.

I close my eyes. *Tonight. I'm coming.*

"Seb?" Eleanor says quietly. I can feel her staring at me.

I open my eyes.

She's sitting cross-legged on top of her sleeping bag, twisting the drawstring slowly around her fingers so the tips of them are going a purply red. Her eyes are wide, and she looks uncomfortable, like there's a pressure building up within her. The muscles in her face quiver.

"Are you all right, Eleanor?"

She suddenly smiles. "Sleep well!" She blows me a kiss, clicks off the flashlight, and wriggles herself into her sleeping bag.

I think she might meet her end by spontaneous combustion. I do worry about that.

"Are you OK?" I say. "You seem—"

"Yep," she says. "Night."

"We can . . . *talk,* you know?"

"It's OK. You're tired." She pulls the hood of her sleeping bag over her head.

I turn onto my back and lie there, staring at the yellow walls, trying to block out the sound of the other couples in the tents around us, until the low hum of their chatter slowly disappears.

Wait. Just wait. A little longer.

And then, from next to me, Eleanor's voice again, but this time muffled, like she's very far away. "In the love ritual. You were talking about . . . *him,* weren't you?"

I pretend I'm asleep.

After a while, I hear her breathing change. Heavy. Deep.

I wait a little longer, just to be sure. And then slowly, quietly, I sit myself up.

I open the nylon door. Poke my head out. All the lights in the other tents are now out. Just the embers of the fire, glowing gently. I zip the door back up, careful not to make a sound.

And then I go. Turn right, out of the cove, along the coastline.

I go to him.

SEVENTEEN
Learning

I stay low as I follow the coast. The moon shines above, a luminous orb lighting my way, its glow bouncing off the rippling surface of the sea.

I clamber up onto the top of a cluster of rocks. And there it is. The pebble beach. Stretching out in front of me, the row of targets still running right along it. I crouch for a moment, letting my breath slow. It's quiet. Really quiet.

I shift my gaze to where the pebbles meet the wood's edge like a curtain drawn across the back of the shore, hiding its secrets. In the distance, the boathouse.

I drop down from the rocks onto the pebbles. They crunch beneath my feet.

I remember his note. *Do not cross the beach.* Why?

Then something catches my eye. At the end of the line of targets, right by the water's edge—a man in black. Black boots. Black gloves.

The Keeper. That's why.

I move back into the shadows of the rocks, watching as he stands stock-still, looking out over the water.

Move, Seb.

I hug the side of the rocks, treading carefully until I'm at the edge of the wood. I duck behind the curtain of trees and slowly move toward the boathouse, never once letting my eyes leave the back of him. When I'm halfway there, I see a trunk wide enough to hide behind.

I press my forehead into the bark. OK. Just take a second. Breathe.

I peer around the side of the trunk and trace the Keeper's outline. *What is he doing?* And then I see something in front of him, out on the water. A light. Moving slowly toward the shore. *Is that a boat?*

Suddenly I feel a hand over my mouth.

"Shh. It's me." Finn. Adrenaline surges through my veins. "Come this way." His hands gently pull me backward, and I move my feet with his. "Keep going," he whispers. "That's it."

I watch the outline of the Keeper growing smaller as we move painstakingly back through the trees, deeper into the woods. Finn's body behind mine, his chest expanding into me with every breath. Then the ground beneath me feels different. Firm. Solid. I stop and look down.

At first, I don't register what it is. A large wooden hatch, beneath the twigs and leaves. A handle. A chain. A padlock. And then I realize. *The bunker.*

"Is that . . . ?"

"Yeah."

"Jesus."

"Come on. *Keep moving.*"

As I move my foot, it hits the handle of the hatch. I try to stop myself but fall sideways. My knees slam into the wood.

Donk. The noise reverberates around the trees, sending birds flying up out of the canopy above.

Shit. I snap my head up, looking toward the shore. The Keeper swings around. He takes a step forward and peers into the darkness of the tree line.

Oh, God.

"Reveal your number!" he shouts.

I look up at Finn. "Boathouse. Now. *Go.*"

I turn and crawl, scrambling on my hands and knees as quickly and quietly as I can through the pine needles, until I see a low thicket of twisted vines. I throw myself behind it.

"Reveal your number!" the Keeper yells again.

I push myself up onto my knees and peer through the vines. I can just make out Finn, still standing on top of the hatch. "Number Five!" he shouts. "I am Number Five!"

The Keeper steps through the trees toward Finn, until he is right in front of him. Then he stops, towering over him.

"Why are you not seeing to your duties?"

"Sorry . . ."

"*Sir.*"

"Sorry, sir."

"You shouldn't be down here."

Finn drops his head. "I just wanted some water."

"You are becoming a problem, Number Five. You are beginning to make my job very difficult."

"I thought—"

"Do not speak." They're now inches apart. "You're slacking. Aren't you?"

"Yes, sir."

"Your duties are for your benefit. They're a vital part of your program."

"Yes, sir."

"You are lucky to be here. She gave you a chance."

"Yes, sir."

"Do you understand me?"

"Yes, sir. I do, sir."

"Say it."

"I am lucky, sir."

"You don't seem to be taking it seriously."

"I am." Finn's voice trembles. "I promise, I am. . . ."

"We just want you better." The Keeper starts to take off his gloves.

Finn looks up at him. "Wait! Please, no!"

"You need to learn." The Keeper pushes his gloves down into his pockets. I watch as he lifts up the sleeve of his coat, revealing his wrist. There's something around it.

A yellow wristband.

Finn takes a step back. "I will. I promise. Plea—"

The Keeper presses his finger onto the band. The tag on Finn's leg flashes red beneath his pants, lighting up the darkness.

zzzzz

Finn's head snaps back. His body contorts, like his muscles have suddenly stiffened. Then he shudders, twitching uncontrollably.

I put my hand over my mouth. Oh my God.

The Keeper lifts his finger from the wristband, and Finn drops to the ground. He groans, writhing in the dirt.

What the—

The Keeper leans forward. "Do you understand me now?"

"Yes, sir," Finn gasps.

"Stand up."

I watch Finn scramble to his feet. The Keeper lifts Finn's chin with his fingers so that their eyes meet. "You need to change. Agree with me."

"I . . . I need to change."

"Good. Now you're learning. Now, go. If I see you back at the dorm before clock-in, you will have to learn again. You will learn and learn, until you understand. Yes?"

Finn slowly nods. Then he staggers away, his tag glowing green, illuminating his footsteps as he limps into the darkness. The Keeper scans his eyes around the trees. Then he walks back toward the shore.

My ears ring, pulsating from the blood churning around my head. The bitter taste of dread coats my tongue. They're going to kill him.

The Never Plan. *Ended.* While we're all up there eating Love Hearts as if none of this is happening. I realize my eyes are wet and I'm dribbling over my hand, still clutched around my mouth. *She controls everything.*

I'm frozen. My body stuck. *You need to move. Come on, Seb.*

I begin to crawl in the direction of the boathouse. I have to help him. We have to get out of here.

Up ahead I see the crumbling wall covered in vines. Crouched behind it is Finn. He puts a trembling finger up to his lips and beckons me forward.

As I sit down next to him, our backs to the wall, he looks at my face and registers my expression. "You saw."

"Yes, I saw. What the hell?"

"Shh . . . ," he hisses. "Stay quiet." His voice is hoarse. "He's still out there."

"Why didn't you tell me?"

He doesn't answer.

I can hear his chest wheezing as he inhales. His eyes are distant. Vacant. Empty. I put my hand on top of his. He flinches. I don't let go. Squeeze his hand.

Finally he peers around the corner. "OK," he says quietly. "He's gone. He'll be back in the bunker by now. But we don't have long. Let's go."

We scramble up the wall, scaling the vines until we're up on the roof. I look out across the water and see the light in the distance, this time moving away from us.

"What is that?"

"Our chance," he says. "A boat comes every other night at midnight to drop provisions for the Keeper." And as I understand what he is thinking—his idea, his plan—I see the sharp icy blue returning to his eyes.

He points to the hole beside our feet. "Go on, then."

I drop down into it, hitting the floor in a cloud of dust. I wait for it to settle and stand up.

Four hooded faces stare back at me from the far wall.

Finn lands next to me. "This is Seb," he says, taking a step toward them. "You might remember him from HappyHead."

He turns to me, his eyes burning. "He's going to help us."

EIGHTEEN

Scrappy

I recognize them all.

Betty. Her black hair hanging into her eyes, the ragged sleeves of her hoodie pulled down over her clenched fists.

"Hi, Seb," she says. "Sorry about the other night. I was just . . ."

Scared? Me too, Betty. Me too. "It's OK, Betty."

Next to her, Jennifer Beale. The angry girl who was dragged out of the assembly hall after Manning told her she needed to find inner peace. Her blond hair is now a filthy brown, her strong features muted. There's a number two printed on her hoodie. She nods at me.

Next to her, Number Four. I remember him from the beach inside the perimeter fence at the facility, the day they took Finn away. He nearly spat in the face of an Overall before he was dragged to his boat. His fair curls fall loosely over his forehead. Green eyes shine through his rough features and stubble covers his cheeks. I notice how broad he is, how tall. He looks alert, ready, the sleeves of his hoodie rolled up to reveal forearms covered in bruises. "Killian," he says. Irish. He looks me up and down, skeptically.

Lastly, there's Number Three. Malachai. The boy from Serenity who liked mixing up his cereals. He looks tiny next to Killian. He blinks at me through his glasses, now cracked and clouded with muck and grime, like a newborn mouse opening its eyes for the first time.

"Hi, Malachai," I say. He holds his hand up.

The Bottom Percentile.

I think of them before, back in the old world. Before Happy-Head, before all of this. I try to imagine them in their own clothes, at home, with their friends, before they ever received the letter telling them they'd been selected. But I can only see them like this. In their tatty, dirty Greens with numbers printed on their chests. While I stand in front of them in a set of fresh Reds.

"Seb is on our side," Finn says. "He wants to help."

As they all look at me, waiting, I begin to feel . . . overwhelmed. Like nothing I have to say can help. I open my mouth, hoping something good will come out of it, but all I end up saying is "I'm so sorry."

"Fine for you, isn't it?" Killian says.

"Killian . . . ," Finn says cautiously.

Killian shrugs, not taking his eyes off me. "What are you doing up there all day? Meditating? Singing songs around a campfire? Kumba-fucking-ya? While we're down here, getting zapped by Electro Man out there."

"Give him a chance," Betty says quietly.

"Yeah, go on, Seb," Jennifer says.

Malachai blinks at me.

"How can we trust him?" Killian says.

"You can trust him," Finn says, his voice stronger now. "Tell them what you know, Seb."

I look back at him. *Everything?*

He gives me a small, reassuring nod. "They need to know the truth."

Shit. OK. The truth . . .

"Killian . . . You're right."

He raises his eyebrows. *Go on, then. I'm waiting.*

"The whole program is a lie. It was never meant to be like this. Manning is not who you think she is. She's dangerous. Dr. Stone was never sick when we were back at the facility. I mean she *was,* but Manning *made* her sick and then hid her away so she could use the program to start her own experiment."

They all stare blankly. Betty chews on her sleeve.

I said that very quickly. Maybe it was too much. At least for an opener.

"How do you know all this?" Killian says.

"I . . ." I falter.

"Spit it out, pal. We're putting ourselves at risk being down here."

Finn's fingers brush against mine.

I exhale. Just tell them. "Me and Finn found something called the Never Plan in Manning's office back at the HappyHead facility, in her safe. She didn't want anyone to find it. It was never meant to be seen. It's why they put the cameras up after the Hide, searched our rooms, recalibrated our chips. It's why Finn got taken off the beach by—"

"So how come *you* didn't get in trouble?" Jennifer cuts me off.

"They didn't know I was there." And still don't. I hope.

"This is why he can help us," Finn says. "They still trust him."

Doubt creeps across their faces.

"But *I* don't trust *them*," I say. "At all." Just need to make that very clear.

Betty lifts her head, taking her sleeve out of her mouth. "What's the Never Plan?"

"It's a document Manning created that outlines what she wants to do with us all here, on the island."

"Oh, yeah?" Killian folds his arms. "And what's that, then?"

"Well. She. Um . . ." Oh, God. "She's decided that you're something she calls the Bottom Percentile."

"Oh," Betty says. "What does that mean?"

"Doesn't sound great, Betty," Killian says. "I wouldn't hold your breath."

"It means . . ." OK, *the truth.* "It means she thinks you're worthless. That there's no hope for you. This Helpers' High program—it's a lie, a pretense. She doesn't want you to be happy. She wants you right where you are. She doesn't care about you. She wants to use this *new purpose,* this *lie,* to keep you in your place."

Betty drops her eyes. Jennifer chews her lip. Malachai sniffs.

"Serving you?" Killian says.

"Yes."

"For how long?" Betty says quietly. "When do we go home?"

"I don't think we are going home, Betty," Finn says.

Betty makes a small whimper.

"What?" Jennifer says.

"And it will get worse for us," Finn continues. "If we don't do something about it."

"What kind of worse?" Killian asks.

Finn doesn't answer. The truth moves across them like a dark spirit, joining them at the back of the room.

"Why would she do this?" Jennifer whispers.

"Because she thinks she's right," I say. "Radical change. Eradicating unhappiness. Ending it. She thinks she's helping."

"Helping?" Killian gives a bitter laugh. "She's off her head."

"I don't think she sees it like that," I say. He shoots me a look as if to say, *Are you defending her?*

"It's the truth, Killian," Finn says quickly. "It's real. The Never Plan is real. I've read it. And so has Seb. We're all in it. All our names are in it."

"And you lot up there," Jennifer says. "What's all that about?"

"They call us the Ten. The Elite."

"The favorites," Killian snarls.

"That's how she sees it."

"And what does she want from you?" Jennifer says.

"She wants the Ten to become resistant to weakness. To become what she would call strong, happy people. And she's pairing us off into couples. This seems to be part of her plan to stop unhappiness. She wants us to fall in love."

That word *love*. It's so far removed from this.

"Eugenics," Malachai whispers. He takes off his glasses and wipes them on his hoodie, then puts them back on, no less dirty than they were before.

"Yeah," I say. "Exactly that."

I think of the Ten, back up there, in their tents, with their marshmallows and fizzy drinks. "Manning calls us special. But we're not. We're just more . . . desperate to impress. To do anything for a reward. To win their approval, their praise. To be liked."

"Why do you want to help us? What's in it for you?" Jennifer asks. "Isn't it easier for you to just, like, pretend all this isn't happening?"

I think of Eleanor. Her face in the tent, looking like she was about to burst, brimming with the strain, the effort of her pretense. And when I answer, I keep my head up, steady, matching Finn's pose.

"Because you're not weak and you don't need to change. If anything, you're the special ones. You remained yourselves, and Manning hates you for it. I wasn't able to do that. That's why I'm up there, with them. I'm there because I was lying. And, if I was honest, I'd be down here, with you. This is where I want to be. I want to be here, with you lot. And I want to help you get out."

My head is reeling. I realize Finn is holding my hand.

Killian scratches his nose. "So," he says. "We're in a fucking pickle, aren't we?"

"That's one way of putting it."

"Right, then." He exhales, long and hard. "Let's do this." He nods at me.

Finn's grip tightens around my hand. "We need everyone," he says. "If this is going to work. It's not going to be easy, but we need to try. Are we all in?"

I remember what he said, all that time ago in our makeshift tent. *We need to stop this. For people like us.*

"Yes, please," Betty murmurs. "I want to go home."

"All right," Jennifer says. "Anything but this."

"I'm not staying here to be killed," Malachai mutters.

"Right," Finn says. "Good." He gestures for them to come closer. "I've been watching the Keeper. He makes some kind of collection on the beach at midnight, every other night."

"What collection?" Betty asks.

"A boat comes to the shore and delivers something to him," Finn says. "From the mainland. A duffel bag. There's just one person on it. They speak together for about five minutes."

Betty frowns. "How do you know?"

"I've watched them from the tree line. Overheard them." The others raise their eyebrows. "Voices travel on a quiet beach."

Killian smiles. "Sneaky, aren't you, Finneas."

"Try my best."

Finn's energy moves among the group, contagious, hopeful, galvanizing. The boathouse begins to fizz with possibility.

"And this man comes on his own?" Betty says.

"It's just the two of them on the beach."

"Does he have a wristband too?" Jennifer asks.

"I'm not certain, but we should assume he does. He wears the same clothes as the Keeper."

"What's in the bag?" Jennifer says.

"Provisions for the Ten. Fresh food. Strawberries and croissants and stuff."

"Fuck's sake," Killian says. *"Croissants?"*

They all look at me, frowning. I put my hands up. Not my fault.

"So the next collection is when?" Jennifer says. "And you're *sure* about this?"

Finn nods. "As sure as I can be—it's in two nights' time. He's just done one now. He's taken the bag down to the bunker, and he'll stay down there for about an hour after the delivery."

"I wonder why," Betty says.

"So he can steal the croissants," Killian says.

Malachai grins. "And do his nightly sudoku."

Killian looks at him, smiling too. "Look at his stash of porn, more like."

I watch the corner of Finn's mouth turn up, so I can see a flash of his teeth.

Smiling. Genuinely. He looks so *good*.

"Or maybe it's a copy of *Lord of the Flies*," Malachai says.

OK, Malachai. A little far. A little close to the bone.

"What's *Lord of the Flies*?" Betty peers at him through her fringe.

Um. Maybe we shouldn't—

"It's about a group of kids who go to an island and start to beat each other to dea—"

"All right!" Killian cuts him off as Betty's eyes widen with horror. "Maybe we just go back to the plan."

Malachai shrugs. "What? It's a good book."

"Seriously, though, guys," Jennifer says. "How do we actually get on the boat?"

"Jump them," Finn says. "When they pass the bag over. It should be dead simple if we're all together. They'll be outnumbered."

"But . . . ," Jennifer says, clearly not convinced, "the Keeper will use his wristband to stop us. And if the other man has one too, then we'll all be fucked."

That's a good point. I watch the others as the excitement begins to fizzle away.

But then I realize something. "I don't have a tag," I say. This is how I can help.

"But what are *you* gonna do?" Killian says. "No offense, mate, but he's twice your size. You wouldn't stand a chance against two of them."

A hit of adrenaline sears through me. I know exactly what we need. "The crossbow," I say.

Finn looks up at me. They all do.

"What crossbow?" Finn says.

"Ares and Artemis—the Couple—have a crossbow. It's . . ." I visualize the bolts, its angular black frame. "Lethal," I say.

"Sounds kind of . . . *perfect*," Killian says.

Finn's eyes widen.

"It's why there are targets on the beach. They're training us. Some bullshit about trust. If I get it, we can use it." The adrenaline intensifies. I feel it buzzing in my chest.

"Do you know how to use it?" Jennifer asks.

I am the Ultimate Sniper King. OK, stop. That wasn't real. "Well, no," I say. "Not really. Not yet."

"But he might not need to," Finn says slowly. "We just threaten them with it."

I nod. "They wouldn't use their wristbands if there was a crossbow pointed at them."

I watch as the group digest my words. As their hope reignites.

"I can make some shanks as well," Malachai says. We all turn to him. "With branches from the forest. I've actually made one already." He lifts up his hoodie and takes a small, pointed stick out of the elastic in his pants.

"Curveball," Killian says, looking at him a little cautiously now, like we might have a live wire on our hands with Malachai. "I love your enthusiasm—and you clearly have a keen eye for woodwork, pal, which is *great*—I just think we might need something better than spiky twigs."

Malachai drops his head. "Could be pretty deadly too."

"I think it looks good, Malachai," Betty says.

I feel like these two have some united love for the macabre

they might want to tap into together. When they're out of here. And I'm not around.

"I think the crossbow will be enough," Killian says.

"OK," I say. "I can get it. I can get the crossbow."

"You sure?" Finn says.

I nod.

"Just . . . make sure you don't put yourself in danger."

"Bit late for that," Killian says. "But yeah, Seb. Keep yourself safe, mate. But also, make sure you get it." He grins. "No pressure."

"Wait," Jennifer says cautiously. "So what happens when we get to the mainland?"

Finn's eyes flash. "We take the man's quad bike."

"He has a *quad bike*?" Killian says.

"Oh, yeah. Thought I'd said that."

"No." Killian laughs, giddy now. "Fucking *awesome*. Shotgun driving."

"Fine by me," Finn says. "And once we're on the mainland, we get help. Once people know, Manning will be stopped and this will be over."

Holy shit. This could happen. We stare at each other, the air between us fizzing. Alive.

Wait. Hold on. "So the collection happens at midnight?" I say.

"Every time," Finn says.

"How do you know that? There are no clocks."

He pulls up the bottom of his pants to reveal the tag. I look at the digital numbers on the screen.

00:36

Ah. That's how.

"That's . . . useful," I say. "But *I* still don't have any way of knowing."

"Wait," Betty says, her eyes gleaming. She lifts up her wet sleeve. "You can have this."

She holds out her arm. On it is an old watch. Delicate. Its thin gold strap loose around her wrist. Behind the slightly steamed-up glass, I can see the hands moving over its ivory face. Ticking gently.

"How did you get that?" Killian says.

"I hid it in my bra back at HappyHead when we had to give our phones in." She smiles up at us mischievously.

"Why would you want to keep *that*?" Jennifer says.

"It was my grandma's. She left it to me, so I wasn't going to let them take it. I've never taken it off." She unclips the buckle and holds it out to me.

"Are you sure?"

"Yeah, you're going to need it."

"Thanks," I say. "I won't lose it. Promise."

I take it from her and clip it on to my forearm. It's tight, nipping my skin, but it fits.

"Suits you," she says.

Everyone looks at me. Hopeful. Waiting for what I will say next. It makes me feel uneasy that they are trusting me, but I try not to show it.

"So," I say. "We meet here, in the boathouse, in two nights' time, at midnight. Me with the crossbow—"

"Malachai with his stick," Killian says.

"And we get the hell out of here," Jennifer adds.

Silence falls. The anticipation ripples through us.

"It's scrappy," Killian says.

"Very scrappy," Finn says.

"But scrappy is better than nothing," I say.

I look at Finn, his hair hanging over his face. He looks so good like this. And suddenly I can visualize him out of here. Away from all this.

He sees me looking and nudges me with his shoulder. "What?"

"Nothing."

"Right, let's get going," Killian says. "Before he comes back out of the bunker." He turns to Finn. "And your boyfriend here gets caught and shot for betrayal." He looks at me and shrugs, then begins to move the crates with the others.

Boyfriend. OK. Interesting choice of words there, Killian.

I steal a look at Finn, but he seems caught up in his own thoughts.

Once the crates are stacked in the center of the room, the others clamber up through the hole and disappear back into the woods to their chores. Leaving just me and Finn.

"Look, if you can't get it, we can think of something else."

"I'll get it," I say. "We're going to do this."

And then I remember. "I have something for you." I put my hand in my pocket and take out the pack of Jolly Ranchers. "Here."

"What are they?" he asks, taking them.

"My favorite ever sweet."

"No way!" He reads the pack. "Jolly Ranchers." The way he says this, in his Manc accent, makes me like them, and him, even more. "You had them stashed in your keks this whole time?"

I don't know what this means, but I like it, so I just nod.

"Not had sweets in ages." He rips open the pack. "What's the best color?"

"Blue."

He takes one and puts it in his mouth. "Wow, this is fucking sour."

"I know. Great, isn't it?"

"My tongue feels like it's gonna drop off," he says. "Ugh. You *like* these?"

"Love them. You just need to push through the sour bit, then it tastes like bubble gum."

I remember what I said to Eleanor at the cove. All the things I should have said to him. "Finn . . ."

"Yeah?" he says, making a face, still powering through the outer layer.

"You make me feel great," I blurt out. "Like . . . really great. I really want this plan to work so we can get out of here and just . . . be. Together."

OK. That's definitely not what I said to Eleanor.

"We will," he says. "I'm glad I make you feel great."

Beep. He looks down at his leg. "Shit. Got to go."

And before I know it, he's on top of the crates.

"Don't piss him off again," I say.

"I'll try not to."

Once he's gone, I scan my eyes around the room, taking it in, picturing their faces in the dark. My head buzzing, searing with something, something *emotional.* I can't quite place it.

Then I realize it's because I haven't ever really felt it before. And it has a name. Belonging.

I feel a heat behind my eyes, and they start to sting.

People like us.

NINETEEN
The Slate List

When I get back to the Love Beach, I gaze out across the sea. The vastness of it makes me feel tiny. Insignificant. It galvanizes me.

We will get out of here. This will all be over soon.

I tiptoe across the sand, looking down at the remnants of the evening. The sweet wrappers, the empty cans, the melted marshmallows glued to the rocks surrounding the dying fire.

I climb into our tent. As I zip it back up, I glance over at Eleanor, buried deep in her sleeping bag. I then lie back on my sleeping bag, allowing the softness of it to envelop me.

It feels like I've only been asleep for minutes when I jolt awake. I open my eyes. The tent is already unzipped. I peer through the gap to see Artemis standing by the firepit, banging a pan against a rock. "Up, everyone!" she calls. "Time to eat, then back to camp."

The couples emerge blearily onto the beach. The debris of the night before is now gone. The boys begin to congregate, and I watch as they laugh, nudging each other suggestively, fist-bumping in a congratulatory way as the girls create a little circle, whispering and blushing.

Where's Eleanor?

And then I see her, sitting alone by the firepit, chewing on the end of a Snickers bar.

She looks a little . . . absent. I realize that she isn't actually chewing the Snickers. It's just hanging out of her mouth like she's completely forgotten it's there.

Rachel bounces over and sits beside her. Eleanor's face immediately changes. She takes the chocolate out of her mouth, leaving a smudge of brown on her bottom lip, and turns to Rachel. Excitable. Giggly. *Coy.*

I watch as they talk, trying to read their lips. But they move so rapidly that it's hard to know exactly what they're saying. Then Eleanor flashes her eyes to me, flutters her lashes like she is in a badly written rom-com, and makes a very questionable hand gesture.

Oh, right. So the rom-com is not a PG.

They both fall about in hysterical laughter. That *definitely* didn't happen.

"Hey, Seb." I look up. "What are you doing, mate?" Raheem says. "You gonna stay like that forever?" I realize I'm still a floating head.

"I was just . . . You know . . ." I look at Eleanor again. "Thinking about last night."

"Yeah?" He sits down on the sand in front of me. "So how was it?"

I pull myself out of the tent and squat next to him, shuffling my bum to make a groove in the sand. "Yeah, you know . . ."

"You had fun, right?" He nudges my arm. "You look knackered."

"Um. Yeah. It was . . . fun. How was yours?"

"It was nice," he says. "Really nice." He glances over at Lucy, now standing talking to Li and Artemis. "We didn't *do* anything. We just chatted. A bit of cuddling. But . . ." He pauses. "She's cool. Really cool. Amazing, actually."

"Yeah, she's lovely," I say, still trying to find the right position for my bum.

"It's weird, isn't it?" he says. "Being here."

I stop. "What do you mean?"

"Just . . . I dunno . . ." He scratches his cheek. "Just strange. This place."

I shuffle a little closer. "Yeah . . . Can be," I say quietly. "Strange is a good word for it."

"I just . . ." He stops and glances at Artemis, who is still deep in conversation. He lowers his voice. "This could all be seen as a bit *mental,* couldn't it? This whole thing."

My stomach tightens. "Yeah . . ."

"And I like you, Seb. I think you've got your head screwed on. . . ."

"Uh-huh."

"And it might be weird to say this. . . ."

"Go on," I say.

"Well, before I came here, I wasn't like this."

"No?"

"No. I was . . ." He starts to whisper so I have to lean in to hear him. "I sometimes feel like a bit of a fake. Cos I was a bit of a bad kid, you know. I had problems at school and stuff. My parents were worried about me at times. . . . I was a bit . . . *depressed.*"

"Right . . ."

"Sorry . . . I don't know why I'm telling you this."

"No . . . it's good. I was the same. Sort of."

He frowns. "And this place . . . This whole thing."

"Yeah?"

"I just wonder . . ."

"What?" You wonder what, Raheem?

"I just wonder *why* I'm here. . . ."

"Yeah, I understand that. . . ."

"Like . . . Sorry. I don't know."

"You mean," I whisper, "it all feels *wrong*?"

"Yeah . . . Exactly." He sighs. *Go on, Raheem. . . .* "Cos I just finally feel *happy*, Seb." I feel my stomach drop. "And I've never felt that before. Right now, I think I'm probably the happiest I've ever been in my life. I think I really love her, you know?" He turns to look at Lucy again.

"That's good," I say. "I'm so happy for you, Raheem."

"And it's all thanks to her, isn't it?"

"Lucy?"

"No. Madame Manning."

Oh. Oh, right.

"I would never have met Lucy without this place. I'd never have had the chance to learn how I could be this kind of person. I'm so fucking happy, Seb!" He laughs. "And she's making that happen. Manning is, I mean."

"Yeah."

"I think me and Lucy could be something really special. And I hope she sees it. *Manning*."

"I understand what you mean."

"But it's all kind of overwhelming. It's kind of *scary*, isn't it?"

"Yeah," I say. "It really is."

By the time we get back to the elm tree, Jing and Matthew are already sitting on their stone, their heads lowered.

Something's not right.

"Everyone, take your seats," Artemis says, joining Ares by the firepit.

I head to our stone, Eleanor by my side. As we pass Jing and Matthew, I look down at them.

"Hi, Jing," I say.

She glances up at me, her eyes red and puffy, sleeves pulled down over her hands.

"Are you OK?"

Matthew glares at me. "We're fine."

"Come on," Eleanor says, pulling me away. "They're clearly frustrated with themselves for not completing the trial yesterday. And rightly so." She says this loudly so they can hear.

I keep my eyes on Jing. She seems unfocused. Distracted. I watch Li go over to her and try to hug her, but Jing shrugs her off. She glances warily at Ares.

What happened?

"Welcome back," Ares says. "You all *really* impressed us yesterday, those of you who had the courage to complete the trial. Some of you are making real headway filling your vessels." His eyes shimmer with what I assume is pride. "And I'm so pleased you could relax and enjoy the full experience of the Love Beach."

"*We* defo did," Jamie whispers. "The *full* experience."

"All right, cocky, reign it in," Rachel hisses back. "So embarrassing, everyone. Sorry. *Not* funny."

The others think it is. They laugh. All except Jing and Matthew, who keep their heads down as if they want to dissolve into the ground.

What's he done to them?

"We have something we need to discuss," Ares says, his voice now somber. "Jing and Matthew have been doing some thinking, up here at the camp, with me. And they have something they'd like to say to you."

They slowly stand up.

"Um . . ." Jing looks at Ares, who nods. "So, we want to apologize," she says, her voice shaky. "We feel like we've let everyone down."

Lucy shuffles in her seat. "Don't be silly, Jing. We—"

"Let them speak," Artemis says, cutting her off. "Go on, Jing."

"Well . . . We just want you all to know that we do *really* care about the program. We know what this opportunity means, and we feel like by not showing our trust, we"—she looks at Ares again—"we *devalued* it in some way." He nods approvingly. "And we *do* trust Artemis and Ares. Of course we do. They're amazing."

"Amazing," Matthew echoes.

"We didn't do the Drop," Jing continues, "because I was too scared. It was a lot for me to process, in the moment. But I regret my decision. I'm sorry, Matthew."

"It's not just your fault, Jing. I should have encouraged you," he says quietly. "Ares has shown us the importance of being committed. So we . . ." He pauses, and I see Ares nod.

He pulls his sleeve back.

Jing does the same.

They both hold their hands up to us in unison, showing us the new bandages wrapped around them, fresh blood seeping through the white cotton.

"We wanted to recommit ourselves," Matthew says resolutely. "Kill our old selves again. To show how much this means to us."

"It was our choice," Jing says, but as she keeps her eyes on Ares, I get the feeling she's not telling us the truth. "And we wanted to use this as an opportunity to remind all of you to give yourselves over to this. Fully. It's *really* important." She flicks her eyes to her sister. In them is something maybe only a sibling could translate, but to me it looks like a warning. "Ares has assured us that he and Artemis will . . ." She pauses, clearing her throat. "They will do anything to get the best out of all of us. So . . . just . . ." She lowers her voice. "Attempt all the trials. We need to make sure we do."

Ares nods approvingly.

What does "do anything" mean? What has he told them?

"Anything you want to add, Matthew?"

"Yes," he says. "All our choices on Elmhallow have consequences that are bigger than we know."

Consequences. Ares nods. "Thank you," he says as they sit back on their stone. "That was very poignant, Jing and Matthew. Your recommitment will not be overlooked. We appreciate this recognition of your weaknesses. If we are scared, we are weak. Madame Manning asked Artemis and myself to watch out for your weakness and gently encourage you when it is inhibiting your progress." Not sure how gentle cutting ourselves is.

Then he flicks his hair out of his eyes and smiles warmly, breaking the tension. "Now, all of you, have a restful morning. Embrace your surroundings, meditate, be at one with your partner. Enjoy your time here at the camp before your next trial. You will need your strength."

As I sit on my bed, I keep glancing at the crossbow leaning up against the wall by Ares's bed. He's lying on his back, completely still, blinking up at the ceiling. I never understand people who can do that. Just be *still*, for ages. Just be there, in their own head.

Matthew is flat-out asleep. Raheem too. Both snoring gently. The others are outside, gathered around the firepit, laughing and chatting.

The crossbow.

My stomach clenches. Fear creeps up into me, and I try to swallow it down.

We don't need to use it. It's a threat.

But . . . what if something goes wrong? What if we actually do need to use it? If I just knew how to *fire* it . . .

Ares suddenly turns to me. Jesus. "Are you OK, Seb?"

"Yeah, all good. Just . . . being."

"I see." He keeps staring. "I could feel you looking at me," he says quietly.

Oh, he thinks I was looking at *him*.

"Um. Just . . . thinking about the example you set."

Actually. You know what? Sod it.

"Can I ask you something, Ares?"

"Anything, Seb."

"So, sort of . . . In light of . . . In light of the example you set. I wondered if you could teach me something that might make me stronger."

"Go on."

"Do you think . . . maybe you could teach me to use the crossbow?"

172

His eyebrows raise. "You want to learn?"

I nod. "Yeah, I do. It looks difficult and dangerous, two things I have struggled with in the past. I want to show my willingness to keep changing. Is that OK?"

"Of course it's OK."

"Great!"

"But you're not ready yet." Shit. "I will let you know when you are. You must keep proving yourself."

"OK, thanks. I'm going to try and get some rest now."

"Good idea, Sebastian."

Artemis and Ares stand in the middle of the stone circle, holding little white stones in their hands, about to tell us how to win more stones. That's one thing I've noticed. There are a lot of stones here. A lot of significance placed on stones.

I look at the ground. There's something on the grass in front of us. It looks like our roof tiles at home. Grayish blue. A slate.

"Welcome to today's trial," Ares says. "Pick up your Sacred Slates and turn them over."

Oh, sorry. *Sacred Slate.* My bad.

Eleanor grabs it before I can. She turns it and holds it up to her face. "Look at this, Seb."

I can't, your big face is in the way. "What is it?"

"A list."

Oh, I like lists. Lists can be fun.

She places it down on her lap, revealing a list of words in what looks like white chalk.

BEING ALONE
REJECTION
VULNERABILITY
FAILURE
COMMITMENT
INTIMACY
THE DARK
PAIN
DEATH

So . . . I have to admit, not the *most* promising list I've ever seen. Not the *most* fun.

"Today we want *you* to choose the trial." Ares looks at us like this is the best news ever. "In your pairs, you must decide which of these words, these *concepts*, on the slate you are most afraid of as a couple." *Concepts?* "You must pick two. Put a tick next to them using these stones." He holds up the little white stones. *Fucking stones, everywhere.* "And be honest. We can only break through with complete honesty." He begins to hand them out. When I take one, he smiles. "Choose wisely."

I watch the other couples looking down at the list.

"Death," Eleanor says, squishing herself up next to me. "Terrified of it. I never want to die."

I sometimes feel like she'll never die. She'll outlive us all, her and the cockroaches.

"Um . . . OK . . ." I seriously don't think we should be picking a trial to do with death. "I dunno. . . . I'm not too worried about it. It's inevitable, after all. What about . . . ?" I look down at the list again. Oh, God. They're all awful. "What about failure?" I say hopefully.

She shrugs. "Never really known what that's like."

I look at the word "commitment." That's a scary word.

"Being alone?" Eleanor says.

I like being alone. Good idea. "Yeah, OK."

"Oh, wait. *Pain,*" she says with a startling amount of enthusiasm.

"But . . ."

"Definitely pain. No one likes pain." Um, *you* do. Inflicting it at least. "Give me the stone." I tighten my grip. "Give it to me, Seb."

I look up to see Ares staring at us. I hand it to her.

She scratches a tick next to the word "pain." Then a tick next to the word "death." "Pain" and "death," each with a tick next to them.

"We have to be honest, don't we?" she says. "Done!" she shouts, shooting her hand in the air.

Artemis and Ares walk around the circle, collecting the slates. When they are done, they stand by the firepit looking through them like they're marking an exam.

Artemis stands, ready to deliver the results. "The vote shows that most of you are afraid of two things: pain and death."

Not a great result, guys. Not sure we collectively aced this one. Any chance of a recount?

"Now, collect your packs and follow us." She pauses. "This next trial is where you must really dig in. Where you must open up your minds to a new way of thinking."

TWENTY
You Are Loved

Something is concerning me. We're standing in the middle of a field, surrounded by a fence, staring up at a wooden sign nailed to a tall wooden post.

WELCOME TO EXPOSURE THERAPY

Wires run up the length of the post. Above the sign, a single light bulb hangs, swaying in the wind. And above that, at the very top, is a yellow plastic megaphone with a HappyHead face on its side. Like one of those speaker things you see in American high-school movies.

But that's not the thing that's concerning me. The thing that's concerning me are the ten canvas sacks and ten pieces of rope laid out on the muddy ground around the base of the post.

"Welcome to the Pen," Ares says, Artemis at his side. "You will be here for . . ." He looks at her and smiles. "Well, as long as you feel you can be. That is up to you."

They seem like enigmas, these two, don't they?

The sun is low in the sky. A cool white sphere in the graying light. The cold starts to bite.

"In today's trial," Artemis says, "you shall face your fear of pain and death."

Brilliant. I knew we should've picked *being alone.*

I scan the faces of the Ten, lined up in their pairs. They just stare, masking any apprehension, any fear of . . . Well, pain and death.

"Dr. Stone's research has indicated that the concepts on the Sacred Slates are the things that teenagers fear the most, increasing stress and anxiety, moving us away from achieving inner peace. If we are constantly worrying about what may or may not happen, we cannot remain present. Fear rids us of the here and now. In the Pen we will teach you how to overcome it." I don't like where this is going. "Exposure therapy is a well-established technique. Through it, we can conquer what holds us back: our greatest and darkest fears. Who wants that?"

People lift their hands. I instinctively do too, because that actually sounds quite good. But then I see the sacks and rope and quickly put it back down.

"Is it going to be like that water torture thing?" Jamie says.

Lucy makes a face. *What?*

I agree. *What?*

"No," Artemis says. "But in a way."

Um. In a way? In a way like that water torture thing?

What the hell does that mean?

I glance at Eleanor. She's holding my hand, remaining stock-still as she stares at the post.

"Fear is extremely inhibiting," Artemis continues. "It ruins people. Ruins their potential. It is time to show us how strong you are." She picks up one of the sacks. "Who would like to go first? Who is willing to look pain and death in the eye and say *I am not afraid of you?*"

Who is willing to tell this woman that she needs to be in a maximum-security prison?

Matthew goes to raise his hand, opening his mouth to speak.

"I will," Rachel says before he can.

"Good," Artemis says. "Very good, Rachel." Matthew shoots her a look, annoyed that she's more willing to be "in a way" tortured than he is. Artemis steps toward Rachel. "Is the fear there?"

"A little," Rachel says.

Artemis steps toward her and Jamie. "You both have no blood-stones yet."

Jamie shuffles. Rachel nods. "No."

Artemis keeps her gaze on them. "It's time to step up, both of you. You remember what Matthew and Jing said." Rachel nods. Jamie shuffles. "We don't want to have to keep reminding you of the consequences your actions have."

Consequences.

Rachel draws herself upright. "We're ready." And suddenly she seems it.

"Good. Let go of her hand, Jamie."

Jamie lets go of her hand, and Artemis places the sack over Rachel's head. Ares comes over with one of the ropes. He ties Rachel's hands behind her back.

"Comfortable?" he says.

Her little sack head nods.

Why is she nodding? She doesn't look comfortable—none of this is fucking comfortable.

Artemis and Ares move around the circle, pulling a sack over each of our heads, one by one, then tying our hands behind our backs. When they do it to Matthew, he says, "So cool," which is both confusing and worrying. When they do it to Lucy, she whimpers.

"It's OK to be scared. We expect it," Artemis keeps saying. As they do it to Eleanor, she remains still, unflinching. Then it's my turn.

The inside of the sack smells like a barn. I feel very restricted. Very penned in.

All I have to do is get through this, then. . . .

"You must stand like this, in total silence, for as long as you can," Artemis says from somewhere nearby. "This is not about physical pain, but mental pain." *Mental pain?* "You must not sit, crouch, or fall asleep. If you do, the ritual will be over for you.

"We want to see how much you can take. It will start to hurt. The cold will begin to burn as the temperature drops. You will struggle. But sacred bloodstones will be awarded to those who manage the most time. The final three will receive them. The person in third place will get one; second place, two; and the last person standing will receive three."

"We can win five in total," Eleanor whispers. "If we both last the longest."

"When you want to end it," Artemis continues, "all you have to do is fall to your knees. Now it is time to face the fear."

I see the fragmented light through the weave of the sack, crisscrossing in front of me.

There's a click from above, like someone is pressing play on one of those old tape players, then a crackling sound. It's coming from the megaphone.

And then the noise begins.

At first, it sounds like . . . a baby.

Relaxed and content, gurgling softly. But then it starts to become more . . . upset. Distressed. The baby starts wailing. And it doesn't stop.

It cuts into my head. So loud.

At some point, it gives way to something else. A siren. An ambulance or police car. *Jesus, that's intense.*

And then . . .

Screeching. Like someone is scraping their fingernails on metal. On and on. I start to picture it. I see fingernails snapping. Blood.

Then some kind of electric saw. Louder and louder until it's right in front of me. I see its corrugated wheel turning, spinning, moving toward me. . . .

Again, it changes.

An incessant, sickening *whummmm* like I'm underwater. Back in the cave. But this time, drowning. I feel the pressure in my head. It hurts, actually hurts, and my breaths begin to shorten. I can't breathe. I'm hyperventilating.

Where's my inhaler?

Then screams. Relentless screams. Men. Women. Children.

Who the hell is that? They sound . . . terrified.

I need . . . something.

Bowie.

I search the corners of my mind for his lyrics and start to sing them under my breath.

But the noises keep pushing them out.

Sobbing. Deep, guttural sobbing. I can no longer tell if the sounds are coming from the speaker, or if they're coming from people in the Pen itself. *"Help me, help me. Help me, please. . . ."*

I suddenly see Lily. *Lily.*

She's tied up in front of me. "Help me! Please!"

An almighty explosion.

Then bombs. Dropping. *Everywhere.*

My muscles are burning. My legs shaking. It's cold. So cold.

Focus on him. Finn. *Us.*

Gunfire.

I flinch. Duck. Nearly fall. Outside the sack, I see flashes of light.

This is not real. It isn't real. It'll all be over soon.

I hear thuds around me. People dropping to the ground. Dogs barking. Attacking.

Another thud.

Hours pass—it must be hours. The image of him completely disappears. The noise drowns it out. Takes him from me.

I pull at the ropes tying my arms, but I can't break free.

Crying.

Is that me? I can't tell. My brain feels like it's dissolving.

Someone shouting. "You're weak. You are weak!"

Who is that?

Mum. Dad. Pastor Johnny?

"You are nothing. You are nothing."

My body can't take it anymore. I start to sway.

A voice speaks quietly in my ear. Ares. "Stay standing, Seb. Stay strong. I believe in you."

Stay strong.

"Help me," I beg. "Please . . ."

But there's no reply.

I hear fire. Burning. Crackling. Consuming. I can smell it.

Then grunting.

Something circles the space inside the darkness. Huge, twisted horns, breathing smoke from its nose. Black eyes staring, watching me. A monster. A devil.

It begins to laugh. Wicked. Awful. Evil.

It moves inside me. Possessing me.

Oh my God. I've never been so scared in my life.

"Help me," my voice says. "Make it stop!"

Where is he? Where is . . . ? Shit, I can't remember his name.

Burning. Burning flesh . . .

And then . . .

Silence.

Complete silence.

When the sack is pulled from my head, the world swims. The first thing I see is the two bloodstones glinting on the ground in front of me.

I'm going to be sick.

Ares smiles down at me. "Well done, Sebastian." He unties my hands.

As he turns away, panic grips me. "Wait!"

"You're OK," he says. He squeezes my arm. It feels warm. *Real.* "You've done so well." He gently wipes the damp hair from my eyes.

"Thank you," I say, my voice trembling.

"Do not be frightened anymore. It's over."

My brain feels like it's on fire.

The sky is now pitch-black, but a dim light shines through it from the little bulb. It illuminates Ares in a golden haze. It feels almost . . . holy. I look around the Pen at the others, all on their knees facing the post.

In front of Eleanor there is one bloodstone.

In front of Rachel there are three.

"Be gentle with yourselves, all of you," Artemis says. "You are safe."

As we drag ourselves up from the dirt, I see her hugging the trembling girls, wiping their tears. Ares supports the boys, helping them stand.

Jamie is crying. So is Sam. And Lucy. They all are.

"The first part of the trial is over," Ares says. "You have done well. In the next part, we will face our greatest fear. Our fear of death."

Oh, God. I had forgotten. . . .

Then I see something in the middle of the circle. Something that wasn't here before. I rub my eyes to make sure I'm not hallucinating.

Pigs.

Six of them. All chained to the post, wearing little yellow collars. Tied to each of the collars is a woven sack, full of what appear to be bloodstones. On the sacks, a HappyHead smile, and beneath, each couple's initials.

"Are they real?" Raheem says.

I think they are.

"Now, go and stand in front of your pig," Artemis says softly. "In your couples."

Eleanor takes my hand in hers. I can feel her trembling, see the fog of her panting breath as we approach our pig.

Big ears, beige skin beneath its bristly hairs. A patch on the side of its tummy. A brown splodge. Its chain rattles as it chews on a bit of grass. It lifts its head and snorts. It sounds like "hi."

"Hi," I say back.

Someone whimpers, and I look up. It's Li.

Artemis steps toward her and takes her hand. "Are you scared, Li?" Li nods. "It's OK to be scared. Everyone is." Artemis kisses her forehead. "Do not feel shame. It's natural for you to think of death as traumatic. But this is because you have been conditioned to. That was the old world restraining us, Li. What if I told you that here, death doesn't have to hold the same power?"

She turns, speaking to us all.

"On a guttural, human level it is not natural to feel this way. Our anxieties are heightened by what other people tell us. The epidemic of unhappiness we are trying to break is being fueled by how we are *told* to feel. *You must feel sad. You must find it difficult. You are bad if you don't.* How would you feel if I gave you permission to *not* feel that way?" She pauses. "Really think about that. How would that make you feel?"

That actually sounds . . . *nice.*

"Relief," I hear myself say.

Artemis looks at me, and her eyes widen. "*Relief.* Exactly, Seb. We want that for you. That is why you are here. Fear has manifested in our bodies, in our generational subconscious, and become real. Back when humanity truly lived freely, it was not. Fear never stood in the way of people being happy because sadness was not instinctual. It doesn't have to be."

It doesn't? *My brain hurts.*

"We must not see death as something that is awful, horrific, and inhumane, but as a natural part of life."

"Like the lamb," Rachel says.

"Exactly, Rachel," Artemis says. "Just like the lamb."

"So . . . we're going to kill them?" Li says quietly.

I look up at the stars in the sky. Tiny flecks of light above us. And I feel very small. But also, somehow, very different. Very . . . other. Very not like me.

"The choice is yours," Artemis says. "We will not force you to do anything you do not feel comfortable with. But in order to gain the sacred bloodstones attached to the pigs' collars, we need you to open yourself—expose yourselves—to your fear of death. Move through it, past it and into strength. You have the opportunity to combat that, here and now. It is a gift. To be free of fear."

Free of fear. That sounds . . . That really does sound . . .

My brain. It feels like pulp inside my skull.

"There are seven bloodstones in each pouch."

"Seven?" Sam says.

"Yes."

Sam looks at Li. She seems terrified. "But . . . ," she says, "I don't know if I—"

"You have to, Li," Jing suddenly says.

Her sister looks back at her. "But, Jing—"

I see Ares watching, his face soft in the light. "Remember, in the Pen you are safe, Li. We will keep you safe. HappyHead will *always* keep you safe. Perhaps some words of encouragement may help, from someone you know well."

He turns to the post and presses a button. The megaphone clicks on again. But this time the crackling gives way to a voice. It rings out above us.

"Hello, our Ten. You are doing so well."

I recognize it. Smooth. Scandinavian. Lindström.

"Commitment, growth, gratitude, and obedience lead to a happy head."

It is. It's her. The therapy lead from HappyHead.

"While you stand here, facing your fears, I'd like to tell you how loved you are. How special you are. How much we admire your commitment. We see it. Your desire to grow. To change. To rid yourselves of the restrictions of the old world. To rewire the way you think. We adore you. You are loved. You are special." Her voice stops.

But then it goes on.

"We adore you. You are loved. You are special. We adore you. You are loved. You are special. You are special. We adore you. You are loved. . . ."

It washes over me. Removing the fear. The devil inside of me. And I feel an odd stillness, like the air after a storm.

"I will show you how easy it is," Ares says. He kneels down in front of the seventh pig. "I will now emotionally detach from what I have learned to be afraid of." He holds up his dagger. The one he cut us with.

We all watch. We watch him *emotionally detach.*

Ares inhales. He holds the blade right up to the pig's neck. Then he thrusts it into the flesh and twists.

The pig makes a disgusting squeal.

"You are loved. . . ."

The other pigs scream too.

"You are special. . . ."

But her words drown it out.

"We adore you. . . ."

He holds the dagger in place for a moment. Then releases it.

The pig drops to the floor. *Thud.* Its legs jerk uncontrollably.

No one speaks. No one moves. We just stare as the blood begins to pour out of the pig's neck and onto the mud.

The words wash over us. They enter me. Fill me up. Am I *loved*?

Eventually the pig stops moving. Ares steps toward it. "The trick is to be quick. Not to overthink. Be pragmatic," he says briskly. "It is time to move forward into a life without fear." He holds the dagger out in front of us, his hands shining wet with blood. "We are here with you. We are here, together. We are united in this."

I watch everyone, wide-eyed as if they are in a trance.

"Do not think," Artemis says. "Thinking leads to fear. Just take it. Take the opportunity. And then we move forward." She turns to Li. "Li, perhaps you and Sam should go first, since you were so scared?"

She takes a small step back. "I—"

"Face your fear, Li." Sam takes her hand. Holds it tight. "We still only have one bloodstone."

Li looks back to Ares. "B-but . . . ," she stammers. "I don't think I—"

"You have to, Li," Jing says. I see how terrified she is.

Her sister looks back at her. "Jing—"

"Listen to me. . . ." Jing lowers her voice. "When Ares spoke with me and Matthew after we didn't do the Drop, he . . ." She stops. "Just do it, Li. Please."

What did Ares say to them?

Li shakes her head. "You know I'm—"

"That was in the old world, Li," Jing says.

"Jing is right," Artemis says. "Here you must leave your old beliefs behind."

"Just think of it this way," Matthew says. "Normalize it." *Normalize.* Normalized pig killing. "We all eat sausages."

"But I don't . . . ," Li says, now sobbing. "I'm vegan. . . ."

Matthew rolls his eyes.

"Please, Li." Jing pulls up her sleeve, revealing the bloody bandage around her hand.

Li hesitates. Then her eyes flash, resolute. "No. I won't."

I see Ares's gaze momentarily meet Artemis's. "That is a shame," he says. "A real shame."

"But . . . Can I do it for both of us?" Sam says, reaching out his hand for the knife.

"I am afraid not, Sam," Artemis says. "Both of you, wait outside the gate."

"What? Now?" Sam says, panicked.

"Yes, now."

"But—"

"Now."

They slowly cross the Pen toward the gate, Sam shaking his head, Li sobbing.

I try to align my thoughts. Voices swirl around my head.

What did Ares say to Jing and Matthew? *Consequences.*

What will he do to us if we don't comply? Will it put the plan in jeopardy?

Finn: *They can't suspect.*

Eleanor: *You don't know what these two people are capable of.*

"We'll do it."

Wait. That was me. I said that.

Oh, God. Oh, no.

What am I doing?

Eleanor turns to me. I can't gauge her expression. I can't tell if she's surprised, impressed, concerned, or all three.

"Good, Sebastian." Ares hands me the bloody knife.

Eleanor nods.

Together, we crouch in front of our pig.

Ares kneels with us. He smiles in a way that instantly warms me. "You are ready," he says. "To allow yourself to be free." I stare at the green flecks in his eyes. Reassuring. Kind. "I know you want that."

I do. I do want that.

But not like this . . .

"Good. Now detach."

My hand moves. With hers. Together.

Thrust. And twist.

Once we are done, once we are back in our places, thick black blood covering our hands, our hoodies, our pants, Ares steps over the pig corpse, toward me. He puts his hand on my shoulder. "Well done, Sebastian." He then whispers in my ear, "You have been very brave. It is beautiful to witness."

I feel numb. "Thank you, Ares."

Something within me doesn't want him to leave my side. It wants him to stay.

But he turns away. "Who is next?"

One by one, the remaining couples are called forward. And each couple kills their pig. Hand in hand. While Lindström speaks.

The dense fog in my brain makes me feel as if I'm watching it all on a screen. Like I'm somewhere far away. It is brutal. But there is something oddly . . . *peaceful* about it.

And as I watch these people facing their greatest fears, as I look at Ares, so proud, at Artemis, encouraging them, I see that there are so many things in my life that I've stopped myself from doing or saying. Fear. It has held me back for so long. Made me so *sad*.

Imagine a world without that. A life without guilt. Without shame.

How would I feel? *Who would I be?*

"You are special. . . ."

I can no longer hear the screams. The squeals.

"We adore you. . . ."

Just the voice. The words.

"You are loved. . . ."

And then it is done. The sun is beginning to rise.

"I am so honored to be standing here with you all," Ares says. "It is a pleasure, a *privilege,* to watch you grow. You are taking a huge leap of faith."

"You are showing us that you are beginning to understand." Artemis joins him at his side. "You are beginning to understand that the old world was wrong. That you can be free."

Free.

Everyone looks . . . dazed but relieved. Relieved they have done it. That they have faced their greatest fears. That they have murdered a pig with a knife.

And I realize through the haze of it all. The golden, bloody haze. This is it.

The Never Plan.

I watch the blood, thick and shiny, pool around our feet. And my whole body begins to tremble. Because this is real. This is actually happening. And we are doing it.

I am doing it.

"We adore you. You are special. You are loved."

TWENTY-ONE
Freedom

I can hear drums. I open my eyes, but it hurts. The beat of the drum vibrates through the window, and I feel a wave of nausea. I want to throw up. Get it all out of me.

I'm back in the dwelling house. It's empty. I pull off my blanket and try to stand.

My body feels weak. Broken. Like there's nothing solid inside, just a jellied mess. I look out through the window to the stone circle. The fire is roaring. I can see dark shapes moving in front of the flames.

What time is it?

I pull my sleeve up to reveal the ivory face of Betty's watch. 6:45.

What? It's . . . the *evening.*

I've slept all day.

The plan. Tonight. We leave.

I look over at the crossbow, leaning up against the wall in front of Ares's empty bed. Shit.

I rummage through the baskets by the fireplace—*nothing*—then head for the Bucket Room. I see my fresh Reds hanging neatly on my hook. I pull out the pockets, my fingers shaking.

Come on, Finn. *Come on.*

A shard of wood. *Yes.*

All set tonight

Midnight

Boathouse

I close my eyes. Inhale through my nose. Soon we will be gone. We will be on the boat, and this will all be some nightmarish memory.

I snap the shard into pieces and push them through the grate in the floor. As I kneel in front of the bucket and stick my head under the tap, I think of the pigs. Of Ares. Of how safe I felt next to him, in that moment.

What have I done?

I let the cold shudder through me, until the water numbs my thoughts and takes them with it.

Come on, Seb. Get your shit together.

Once dressed, I step outside and into the icy night air.

They're all here. All in their yellow robes. Gratitude Garlands on their heads. Smiling. Laughing. *Dancing.*

Artemis is banging her drum, while the others spin and turn to its rhythm, arms in the air.

"Finally, the boy is up!" Ares shouts over the noise. He weaves his way over to me and puts his arm around my shoulder. "We've been waiting for you."

He pulls me forward, leading me through the turning bodies, the grinning faces, into the stone circle.

Lucy's face. "Seb! You're up!"

Raheem's face. "You did great, mate. They're really impressed."

Rachel. "Buddy! Risen from the dead!"

Then Sam. A new bandage on his hand. "Get some food, Seb. You must be starving."

"But . . . What's he eating? Is that . . . ?"

It is. It's meat.

I look into the fire, where a pig is roasting on a spit. One of the pigs we murdered.

"What's wrong, mate?" Raheem says.

"What's . . . what's going on?" I stammer.

"Tonight, we are celebrating." Ares takes my shoulders in his hands, turning me to face him.

"Celebrating what?"

"Freedom." His eyes glow.

"Seb!" Ares steps aside and watches as Eleanor kisses me on the cheek. "Well done, honey."

"I'll leave you two to it," he says.

Eleanor guides me to our stone. "Look." She points to our bowl. There are loads of bloodstones. *Loads* of them. "Look how we did." She lowers her voice. "Ares *loves* you. Thinks you're amazing. I overheard him." She looks so excited. So happy. "Sam and Li only have one, which is a bit of shame for them, but hey, they need to buck up their ideas or they have no chance. Rachel and Jamie have ten; Jing and Matthew have eleven; Lucy and Raheem, fourteen; but, Seb"—she pauses and grabs my arm, digging her nails in—"we have sixteen. *Sixteen*. We're *winning*, Seb."

At the Never Plan.

I'm coming, Finn.

"I'm a bit concerned about Sam and Li," she goes on. "They're really struggling. . . ." I look at Li, sitting quietly on her stone, cradling her bandaged hand.

"Struggling?" I say. "Because they didn't murder a—"

"What a sight!" Ares shouts, now standing on top of one of the stones. "It fills me with joy. Look how happy you all are!"

Everyone cheers. Then the drumming stops.

"We have an announcement to make." Why now? Please not another task, please not another ritual. "You have reached the end of phase one on the island." *Phase one?* "Tonight, we not only celebrate freedom, but our progression to the next chapter." *Next chapter?*

Well, I won't be here for it. Thank God.

The others begin to whisper around me, excited, giddy. Ares holds up his hand to quiet them. "You are showing exceptional strength. We need to see you continue to do that. We are watching. Always watching. More than you might think." His eyes fix onto mine. "We see you. We love you. You are ready." And then he opens out his arms. "Now, eat, drink, and dance. Because tomorrow we will be moving forward."

He leans his head back and screams into the night, "To freedom!"

"To freedom!" everyone cries.

The drumming starts up again. And everyone dances.

I watch them moving together—uninhibited, laughing, *free.*

But not.

Not at all.

Ares is the last to come back to the dwelling house. He pushes the door shut and turns the key in the lock.

"Night, brothers," he whispers as he lies down on his bed. He pulls the cover over himself and turns on his side. I watch as his eyes begin to close and his breathing slows.

I lift up my sleeve and look at Betty's watch. 11:15.

I look back to the crossbow in its place against the wall. At the yellow feathers of the bolts, sitting snugly in their sheath.

Not long now and we will be gone. No more HappyHead. No more of this. We will stop it.

Finally, it's time.

When I reach the foot of Ares's bed, I look at him. His mouth wide open. His chest rising and falling. His beautiful face.

I put my hand on the cold metal of the crossbow and lift it up slowly, carefully. It's heavy. I pick up the sheath in my other hand.

His bed creaks, and I snap my head to him, just as he rolls onto his side. Shit.

His eyes remain shut. I hold my breath, frozen, as he mutters something through the thickness of sleep. I only catch his final words. *"I am loved."*

Then he is silent. Still again.

The fear moves me like a hand placed firmly on the bottom of my back, pushing me toward the Bucket Room door.

Just get out.

Before I know it, I'm opening the window, dropping the crossbow and sheath through it, perching on the ledge.

I jump. And then I run. Hurtling through the night, down the hill, through the grass, the mud. To the woods, to the boathouse, to him.

To freedom.

TWENTY-TWO
Apple Seed

I dart between the trees, the crossbow on my back, feeling a rush of exhilaration as I run.

Is this what Legolas felt like?

As I reach the edge of the wood, I slow my pace, then stop.

Careful. The Keeper could be out here.

Uncertainty tugs at me. I still don't know how to *use* the crossbow. How it works, how any of this will work. I start to feel like a six-year-old kid holding something that is only meant to be used by adults.

Don't spiral. Now is not the time to spiral. . . .

We just need to threaten them with it, Finn said.

I move on, going through the plan in my head for the hundredth time—*get the boat, lock the Keeper in the bunker, cross the sea, find the quad bike*—until the back of the boathouse comes into view.

It's quiet. I edge forward through the trees, until I'm pressed up against the wall. I peer around the corner and see the beach spanning out in front of me. The sea lapping against the shore, the sand churning under the weight of the tide. The targets.

And then I see him. Right at the edge of the shore, with his back to me. The Keeper.

And in the distance, the light of the boat. Moving closer. Toward him.

Oh my God. *It's happening.*

I take the sheath of bolts under my arm, make sure the crossbow is firmly on my back, and scale the wall. I crouch on the iron roof, keeping myself low.

Go now. Before he sees.

I look down into the hole. Into the blackness. I swing my legs over the edge, then drop. *Thud.* The sheath falls from under my arm and rolls across the floor. That's strange. . . . Where is every—

Panic courses through my body. It's empty. The room is *empty.*

I scramble up. Swing around. *They're not here.* The crates. Everything. All gone.

Shit. *Shit.* Terror engulfs me. I feel it in my skin, taste it on my tongue. I move around the room, looking into the corners, as if they might be there, all five of them, huddled in the darkness.

Maybe they're just late maybe they're just late maybe they're just—

And then I see something, lit by the single pool of light cutting through the dust from the hole above. A message scrawled across the floor like someone has written it in a hurry with a chalky stone.

Go back

OK. There's an explanation. There has to be.

Something creaks. I spin around to see that the front door has blown open a fraction. *Why isn't it locked?*

I step slowly toward it. *Maybe they found a key?*

I peer out the door. The Keeper still stands on the beach, waiting. The boat is closer now, a white mark on the black sea.

I pick up the sheath of bolts and turn back to the door, adrenaline firing in my veins as I step outside. I keep my eyes on the Keeper as I move around the side of the boathouse, pressing myself into the shadows. Then I start to run, back through the trees toward the bunker. They must be there. They *must* be. . . .

Where is it? I try to remember. Halfway down the shore, about ten yards from the tree line . . . But everything looks the same.

I pause to catch my breath and look through the trees. I can just make out the back of the Keeper. The boat is nearly at the shore now.

Oh, God.

Finn's note said *all set*—it said they were ready. *Where the hell is the bunker?*

Quietly now . . . steady. That's it. . . . It's there. . . . The hatch is open—wide open—revealing a gaping hole in the forest floor. A set of concrete steps leads to a low light at the bottom. I take one last look behind me; then I step down into it. The air is dense. Humid.

"Finn," I whisper. "Finn!"

As I reach the bottom of the steps, I pause. Ahead, a low corridor leads to a small room. There are three sets of bunk beds, pushed up against the walls. At the far end, an open door leads off into another room. I can just make out a sink. Pots and pans hang from the ceiling.

I look at the beds. There are no blankets. I look around. There are no clothes. No shoes. No . . .

No sign of them at all.

Then I hear something. Heavy footsteps. *Boots.* Someone moves at the back of the second room, stepping out from behind the doorway.

A man. All in black.

My body moves before my mind. I dart back up the steps. As I emerge aboveground, I see the Keeper through the trees, walking toward the bunker, a duffel bag in his hands.

There are two of them? Did he come on the boat?

Go back.

I turn and tear through the forest. My legs aching, head screaming, eyes streaming. Back up the hill. All the way to the dwelling house.

I pull open the window, drop the bow and sheath of bolts through it, then jump down myself. But I know before he speaks that he is there.

"Hello, Sebastian. I wondered where you had been. With my crossbow as well."

Minutes pass. They feel like hours. I'm too exhausted, too drained to think. If I say anything, he'll know. He'll hear it in my voice.

Ares doesn't speak. He just stares.

"I . . ." *Know what this place is. Know what you're doing.* "Wanted to practice my aim."

"With my crossbow? In the middle of the night?"

"Yes."

He remains motionless, his gazed fixed. "And where did you go?"

"To the beach . . . To the targets."

He pauses. "When?"

"A few hours ago."

"Did you see anything?"

"I—"

"At the beach?"

I shake my head.

"Why did it take you so long to get back?"

"I got lost in the woods."

"You got lost?" He doesn't move his eyes from me. "I told you, you are not *ready*. You went against my wishes. Against the rules of the island. Rules that are in place to keep you safe. Why would you do that?"

My mind is on the verge of snapping. "I . . . I can't say."

"You can't say?"

I look at the floor.

"Well, if you can't say, Sebastian, then we'll have to think of a way of helping you try. Do you understand?"

Consequences.

"It's just . . . It'll sound stupid."

"I'm waiting."

"I wanted to . . ." I lower my voice. "I wanted to impress you, that's all."

His eyebrows raise. "You wanted to impress me?"

"Yeah, I . . ." I remember how he made me feel, before the Pen. How safe he made me feel. How I never wanted him to leave my side. How real that felt. "I just feel like you're everything I've always wanted to be. I don't want to make you uncomfortable or anything, but in a way, I sort of . . . idolize you."

"*Idolize* me?"

Do I? No. *No.*

Detach.

"I can't help it. I'm sorry. I want to be like you. Your strength.

Your beauty." I look up at him. "Sorry if this is all a bit much. I just . . ."

He chews his lip. Then he turns his face away, toward the window. He stands like this for a very long time.

"Sebastian . . . ," he says. His voice is different. It drops, as if it is coming from somewhere in the center of him. "I have felt . . . perhaps . . . in a way, we are kindred spirits."

Are we?

Stop it. Get out of my head. You are wrong.

"I feel that too."

He turns to me. "Like you, I've moved away from a life of sadness. When I think back, which I rarely do now, it nearly ended me." *Ended.* "I had a toxic apple seed in my core. It grew and polluted me. Everywhere I looked, in every face, every remark, I saw its poison reflected back at me. It was no way to live. And here, I don't feel like that anymore. I don't have to. I have been saved from all that inner turmoil. That hatred of myself."

He smiles sadly. "We can't change the world without changing *ourselves* first. It's the only answer." I realize I'm nodding. "And you don't need to take my crossbow and sneak out at night to try and impress me. You've already done that, Sebastian." He narrows his eyes. Kind. Strong. "You are on the right course. Don't get distracted. Stay focused on what you want. And don't let anything get in the way until you have it."

"I won't," I say.

He takes the crossbow and sheath of bolts from the floor, then goes to the Bucket Room door.

"I'll give you a moment to think about what you have done." He looks back at me one last time. "Kindred spirits, you and I."

TWENTY-THREE
Path to Greatness

Zumzumzumzumzumzumzum.

The drill is less than an inch from my temple. Deafening. *Sickening.*

Someone is holding it, but I can't see who. Their face is a shadow under their hood. *Zumzumzumzumzumzumzum.*

The spinning shank moves closer and closer to my head.

Zumzumzumzumzumzumzum.

The hood lowers. The face has no form. No flesh. Just a dripping smile.

"Wake up," the smile says. "Wake. Up."

I open my eyes. Raheem looms over me. My body is covered in a film of sweat.

Zumzumzumzumzumzum.

"What's that noise?" I croak.

Raheem holds out my Reds and my yellow cloak. "Hurry up, mate."

As reality rushes back in, part of me wishes the drill was real. That this was all over.

Where's Finn? What have they done to him?

"Come on, Seb, or we'll be late."

I push myself up onto my elbows and look around. The other boys are standing at the ends of their beds. Cloaks on, hoods up, hands behind their backs.

In front of them stands Ares. "Quickly, Sebastian."

I dress as fast as I can. And then I line up behind the other boys by the door. As Ares turns the handle, it smashes open in the wind.

We step outside. The air is moving so fast that it stops the breath in my lungs.

The girls are already there, standing by their stones, their cloaks whipping around them, Artemis in the middle. They look up, shading their eyes against the sun.

And then I see it. A bright yellow helicopter, hovering above the camp.

Zumzumzumzumzumzumzum.

"Go and stand with your partners!" Ares yells over the noise.

We push our way through the thrashing air toward them. When I get to Eleanor's side, her eyes remain up, tears streaming in the whipping wind.

We watch as the helicopter lowers itself to the grass, about twenty yards outside the circle. As the blades slow, my stomach turns.

What is going on?

The end of phase one. A new chapter.

The blades stop. The door on the side slowly opens. A set of steps drops down to the grass below.

I smell her before I see her.

Citrus.

And then she appears. Fur coat. Neat bob. Stylish rain boots. A HappyHead badge pinned to her coat.

Manning.

She waits at the top of the little set of steps. "My Ten," she says brightly, and waves her leather-gloved hand.

"No way!" I hear someone say, and the others begin to whisper, excited, *pleased*. Pleased to see the person who made all this happen.

She makes her way down the steps and toward us across the muddy ground.

Behind her, out of the shadows, comes someone else, tottering forward using a cane to steady herself.

Stone.

Applause breaks out. I clench my fists so my nails dig into the palms of my hands. As they make their way into the stone circle together, a storm of questions brews inside me.

Where have you been?

Do you know what's happening here? Do you care?

Whose side are you on?

A pressure builds; it feels a lot like rage, threatening to make the words spill out of me.

Don't. If they know. If they find out I've been with Finn . . .

To serve unseen.

She will punish them.

But what if they're already . . .

"Look at you all," Manning says as she stands by the firepit, eyes glistening in the way I remember from back at the facility.

Stone hovers behind her, staring down at her hands, clutching her cane. She won't look up.

Why won't you look up?

She looks just like she did on the video in the assembly hall, the last time I saw her on our final day at HappyHead. Her hair all clean and shiny in a bun. She's wearing a posh coat. No cardigan. *See you at Elmhallow. Stay strong.* That's what her message said. But as I watch her taking in the applause, the hope I held on to that she'd been lying to Manning—making Manning believe she was on her side for *our* benefit, to somehow help us get out— begins to dissipate.

Because now I don't recognize her at all.

"You have faced so much," Manning says softly. "And yet you all look even more beautiful than I remember. So much *stronger.*"

She turns on the spot, taking a moment to look each of us in the eye. When she looks at me, I hide the storm inside me with a smile. But it hurts. It hurts to smile.

She inhales deeply, like she's breathing in the sight of us, letting it fill her body. "I can already see from your faces that you are undoing so much of what has kept you from reaching your full potential back in the old world." Those words. They're hers. "But here, where you can be free, I feel that you are *so close* to achieving it. We wanted to see you in action," she says. "Didn't we, Dr. Stone?"

Stone lifts her head and nods at us. She looks so *different.* Her expression, the creases in her skin, her composure, the way she's holding herself.

"And as you can see, the doctor is making good recovery under the specialist team we had looking after her while she was in the hospital," Manning says. "Would you like to say a few words, Doctor?"

Stone clears her throat. "Thank you, Gloria. I would." When

she speaks, her voice is flatter than I remember it, the gentleness of the Irish lilt somehow dulled. "I wasn't feeling myself for quite some time, but thanks to my friend here, I am back to where I should be."

It's true. I've been wrong. I've been so wrong. Tears sting my eyes as I fight against that simmering rage trying to force its way out. *Don't.*

"We wanted to see how you are taking to our program, out here in the wilderness. If you remember, I always like to be in nature. This is where all my ideas come to me. Where I feel free. Where my mind is unconstrained. I hope you are experiencing the same." Stone looks around the circle, scanning her eyes over the faces. When she gets to me, she turns away.

Why won't you look at me?

Her eyes rest on the fire, her composure faltering for a moment as she realizes what's in it. The charred remnants of the pig carcass from last night. "I can see you have been bravely facing your fears. One of the most important parts of your work here. You are all doing so much more than we could ever have imagined. You are on your path to greatness."

"Exactly," Manning says. She touches Stone on the arm. "We have *greatness* in our midst. You have been working hard to gain sacred bloodstones, and I, for one, am *very* intrigued to see how you have been getting on."

She begins to walk in a circle around the firepit, looking down into our bowls. I watch each couple's faces as she passes them. Nervous. Hopeful. *Embarrassed.*

She stops in front of Li and Sam, and their single bloodstone. "Work to do," she says quietly. "What a shame."

Sam drops his head.

"Well," Manning says when she reaches me and Eleanor. "This is really very impressive."

"Thank you, Madame Manning," Eleanor says.

Then she looks directly at me, eyes gleaming. "I've heard how well you are doing, Sebastian."

Where are they, and what have you done to them?

"Trying my best," I say.

"I can see that." She pauses. "Shelly," she says quietly. *Shelly? What?* "She's your friend, isn't she?"

"Um . . . ," I mumble. "I . . . know her." My voice sounds alien to me. Like it's being projected from somewhere outside of my body.

"She's doing very well," she says. "Already in one of the top bedrooms. Number six. We have high hopes for her."

I can't quite compute her words. "Oh . . . Great."

Shelly. *My* Shelly? In room 6?

Manning smiles. "She was a little . . . resistant at first, but like you, she has really begun to take to the process."

What am I doing? Carrying on like this?

She then turns back to the firepit without so much as looking at Eleanor. At her niece. Eleanor swallows hard, like she's pushing something down inside her.

For a fleeting moment, it feels as if we are experiencing the exact same thing. But I know it's for very different reasons.

"Artemis and Ares. Come, stand with me," Manning says. They approach her from the edge of the circle, and she takes their hands. "These are two of the most formidable, courageous, and inspiring people I've ever had the pleasure of meeting. You are lucky to know them. To be *led* by them."

I wouldn't put it past them if they were related too. The lot of them. One big, fucked-up family.

"We are a family here," Manning says.

There you go.

"You are inspiring. You have peace. You have partnership. You have love." I look around the circle at the faces beaming back at her. "Many people spend their whole lives searching for those things." She stares at us with an eerie intensity. "You have worked so hard to be where you are. Given so much of yourselves. Now is your chance to use what you have learned for a higher purpose."

What the hell is she talking about? What higher purpose?

What about the others? Finn. The Bottom Percentile.

Why are they acting like they don't exist?

Why am I not saying anything?

The pressure, the *rage,* surges inside me, until I can't hold it back anymore. "Why are there other people here?"

Silence. Everyone turns.

Eleanor bristles next to me. "Seb?"

But I don't care. I don't care anymore. "Why?"

Ares darts his eyes at me like he's firing a bolt into my head.

"Excuse me?" Manning says.

"Why are there other people on this island? What are you doing with them? Are they in danger?"

I stare at Stone, and for the first time since she arrived, she looks back at me. But it's like she doesn't even recognize me.

"Why would you say that, Sebastian?" Manning asks.

"Because I saw them."

Then she does something I don't expect. She smiles.

"Well, that should never have happened. What a shame. Now,

if you all come with us, while the sun is shining, we have something to show you."

We follow them, Manning and Stone, as they walk side by side, flanked by Ares and Artemis.

I scan the open terrain around us. I could just run. Couldn't I?

The Keepers. Ares. Artemis.

No.

And I need to talk to Stone. . . .

"Seb." Eleanor grabs my arm and pulls me into her. God. The last person I need right now. "Who did you see?" I don't answer. "Who did you *see*, Seb?"

"You wouldn't care, Eleanor." She wouldn't. I pull away from her grip.

"Seb, *wait*," she hisses. "Why won't you . . . ?" Then she stops. Because she sees something ahead of us.

I look up and see it too. A waterfall. Gently tumbling over a low, rocky shelf down into a huge, deep blue pool.

As we approach, its spray hovers around us, shafts of sunlight cutting through it so colors dance in the air. It smells fresh, like wood chips and flowers. The ground beneath my feet becomes soft and mossy. Trees hang low around the water's edge, forming a near-perfect circle. It's like we've just stumbled into an oasis.

But something doesn't feel right. It's too . . . peaceful. Too still.

Manning turns to us, standing at the water's edge. "Welcome to the Sanctuary. Here, today, happiness will reveal itself in its greatest form. You will show it. And in doing so, you will have the ultimate opportunity to show benevolence."

Eleanor gasps. "Look."

But I've already seen them.

Standing on the grassy bank on the opposite side of the pool are five hunched figures. On either side of them, two men, all in black.

I scan the numbers printed on their filthy green hoodies.

One. Two. Three. Four. And then, number five.

TWENTY-FOUR
Becoming Whole

I was baptized when I was thirteen.

It was a weird one.

Pastor Johnny asked all the young people at church if they wanted to do it, if they felt ready, and quite a few of them said yes. He was the one who was going to be doing it, so I said yes too.

I said yes because I thought he was cool and trendy. I wanted a cool and trendy baptism.

Everyone at the church was so excited. Everyone was so *nice* to me. Constantly.

I understood what was happening. And I wanted to do it. I chose to do it. I'd learned through Pastor Johnny's sermons that this was a pivotal part in our development as young people of God. We understood that we were sinners, we were actually *born* sinners, and that it wasn't our fault. By being baptized we chose to turn our lives over to Him. We would be turning away from an old life of sin to a new one, full of light.

But what I really liked about Pastor Johnny was that he didn't like that wording. He said it was archaic. A little *doom and gloom*. He said that what we were really doing was becoming whole.

And that sounded really, really nice.

I had always felt a little bit un-whole. A little bit the opposite of whole. A little bit incomplete. He said that once we had done it, it would be like joining a huge family of people who were also now living in the light. Free.

I remember in the car on the way to church, Mum was chatting with her friend (one of the inner circle) on her phone. She was laughing and smiling and kept looking back at me, saying things like "Yes, he's here now. He looks a little bit nervous, but he has a big smile on his face" and "Oh, I'm so *glad* you're coming" and "Yes, we'll have vol-au-vents in the oven by twelve."

Because there was going to be a party at our house afterward. A party. For me. Loads of people were coming. Granted, I hardly knew any of them and they were all middle-aged, but still. They were coming because they knew this was important and they knew I had chosen to do something really *good*.

When we got to the church, Pastor Johnny was wearing these white robes. He was standing in front of this tall paddling pool thing that had been put up especially at the front by the pulpit. It made me feel a bit strange, a little overwhelmed. But no one else said it was strange, no one else seemed overwhelmed, and that made me feel better.

I watched all the other young people of God do it. There was clapping and cheering.

Then it was my turn. I walked up the little set of steps and went down into the pool, where he was waiting for me. And I felt safe.

When I went under, I remember it being a very long time, but I didn't panic. And as I came up from the water, with all my family, all my (mum's) friends staring back at me from the pews, I felt so much hope. Hope that I'd be whole now.

Because that's what he said would happen. That's what Pastor Johnny said.

TWENTY-FIVE
What Happiness Looks Like

A blend of relief and terror hits me like a bowling ball in the stomach.

They're here. They're alive. *He's alive.*

But . . . *What is this?*

I scan my eyes over the low waterfall cascading into the pool of water in front of us. I then try to catch Finn's eye, but he has his head down.

The hushed voices of the Ten swell around me.

"Who are those people?"

"Aren't they the ones who failed at HappyHead?"

"Why are they here?"

"I thought they'd been sent home."

"Is that Killian? He's . . ."

"A nutter."

"And Jennifer."

"Oh my God. Malachai. Betty . . ."

"They're the ones from the beach. The ones that rowed us."

"And that's that boy, Finneas. The one who went into Manning's office. Looked through all our stuff. Remember?"

"I thought they'd dealt with him?"

"Silence, please!" Manning raises her hand. She turns to me, and a tingling heat surges inside my head. "Yes. You were correct, Sebastian. There *are* other people on the island." She holds my gaze. "Ares has told me that you were very honest, for which we are grateful."

What? I see him watching me carefully.

"He said that you left the camp on your own in order to practice your archery skills and that's when you saw them, on the beach. He said you went straight to him. Is this correct?"

Eleanor turns to me, then looks back at Finn, mouth open.

"Sebastian?" Manning says.

Ares lied for me. . . .

"Sebastian?"

"I . . ."

I look at Stone. She blinks at me, expressionless.

"Yes," I say. "I wanted to impress Ares." I clear the dryness in my throat. "And you. I wanted to impress you too."

I glance at Finn. Head still down.

"Thank you." She pauses, studying my expression. I hold her gaze. "You cannot be blamed for your desire to impress. It was dangerous and risky, and you should never have left the camp. But you were showing initiative and commitment, and sometimes taking a risk has benefits. If anyone should understand that, it's me." Her voice softens. "You look upset, Sebastian. Don't worry, it's not your fault. That was not *your* duty."

Artemis and Ares glance at each other, and a look of something—fear, perhaps—passes between them.

Manning exhales. "Now," she says, her voice regaining its power as she addresses us all, "you may remember these people from the HappyHead facility." She gestures to the grassy bank. "Unfortunately, they proved resistant to finding happiness. If you could all please look at them. Look at how unhappy they still are."

We do. We all look at them. At how unhappy they still are.

"They have been undertaking their own program," Manning says. "Here, on the island."

A gasp.

"No way."

"What?"

"That's mad."

"Where?"

"Quiet! Dr. Stone, if you will?"

"Thank you, Gloria." Stone's voice is stern. Strong. *Different.* "My research has shown that by embracing a mindset rooted in the principle of *giving*, purpose and meaning can be ignited in people's lives. The science is steadfast. Helpers' High is a program that encourages the participants to undertake selfless actions for others. Demonstrating pure compassion activates a part of our brains that is responsible for our emotions. It awakens it, releasing endorphins. Oxytocin and dopamine levels increase. They lift the mood. Reduce stress, aggression, suicidality. It's a proven way of bringing people out of their darkness."

She lifts her hand, gesturing across the pool. "They have been here, on Elmhallow, following this very program. They have cut your firewood, washed your clothes, prepared your food. And slowly but surely it's making them better."

"I thought it was Ares and Artemis doing that?" Raheem whispers.

"But," Stone continues, "it is now time for the two programs to be joined together."

What?

The Ten begin to murmur around me.

"Each couple will now be assigned one of them."

"You're kidding?" Matthew looks nervously across the pool like he's at a zoo watching some particularly volatile caged animals.

Manning takes over again. "They will continue to undertake their duties selflessly. That will be their drive. Their *purpose*. But they now need something more. So *you* will help them. They will join you in the betterment trials and rituals. They need direction and discipline. They need to break the habits the old world has taught them, which are so deeply entrenched. You will help them comply. And you will be rewarded for doing so. You will show them benevolence in its most robust form."

Benevolence. The most benevolent thing. The lamb.

"This is their last chance," Manning says. "They were resistant to HappyHead and many other treatments back in the old world. Everything else has been tried with them and everything else has failed. I have spoken with professionals, doctors, consultants, their parents, guardians, carers. We all agree, this new way must be trialed. They remain deeply unhappy. If you can save these people, you can save anyone. Show them the strength it takes." Her eyes glint in the low sunlight cutting through the trees. "Show them what happiness looks like."

I look across to the Bottom Percentile. I think of how they were in the boathouse, laughing and joking together. They were not unhappy.

"They have been kept safe while they have been here thus far."

Manning gestures to the Keepers on either side of them. "The two gentlemen you see have ensured that." *Gentlemen?* "They've been working with them using a Therapeutic Behavioral Model." *So that's what we're calling electrocution now?* "But it is time to pass them into your care." She claps her hands together. "Right! Would you like to get to know them? It would be useful for you all to learn a little bit about each one as we assign them." She's enjoying this. Like this is all the work of a total genius. Her plan in action. "Let us begin with Number One, Betty."

She turns to Betty. We all turn to Betty.

"Betty. You are here because you are still resistant. You lied at HappyHead." Betty's body stiffens. "You told us during the Sharing Circle that your friend Jenna gave you a drug that you reacted badly to and that you never saw her again. But that's not true, is it, Betty?"

Betty looks up. "I—"

"Jenna contributed hugely to your unhappiness. She was a bad influence on you, but you kept going back to her. Taking drugs together. Drugs that made you very unwell."

"Um . . . ," Betty says quietly. "That's—"

"You ran away from home to see her. Your mother couldn't cope. She wanted you to go to rehab, but you kept disappearing. Leaving her, for nights on end. And your grandmother, your biggest support, struggled with the stress of it. Didn't she?"

I feel the watch around my wrist. *Her grandmother's watch.*

Betty's face goes completely white. "I—"

"Last year, she passed away. And you missed her funeral. Because you were with Jenna. *Taking drugs* with her."

Betty's hands start to shake. Tears streak through the dirt on her cheeks.

"I—I . . . ," Betty stammers. She balls up her fists, clenching her sleeves.

"Denial is not the way to move forward, Betty. You do not know what is good for you. You must accept that you need help."

"But . . ."

"You will be assigned to Jing and Matthew."

Matthew narrows his eyes at Betty.

"Now, Number Two. Jennifer," Manning says. "You struggle with your impulses. You were physically abusive to one of my Reviewers back at the facility, weren't you?"

Jennifer looks up, barely concealing her fury.

"You have a lot of anger, don't you, Jennifer?"

"No," she says quietly.

"You do. Your parents are scared to have you home."

Jennifer's face floods with panic. "You don't know my parents."

"They worry for their safety around you."

"Why are you saying that? You . . . *You don't know my parents.*"

"I have been speaking with them a lot over the past few weeks. They are incredibly worried about who you have become."

"What?"

"They want robust intervention because you are frightening not only them but your younger siblings too."

"No . . . That's not true. That's a lie," Jennifer yells. *"That's a lie!"*

Manning turns to us. *See what I mean?* "Jennifer will be assigned to Jamie and Rachel."

Jamie and Rachel stare at Jennifer, both shuffling uncomfortably.

"Now, Number Three. Malachai," Manning says. "You are disconnected from the world you live in."

Malachai blinks at her through his steamed-up glasses.

"You have retreated from everyday life and do not engage with anyone. Isn't that right?"

He doesn't answer. Just keeps blinking.

"You have spent most of the past year in your bedroom, alone. You have no purpose. You feel your life is meaningless. Am I correct?"

Blink. Blink. Blink.

"You will be assigned to Sam and Li."

Sam puts his thumb up to him.

"Now, Number Four. Killian."

Killian spits on the ground in front of him.

Manning cocks her head. "Need I say more, Killian?"

"Fuck you."

"Apparently not." Manning crosses her arms neatly in front of her. "However, it is in the interests of the couples that they know who you are. You have a history of not being able to contain yourself."

"What?" Killian shouts. "*Contain* myself? You're fucking nuts."

The Keepers take a step toward him.

"You lash out, even when not provoked. You become intimidating and often threatening, as you have just shown. You have a history of fights, of aggression, of violence. You will be assigned to Lucy and Raheem."

The muscles in Killian's jaw tighten. He clenches his fists.

I look at Lucy and Raheem, the shadow of terror crossing their faces.

"And finally," Manning says, her voice lowering like she's trying to keep it free from emotion, "number Five." She looks at Finn. "You are the most resistant."

He stares at her, his eyes burning red.

"You have shown a persistent disregard toward authority throughout your life. You were—prior to coming here—*arrested*. Weren't you?"

"Told you," Eleanor whispers.

"Can you please tell us why?"

He drops his eyes to the floor.

"Tell them, Finneas. They need to know."

"No," he says.

Manning's eyes widen. "Then I will have to tell them for you. You broke into someone's house."

He keeps his head down.

"You broke into a family home, in the middle of the night. Didn't you?"

He is trembling.

"You put them in danger. Why? Why, Finneas?"

Finally he speaks through gritted teeth. "You wouldn't understand."

"Let me make it clear to everyone how much you need the help we are offering you here. It is important that they know. You were expelled from your school for antisocial behavior. You have no friends, no real family. You refuse any help. Your social workers don't know what to do with you. You have been in the hospital numerous times for low mood, on various medications. You are completely lost."

He looks like he wants to scream. His face taut with anger. With *loathing*.

"You were brought to HappyHead as part of a deal. A deal that *you* agreed to. You were given a chance, by me. We did not want you to go back to the hospital again, Finneas. We wanted to do anything we could to avoid you going back to being *locked away in a room.*" I hear her voice break. "We wanted to *help* you, so Dr. Stone and I took a risk and we took you into our care. But since then, you have shown complete contempt toward us. You have undermined our program from the very beginning.

"At the facility you broke into my office and looked through your fellow cohorts' personal details—these people who stand with us today—and put them all at risk. You attempted to leave, and again, *here*, you have attempted to flee.

"Last night we found out you had been trying to manipulate your peers, trying to convince them that leaving would be better for *them*. Planting ideas in their heads that this process is bad for them. Even though, *even though*"—she begins to raise her voice, her composure faltering—"this is the *one* place where they are being given the opportunity to have a new start. You cannot keep trying to escape the help you so badly need, Freddie."

Silence.

Freddie? Who the fuck is Freddie?

Finn looks up, confused.

Eleanor's hand goes to her mouth. She makes a small gasp.

"Finneas," Manning says, clearing her throat. "*Finneas.*"

I look at him. His whole body is shuddering. And then I realize—so is hers.

"Number Five." Her voice becomes flat again, emotionless. "I will be assigning you to the couple who has shown the most strength thus far. To those with the most sacred bloodstones. Sebastian and Eleanor. They will be given the opportunity to try and change you."

My head reels. I turn to Eleanor, her hand still over her mouth.

"Now," Manning says brightly, "let us undertake their Commitment Ceremony." Like ours . . . "In this beautiful place, we shall experience this sacred moment together." She looks across the pool. "We will see your willingness to acknowledge that you need to change and accept the help on offer."

Ares and Artemis begin to take off their shoes. They then step into the pool and wade through it, until they are waist-deep. The water seeps up into their yellow robes, darkening them.

Finn's eyes narrow. *What is this?*

I don't know. *I don't know. . . .*

I look at Stone. Completely still. Quietly watching.

"Come, join us in the water," Artemis says, holding her hand out.

Finn looks as if he might do something. Like he might explode.

"Don't be afraid," Ares says.

And then slowly, very slowly, the Bottom Percentile begins to shuffle forward toward the water, toward Ares and Artemis. All except Finn.

"It appears Number Five is resisting," Manning says.

Come on, Finn. *Come on.*

"Do you need some encouragement?" she calls.

He doesn't answer. He doesn't move.

The others shiver in the water as they join Ares and Artemis.

Move, Finn. *Just move.*

"Number Five, do you need some help?" Manning calls again, impatient now. "Number Five."

He looks up, directly at me. *I'm sorry,* he mouths.

And then he turns. And he runs. Toward the back of the bank, to the trees.

I hear people gasp.

I step forward, but someone takes my arm. Eleanor. "Don't, Seb."

I look on in horror as the Keepers sprint after him. Just as he makes it to the tree line, they grab him, pulling him down to the ground.

"No!" he screams. "Get off me!"

Manning watches. Stone watches. We all watch as he resists. Screaming, pulling at their clothes. Wild. Frantic. *Terrified.*

I try to move again, but Eleanor tightens her grip. "Please, Seb."

"What's wrong with him?" Jing asks.

"Is he OK?" Lucy says.

"No," Manning says. "He is not."

He keeps screaming, his arms flailing, clawing at the Keepers' faces.

"This will not do." Manning turns to face me and Eleanor. She holds out her hand.

In it is a yellow rubber wristband like the one on the Keeper's arm.

Oh, God. No.

"What's that?" Eleanor says, her eyes wide.

"It will help him," Manning says softly.

I can still hear Finn screaming. "No! Please! Stop!"

"Take it," Manning says, firmly now.

"What does it do?" Eleanor says, an edge of panic in her voice.

"Take it, Eleanor."

"But—"

"He is your responsibility now. Both of yours."

Eleanor stares at her. At her aunt.

"Eleanor, you do not want to disappoint me. We both know you can't afford to do that."

Eleanor's face suddenly hardens. She takes the wristband from Manning.

"Good girl."

"Eleanor," I say. "Wait."

Manning looks back to the bank. "Step away!" she calls to the Keepers.

They release him.

Finn scrambles to his feet. He turns to the trees.

"Press it," Manning says. "The button. *Now.*"

"Eleanor! No—"

zzzzz

His body goes rigid. His head snaps back.

No. *No.*

He falls forward onto his knees. Puts his hands out in front of him, panting, on all fours.

"I had hoped it would not come to this," Manning says. "But it appears to be the only way to ensure everyone's safety. Including his own."

"What *was* that?" Raheem gasps.

"Does it . . . *help* them?" Rachel says, her mouth hanging open with shock.

"Yes," Manning says. "It does."

"Does it, like, calm them down?" Jing whispers.

"Exactly." Manning nods. "Dr. Stone?"

"The shocks help ignite neurotransmitters in their brains," Stone says calmly as Finn slowly tries to stand back up. "It boosts dopamine and serotonin at a much quicker rate than other interventions. It has been licensed for small-dose use here."

Small-dose use?

"Does it hurt?" Jing asks.

"The physical reaction displayed is far more extreme than what is actually happening inside the body," Stone replies, her face remaining completely blank. "Proportionally, it is much less than the emotional pain they are currently in."

"So . . . will we all get one of those?" Matthew asks.

Manning nods. "It appears that will be necessary. They are still so unwell."

Finn staggers toward the pool.

"That's it," Manning says. "That's it, Number Five. Well done." She turns to us. "Do you see? He is much calmer now."

We watch as he stumbles into the water—head down, hair hanging over his face. He trips as he enters it, falling forward onto his knees with a splash.

My body moves.

"Where are you going, Sebastian?" Manning calls out.

"To help him," I say, not looking back. "He needs help."

As I enter the water, I see Artemis start to move toward me.

"Let him," Manning says. "Let him help."

The stabbing cold jabs into me as I wade past Artemis and Ares, to the Bottom Percentile.

Finn begins to stand. When we meet, I take his arm in my hand, steadying him. *I'm here.*

I turn with him, guiding him away from the bank, away from the Keepers, into the middle of the pool. As I do, I realize the other couples are now wading into the water too, standing with their assigned number, steadying them as they tremble from the cold.

Eleanor appears opposite me, on the other side of Finn. She doesn't look at him. Doesn't touch him.

"What a beautiful thing to see," Manning says, her voice filled with emotion. Stone stands beside her, watching us intently. "Let us continue."

Manning nods at Artemis, who momentarily hesitates, unsure. She then turns to us. When she speaks, her voice bounces off the surface of the water, resonant and powerful. "You shall now initiate the Commitment," she says. "Lower them so their shoulders are beneath the surface."

Eleanor takes Finn's arm. As I take the other, his eyes meet mine. In them I see so much desperation and terror and confusion that I have to force myself not to look away.

It's OK, Finn. But I know that it's not. How can it be?

We lower him so his chin is just above the surface.

Then Ares speaks. "Here in this Sanctuary, you shall be immersed by your assigned couple. When you come back up, you will begin your journey to leave your old selves behind. You will make a commitment to change. You shall move forward, accepting this help on offer, away from the darkness and into the light. Now repeat after me: The Ten. We commit ourselves to you."

"The Ten. We commit ourselves to you."

"We trust you to help us."

"We trust you to help us."

"By giving us a new purpose."

"By giving us a new purpose."

"We thank you for this opportunity."

"We thank you for this opportunity."

"For showing us what happiness looks like."

"For showing us what happiness looks like."

"Now," Ares says, "submerge them."

And we do. Together, Eleanor and I lower Finn beneath the surface. The bubbles congregate above his head as we hold him down.

"Release them."

Finn breaks free from the surface, gasping, gray.

"Well done," Ares says. "You have taken the first step. We know that accepting help is difficult, but you are here. You are with the people who care the most. Who will do anything to end the pain you are in."

Ares looks at Manning, and she smiles back at him, tears in her eyes. "They are ready," she says. "Phase two will begin tonight."

TWENTY-SIX
Icebreaker

On my first day of sixth form, we had to do an icebreaker.

Icebreakers are the worst thing ever invented, and that includes Andrew Lloyd Webber musicals. The teacher got us all to stand in a circle. "This is called Master and Servant," he said. "It's just a bit of fun to ease you into the class."

It was right after the summer vacation following our exams. My results letter came, and they weren't as great as everyone expected. Some people seemed a bit upset. My teachers. My parents. Even Pastor Johnny and his wife wrote me a card to say they were thinking of me.

I was fine with it all, until Mum actually cried when she looked at the letter. The one from Pastor Johnny. Not the one with my results. She said we had to regroup immediately.

We sat around the dining table, regrouping. We were weighing my options, and she said that I might just scrape into psychology, since I did OK in the humanities.

I said I didn't want to take psychology because I didn't like overthinking things and that appeared to be My Main Problem.

She said because I "feel things deeply," I might be really good at it. And it was a "proper" subject, not like art or drama. She gave a passionate speech about making the most out of tough situations, and somehow I ended up saying yes.

The psychology teacher was this old man called Mr. Clifford, with a gray beard and a side part. He paired us up, and we had to pick who would be the master and who would be the servant.

I was assigned the role of servant. We had to do whatever the master asked of us. That was the only rule.

The masters started getting the servants to do stuff like sharpening pencils for them. But then it started to get a bit weirder. People were told to go to the vending machines and buy their master a can of Coke, or do bits of homework for them. At one point, someone asked their servant to kiss their feet. And the servant did.

Everyone laughed. It wasn't really funny, though.

We were told afterward that it was based on an experiment about the power of authority and our intrinsic propensity to be obedient. To want to impress. Some guy called Milgram back in the 1960s got people to willingly electrocute each other. Apparently, the authority went to their heads and people just fell into their roles.

"That wouldn't happen nowadays," one of my classmates said.

"We're still hardwired to follow the rules. To impress those in charge. Even to deny our own consciences. Their authority over us makes us feel as if everything is safe and right. We're conditioned to think differently to how we truly feel. You're all here, in school, aren't you? But how many of you actually *want* to be here? *Why* are you here?"

We all looked at Mr. Clifford, not really sure how to answer.

He smiled. "Now, be honest, did any of the masters enjoy it? The power?"

The masters nodded. "It was kind of fun. Seeing what they would do for us."

"Exactly."

He was a strange man.

When the class finished and we all walked outside, no one spoke to each other. The reality of it didn't make sense anymore as we stood in the stark lights of the corridor.

But while we were in class, we didn't question it. We just did as we were told.

TWENTY-SEVEN
Originals

The sky is dotted with stars like someone has taken a pin and pricked holes into a heavy black sheet draped over the camp. Each one a tiny suggestion that something might be glowing brightly behind it.

I glance over at the brick shed just beyond the dwelling houses. The Keepers stand guard on either side of the thick iron door, two dark shadows in front of the windowless walls. Finn and the Bottom Percentile are now locked inside.

I feel sick. I have ever since we came back and were told to dry off, change into our cloaks, and wait on our stones while Artemis and Ares took Stone and Manning on a "tour of the camp" like it's a summer holiday retreat.

"Before we begin phase two," Manning says, standing next to the fire as it sends a thick, woody smoke up into the night, "there is something I would like to share with you. To inspire you as you move into this next chapter." She looks to the periphery of the circle. "Artemis and Ares, come and join me."

As she holds their hands, I see her red nail polish bright against their skin. An energy passes between them. It is intense, *private*. I want to look away, but I can't, and I'm reminded of a YouTube video Shelly showed me of people lancing boils on their backs.

Shit. Shelly. *Bedroom 6?*

The energy radiates outward into the circle, drawing us in.

Eleanor leans forward. She hasn't said a thing to me since the waterfall. Since she pressed the button. She stares at her aunt. Emotionless. I realize she still doesn't know that I know she is Manning's niece.

"My Originals," Manning says. *Originals?* "When we first met all that time ago, who would have known how far we would come?" They beam back at her. "Look at what we are achieving. Can you remember when this was just an *idea*? A seed of hope?"

I glance over at Stone, her face shrouded in shadow at the circle's edge.

They look at each other. Just . . . being. For *ages*.

"Madame Manning?" Matthew says tentatively, lifting his hand into the air.

She snaps her head around to him as if she'd completely forgotten that we were all here.

"Yes, Matthew?"

"What are . . . *Originals?*" I don't like him, but he does ask important questions.

"They are the first," she says. "They are the past. They are the present. They are the future."

OK. A little vague. A little convoluted. A little *full of shit*.

"Cool," he says. "So . . . Like . . . But . . . What does that *mean*?" Another solid question from Matthew.

"It means I would like you to understand just how important these two people are. How their journey with us began. How we came to meet." Tenner bet it was in the depths of hell. "I was their therapist."

An image drops into my head of Gloria Manning in a big white chair, wearing a white suit, surrounded by white walls, handing Ares and Artemis a box of tissues while they weep together on a big white beanbag.

"What, like *couples therapy*?" Rachel asks.

Ares and Artemis look at each other and share a small smile.

"No," Manning says, smiling too. "They didn't know each other back then." Her tone shifts. It becomes . . . thoughtful. A bit . . . *sad.* "They were two very unhappy people when they came to me. They were so lost. Each of them had had their own experiences with a system that was supposed to be there to help them. But they found that it was broken.

"It wasn't working. *Nothing* was working. The system was on its knees due to the overwhelming demand and the lack of resources, and it was letting the patients down. I had just set up a therapy clinic for young people, after . . ." She suddenly falters. "After I had truly understood just how bad things had become.

"I knew from my early sessions with Ares and Artemis that they each had something incredibly unique. They questioned the status quo. Constantly curious as to why things were the way they were. And I saw how strong they each were. Two brilliant, inquiring minds. Not afraid to think and say things about the state of the world that others might not. They were so *honest*. When I introduced them to each other, it was undeniable. Together, they were brimming with possibility. And I saw the potential for real, *sustained* happiness."

"Then Gloria brought them to me." Stone steps forward from the half-light. "She and I were already collaborating on the Happy-Head project, and she told me that she knew these two special people who could work with us to understand how happiness could not only be sustained, but *taught*. She pitched the idea of adding a further element to the program, using this bright young pair. For them to oversee the strongest from the facility in a place where they could solidify their strength and teach it to those who were struggling the most." She flicks her eyes to the shed. "Away from distractions. Back to basics. The strong leading the weak. Pushing them. *Inspiring* them. Ultimately, showing them what it takes."

Jesus. I don't recognize her. I don't recognize her at all.

Manning turns to Stone, her features softening. "It was about six months before the building of the facility that I came to you, wasn't it?"

"It was."

I remember what Stone said to me back in the hut beneath the lighthouse. *Gloria came to me and said we had been asked to create something called a Never Plan.*

Manning smiles. "You took a little convincing."

"I did." Stone narrows her eyes, and through the pluming smoke, they become a reflective black. "At first, I was a little unsure about the idea. I thought that it would never work, letting young people lead *each other*." She raises her eyebrows at the memory. "I was, frankly, worried that it could go badly wrong.

"But after Gloria trialed the assessments at the facility with Artemis and Ares, I saw how much potential they had to become *teachers*. To use their newfound strength for others. I could see they had the power to bring anyone, even the most lost, back into the light. It convinced me that this new element could really deepen the effect HappyHead could have." She pauses. "She told me that she thought it could change the world." She smiles. "And something inside me—despite my fears, my reservations—told me that Gloria's plan could do exactly that. Rid the world of unhappiness for good."

Gloria's plan. The Never Plan.

Oh my God. She really *is* gone.

"And now we are here," Stone says.

"And now we are here." Manning smiles. "Ready to change the world."

Their gazes linger on each other for a moment as if they are speaking in a wordless language to one another.

Manning then turns to us. "From this point on, in order for you to be awarded sacred bloodstones, you must ensure that your Number complies with their treatment." *Our Number?* "They will continue their duties from the shed, but you must also help them with upcoming trials and rituals. Some of them may feel alarming and, at times, very difficult, but I need to see that you are ready." Well, that's promising. "I have faith that you will be able to show them that kindness."

Kindness.

"So they'll be winning bloodstones for us?" Matthew says.

Manning nods. "If you are able to inspire them to show change, then yes. This is your responsibility now. Your higher purpose. It is a *privilege* to alter the course of someone's life. Not many would be capable, but I believe you are all strong enough, *special* enough. I hope you can prove me right. So much is at stake, for all of you."

Privilege . . . Higher purpose.

"Tomorrow night, we will both be returning. And when we do, we will count the sacred bloodstones. Whichever couple has the most will have proved their leadership. Their influence. And that couple will receive their prize. They will be the winners. And they will be leaving the island."

I look at Eleanor, but she keeps her gaze fixed on her aunt.

"What is it?" Matthew asks. "The prize?" Again, good question.

"I do not want to alter the course you are on. I want to see you want it because of what you are becoming, not because of what you shall receive." God. "But know this—it will change your lives forever."

"Will we be going back home?"

"Do you want to go home, Jamie?"

"Um . . . not particularly."

Manning smiles. "You like it away from all the mess of the old world?"

"Yeah. And it sort of feels like . . . we're just getting started, really."

She smiles at him. "It does."

"Will we get money?" Matthew blurts out. Jing turns to him, embarrassed, but he doesn't seem to care. "Is the prize *money*?"

"If you win, you will never have to worry about money, Matthew."

"Awesome." His mouth hangs open.

"Will we become *famous*?"

"Lots of people will learn who you are, Rachel. You will have achieved so much, and they will see that. You will be recognized for what you are capable of. For your happiness."

"No way," Rachel says, her eyes bright. "So, like, influencers? Like, *happiness influencers*?"

Manning smiles. "I like that."

Rachel turns to Jamie. "We could make a joint profile," she whispers excitedly. "I wonder how many followers we'd get."

"And what happens to the rest of us?" Sam says. "What if we don't win?"

"You will all leave when you are ready. Which you all *will* be. It may just take some of you a little longer."

"So what about them?" I point to the shed. "What happens to them?"

"They will be going home with the tools and knowledge you have taught them, Sebastian. Free, I hope, of the pain they are in. Just like you." She smiles, with an air of melancholy again. "You are already showing how compassionate you can be. It is time to persevere. Now, shall we begin the first trial?" She nods at Artemis. "Bring out the Trauma Boxes."

The *what*?

Artemis leaves the circle, stepping into the darkness. When she returns, she places something at the feet of each of couple.

An old shoebox.

I look down at the one in front of me, his name scrawled on its lid in thick marker pen.

FINNEAS OLIVER BLAKE

I didn't know that was his middle name.

Finn's Trauma Box. *What's inside it?*

Matthew raises his hand. "And . . . what if they don't comply?"

"I trust you to know when they will need your encouragement."

Matthew looks down at his wrist. We all do. At the yellow wristbands strapped around them.

TWENTY-EIGHT
Trauma Box

"Number One," Manning shouts.

The Keepers unbolt the shed door. The clonk of the latch reverberates through the air. As it swings open, I see a figure in the doorway. Head down. Hood up. Betty.

One of the Keepers takes her arm, pulling her toward us.

I catch a glimpse of the others, huddled together at the back of the small room. *Clonk.* The door swings back, shutting them away.

"Now, stand facing your couple," Manning says to Betty as she enters the glow of the circle. She hesitates, chewing her sleeve. "You are safe, Betty. Your couple is here to help you."

Betty shuffles forward until she's in front of Jing and Matthew.

"Well done," Manning says. "This is an act of erasure. An erasure of your pain, Number One."

Betty whimpers.

Manning turns to Jing and Matthew. "Please pick up Betty's Trauma Box."

Matthew picks up the shoebox at their feet, name facing outward, toward Betty.

ELIZABETH ABIGAIL EVANS

"With this act we want you to help Betty move on from her past experiences, which are the root of so much of her trauma." Manning speaks loudly, making sure we can all hear just how much trauma Betty has. "By letting go of this," she continues, "Betty will move forward into a new way of being. And after, she shall be referred to only as Number One. All the pain associated with her name will be destroyed." She smiles. "Open it."

Matthew lifts the lid. Jing looks down into it. I see her frown.

"What is it?" Betty whispers.

"Show her," Manning says.

Matthew tilts the box toward Betty.

She puts her hand to her mouth. Inside it, I can just make out two tatty, fluffy ears. A teddy bear.

Matthew stifles a laugh as he begins to rummage through the items, lifting them up so they're illuminated by the firelight.

A photo frame. In it, a picture of Betty with her arm around another girl with bright red hair, sticking her tongue out at the camera. *Is that Jenna?*

A baby blanket.

A diary.

Betty looks at Manning, her eyes wide. "Have you . . . ?"

"Read it? Yes, Betty. It is very important I know what's going on in your mind."

Betty's face crumples.

Matthew lifts up a black rectangle, reflecting the light. Wait. Is that a phone? It looks so strange, out here. I haven't seen one for—

But why her phone?

"The internet is poisonous," Manning says. *You're poisonous.* "It is a distraction. And there are many negative people in your life, Betty, whose contact details are stored on that phone. You must detach from them."

Betty's lip wobbles. "Bu—"

"It is time to let go. It is time to burn your trauma."

Betty begins to silently cry. "But this is all my—"

"It's OK, Betty," Jing says gently. "This is going to help you."

Manning nods encouragingly.

"We are helping you," Matthew says impatiently, clearly wishing he wasn't. "Just . . . hurry up." He holds up his arm, flashing the yellow wristband.

Betty flinches. "Please," she says. "Please don't."

Manning looks at him. "Easy, Matthew."

I see him fight the desire to roll his eyes. "Come on now, Betty," he says, using a soft voice, attempting compassion. "This is for your benefit."

"I'll help you," Jing says. "All you have to do is take this one step at a time."

Betty slowly nods. Then she takes her Trauma Box in her hands.

"Good," Manning says.

"Good," Matthew repeats.

She turns toward the flames, shaking so much she nearly spills the contents all over the ground.

"Join her," Manning says to Matthew and Jing.

Jing gently puts her hand on Betty's back as she holds the box over the flames.

"Now, Betty," Jing says. "It's going to be—"

Matthew nudges Betty's back with his elbow, making her drop the box so it lands right in the flames.

Betty puts her hands over her mouth.

We watch in silence as the contents turn black. The air smells sweet. Toxic. My eyes tingle as her trauma burns.

This is sick.

I feel Betty's grandmother's watch, still tight around my wrist. *You're getting this back, Betty. I promise—*

When the box is gone, Manning holds her hand out to Betty. "Here, Number One," she says. "Put this in your couple's vessel."

Matthew smiles, teeth glinting, as Betty drops the bloodstone into their bowl.

Manning then signals to the Keeper, who takes Betty's arm and takes her back to the shed. "Number Two," she calls.

Over the next hour, or however long it is, we sit on our stones and we watch. We watch as Jennifer Emily Beale, Malachai Aaron Cohen and Killian Ronan Kelly are called forward. And I feel myself slip into a strange trance. A heavy stupor.

But then.

"Number Five," Manning calls.

Finn moves toward us through the circle, trying to keep his distance from the flames. And I suddenly remember what he told me about his parents. About how they died. In a fire.

As he takes his place in front of me and Eleanor, I try to catch his eye, but he is just a dark shape in front of us. An outline.

"Pick up Number Five's Trauma Box," Manning says.

Use his name. Why won't you use his name?

"Come on, Seb," Eleanor says. My stomach churns as I see Finn's name on the top of his box in her hands. As he sees it.

It's OK, I try to tell him. *It's OK.* But he drops his eyes to the ground.

I scan the circle, looking for Stone. *Where are you?* And then I see her, standing between Artemis and Ares at the circle's edge, right where the light of the fire meets the darkness. Watching. Eyes dead. *Where have you gone?*

"A fresh start lies ahead," Manning says. "Now, Eleanor, open it."

I don't want her to. I don't want to see what's inside.

I look at her hands, holding it steady. Then she slowly lifts the lid. I glance down into it.

An old camera.

And . . . that's strange. Sheets of paper.

Are they . . . ? I lean forward. Photographs. A whole pile of them.

"Please, show your Number his trauma."

I reach my hand into the shoebox and pick up the photos. As I hold them out between us, I feel them shaking in my fingers. I start to sift through them, and as I do it's as if his entire life flashes in front of me.

There are so many of them. I drink them in.

Him as a little boy, in a park, on a swing.

On a bike, wearing a bright green helmet.

In his school uniform in front of a blue door, holding a lunchbox.

Older, in a black hoodie, grinning, giving the camera the middle finger.

Finn with his hand up over his face, his nails painted all different colors.

Holding a rabbit, kissing the top of its head.

Smoking a cigarette on a rooftop, looking out over a skyline.

Showing off a new tattoo on his arm.

Smiling. *Laughing.*

And then I stop on one. It's older than the others. Tatty edges.

As I look at it, I nearly laugh. I don't know if it's because it's funny, or because I'm shocked, or because it's beautiful. My eyes start to sting.

He's about four years old, in a pair of denim overalls. His face warm and open, his smile so wide I can see all his teeth, holding the hands of two people on either side of him. All three of them beaming into the camera. A woman on his left with the same ice-blue eyes. A man on his right, tall and angular, with jet-black hair.

His parents.

I look up at him. He's staring at it. And his face starts to shake, straining, *fighting* with every ounce of strength to keep himself from spilling over.

"Put the items back in the Trauma Box," Manning says. But I don't. I can't. "It is not fair to prolong this, Sebastian."

Eleanor grabs the pictures from my hand. She drops them into the box, turns to Finn, and thrusts it into his stomach. "Take it."

"No," he says quietly. "I won't."

"Sebastian?" Manning says. "Maybe some encouragement?" She looks at my wrist. At the wristband.

"I—"

"Take it, Finn," Eleanor says. "We want to help you. This will help you get better."

"It won't."

"Sebastian," Manning says again. "You know what to do."

I look at Finn. Hunched. Head down. Trying to hide. To disappear.

"Finn," I say. "It's OK." He looks up at me. And when he does, I see everything he is feeling, all at once. Fear. Hatred. Loathing. Disgust. Shame. Betrayal.

His gaze is so intense that it makes me take a step back.

But then he turns to Eleanor. He takes the box.

"Good, Number Five. *Very* good," Manning says. "Now burn your trauma."

Finn edges forward toward the flames.

"That's it," Manning says. "That's it."

I look at the back of him, his silhouette, as he holds his entire life in his hands. And then he bows his head and he tips it.

The photographs flutter down through the smoke, catching the light as they fall through the air. He throws the box on top of them.

And then he turns, his eyes streaming, and looks toward the shed. "Come on," he shouts. "What are you waiting for?"

The Keeper steps forward. Finn lets him take his arm and pull him away. The shed door closes behind him.

"Well," Manning says. I turn to see her holding a bloodstone in her hand, smiling. "Congratulations. This is yours."

She turns back to the others. "Well done, all of you. Now sadly it is time for us to leave. Assessments are well underway at the facility, and I'm itching to take part again. I had such fun last time."

I glance at Stone, who is still gazing into the fire.

"Let us all say our goodbyes." Manning motions for Artemis and Ares to join her in the middle of the circle. She hugs them, then kisses their foreheads like they are seven years old.

As the others gather around her, saying goodbye in an excited blur of chatter, I keep my eyes on Stone.

I need to talk to her. This could be my last chance. I weave my way through the mingling bodies.

"Dr. Stone. I—"

"Hasn't this evening been so powerful, Sebastian?" she says brightly, cutting me off.

"Dr. Stone, the pager—"

"It was so encouraging to see them being so brave. Number Five is very lucky to have you guiding him." She smiles, her eyes dead.

Number Five. She is gone. There's no use.

"Yeah." I slowly turn around.

"Sebastian?"

I look back at her.

"Good luck tomorrow."

"Right," I say. "Thanks."

"A hug," she says. "To say goodbye."

She opens her arms and steps forward. I feel the papery skin of her cheek pressing gently into mine. And then she whispers into my ear, "No one is going home, Sebastian. No one. This is just the beginning. There is another phase in a new location. I still have a plan. I will help you. Trust me. Look under your pillow. Stay strong. Do not lose hope."

She lets go of me and takes a step back. I stare at her.

Her eyes blaze back at me. Fierce. Amber. Alive again. "It is so good to see you, Sebastian."

"You're here," I say.

She smiles. Then she speaks, her lips hardly moving. "I am here."

And then she extinguishes the fire behind her eyes, snuffing it out with a blink.

She is here.

I watch as she moves through the crowd toward Manning, her words churning over in my brain.

I have a plan. Look under your pillow.

How did she—

The tour of the camp. Sneaky. *Very sneaky.*

I try to hide my smile.

"Good night, all of you," Manning calls. "We will see you at the Counting Ceremony tomorrow. Please remember to put your absolute *all* into the final phase of your journey here. Elicit change. End suffering. That is your duty."

With that, Manning and Stone head toward the helicopter. We stand back as its blades begin to whip the air into chaos around us.

"To bed, everyone," Ares says. "Another big day ahead tomorrow."

The others say good night to each other, then begin to trickle off into the dwelling houses.

As I go to follow, I see Eleanor staring into the embers of the fire.

"Eleanor?" I step toward her. "Are you OK?"

A hand grips my shoulder. Ares. "Come on, Sebastian. It's late."

As he leads me away, I look over my shoulder to see Artemis appear by her side. She puts an arm around Eleanor, and I see her flinch.

"Come now, Sebastian. You will see each other tomorrow."

I lie on my bed, staring up at the bee etched on the beam above me as the other boys talk about the power of change. The power we all have. The responsibility. I listen as Ares speaks earnestly in reply.

I wait for the lights to go out. For their voices to quiet, until all I hear is my heart thumping against my ribs.

I push my hand under the pillow, and my fingers brush against something.

I pull out two pieces of paper. Both folded over and taped shut. Each with an initial on the front.

- S-   -F-

I take the one marked "S" and peel off the tape, trying not to make a sound. It appears to be a blank page that has been torn from the back of an old book. Thick and smelling of dust. A page number in the top corner.

I unfold it.

There's tiny handwriting scrawled across the other side. Familiar. I lift the paper so it's a few inches from my eyes, and I begin to read in the light from the dying fire.

I am sorry, Sebastian. Gloria is still so very cautious of me. I must keep her believing I have faith in her, or we have no chance. By the end of this note, I hope you will understand this and forgive me. I have tried many ways, but she is clever. And so we must be cleverer.

She will only give me limited information. She has someone watching me at all times, except when I use the toilet, which is what they assume I am doing as I write this in the room she keeps me in at the facility. I have grappled with the idea of not disclosing what I have discovered—of not putting you in further danger for being the recipient of this knowledge. But I have no choice. You must know so you can expose her. There is only one real way to stop this, and it must come from you.

No one is going home, Sebastian. Not the winners, not the Ten, not the Bottom Percentile. There is more to come. More than I ever thought she was capable of. There is another location. Another phase. A place that I have heard her call Ash Farm. I do not know the exact location or her full intentions, but I do know this: She is planning on taking the winning couple there in two days' time. And their assigned Number will be going with them.

She does not want the Bottom Percentile to "get better." She has decided that this is now an impossibility. She is using Elmhallow to test their submission and your ability to elicit it. Over time, each couple will join the farm, when she deems them "strong" enough. I have no details of what will happen there, only guesses and grave assumptions.

· I have attempted to explore every other feasible option for your escape, but can think of only one. And it is this. In spite of everything, you must win. <u>You</u> must be the first to be taken to the farm.

I have appealed to Gloria's ego by convincing her to conduct a short press interview with the winning couple before they move forward to Ash Farm. This would be your opportunity to expose her.

Tomorrow's trials will not be easy, and I am aware that I am asking for your faith. Blind faith, perhaps. But if you give it to me, I hope that we can find a way to stop this. All of it. For everyone.

Gloria is, as I have always known, a genius with incredible potential. However, her ego and past trauma have driven her to believe that what she is doing here will change the world. But it is her ego that may, in the end, help us.

I must end with a warning. If anyone finds out what I have told you, you will be silenced. She has already silenced Mark.

James and Mia (or, as you know them, Ares and Artemis) are firmly under Gloria's control. I fear for what they will do to you if they have any inclination of our intentions.

Eleanor's desire to win should serve us well. Her relationship with her aunt is complex. She is very afraid. She will do all she can to please her.

Please give Finn his envelope. He must now show real strength. He must battle against his instincts and win you bloodstones. This is vital. His safety is crucial. Keep him alive.

You both must show your strength now more than ever before. You are special, both of you, together. You are special because you know that truth is the most important thing.

We will reveal it. We will.

Destroy this.

ES

I read the words again and again until they are etched into my brain. Then I tear the letter up into pieces and gather them in my hand.

I look over at the sleeping boys, at Ares. Then I move across the sheepskin rugs toward the fire, which is still a glowing bed of embers. I take one final look at Ares before I scatter the fragments into it like gray confetti. They ignite, sending a glow out across the room.

Shadows dance over the walls, over the ceiling, over me. I watch until the paper is all gone. Until there is nothing but ash.

When I am back under my covers, I take Finn's note in my hand. It's a little thicker than mine. As I lie there holding it, the fear of what is to come makes my brain fizz and crackle. It is dense, *electric,* like the moment just before a storm.

But there is something else too. A strange, unfamiliar feeling cutting through it all. It flashes, bright and jagged, against the darkness.

I push the envelope down into my sock to keep it safe.

Her words ring in my ears like she is right here with me.

Do not lose hope.

TWENTY-NINE
Let's Dance

Music is playing. Bowie. "Let's Dance." I'm with Finn. In the sunshine. And we're dancing together. No one else for miles and miles . . .

I look at his beaming face as we dance. Jumping. Spinning. *Laughing.*

And it is . . . fucking amazing.

But somewhere, underneath it all, there's a nagging awareness that this isn't real. That at some point I must wake up. And this moment will no longer exist. It will be replaced with something very different.

So I dance harder. We both do. We dance and dance and dance.

And I hope that somehow, inside the brick walls of the shed, he is dreaming the exact same thing.

A noise. Rustling. I open my eyes to see someone crouched in front of the fireplace.

I focus on his hunched frame, the arch of his spine protruding through the back of his hoodie. His dirty hands. For a second, I don't realize it's him.

I panic, wondering if he's searching for the remnants of the note I dropped into the fire last night. But then I see a set of tools on the floor beside him—a small spade, a sponge, a bucket—and I realize he's cleaning it.

The pale morning sunlight creeps over him through the dwelling-house window, making him appear drained of all color. Like how I imagined a character from a Dickens book that we read in GCSE English.

The gaunt one. The poor one. The *servant* one.

"Finn," I whisper.

He snaps his head to me. Our eyes meet, and his face drops. He shrinks back. Embarrassed. *Humiliated.*

I open my mouth to speak again, but he puts his finger to his lips. He flicks his eyes to the dwelling-house door. It's slightly ajar. Through the gap I can just make out one of the Keepers, standing with his back to it.

The other boys are still asleep in their beds, breathing heavily.

But not Ares. His bed is empty. I squint through the window opposite, into the pale sunlight. He is standing in the middle of the stone circle. Top off, muscles gleaming, talking quietly with Artemis.

The Bucket Room door slowly opens. And Betty steps out, clutching a basket full of dirty towels.

Wait, I mouth.

She frowns. *What?*

Just . . . Wait.

She flicks her eyes nervously to the Keeper.

I feel for her grandmother's watch around my wrist. Unclip it so it drops to the floor into my pile of dirty Reds. Her eyes widen.

Betty tiptoes over, picks up the Reds, and puts them in her basket. She smiles at me, then lowers her head and scurries toward the dwelling-house door. The Keeper steps aside, letting her pass.

The Keeper then turns to Finn. He frowns and taps his watch. *Hurry up.*

Finn picks up the small spade from the floor next to him. His hands shake as he begins to shovel the ash into the empty bucket, careful not to make a noise, not to spill it.

Helpers' High. More like *Oliver Twist.*

I watch the Keeper watching him. I take in the width of his shoulders, his shiny, bald scalp peeking out from beneath his cap, the wrinkles, deep like scars, between his eyebrows.

And then he looks up.

Black eyes. Staring straight at me.

Hi, I mouth.

Fuck you. I meant *fuck you.*

He raises his hand and beckons me toward him.

Um . . . What? Me?

He nods. *Yes. You.*

Oh, God.

As I pull the blanket off and step onto the floor, I feel the note in the side of my sock. Shit.

I force my mouth into what I hope resembles a smile. It makes the muscles in my cheeks throb. ·

Finn keeps his eyes on the fireplace as I head over to the Keeper.

When I am right in front him, I stop. His dark gaze hovers over me. Just keep smiling.

"Make sure he gets it done," he whispers gruffly. I can see

yellow stains on his teeth and smell the staleness on his breath. "He's your responsibility now."

I nod.

"He has half an hour. When I come back, I want to be able to see my reflection in it."

"Sure."

He then turns and heads through the door. It swings shut behind him, and I hear the key in the lock.

Half an hour.

I scan my eyes over the boys again. Still sleeping. Then I step toward the fireplace.

Finn's hands go still. He looks up at me. I gesture with my head to the Bucket Room.

He wipes the hair from his forehead, now clammy with sweat. He nods.

I tiptoe past him toward the Bucket Room, sensing him directly behind me as I step inside. He closes the door after us, but he stays facing it.

As I watch the back of him, his head hung low, he seems to *vibrate* with a strange, frenetic energy. I can almost *taste it*. Thick. Bitter. His fear and terror and shame, all swirling together.

"It's OK," I whisper.

That's a stupid thing to say. Say something else.

"Hey," I try.

He slowly turns, and as he does, he scans my body with his eyes. His mouth flickers with a tiny smile.

"What?" I say. He grins, wider now. "What is it?"

I look down and realize I'm only wearing my HappyHead boxers and my socks.

"Nice," he whispers.

"Oh, yeah, thanks," I say, my cheeks prickling with heat. I hold my hands together in front of the boxers, mortified that I ever said I *liked* them. The HappyHead symbol is right there. Right on my—

"Do you sleep in your socks?"

"Um. Yeah."

We stand looking at each other, and the fragments of my embarrassment meet his somewhere between us. For a moment it calms me, it's like we are *the same*. It makes me smile with him. But then I remember we are not the same. Not at all.

I step forward and wrap my arms around him. I feel him resist, but I squeeze tighter and he gradually lets his body ease into mine.

"I'm so sorry," I whisper. "I tried. I got the crossbow, but you were—"

"Don't," he murmurs into my shoulder, and I feel his chapped lips against my skin. "We all tried. Just . . . Can't fucking believe this. *Her.* Manning. She's so . . ." He exhales slowly through his nose, into me, his breath warm.

"It's going to be OK," I whisper.

He lifts his head. "It's not, Seb." His tone shifts. "None of this is OK."

He steps back.

No. *Don't go.*

As he moves away from me, I can tell that he's . . . *irritated.* Irritated that I could say that. That I could *believe* that.

"Finn—"

But he isn't listening. He runs his hand through his hair, his eyes darting around the room, searching desperately for something.

"There's no way we're getting out of here now," he says quietly.

"There is," I say. "Finn, look at me. There is a way." I lower my voice. "I spoke to Stone."

The muscles in his jaw tense at the sound of her name. "When?"

"Last night. Before they left. She's still with us, Finn. *She's still with us.*" I feel the anticipation spilling out of me.

He drops his head. "Right."

"Finn, this is good. She's still helping us."

"Is she?" he hisses. "It seemed pretty clear to me that she *didn't* want to help us, Seb. More like the complete opposite."

"That's not—"

"She just stood there and watched. She let all of that happen. *All of it.* She isn't *helping* us. She's with them." He scratches the stubble on his cheek. "Nah, Seb. She can fucking . . . *do one.* The lot of them can."

"She was acting that way to try to convince Manning she can be trusted. So she *can* help us."

"Bullshit," he snaps, and I flinch. "If she wanted to help us, she would have found a way. We can't trust her, Seb." His whisper becomes louder now. "We can't trust any of them. We're on our—"

"Shh." I signal to the door, but it only makes him more agitated. He starts pacing the room, his feet padding heavily on the tiles. Like a prisoner in a cell.

He stops in front of the window and stares at it, chewing the skin around his thumbnail. It's red and shiny with bloody splotches where he's already torn most of it away with his teeth.

"Finn, just let me tell you what she—"

"I don't want to hear it, Seb. There's no point. We can't believe a word she says. Manning's got to her. I know she has. The way she was just *standing* there . . . like she couldn't give a flying fuck, while we . . ." He stops.

"Finn, please. Just—"

"No, Seb."

"*Please.* Look at me. Just look at me for a second, Finn."

He exhales slowly. And then he turns. As he does, the sharp blue of his irises catches the early morning light so they shimmer behind a thin, watery film. His whole body begins to shake as if he's being pulled in a million different directions. He tenses his muscles like he's trying to control it. Trying to stop himself from being ripped apart.

"She didn't say anything, Seb. She didn't even try." He looks at me dead in the eyes in a way that makes my insides ache. "And neither did you."

My mind goes blank. "I—"

"Why didn't you say anything, Seb?"

"I thought—"

"You could tell them the truth, you know."

"But . . . Tell who?"

"All of them. Your little group. The sacred Ten."

My little group.

"It wouldn't work, Finn. They'd never believe me. We have no proof."

"It's written in the Never Plan. It's there. In black and white."

"But we don't have it. Ares and Artemis would call us liars, and the Ten would believe them. Ares and Artemis, they—I dunno— have them under their spell, thinking this is all good and a chance to *change the world.* If I told them, it would ruin everything."

A noise escapes his lips, like a laugh, but not. The *opposite* of a laugh. "*Ruin everything*. Right. I see." He shakes his head. "You know what, Seb? You're starting to sound like you're protecting them, not us."

"I'm just trying to be careful."

"What's the point? We're fucked anyway." He shrugs.

"I'm trying to keep us alive, Finn."

"Us?"

"Yes."

"I don't think you have to worry about yourself there, Seb. I'm pretty sure you'll be just fine."

"It's not easy. . . ."

He lifts his head, and his eyes bore into me. "Oh, I'm sorry. Would you rather be in my position? Would that be *easier* for you?"

"I don't—"

"Nah, go ahead. Take my spot. Let's swap."

"No, Finn."

"No? Why not?"

"Because—"

"Because maybe a part of you actually *likes* it?"

"What?"

"Being part of that little group. Being the favorite."

"No, Finn."

"Being called special. *Winning*. Winning at life, side by side with the incredible Eleanor Banks." He spits out her name, white flecks flying from his mouth.

"None of us are winning here, Finn."

"That's not true."

"You really think this is easy for me?"

"It definitely doesn't look awful, Seb."

"You think it's easy waking up every day knowing I have to lie, over and over again? Having to constantly pretend to be someone else?"

"Well, it seems like you're doing a pretty good job, Seb. But I guess you've had practice."

My body goes numb. "Yeah. You're right. I have. But then I met you. And it changed. *I changed.* You did that, Finn. And now I know what I want. I know *exactly* what I want, Finn. So actually, it's *worse*. Because I have to pretend you don't matter. That you aren't important to me. So yeah, it's awful. It's absolutely fucking *awful*."

"Why are you doing it, then?"

"Because I have to."

"Why? Why do you *have to*?"

"Because if they find out about us, I'll become redundant to them and they'll separate us. I'll probably never see you—"

"If they *find out about us*?" He makes that noise again. "*Redundant?* What do you think this is? *Downton* fucking *Abbey*? You can't be seen with the servants? Well, this isn't an episode of shit TV, Seb. This is real. This is happening, mate."

Mate. I feel my stomach drop, dragging me with it.

He puts his hands over his face. "Fuck," he whispers into them.

He clenches his fists so tightly that his knuckles go white, then pulls one of them back, away from him. He turns it toward his face.

"Finn, what are you—"

He smashes it right into the side of his head. Hard. Again. And again.

I grab for his arm.

"Finn, please, stop. *Stop.*" He struggles, trying to yank it out of my grip. "It's all right, Finn." I pull his arm down and hold it by his waist, pushing myself into him so I'm right in front of his body, closing him in. His chest heaves as he inhales, phlegm rattling at the back of his throat. "Hey, it's all right."

I hold him tight, and gradually his breaths begin to slow.

"You're OK," I say. I squeeze my fingers, trying to press what I'm feeling deep into his bones. "We're OK."

And then he goes completely still. "Shit," he whispers. "Shit, Seb."

"It's OK. Shh. It's OK."

"I'm sorry. . . . I'm . . . so sorry."

"It's all right."

"I should never have said that. I didn't mean any of it."

"It's all right. It is."

"It's not. I'm just so . . . I'm so fucking *scared*, Seb."

"I know."

He lifts his head, his face inches from mine, tears flooding down his cheeks. "I'm scared that I'm gonna lose you to them as well."

As he rubs his face with his sleeve, an image sears into my brain. Him, by the fire, looking at the picture of his parents as it burns. As they disappear.

I gently pull him back toward me until his forehead meets the inside of my shoulder. I feel the heat of his tears trickling down onto my bare chest, my stomach.

"I'm sorry that Manning took those memories from you, Finn," I whisper. I put my hand on his back, drawing him closer. "But I promise, she won't take me. That'll never happen. I won't let it."

He breathes into me. In and out.

"They looked just like you," I say. "They looked like really good people."

"They were." I listen to him exhale, long and slow. "You know what?" He lifts his head.

"What?"

"She didn't take everything. I still have . . . something."

"What?"

"I still have this . . . thing. This . . ." He pauses. "*Feeling* . . . that they left me with."

"Yeah?"

"Yeah."

"What's it like?"

He closes his eyelids, and they begin to flutter, like he's conjuring something behind them. Something that only he can see. "It feels . . . calm. Good. Safe."

As he says this, I realize my cheeks are wet too. "So . . . *happy*, then?"

"Yeah, I suppose so."

"Well, she can't ever take that," I say. "She won't ever take that from you."

"No." He sniffs and wipes his face with his sleeve again. "Listen, Seb. That wasn't me. I promise I'm not . . ." He stops.

"Not what?"

He drops his head. "Bad."

I remember what Shelly once told me. *Good isn't a thing. It just doesn't exist.*

"It doesn't exist."

"What doesn't?"

"Bad. Good. They're not real. You can't just *be* either of them. I think we're all in the middle somewhere, just . . . sort of . . .

floating around." Oh, God. It definitely sounded better when Shelly said it. "Sorry, that didn't really come out right."

"No," he says quietly. "Maybe you're right." He rubs his nose with the back of his hand. "Listen, Seb. The burglary thing—"

"It's OK."

"I want to explain."

"You don't need to."

"I did do it. And I want to tell you why. I want to tell you everything. I do. But not now. When we're out of here. And it's just me and you. Together." *Just us.* "I'll tell you everything. All of it. My whole life."

And then I remember. *My dream.* Us. Dancing together. In the sun. To David Bowie.

"Finn . . . ," I say. "Can I ask you a weird question?"

"Course."

"Did you dream last night?"

He looks at me, confused. "I dunno. I hardly slept. Why?"

"No reason."

A smile creeps across his face. *His smile.* He cocks his head, and his eyes move over mine, suddenly playful. "Wait. Have you been *dreaming* about me, Seb?"

"Um. No."

"You have." He keeps smiling.

"OK. Maybe I did. Just a little bit."

"Just a little bit."

"Yeah. A small one."

"A small one. Right. What were we doing?"

"Um. We were . . . dancing."

"No way."

"What?"

265

"I've had that one."

"Have you? Oh, cool. Was it . . . *sunny* in yours too?"

He laughs. "No. We were in Manchester, so it was nonstop rain."

"Right. Of course." I pause. "It would be fun to do that one day."

"It would."

And then he takes my hands in his. Tight.

"What song?" he says. "Or do I even need to ask? Mr. Bowie."

He starts to rock from side to side, still holding my hands.

"Um . . . Finn. What are you doing?"

"I'm trying to dance with you, knobhead."

"Oh, yeah. I can see that."

He stands on my foot. "Oops, soz."

Soz. I laugh.

"Just do it with me, for a second."

"What, as your *mate*?"

He drops his eyes. "Oh, God. I'm such a dick." Then he looks back up at me. "Is boyfriend maybe better, then?" He winks.

He should do that more often. It makes my whole body hum.

"A bit better, yeah."

"Never had one of those before."

"Me neither."

"Are you ready?"

"Yeah. Why not."

"Mint." He pauses. "Mint means 'good,' by the way."

"I know."

"Oh, you know that one?"

"Yep."

I move with him, holding his hands, rocking from side to side.

I don't know how long for. I don't care. But then I feel the edges of the envelope in my sock, digging into my skin.

I stop rocking. "Let me tell you what Stone said, Finn. It could get us out of here."

He stops too. "OK."

"Just . . . bear with me." Oh, God. "Stone said that no one is going home. She said that the winners are going to another location. Another phase. And that their Number will go with them."

He takes a step back, dropping my hands. "See, I fucking knew it—"

"Wait. Hold on. She said she has a plan. To help us. To help you five get out of here. All of us. To stop it all."

His eyes narrow. "What plan?"

"We have to win."

"Right. This isn't really filling me with confidence, Seb."

"She said that winning is the only way off the island and that she'll be able to help us once we're off. She said that she'll make sure there'll be an opportunity."

"She'll *make sure*?"

"Yes."

"So . . . not really a plan, then, Seb."

"She's asking us to trust her."

"And do you?"

"Yes." I lean down and reach for my sock.

"But what if she's lying? How can we even trust her? Seb—*are you listening*? Why are you taking your sock off?"

He looks down at the note that has fallen out onto the floor.

I lift it up and hold it out to him.

267

- F -

"She wanted me to give you this." His eyes scan cautiously over it. "Might as well see what she has to say, Finn."

He takes it in his fingers and begins to peel off the tape.

"Oh, shit," he whispers. "No way."

"What is it?"

As he stares at it, his eyes glint again beneath the watery film. He puts his hand over his mouth. "Whoa."

"What is it, Finn?" I look over his shoulder.

A photograph. Three faces. Him, between his mum and dad. *The same one.*

"But *how*—"

Then I realize it's not the same. Not completely.

Their faces are the same, their smiles are the same, their clothes are the same. But in this one, they're looking off to the side of the lens as if they weren't quite ready. As if it was taken just a few seconds earlier.

"How did she get this?"

I shrug. "See," I say. "Told you."

"Yeah. You did." He scratches his nose. "Wow. That sneaky woman."

"She's with us, Finn."

"So we have to *win*. I have to comply. Show I've changed. Win you bloodstones. And then she's getting us the hell out of this place?"

"That's what she said."

"What if it doesn't work? Our success rate with getting out hasn't exactly been stellar, has it?"

No. It hasn't. "I don't think we have any other option."

He nods. "Fuck. I wonder what the next location is."

Personally, I'm trying my best not to do that. "We don't have to think about that, Finn. If we just do what she says, we—"

Suddenly a noise. From the bedroom. Voices.

"Through there."

"I thought he was cleaning the fire?"

"Sebastian was supposed to be watching him."

Heavy footsteps. Coming closer.

"Shit," Finn hisses. He shoves the photograph into his pants pocket.

"What do we do?" I whisper.

His eyes move to my wrist.

"Press it," he says.

"What?"

"Now, Seb."

The door starts to open.

He grabs my arm.

"Finn—"

zzzz

I feel the pulse of the shock as his finger is thrown from the button.

His head jerks back just as Ares steps into the room, followed by the Keeper. Finn drops down to his knees in front of me, his scream cutting through the air.

"What's going on?" Ares says, staring at me.

"I—"

"I'm sorry," Finn groans. "I won't do it again. I swear."

Ares keeps staring. "What happened, Sebastian?"

"He . . ." I look down at Finn, curled up on the floor. "He was upset," I say. "He came in here, and I followed him. I . . . I knew he needed help. I knew he needed some support." I lift up my wrist. "Some encouragement."

Ares looks at the wristband and nods. "Well done," he says. He then turns to the Keeper. "Take him back to the shed."

The Keeper steps toward Finn. He leans down and grabs the back of his hood, pulling him up off the floor and dragging him across the tiles toward the doorway. I see the other boys all huddled there, watching. He pushes through them, hauling Finn with him.

We stand completely still, until we hear the dwelling-house door slam shut behind them.

The other boys stare at me. Their faces all puffy with sleep.

"He's still so resistant," I say. "It's awful."

"You're right," Ares says. "It's heartbreaking." He nods solemnly. "You have done well, Sebastian. You should be proud of yourself."

He takes in the boys behind him. "Clear your minds. The trials today will be . . . *intense,* to say the least. So gather yourselves, brothers. The first one will begin shortly."

They nod in unison.

Yes. Yes, brother.

Ares turns back to me. "You will have the opportunity to do some really important work with him today, Sebastian. But you will need to push him. You will need to be strong."

"I will," I say. "I promise."

THIRTY

Typed, for Convenience

EMAIL TRANSCRIPT 12:
Dear Mr. and Mrs. Seaton,

It was so lovely to speak with you again earlier today. We are thrilled with how excited you were by the latest update on Sebastian's progress and what might be in store for him. Thank you for your consent for him to continue his journey with us, which we are delighted to say may extend. He is taking to his new role so well. As you know, the removal of technology plays a vital part in the program, but we are happy to enclose a short letter from him. He wrote it, but we have typed it up for you, for convenience.

It fills us all with joy to see the progress he is continuing to make. If you have any questions, we are just here.

Yours in faith,
Professor Gloria Manning and Dr. Eileen Stone
Lead Psychotherapist and Psychiatrist of HappyHead Inc.
☺

Attachment 1 of 1:
Hi Mum and Dad!

I miss you, but I am having an amazing time. It is intense, but I seem to have taken well to that! I have become so much more open as a person. I have opened myself up to knowing that with someone else, I am a better person. I am so happy. I never thought I would say that. And despite everything that has happened in the past, I know that I am becoming stronger.

Love you,
Seb

P.S. I want you to let Lily know that I miss her too. She might not believe me, but it's true.

EMAIL TRANSCRIPT 18:
Dear Mr. and Mrs. Khan,

It was so lovely to speak with you again earlier today. It is wonderful to hear how much you care about Finneas. He is lucky to have you. We were thrilled with how excited you were by another update on his progress, and for you to give your consent for him to carry on his journey with us, which, as you know, may continue.

We know how difficult it has been for you and are glad to give you good news about him opening himself up to this opportunity. We are working closely with him to move forward with his newfound purpose. As you know, the removal of technology plays a vital part in the program, as it can be so dangerous to the mental health of our young people. However, we are happy to enclose a letter to you from him. We have typed it up for your convenience and have added it as an attachment.

If you have any questions, we are here.

Yours in faith,
Professor Gloria Manning and Dr. Eileen Stone
Lead Psychotherapist and Psychiatrist of HappyHead Inc.
☺

Attachment 1 of 1:
Hi guys,

I miss you both. This has been difficult, but I am learning that I am in the right place. They are pushing me, and it is hard, but I am glad that I have been given this chance. I know you will want to know I am OK. I am. I am getting there. I am so sorry for how much I have put you through, but I feel like I am learning to cope now. It seems commitment, growth, gratitude, and obedience really do lead to a happy head.

Thanks, love you,
Finneas

THIRTY-ONE
The Truth Train

The others chat quietly as they take their places in the stone circle, whispering about tonight's Counting Ceremony, about the prize.

The prize the prize the prize.

As I watch, I think about my conversation with Finn in the Bucket Room. About how I've been left with a strange feeling. A strange sense of . . .

I don't know what. There must be a word for it. It's like that thing my dad says he always admires in people. *A quiet confidence.* That's it. *That's* what I feel.

I'm not going to question it because it feels a little thin. Like it could be blown away at any moment. But it feels good. *I* feel good. Emboldened. A little . . . indestructible.

Tonight. We could be out of here. If we win . . .

My stomach clenches at the thought.

I look toward the shed. Only one of the Keepers is standing guard, which is a little odd. *Where's the other one?*

Eleanor makes her way across the circle. She still seems . . . distracted.

"You OK?" I ask as she sits next to me. She doesn't answer. She begins to fidget, tugging at the collar of her hoodie like she's trying to cool herself down. "Are you hot? It's freezing, Eleanor."

"Just a bit . . . I don't know. *Uncomfortable.*"

"Right."

Her eyelids look red and sore, as if she's been rubbing them.

"Fuck, argh," she says. She puts her hands on top of her head and starts to move her fingers around it, until they find her little pink clips. She presses down on them. *Click.*

I watch, confused, but also a little fascinated, as she slides them out and puts them between her teeth. She then pulls out the elastic band holding her ponytail in place, so her hair falls loose around her face.

"I've never seen you like that," I say.

"Hmm?" she mutters through a mouthful of clips.

"You look different."

She doesn't seem to hear me. She loops the elastic band back around her hair, then pulls it so tight that it tugs at her forehead. For a second, I worry she's going to pull her entire face off.

"Isn't that . . . painful?"

She gives me a look to say *What would you know?* then takes the clips from her mouth and slides them back into place. *Click.* Her eyebrows now appear to be stuck halfway up her forehead.

"That's better." She turns to me and smiles. "Sorry. Yes, I'm good, Sebby." She's all chirpy now. Back to her usual self. "I had a nice chat with Artemis last night. She was so helpful. She saw I was a bit . . ."

"A bit what?"

"I don't know. Flustered, maybe."

"Why?"

"What?"

"Why were you flustered? Was it Mann—"

"And"—she cuts me off—"they really think we've got a good chance of winning. Which would just be amazing, wouldn't it?"

"Yeah," I say, and I mean it. "It would."

She wafts her hand at a fly buzzing near her head. As she does, she spots her yellow wristband. She quickly pulls the sleeve of her hoodie back down over it.

"How did it feel?" I say quietly.

She frowns. "How did what feel?"

"It must have felt good for you, right?"

"What must have?"

I shrug. "A bit like revenge?"

Her eyes widen with realization. "Oh." She begins to frantically brush her pants. "I'm happy to help him if he needs it. Which he does. It's the robust training they all need." She says this like a robot. "And he's still very unwell."

"I heard you in the tent."

Her hands stop moving. "What?"

Emboldened.

I keep my voice lowered. "When you asked if what I said about love was about him."

She forces her mouth into a smile, darting her eyes around the other couples to check they're not listening. "I don't know what you're talking—"

"Yes, you do. You asked me if it was about Finn."

"You mean Number Five," she hisses.

"No, I mean Finn."

"Keep your voice down."

"It was," I say. "It was about him. I think I love him, Eleanor." A vein emerges in her forehead like a worm has wriggled out of her brain, desperately trying to escape it. "He isn't who you think he is."

The muscles in her cheek twitch. "You're very *chatty* this morning."

"He's not a bad person. He's not *unwell*. None of them are. They just didn't try to change. That's all. And she's punishing them for it. *We* are punishing them for it." I pause. "Do you know what the prize is, Eleanor?"

She looks at me, still smiling. "No, Seb. Why would I? And anyway, she doesn't want us to talk about it."

"I wonder why."

"Huh?"

"I wonder why she won't tell us." *Sod it.* "Don't you ever wonder if this is all going to end very, very badly?"

"No, Seb. This is all going to end very, very well." Robot. Smiling Robot.

"Right." I stare at her.

"*What,* Seb?"

I keep staring.

"What are you doing? Stop looking at me like that. *Stop it.*"

"I guess you would know if something bad was going on, wouldn't you?"

"Huh?"

"I guess she would have told you."

"Who?"

"Your aunt."

The vein pulsates like it's about to burst. She turns to me, eyes bulging, teeth glinting like a windup toy about to malfunction. "How did you—"

"Wouldn't she? I mean, you *trust* her, don't you?"

"I—" Her face flushes.

"Well, you shouldn't." *What are you doing, Seb?* "Look what she's making you do. Open your eyes, Eleanor. *Open your eyes.*"

She widens them so much that I can see little squiggles of red on the whites of her eyeballs. "They are open." She points at them. "Look."

"No, they're not." I put my hand on hers. "I've seen you. *You.* Maybe for only a second, but it was enough to know that this isn't you. This is all bullshit. It's horrible. It's a lie. All of this is. I'm *gay*, Eleanor. And you know that. What are you doing? *What are we doing?* Stop trying to be what she wants. It'll never make you happy. So take your fucking pink hair clips back out and just be *you.*"

Her mouth hangs open.

Well, shit. "Emboldened" was definitely the correct word.

I feel like I'm on a very fast train that I can't get off. That I don't *want* to get off. And the train has got a name. It's called the Truth Train, and it feels absolutely *mint*.

"Did you know they're called James and Mia?"

"What?"

"Artemis and Ares. They're called *James* and *Mia*. Funny that, isn't it? Doesn't really suit them."

She stares at me. "How—"

"Who's Freddie, Eleanor?" Her bottom lip begins to wobble. "Who is he?"

"I—"

"Settle down, everyone!" Ares calls.

Damn it.

"We must begin. The next trial will start now." The circle falls silent. "Artemis and I will take turns leading each couple to the trial site. We will begin with the couple that has the most sacred bloodstones."

As he turns to me and Eleanor, he clasps his hands in front of him. In his robes, his long hair blowing around his face, he reminds me of someone. A priest. A handsome priest. A *trendy* one. One who knows how to get people to listen to him. To follow him blindly, into the light.

"Come now, Sebastian and Eleanor." I sense the other couples eyeing us, trying to hide their jealousy. "Number Five is already there. I don't think it would be wise to keep him waiting."

Please just . . . *Let this one be simple. Let it be quick. We are so close.*

As we follow Ares down the hill, through the fields, weaving our way through the heather and gorse, across the island, I try to shake away the twist of fear that's tugging at me, threatening to pull away that quiet confidence, that emboldened feeling.

Don't go. Please stay. Just for a bit longer.

"This way!" Ares calls as he walks toward a rocky incline.

We start to ascend. Up and up.

And I realize I know this place. I have been here before. It's where the Drop is. Where we fell backward into nothing. I can tell by the rubble, the gradient.

It levels out, and as we move across the top of a huge pillar of rock jutting out from the ground, I see the sea all around us in every direction. Just sea. Black water beneath a gray sky.

Then he stops. Because there is a gap. A gap in the ground. Across the gap, about ten yards away, the land starts again. And there, standing facing us, his arms folded across his chest, is the Keeper, next to a signpost.

WELCOME TO THE BRIDGE OF HAPPINESS

I look down. Between us and him there's a drop. The height of a church spire. Maybe more. At the bottom, there's nothing but a twisted jumble of rocks.

I stare at the narrow wooden plank laid between the two ledges. Right across the gap.

I stare at the middle of it where the plank bends down slightly.

Someone is standing on it. Arms out to the side, steadying himself as the wind whips around him.

"Oh my God," Eleanor whispers.

Here we go.

THIRTY-TWO
Bridge to Happiness

Finn stands in the middle of the plank, keeping as still as he can. His feet pressed together, the sides of his sneakers right up to its edges.

Circling his waist is a rope. I follow the length of it with my eyes as it stretches across the plank and ends in a coiled pile on the ground at our feet.

"Let us begin," Ares says. "As you can see, we do not want to keep Number Five waiting."

No shit.

Eleanor peers over the edge at the jagged rocks below. "Where's the water?"

"This is a slightly different location than that of the Drop," Ares says. "A little farther along. Similar, but different."

Just a bit. That quiet confidence has now completely left me. Snuffed out like it never existed.

"The trial is simple," Ares continues. "All you must do is encourage Number Five to step toward you. As you can see, he's already halfway there." I keep my eyes on Finn as he speaks. "All he must do is comply."

OK. You can you do this, Finn.

He keeps his eyes on the plank as it bounces gently beneath him.

Can we just hurry up?

I look at the Keeper on the ledge behind him. Watching.

Hurry up hurry up hurry up.

"However," Ares says. *Of course there's a fucking however.* "There are a few rules he must adhere to."

Ares takes his pack off his back and lifts something out of it. One of the slates. *The Sacred Slates.* I can just make out the white writing etched into it. "On this slate are the instructions for the ritual. One of you must read from the slate while the other holds the rope."

I turn to Eleanor. Her face is gripped with fear. I remember her panic attack in the cave. Shit.

"I'll hold the rope," I say quickly. "You read, Eleanor." Her eyes remain fixed on Finn as she nods.

"Have you chosen?" Ares says.

"I'm holding the rope," I say. "Eleanor will read."

"Wonderful." No. Not wonderful. Definitely not wonderful. "Sebastian, if you would now take hold of the rope."

The drop looms in front of me, making my head swim and my knees feel weak. I lean down and take the rope in my hand.

Stop shaking, Seb.

"Stop shaking," Ares says. *Please fuck off.* "It won't help."

"I'm good," I say loudly so Finn can hear. "I'm all right."

I grip one hand around it, followed by the other, then stand up straight. I gradually pull it taut, not wanting to startle him. As it lifts up off the plank, he watches it rise. Then his eyes move up to me.

It's OK, I mouth to him.

He's terrified. Completely terrified.

Breathe, Seb.

I wrap the excess rope around my waist, careful not to pull him with it, until I can feel it digging in around the middle of my stomach. I then lean away slightly so my weight is back, my feet pushing hard into the rubble.

I've got you. I've got you, Finn.

"Sebastian, are you stable?" I hear Ares say.

Are you? "Yes, I'm good."

"Fantastic." Another peculiar choice of words. "Eleanor, please take the script."

Script?

I hear her move toward him. The soft thud of stone against skin as she takes it in her hands.

Come on, Eleanor. Just hit him over the head with it.

"Now, join Sebastian at the end of the bridge."

It's not a fucking bridge. Bridges have sides and supports and are typically made of concrete.

"Here?" Eleanor says, shuffling up next to me.

"That's right," Ares says. "Now face Number Five."

I can feel Eleanor next to me, shaking. "Oh my God, Seb."

She puts her hand on my arm, making me jolt. The rope tenses, pulling at Finn's middle. He leans forward.

"Whoa!" He swings his arms to steady himself.

"Sorry," I shout. "Sorry."

"Let us not delay any further," Ares says. "Eleanor, if you would like to read the instructions on the slate. Address your Number as you do so."

"Number Five." Her voice croaks, and she clears her throat. "Learning to control your emotions is vital in order for you to achieve the happiness you so badly need. We are proud of you for what you achieved yesterday. Clearing your past in order to move forward is vital, and it paved the way for you to be halfway to where you need to be. This is why you are starting in the middle. You are on your way. However, you must now learn to deal with the"—she pauses as if trying to make sense of the words—"the *residue* of your trauma that still lies within you. You must learn to deal with your emotions. You must learn to *control* them. This will help you move forward to happiness."

She glances up at Finn.

"Continue, please, Eleanor."

"The distance from you to us is approximately five strides. I will now ask you five questions. Each question has been designed to elicit an emotional response. As you answer, we need to see you control yourself as these emotions come to the surface. The bridge should help you to tame them. If you allow yourself to become overwhelmed, you may fall."

Who wrote this? Who came up with this?

"Only once you have processed the emotions, controlled them, and given an honest answer, may you step forward. Ares will alert us if you have." Oh, great. "Each step you take will earn your couple a sacred bloodstone. Please turn over for questions."

Oh. My. God. Seriously? Do they all just sit around in a white room thinking of the most messed-up things they possibly—

"Wait," Eleanor says, turning to Ares. "What happens if he *doesn't* answer them?"

"Then it will be your job, Eleanor"—he raises his voice so that Finn can hear—"to offer Number Five some *encouragement*. You have your wristband to help with this."

The rope tenses in my hands as Finn looks up. He stares at Ares with so much loathing I wonder if he's about to jump at him.

Careful, Finn.

"Fuck you," he spits.

"Save it," Ares replies calmly. "Save all this emotion for the ritual, Number Five. You will learn to harness it. They are going to help you."

"But . . . ," Eleanor says. "If I do that—if I *encourage* him—won't he fall?"

Ares answers, his voice somber in a way that makes me want to punch him. "It is your job to ensure Number Five works with you to prevent that from happening. But if it does, Sebastian will be right there to catch him. However, you will not win any sacred bloodstones this morning." Yeah, I definitely want to punch him. "Let us begin."

Eleanor turns the slate over in her hands. "Question one," she says. Her voice sounds small. Thin. Weak.

"Louder, please, Eleanor. Make sure he can hear you."

She inhales, filling her lungs. "Question one. Have you spent most of your life feeling completely alone?"

What? What kind of a question is that? Everyone feels alone. *Don't they?*

Finn moves his eyes down to the beam. He exhales.

"That's it," Ares says from somewhere behind us. "Experience it. Experience the loneliness."

We watch Finn. Watch him experiencing his loneliness.

"This is hard for all of us," Ares says. Well, you seem fine to me, on the solid ground, you hippie nutjob. "But we need an answer, Number Five."

Say something, Finn. Please.

"We are waiting, Number Five."

He is fuming. Seething.

"Perhaps it is time for a bit of encouragement. Eleanor—"

"Wait!" Finn wobbles, and the rope sways. Shit. I grip, my knuckles white. "Yes. Yes, I have. I've always felt alone."

This is horrific.

"That is so sad," Ares says. "No one should have to feel that way. Is it still like that now?"

That's another question, Ares, but I'm pretty sure it's not on the slate. Stop wasting time.

Finn looks up at me, and our eyes meet. "No."

"No?" Ares says.

"Recently I've felt better."

"That is very interesting, Number Five. It's a joy to hear that Helpers' High is working for you. You have answered honestly. Take a step forward on the Bridge to Happiness."

Finn raises his foot, his arms out by his sides. As he takes a step toward us, I move the rope with him, drawing it into my body.

"Well done," Ares says. "One sacred bloodstone. Next question."

"Question two," Eleanor says. "Have you always been angry?"

His eyes flash. His body tenses. "Yes," he replies. "Yes, I have."

"Another honest answer. Take another step forward."

He does. Slowly. Very slowly.

I draw him closer. That's it. *That's it.*

"Next question, Eleanor."

"Question three. Tell us why you robbed the house."

That's not a question. That's not a fucking question. I remember what he said in the Bucket Room: *I haven't told anyone this stuff before.*

"Eleanor?" Ares says.

"OK, OK. I'll tell you."

"That's it, Number Five. Well done."

I see Finn's face contort. Humiliation. Fear. Shame. All of it, all at once. He speaks quickly, spitting out each sentence. "I'm not proud of it. I was hanging around with the wrong people. I wanted to impress them. They told me it was empty. I had no idea there were children in the house—"

And then he loses his balance. Eleanor gasps as he staggers backward, his feet taking tiny steps, his arms swinging. I grip tightly as the rope pulls.

"Oh, God," Eleanor whispers. "Oh, God."

"I've got you," I say. "I've got you." I hold the rope stable, firm, as he steadies himself. "Look up," I hear myself say. "Look at me."

"We need more," Ares says. "That is not enough, Number Five. We need more detail for you to move forward. We need the why. *Why* did you do it? Ask the question again, Eleanor."

"But—"

"Ask it."

She looks back down at the slate. "Question three. Tell us why you robbed the house."

Just me, I mouth. *No one else.*

He slowly nods. "After my parents—" His voice cracks. *Keep looking at me. That's it.* "After my parents died, I didn't know how to be around anyone. For a long time. Years. I was lucky that two very kind people took me in. But I caused so many problems for them. I *was* angry. I *was* lonely. I felt like I was a piece of shit.

I just wanted to be anyone else. So I started fucking about and I met some people who weren't like me. And that's how I wanted to be. Anything but me. So I did it. I robbed the house for them."

"Take a step forward, Number Five."

Careful. Nearly there.

"This is better. You are controlling yourself. You are managing your emotions, Number Five. Next question."

I stare at him, focusing on his face. Everything else fades away.

"Question four," Eleanor says. "Your parents died in a fire. Who was responsible?"

His eyes widen. His lips tremble.

It's OK. I'm here. He fixes his eyes on mine. *Just us.*

I watch as he mumbles something.

"I can't hear you," Ares says. "Louder."

"I was. I was responsible."

"Well done. Take a step forward. Four sacred bloodstones. One more to go, Number Five. You are controlling your hatred. Your hatred of yourself."

He steps forward, until he is about three feet away from me. *Nearly there.*

"Question five," Eleanor says. "How . . . ?" She stops. "I don't—"

"Eleanor," Ares says. "He must push through this."

"But—"

"Nothing else has worked."

The air is silent for a moment.

Then. "Question five. How did it happen?"

His face tenses. "I . . ." *You can do it.* "I was playing with a candle. I was six. I didn't mean for anything bad to happen."

That's it, Finn. You're done. Come on.

I pull gently at the rope. He lifts his foot.

"Stop," Ares says. "We need more."

"It's enough," I say. "He's said enough."

"No. This is his breakthrough. Come on, Number Five. More. *Dig in.* We need to hear it. We need to hear how you felt. How you *still* feel. Then you will be free of it."

Tears well in his eyes. The plank begins to shake under his feet. I hear it creak.

"Eleanor," Ares says. "Will you encourage him." Silence. "*Eleanor.* This is important."

"No," she says, her voice strong. Firm. "I won't."

"*Eleanor . . .*"

"Go on, Finn." She keeps her eyes locked on him. "It's all right. Just tell us. Then it's done."

Ares steps toward her. "Eleanor, you—"

Finn cuts him off. "I went downstairs." *Look at me. It's OK. Nearly there.* "After they went to bed. The candle was still alight. I stuck my finger in it to feel the wax. I dunno why, I was fucking six. I don't know why I fucking did it." Tears trickle down his cheeks, dropping through the air. "It fell onto the carpet. I had to get out of the window, away from the smoke. I was too scared to scream. I couldn't breathe."

This is awful. *This is so awful.*

"More," Ares calls. "We need more. *This* is your breakthrough, Number Five."

"I can't," he says. "There is no more. There's nothing else to say."

"There is," Ares says, his voice sharp. Impatient. "You *must* experience this. You *must* rid yourself of all your anger. All your *hatred.*"

"Fine!" Finn screams. The rope pulls. Wobbles in my grip. "I feel guilty! Is that what you want to hear? I feel fucking *guilt.* I feel it all the time. They couldn't get out. It was too late. And it makes me angry and lonely and I hate myself because of it. I've hated myself *every day of my fucking li*—"

And then it happens. An almighty jolt. So quick I can't make sense of it.

He's no longer on the plank.

And I am no longer on my feet. I'm on my stomach, being pulled toward the edge. Across the rubble.

Someone screams, "Seb!"

I fly forward. and my body turns on its side. Suddenly horizontal. My stomach smashes into the rock in front of me.

"Oh my God!"

Then hands on my body. Eleanor's.

A weight. *Her* weight. On top of me. Pinning me to the ground.

My back is being crushed. I'm being crushed.

"Seb!" she cries. "The rope!"

I see her hands scrabbling for it, grabbing it. . . .

"Help me, for God's sake!"

My arms are beneath me. I can't move. Can't breathe.

"Roll back," she shouts. "Roll away from the edge, Seb!"

I twist my body underneath hers.

Another scream. This time from below. *Finn.*

I keep twisting, grinding against the ground, until I feel a rock with my feet. I push against it.

Push.

My legs straighten out.

Eleanor's weight shifts off me. I gasp. Air floods into me.

I feel the rope running down my legs. I grab it.

Pull. *Pull.*

"Take my hand!" Eleanor yells. "Take it, Finn!"

I pull and pull and pull.

I see Eleanor leaning forward on her stomach. Over the edge.

Pull. *Pull. Fucking pull.*

Where is he? Where the hell is he?

Come on, Finn. *Please . . .*

And then . . .

I see his hair.

His hands.

His leg as he drags himself over the ledge.

His body on the ground.

"He's up," Eleanor says weakly. "He's up."

As I let go of the rope, the pain floods through me. I stare at the sky, dots dancing across it. I feel them crawl next to me. Her, on my right. Him, on my left.

And then, from somewhere, Ares's voice. "It a shame you were not able to help him contain himself. This is incredibly sad." His face comes into my vision, looming over us. "Because of this, you will not win any sacred bloodstones. You will have to work hard this afternoon if you still want a chance of winning."

I hear careful footsteps, across wood.

"Take him," Ares tells the Keeper. "Prepare him for the final ritual."

And then Finn is gone.

I turn to Eleanor. Her pink clips have slipped. And her face is different. She's crying.

But it's not that. It's something else.

"This isn't OK, Seb, is it?" she whispers. "This is not OK. . . ."

That's what it is.

I can see her.

Finally.

Her.

THIRTY-THREE
No Other Sheep

It starts to rain. Slowly at first, individual droplets hitting my face. As the drops land, each one awakens a thought in my head. A single snapshot of clarity.

Eleanor called him by his name. She called him Finn.

She stopped us falling. She saved him. She saved us.

We didn't win any bloodstones.

We need to win bloodstones. To escape. To stop this.

There is an opportunity.

He nearly died. We nearly died.

Pull it together, Seb. You need to win.

One more trial. Just one more.

I keep my eyes on Eleanor up ahead of me as she follows Ares, his yellow robes billowing around him in the wind. A guiding light leading us back toward camp.

I slow down, trying to put some distance between us as the thoughts reel inside my head.

The cold air whips into my body, but it still can't numb the pain. I feel where the rope ripped the skin from the palms of my hands, leaving them shiny and torn. Where the rope constricted around my stomach. Where the rock smashed into me.

Everything aches. My muscles, my joints, my head.

My insides. My core. My heart.

How could they make him do that? How could they make him say all that?

The rain is heavier now, hammering into me. I keep my eyes on Eleanor as she staggers up the hill, Ares way ahead. Then I see her stop. She gazes down into the long grass by the side of the track, completely still. She looks eerie. Like something from a Gothic painting.

I make my way toward her. "Eleanor . . ." My voice hurts. *Everything hurts.* She keeps her eyes down. "Eleanor, listen," I croak. "Thank you for—"

And then I see it. I see what she's looking at. Almost completely hidden by the long grass. But not quite.

The *lamb.*

Its small, stiff body bent out of shape. Its crusted black eyes. The bloody, mangled hole gaping in the side of its stomach where something has pecked and torn at its decomposing flesh. Flies. Everywhere. And maggots. Crawling out of its stomach.

"Eleanor?"

She doesn't answer. She just . . . stares. "There are no other sheep on this island," she says very quietly.

"Sorry?"

"I said I haven't seen any other sheep since we got here. There are no other sheep."

I watch her squinting at it through the rain, studying its lifeless body. Its matted coat of wool, the gray-blueness of its lolling tongue, the fluid that's solidified around its tiny nose. It's like the lamb is revealing something to her. But she doesn't look sad. She doesn't look scared. She looks calm. Aware.

There's a moment sometimes, when I just wake up. I really like it, even though it lasts only a few seconds. In that moment, none of the noise in my head has downloaded yet. I like it because it isn't really anything. It's just . . . a state of awareness. No emotions. No opinions. No voices. No noise.

"He's my cousin," she says, without turning. "Freddie. He's my cousin. He *was* my cousin."

"Oh . . ."

The rain trickles down the profile of her nose. When she speaks again, she's completely unemotional, like she's recounting a series of facts. "He died. Two years ago. He killed himself. He killed himself in a hospital."

"Oh, God." Oh, *God*. "That's awful. I'm sorry, Eleanor."

"And she was so angry. She was angry because they didn't look after him. He was supposed to be kept safe. But he wasn't."

And then I understand. Freddie was Manning's son.

I watch the droplets collect on Eleanor's eyelashes. She blinks. "The night before it happened, I visited him in the hospital. He told me he wasn't feeling good. He told me he was scared of himself. I spoke to the staff, but I didn't tell Gloria. That night he stole a key from the nursing office while the team was dealing with an emergency. He went into the courtyard, climbed up onto the roof, and . . . he jumped."

The wind blows loose strands of hair into her eyes, but she doesn't brush them away.

"I'm so sorry, Eleanor."

"It's fine. I mean, it's not. But it can't be changed."

"Is that why you struggled with the Drop?" I hear myself say. I meant to think it, but it just came out of me. "Why didn't you tell me before? I would never have made you do that."

She blinks again. "I think she created the trial for me."

"What?"

"To help me get over it."

"Eleanor, that's messed up."

"She said she could have helped him if she knew. If I had told her."

A horrible feeling creeps over me. *She was punishing her. Manning was punishing her. She still is.* "It's not your fault, Eleanor."

"She was so . . . *mean* to Freddie. I always thought she hated him," she says quietly. "But I don't know if she did." She turns to me and fixes her gaze just below my face, avoiding meeting my eyes. "Freddie didn't care about impressing people. He didn't give a shit about what anyone thought or said. And I think that confused her. *Hurt* her. She thought it was why he struggled.

"He failed his exams. Didn't have many friends. Got bullied for being odd. Got in trouble. 'Aimless,' she always called him. He'd get really angry sometimes. Really sad. And aggressive. She wouldn't stop criticizing him. Trying to change him. I think she thought she was helping him. And then it was too late." She pauses. "She blames me. She's told me that. Many times."

"Eleanor—"

"And ever since, I've wanted to be . . . to be everything she always wanted Freddie to be."

"But . . . *why?*"

She looks up, right at me, as if I know exactly why. And I do. "Because I'm so . . . *scared,* Seb." She begins to tremble. "Sometimes

I choose to forget the truth. But when I let myself think back, think about him, just him and me, together, I remember it differently."

"What was he like?"

"He was happy, I think. In his own way." Tears swell in her eyes. She quickly wipes them away with her sleeve. "He liked jigsaw puzzles. He was really good at them. He liked singing too. But he wasn't so good at that. . . ." The smallest flicker of a smile crosses her face. "He was my best friend, Seb. We spent all our time together. We loved each other, you know? We did." She pauses. "He was actually a bit like you." She closes her eyes and exhales slowly. "And a bit like Finn too."

Tears begin to fall, mingling with the rain on her cheeks. But this time, she lets them flow.

"Why are you telling me all this now, Eleanor?"

She looks back down at the lamb. "Because they did this. They killed it. Artemis and Ares. James and Mia. For *her*. And I knew that, back when we first saw it, but I didn't say anything because it was easier not to. Part of me . . . part of me didn't want to believe it. Because if it was true, something was wrong. And I didn't want to go back to all that, at home. My parents have been different with me, ever since. . . . And here, none of that exists. I'm someone else."

"But you're not," I say.

She sniffs, then turns back to me. "I don't fancy you, Seb."

Well, no. That's been apparent for some time now.

"Yeah. I think I'm aware of that. But . . . thanks for clearing it up."

"I just wanted to win."

Also apparent. "I know."

"And . . ." She hesitates.

Come on, Eleanor. I take her hand in mine. She lets me.

"You're already on the Truth Train, Eleanor. Just say it."

She frowns. "The what?"

"Just . . . open your eyes. It's right here in front of you."

She pauses. "The truth is . . . I know you love Finn."

"Yeah, I do."

"And I know this place isn't going to stop that."

"No. It's not."

"And I don't love you."

"Right, we've established that."

"I also know that something bad is going to happen, Seb. You're right. Something really, really terrible is going to happen. I think someone is going to die."

She looks at me with such complete conviction that I feel a heat rising inside my chest.

I glance up the hill. Ares is now nearly at the top.

Right. Quick.

"No one is going home, Eleanor," I say.

Her eyes widen. "What?"

"Dr. Stone told me everything she knows."

I watch her absorb my words. "What do you mean, Dr. Stone? But—"

"Manning is controlling her. Stone never wanted it to be like this. Dr. Stone is trying to stop the Never Plan."

"The *what*?"

A part of me always thought she knew. But it's suddenly very clear that she didn't.

"There's another phase, Eleanor."

"What *other phase*?"

"A place called Ash Farm."

She suddenly looks panicked. "What kind of *farm*?"

"I don't know. But I do know we're going to be taken there. All of us. The winners will go first, and they'll be taking their Number with them. It's a plan based on eugenics—"

"Eugenics?"

"You two!" a voice bellows. Ares. Now just a dark shape, watching us from the top of the hill. "Get up here, now."

Smile. Smile and wave.

"Coming!" I shout back.

I then whisper out of the side of my mouth, "But there's a way we can stop it all, Eleanor." She is waving too. Smiling widely. "We have a plan."

As Ares turns back toward the camp, she looks at me, her eyes steady. Focused. Strong.

"Tell me."

Ares stops us just outside the stone circle. "You must go straight to your dwelling houses, both of you, until the other couples have completed the trial. You must not talk to them. We do not want you distracting anyone."

You mean you don't want us to tell them how messed up it was? Sure.

"Of course," Eleanor says brightly.

Ares pauses. "What were you doing back there?"

"We were just discussing how we can be better," I say. "We're so sorry we didn't show the strength we needed earlier."

He looks at me. I smile.

He looks at Eleanor. She smiles.

"You only have the next trial to make up for what you have lost this morning. I was disappointed, to say the least."

"Don't worry, we will prove ourselves," Eleanor says. "It was just a blip."

"Good."

She smiles at him toothily. "We *really* want this. Don't we, Sebby?"

"Yes. We want this more than anything."

"Well," he says. "I'm glad this morning hasn't deterred you."

"No, it's only made us stronger," Eleanor says.

He nods. "We shall see."

She kisses me on the cheek. "I love you, Seb. I really do."

"I love you too, Eleanor."

"Commitment, growth, gratitude, and obedience," she says to Ares. "That's all we need. And we will show Number Five exactly what it takes. We will not let his weakness infect us again. We will show him exactly what he needs to get better."

And then she heads toward the dwelling house, pulling her ponytail sharply back into place.

God, she's brutal.

But she's *good.*

THIRTY-FOUR

Trust

I watch through the dwelling-house window as the rain finally stops and the sun begins to appear through the clouds.

The door opens.

"It is time for your final ritual," Ares says.

The other boys bolt up from their beds. No one has said much since they returned, but from what I can gather, none of the other Numbers fell. None of the others failed.

They all seem . . . confident. Assured.

"Quickly, Sebastian," Ares says. "This is your last chance."

Yes. I'm well aware. But I smile broadly. "I'm looking forward to it."

Once I'm out, he shuts the door behind me.

I join Eleanor in front of our stone. As the other couples take their places, I dart my eyes around the camp. The Keepers are not here. The Numbers are not here. Neither is Artemis.

Where are they all?

Ares addresses us from beside the unlit fire. "Now, as we draw closer to the end of phase two, I would like to give you some final motivation, to encourage you to really push yourselves and your Number in this final challenge, by announcing the bloodstone totals as they currently stand."

Eleanor takes my hand.

"Li and Sam have seven." Sam shuffles next to Li, who drops her head, embarrassed. "Rachel and Jamie have sixteen, Matthew and Jing have seventeen." Matthew eagerly bites his lip. "Eleanor and Sebastian also have seventeen. And in the lead are Lucy and Raheem with twenty." Lucy and Raheem look at each other, surprised. "We will now be heading back to the shore for your final trial, where there will be the opportunity for things to really change. Remember, here on Elmhallow, all our choices have consequences. So my advice is, choose wisely. Sometimes the most difficult choices reap the greatest rewards."

With that he turns.

We follow him in our couples. Side by side. Two by two. Down the hill and into the wood. I stay at the back of the group, with Eleanor by my side. Trying not to picture what will be waiting for us. The pine needles turn to pebbles beneath my feet, which crunch as I step out onto them.

"Shit," Eleanor whispers.

I look up to see the Numbers lined up along the width of the shore. Each standing directly in front of one of the targets.

"Before we begin," Ares says, "I need to ask you to really push yourselves. To really push *them*. Your Numbers. This is your final chance to win sacred bloodstones before the Counting Ceremony tonight. Remember, what may feel difficult will ultimately reward you. Will reward *them*. Be brave. Be fearless."

I see Finn right at the far end of the row, head down, hair hanging over his eyes.

"Now all line up behind the rope in your couples, facing your Number."

We shuffle forward across the pebbles. I take in their trembling faces, their dirty clothes, the faint green light of their tags glowing at their ankles. The numbers on the front of their hoodies as I walk along the length of rope, stepping over the yellow plastic bows placed along it.

One.

Two.

Three.

Four.

Then five.

Eleanor and I stop opposite the final target. I look at the circular wooden board, yellow and white rings alternating inward toward the yellow bull's-eye. Just above the top of Finn's head.

Behind him, I see two dark figures walking toward us. The Keepers. They take their places on either side of the row of targets. Then they turn to face each other, folding their arms.

But where is Artemis?

"Welcome to your final trial," Ares says. "This is about trust." He moves his eyes over each of the Ten, taking us in. "We want to see how much your Number trusts you. It is so important, moving forward, that they do." He smiles. "Pick up your bows."

I look down at the plastic bow with a single arrow next to it, rubber sucker at the end.

Eleanor stares at it, frowning. "This doesn't feel right," she whispers. "Something's not right."

"Let's just . . . keep going," I whisper back, and she nods.

I lean down and take the bow. It feels so *light* in my hands in comparison to the crossbow.

Where the hell is Artemis?

Ares begins to pace back and forth in front of us. "The ritual is very simple." You said that about the last one. Liar. "You will fire at the target, aiming for the bull's-eye. In order for your Number to win you sacred bloodstones, they must show you their trust. If they so much as take one step away from the target, not only will you not win any sacred bloodstones, but you will *lose* five of them."

"Fuck's sake," Matthew hisses, glaring at Betty. Her hands are clenched so tightly around her sleeves that I can see the outline of her knuckles.

"Each couple will only have one shot," Ares continues. "So make it count. Now, decide in your pairs who will fire the arrow."

Eleanor turns to me, panicked. "Seb, I'm terrible—"

"It's OK. I'll do it."

"Are you sure?"

I nod.

"You can do this." Well, kind of depends on what "this" is. "Didn't you say someone once called you the Ultimate Sniper King?"

"Yeah." But that wasn't real. This is. This is very real.

"You have good aim. Trust yourself."

"Yeah. OK." Oh, God.

"Now," Ares says, "those who are *not* shooting, take a step back from the rope."

Eleanor places her hand on my arm and gives it a reassuring squeeze before stepping away. I look down the row of people left standing behind the rope, plastic bows in hand. Matthew, Raheem, Rachel, and Li.

Ares stops pacing. "I have something important to tell you." Please, just let it be over soon. Please. "There is another element to this ritual. A choice."

Something moves in the periphery of my vision, and Artemis steps out from the tree line. The clack of pebbles grinding together beneath her feet punctuate each step until she's right beside Ares. In her hands, I see its black angular frame. The yellow feathers of the bolts protruding from the sheath on her back.

The crossbow.

I knew it.

"No way," Matthew says. "So cool!"

There's a gasp from the direction of the targets. I turn to see the panic-stricken faces of the Numbers.

Finn's eyes stare straight at me. Completely gray.

"Do not worry about your Numbers," Ares says. "They have had their instructions. This is the robust teaching they need, and they know that. Remember, this is about trust. *Faith.* They must have faith, or there is no point. No purpose."

Artemis stands next to him, nodding along as he speaks.

"The choice is this: if you choose to shoot with your plastic bow and your Number does not move from the target, you will receive one sacred bloodstone."

"One?" Sam mutters. "Is that it?"

"But if you choose to shoot with the crossbow"—Artemis steps forward, holding it out in front of her—"and your Number does not move from the target, you will be awarded *ten* sacred blood-stones." Her eyes glimmer.

They think they're so clever.

"Ten?" Rachel says. "Wow."

Artemis nods. "And if you hit the bull's-eye—*only* if you use the crossbow—a further five bloodstones will be awarded. This could change everything for you."

I look at Eleanor, eyes ahead on Finn, focused. I know what she's thinking. We might need to actually hit the bull's-eye to win.

"Now," Ares says, "we will undertake the trial *in complete silence*. We do not want anyone to be distracted. Do you understand?" Everyone nods obediently. "Good. We will start with Li."

Li looks at him. "Me?"

He nods.

Li steps forward until her feet are right up to the blue rope. Her eyes fix on Malachai opposite her. She takes in his dirty face. His cracked glasses. The steam rising in them each time he exhales.

"Which bow will you choose to shoot with, Li?"

"I . . ." She falters. Turns her head to Sam.

"The choice is *yours,* Li," Ares says. "*You* must make it."

She looks down at the ground and mumbles something.

"Speak up, Li."

"The plastic bow," she says. "I choose the plastic bow." She keeps her eyes down. "I'm sorry."

I see Sam's face fill with an emotion I haven't seen in him before. *Anger. He's angry.*

"Very well," Ares says somberly. "It's a shame."

Artemis nods. "I was hoping we would see a little more strength today. What with so much at stake. This trial is really going to narrow down who will win the prize."

The prize. The fucking prize.

I look at Finn, and I'm overwhelmed with the urge to shout, to *scream*. He shakes his head. *Don't.* Stone said it. This is the only way out.

"Wait . . . ," Li says. "Can I . . . can I change my mind?"

Artemis smiles. "Good girl." She steps toward her, holding out the crossbow. *Presenting* it to her.

"It's very easy to use," she says. *Easy.* "It has a fantastic aim. I will load it for you." She kneels down in front of Li and turns the crossbow, angling it toward the pebbles.

It's as if something sucks all the air from the beach. Every noise is heightened. The *whip* of the bolt as she pulls it from the sheath on her back. The *rustle* of the feathers as she attaches it to the string. The *thrum* of its vibrations as she pulls it taut. The *click* signaling that it's in place snapping through the air.

Artemis stands. "I will talk you through it," she says. "It is simple." *Simple.*

Li takes it in her hands. "It's heavy," she says.

Artemis nods.

Then Li slowly lifts it up to her shoulder. She points it toward Malachai.

"That's it," Artemis says. "Now, look through the scope. Can you see the marker? The cross?"

"Yes," Li says. "I see it."

"It is called the reticle."

I don't think we care what it's called.

"Move it over the bull's-eye."

"OK."

"Then all you need to do is pull the trigger," Artemis says. "Are you ready?"

Li makes a tiny nod of her head, but I can see her fingers shaking.

Malachai is completely still. He doesn't even close his eyes. He just . . . blinks.

"Oh, God," Eleanor whispers. "Seb—"

Thwack.

The noise ricochets around the shore. Malachai's glasses slide down his nose as the wooden target reverberates behind his head. The bolt juts out just above his hair, a few inches away from the bull's-eye.

The other Numbers turn to Malachai, their mouths hanging open in horror. All but Finn, who keeps his eyes fixed on the ground.

"A little out," Artemis says. "But good."

Li lowers the bow and hands it back to her. "Wow," she says. "That was . . ." She smiles. "Well done, Malachai!" she shouts. I can hear her voice wobble with relief.

Malachai pushes his glasses back up his nose with his finger, tears streaming down his cheeks.

"Don't call him that, Li," Ares says. "He is Number Three."

"Right, yeah," Li says, still smiling.

Ares turns back to us. "Next." Oh, God. Raheem steps up to the rope. "Which bow do you choose?"

He stares at Killian directly ahead of him. His eyes narrow as he chews the inside of his lip, turning the decision over in his mind.

He looks back at Lucy, unsure.

"Your choice, Raheem," Ares says.

Raheem exhales slowly. "Go on, then, I choose the crossbow."

"Good boy."

Lucy makes a small, stifled noise. A squeal. A squeal that sounds a lot like . . . *excitement.*

Killian's eyes widen in terror.

Artemis kneels in front of Raheem. Puts the crossbow down in front of her.

Whip. Rustle. Thrum. Click.

His hands shake as he lifts the crossbow up to his shoulder, as he feels the weight of it, as he looks through the scope. "Wow, OK."

"Breathe," Artemis says. "Just breathe."

Killian's body tenses as if he is about to bolt. Run. But then he sees the two Keepers on either side of him, their yellow wristbands glinting in the cold sunlight.

He turns to face Raheem. "Mate, please," he says quietly. He sounds like a completely different person. "Pick the other one. Go on, mate. You can swa—"

Thwack.

Suddenly the bolt is trembling above Killian's head, on the outer ring of the target.

"Oh, fuck." Raheem drops to his knees. "Oh, thank fuck."

I look at Finn. Still with his head down.

"Good, Raheem. Very good." Artemis places her hand on his shoulder, and he smiles up at her.

Lucy puts both her thumbs up. "Ten bloodstones!"

"Next," Ares says. "Rachel, which bow do you choose?"

Rachel tugs at the sleeves of her hoodie as she gazes at Jennifer. She then looks back at Jamie.

He winks at her. *Do it.*

"The crossbow," she says. "I'll use the crossbow."

Artemis joins Rachel. She loads the bolt.

Whip. Rustle. Thrum. Click.

As Rachel takes it in her hands, she becomes oddly calm. She raises the bow to her shoulder. Steady. Her eyes alert.

"Ready?" Artemis says. Rachel nods. "Good."

Then. "Please, no!" Jennifer holds her hands out in front of her and begins to lift her foot so her body angles slightly. "I promise. I'll get better. I promise—"

Thwack.

The razor-sharp point pierces through the back of her hood, right beside her neck.

Rachel gasps.

Jennifer freezes. Her eyes move to the bolt pinning her to the target.

I see red on her neck, forming a line in her skin. Blood begins to pour from it like thick red tears. Her hand moves to the gash, and she makes a small, feeble noise as she feels the wetness. She begins to sob.

"Is she OK?" Rachel whispers.

"It's just a scratch," Artemis says.

"This is why you must remain *still*," Ares calls.

But Jennifer isn't listening. As she studies the blood coating her fingertips, her face changes like someone has flicked a switch inside her, turning off the panic, the fear, the sobs. She clasps her hand around the bolt and yanks it out of the target.

Jennifer looks up. She lifts her arm and points the bolt dead ahead of her. Right at Rachel.

"You bitch," she says quietly. Her face begins to fizz with something I recognize. Something I've tried to push back down inside me. *Rage.*

She steps forward. "You're a fucking bitch, Rachel. Standing there like you're better than me. Like you're worth more than me." The bolt trembles in her hand. Her eyes pulsate with intensity. "But you're not. I know you. I know your type. You're just a scared, needy little bitch who can't think for herself. I'm sick of this shit! You nearly fucking killed m—"

zzzz

Her head snaps back, and she drops to her knees.

Ares steps forward, his finger on his wristband. "You shouldn't have moved, Number Three," he says as she writhes on the ground. "You should have trusted her. We are trying to help you." He turns away. "Next."

Jennifer crawls back to her target, her fingers leaving red smears on the pebbles.

I feel tingling that starts in my fingers, then moves up through the arteries in my neck and into my brain.

Calm down.

"Matthew," Ares says. "Which bow do you choose?"

Matthew steps forward. "Easy. The crossbow." He stares at Betty ahead of him.

Artemis approaches. She kneels. Loads the bolt into the string.

Whip. Rustle. Thrum. Click.

She hands it to him, and he smiles like a child being given a free pack of sweets.

"Fucking ace," he says, holding it up to his shoulder. "Kind of . . . *007,* isn't it?" He narrows his eyes as he looks down the scope.

But then Betty moves. She steps forward, away from the target.

"No!" Matthew screams, dropping the bow. "What are you doing?"

She starts walking toward him.

"Number One," Ares barks. "Get back to your place."

But she continues to walk. Her hand up by her side. Fist clenched.

"That's *enough*."

Picking up her speed. Unwavering. *Determined.*

Like she's going to—

zzzz

Her head snaps back. She falls to the ground.

Matthew stands with his finger on his wrist. "How dare you!" His face twists with disgust as he strides toward her. "Do you understand what you've done?" He stops and leans down, his face inches from hers. "Look at you! You're pathetic!" His spit sprays out over her face.

"Gently now," Ares says. "Remember, she is struggling."

Matthew turns to Ares. "It's . . . it's not my fault. . . ."

"You clearly haven't shown her that she can trust you yet."

"But—but . . . ," Matthew stammers as Betty scrambles to her feet and hobbles away, back to her target.

Ares keeps his eyes on Matthew. "Sadly she has lost you five sacred bloodstones."

"What? Five?" Matthew steps back across the pebbles until he is next to Jing. "There's no way we're going to fucking win now."

In Jing's eyes I see utter *revulsion*.

"Seb," Eleanor hisses.

"Do I have to hit the bull's-eye?" I whisper.

"Yes," she whispers back.

Shit.

313

"Sebastian," Ares says.

The panic trips a fuse in my brain. I feel like I'm floating. Like my body is not my own and I'm no longer real. It's like I'm in a video game and someone is moving me with a controller, looking at me through a screen.

You must win. It is the only way out.

"Sebastian," Ares repeats. "Which do you choose?"

I swallow hard. "The crossbow."

"Good."

Whip. Rustle. Thrum. Click.

Then Artemis is holding it in front of me.

"I am interested to see how much Number Five trusts you, Sebastian," Ares says.

I stare back at him.

You're evil. You're fucking evil.

"Sebastian," he says again. "We're waiting."

Things don't feel real. I'm not real. Nothing is real.

Detach. Now detach.

I feel my hands move, but it isn't me doing it. My fingers hook around the bow. They lift it up to my shoulder. Turn the bolt toward Finn.

Someone else is in control. Of me. Of all this.

"Are you ready, Sebastian?"

I look through the scope, and the whole world shrinks. I move it so the cross hovers over Finn.

I see the gray of his eyes as he looks back at me.

As I focus on his irises, I see a flash of ice blue behind the gray. It floods through me like a drug, filling the synapses in my brain, forging them together with color, clearing the panic, the dread, bringing me back into myself. The hairs on my arms prickle, and a heat explodes in my head, right below the base of my skull, like a connection has been made. A plug has been pushed firmly into its socket.

This is real. Me and you.

He nods at me, scared, *terrified*, but he understands what I have to do. I have to do this so that we can win.

So that we can get the hell out of here.

His color is so bright. So vibrant. It's all I can see.

Thwack.

THIRTY-FIVE
The Edge of Sadness

We have been told not to speak to each other. To remain silent and respectful as we make our way back to camp. All I hear is the scuffle of shoes through the pine needles and the rustle of birds above as they return to their branches after being shocked out of them by the noise of the darts. Jennifer's screams, her sobs. The applause.

When I hit the bull's-eye, people cheered. They clapped.

"No way!"

"Wow!"

"Holy shit, Seb!"

But when I saw the bolt jutting out of the board just above Finn's head, I did not feel good. I did not feel proud. I felt pain. I felt as if the dart had hit *me,* injecting me with a deep sadness.

When Eleanor took my hand and whispered, "God, Seb, well done," I felt like bawling.

As Finn nodded at me from across the pebbles—*You did it, Seb*—I saw relief in his eyes. And *gratitude.* It hurt to see him so grateful. Grateful for not hitting him with a serrated metal bolt.

Ares then put his hand on my shoulder and squeezed it in a way that made a prickling sensation crawl all over my body. I couldn't tell if I was going to be sick or cry.

But I did neither. I just stood still. Fighting against the tingling sadness.

Don't let him see it, I told myself. *He can't see it.*

"You have proved yourself," Ares said quietly. "You have shown us just how much Number Five trusts you."

When he removed his hand, I felt like it was still there. I still do. I keep rubbing my shoulder to try and remove its imprint. I can still feel it. His impression on me.

And I can't stop thinking about what Artemis said, just before the Bottom Percentile were led away by the Keepers.

Total surrender, she said. *Total surrender is the only way forward. Surrendering brings the birth of a new being. A new way of life. Submit. Submit to this new way of thinking and strength will flow from within you. Your higher purpose will be unleashed. Prove yourself. The time is upon us.*

I now realize that Artemis was not only talking to us, but to herself. None of this is about the Bottom Percentile. None of it is about the Ten. Not really. The Couple need us to prove ourselves so that they can do the same. Stone was right. We are nothing but pawns in their game. We are all here, on this island, being pushed about by someone else. All of us. And everyone wants to win.

Approval. *That* is the reward.

In this moment I see them—Ares and Artemis, James and Mia—for the first time. What they really are. Two scared human beings desperate for their reward. To be seen. To be liked. To feel important. To be happy.

And as they lead us back, speaking with each other in precise, covert whispers, I understand how dangerous that is. I look at Eleanor—her eyes fixed forward, not moving from the back of the Couple—and I wonder if she is thinking the exact same thing. "Drop back a bit," I whisper.

When there is enough distance between us and the rest of the group, we speak, keeping our voices low.

"You did great, Seb. I thought maybe you wouldn't—"

"I did too. Have we done enough?"

She nods. "Yes," she says. "Just." She pauses. "But I have this weird feeling. . . ."

"It's fine. We're right where we need to be."

"Something's not right. Something's off."

"It's all *off*, Eleanor."

"I know, but . . . I just . . . I feel like something's coming. Something more. Those two"—she motions to Ares and Artemis—"they'll do anything for Gloria." Yep. I'm glad she sees that. "And if they find out about what we're doing . . ."

"They won't find out," I say, taking her hand in mine. "We just need to get through these next few hours, and we can leave tonight."

"But . . ." She pushes her fingers into the bridge of her nose. "Fuck, Seb."

"Don't let them see you're upset. They can't see."

"I know." She exhales slowly. "I know."

I move closer, keeping my voice low. "Stone said we must win, and she has this press interview set up for the winners, where we stop this. That's it. There is nothing more."

"She *definitely* said that?"

"Yeah, she did."

Did she?

Stop it, Seb. Stop doubting.

"OK. So before we go to this *Ash Farm* place?"

"Yes. We have to trust her, Eleanor."

"I have to trust *you.*"

"Do you?"

She nods.

"Good."

Up ahead I see Ares turn. "Pick up the pace, you two!" he shouts, making the rest of the group turn their heads.

"Come on," I say, pulling at Eleanor's hand.

As we join the back of the group, I try not to listen to what they're saying, but it carries across the cold air.

"Do we know who's won?"

"I think we know who hasn't."

Matthew is walking alone, a little outside of the group. His head is down, but he's listening. Calculating.

"Knowing this place. Anything could happen."

Matthew lifts his head. He turns to me, chewing his lip, leaving a smear of blood on his front teeth. As our eyes meet, he spits pink saliva out onto the grass.

Ares suddenly stops, leaving Artemis to continue on.

"What's he doing?" Eleanor says, watching him step a little off the track and wait.

As we approach him, I smile. *Everything is fine.*

He holds up his hand. "One moment." We stop, and I feel Eleanor's grip tighten. "Sebastian, I would like to speak with you."

Oh, shit. He knows. Finn. The escape plan. All of it.

"Sure." I shrug. "No problem." I turn to Eleanor and kiss her on the cheek. "See you back at the camp, hon." I say breezily.

"Thank you, Eleanor," Ares says. "I won't keep him from you for long."

Why does he sound so serious?

"You'd better not," she says, grinning.

We watch her walk away. Then it's just us. Me and him.

He closes his eyes and turns his face up to the sky as if drinking in the final rays of the sun.

Oh, God. Here we go.

"Come with me back down the hill a little," he says. "I don't want anyone to hear what I have to say."

I'd rather not. "Can't you just tell me here?" I say, but he is already moving down the track. I follow until he stops at a point where the camp is no longer in view.

"Sebastian."

So intense. "Hi."

"I wanted to say well done."

Oh. Right. That's not so bad. "Sure, thank you."

"I nearly didn't believe you had it in you. I thought you . . . Well, I should never have doubted you."

"It's fine. Really. Don't worry about it."

"I just wanted to tell you I'm sorry and that I think you're an inspiration. A true representation of all the work we are doing here."

"That's very kind. . . ."

"You are growing into such a wonderful person. Strong. Confident. Assured."

"Ah, well, you know. It's all thanks to you two."

He flicks his eyes up to the top of the hill, checking we are alone. "I need to ask you something, Sebastian."

Why now? Please don't. "Yeah, of course. What is it?" I try to keep my voice level.

"Are you sure you're OK?"

Huh? "Yeah, course I am."

"You seemed . . . emotional."

"What? When? I'm fine. Great, in fact."

"Earlier. On the beach. After you hit the bull's-eye."

"Oh. Did I? I don't remember."

"You were upset. Sad."

"*Sad?* What would make you think that?"

"Because it looked like you were about to cry."

Oh, right. So he did see. Shit.

"Well . . . Maybe I was a *bit* emotional." Stop looking at me like that. "It's been a lot. Honestly, Ares, I was probably just overwhelmed. Recognizing how far I've come."

"You are very sensitive, Sebastian."

All right. *Can this end now?*

"Sorry, was that a question?"

"No."

Silence. More staring. *Stop it.*

"I can't help but find myself wondering . . ." He glances back up the hill again. "Where the source of that emotion, that sadness, comes from." He knows something. *What does he know?* "If there's something else going on."

Oh, God. "I'm not sad. I'm very happy."

He narrows his eyes. Doubt.

Come on, Seb.

"I think it was just a lot, shooting a bolt at someone with an actual crossbow, regardless of how sensitive I am."

Can everyone please stop thinking? Bad things happen when people think.

"I have wondered if perhaps you are not being fully honest with yourself," Ares says.

That's not good. He doesn't know. *He can't.*

"Well, I am. Rigorously so."

He sighs. "All right, Sebastian."

"OK. Great. Good chat, Ares." I begin to walk away, but he takes my sleeve in his hand.

"Sebastian?"

I turn back. "Yep?"

"If there's something you need to tell me, I am giving you the opportunity to do so now. It is important. Imperative for the program. Before you move forward tonight. Before you win."

"So we've . . . won?"

He lowers his voice, still holding on to my sleeve.

"I can help you," he whispers. "We are very similar, you and I." We are not. He inhales, readying himself. "Sebastian, I know."

"Um . . . Know what?"

"I know that you do not love Eleanor."

What? "Excuse me?"

"You do not love her." His eyes flick up to the hill. Back to me.

"Yes, I do."

"No. You do not."

"I'm confused because I really, *really* do."

"I've seen it."

"Seen what?"

"There is someone else."

Oh, shit. *Shit, shit, shit.*

Not now. Not now. We are so close.

"Someone *else?*" I force a laugh. "That's just ridicu—"

"I first noticed it a while ago. Your . . . little signs." The notes. He's seen the notes. The pieces of wood. The bee. "Coded exchanges." Oh, God. No. *Please no.* "And I saw it today on the beach." Finn. His color. So bright. "Eye contact."

"Eye contact?" Are we going to lose this opportunity because of *eye contact?*

"An energy you give . . ."

"I don't give an *energy.*"

"There is someone else. Do not lie. I need to know."

He stares at me as if trying to see right inside me. But I won't let him. *I won't.* "There is no one else, Ares."

"I don't believe you."

"I love Eleanor. I love her. I am in love with Eleanor Banks."

He steps toward me. "You are not."

"I am."

"No."

"Stop saying no."

He puts his hand on my shoulder and squeezes. Then he leans forward, so our faces are a fraction apart. "You're the one who is saying no, Sebastian. To yourself."

When he takes my cheeks in his hands, when his lips touch mine, I freeze. Completely paralyzed as fear and disgust and shock and anger overtake me.

Ho-ly shit. He thinks it's *him.*

He steps back. I try to catch my breath as he looks at me tenderly. "Seb . . . I—"

"No!" I say. "Stay back."

"We are the same, you and I." *The same.*

"Get away from me!"

"Please, Seb. This is difficult for me too. . . ."

He steps toward me, but before he can reach me, I push him. Hard. He stumbles backward.

"Don't come near me. I don't want this."

Shit. *Shit.*

He slowly straightens himself up, wipes his hair out of his face. "Are you sure about that, Sebastian?"

"Yes," I say. "I've never been more sure."

"Right. I see. OK."

Then something strange happens. He puts his face in his hands. And he laughs. A horrible, wicked laugh.

He looks up at me. "Well," he says. "That was interesting."

What the—? I can feel my whole body trembling.

"It's not interesting. It's not funny either. I'm going to tell them. Artemis . . . Manning . . ."

He frowns. "Tell them what?"

"That you're lying to everyone. That you—"

"But that's not true."

"It is."

"It is not, Sebastian."

What is happening? "You're a liar."

"Fine." He shrugs. "Tell them."

"What?"

"Tell them. If that's what you feel you need to do." He holds his hands in front of himself like a priest at an altar. Completely calm. Composed.

What is he doing? "I will."

"Sebastian, listen. They already know."

"What do you mean?"

He sighs. "She asked me to do this."

324

"Who did?"

"Madame Manning."

"Manning asked you to kiss me?"

"It was a test, Sebastian."

My brain stalls. "A *test*? Why?"

"We needed to know if our concerns were true."

"What concerns?"

"Ever since you spoke to me in the bathroom after you snuck out in the middle of the night, I felt that you had shown some . . . *complex* feelings toward me." *What the actual fuck?* "I discussed it with Artemis. We needed to understand where your attractions lie. It was important for us, for the program, and of course for Eleanor. We spoke to Manning, and we agreed that if you were lying to us, to yourself, then sadly you could not move forward. You could not win."

He thinks I love him. He thinks I love *him*.

Oh my God.

"Right," I say flatly.

I try to keep my breath calm. My face unreadable. My brain silent.

"Don't you want to know if you passed?" I hear him say. I look up. "I am still undecided."

If I *passed*?

This is so messed up. *You know what? Fuck this guy. Fuck all of this.*

I step toward him. "Actually, Ares," I say, keeping my voice completely level, "I think you're right."

A flash of confusion. "Excuse me?"

I put my hand on his shoulder and squeeze. Hard. Firm. "You were right."

He flinches. "I was?"

"Yes." I look right into his eyes the way he looks at me. As I do, his body begins to tremble ever so slightly. There is something in him. Something I recognize. An edge. An edge of something deeper. More real. A sadness I have understood and battled with. A pain that comes from a place so specific, so deep, so gentle and soft and angry, born of such denial and struggle and resistance, that I do know him. And suddenly everything makes sense.

He lied. This was not a test. For a split second, I want to hug him. To say how sorry I am. Because I know. I do.

"We *are* the same, you and I."

He swallows. "And why is that?"

"You know why." As I squeeze harder, his eyes begin to prickle with tears.

"Do I?" he says, panic rising in his voice.

"Yes." I lean toward him. "We're both *winners,* aren't we?"

Relief floods his face. "Yes. Of course. *Yes.* We are."

"And we both know exactly what it has taken from us. How hard it has been. How painful. But we've overcome it, haven't we?" He tries to lean back, but I keep hold. "Look at us. Look at us both now. Free from all that pain." I watch as his eyes flicker. "I'm excited to have exactly what you have. Because you seem so *happy,* Ares."

I see you, Ares. *And I will never let myself become that.*

I let go and I walk away.

"Sebastian," he says.

I turn back to see him holding his hand out toward me. In it is one single bloodstone. "Here. You won this."

I don't want it. I don't.

I step forward and take it. "Thank you," I say, feeling its weight in my hand.

"Keep this one for yourself," he says quietly. "When things get difficult, remember this moment."

"Don't worry." I push it down into my pocket. "I will."

By the time I reach the camp, the rest of the Ten are sitting in their pairs, now cloaked, the crack of the roaring fire cutting through the cold, graying sky. The shed door is shut, the Keepers on guard outside it.

Artemis is prowling around the stone circle. She looks at me as I take my place next to Eleanor, who hands me my cloak.

"Where's Ares?" she asks, frowning.

"He's coming," I say, pulling it on. "He said he needed a moment."

"A moment?" She pauses. "Is everything all right?"

"Absolutely. He's helped me understand something very important. And I am so grateful. He is such a wonderful man. You are very lucky. Both of you."

She smiles. "Thank you, Sebastian. We feel very fortunate to have found each other."

I sit next to Eleanor.

"What happened?" she whispers. "What was it?"

"A test."

"A *test*? What kind of test?" She puts her hand on mine. "What did he say? Did you pass?"

Before I have the chance to answer, I see Ares walking calmly toward us. I watch as he joins Artemis, smiling. But as he kisses her and says, "My love," and strokes her on the cheek, I recall a sharp edge of sadness once more.

"Let us celebrate our last few hours together as a group," he declares. "Tonight we have so much to be thankful for. And then the winners shall be announced."

I feel the weight of the bloodstone in my pocket.

"Yeah," I say quietly to Eleanor. "I passed."

THIRTY-SIX
My Little Pony

"Before Madame Manning arrives," Artemis says, glowing in the firelight under the heavy sky, "we would like to take a moment. We have something special for you all." She smiles. "Your Numbers would like to thank you."

She nods to the Keepers. They unbolt the door. *Clonk.*

The Numbers file out, finding their places in front of their pairs. I see Jennifer, a large gauze dressing over the cut on her neck. She won't look at Rachel. She won't look up at all.

They are each holding something. Envelopes.

"Your Numbers are so grateful for what you have taught them." Artemis turns to them. "Aren't you?"

They nod. *Yes. We are grateful.*

Artemis looks back at us. "Madame Manning told you that she has been updating your families, your loved ones, on your progress. They are so proud of you. And so they have written each of you a letter, which you will now receive."

Whispers rise up around the circle.

"No way."

"Oh my God. Really?"

"That's so sweet. . . ."

"And," Artemis continues, "your Numbers have decided that they would like to read them to you, as a token of their gratitude. Isn't that nice?"

An awkward silence descends. Behind her, at the edge of the circle, which is now falling into darkness, Ares stands, watching.

"Let us start with Number One." Matthew glowers at Betty. She shrinks back from him, then realizes she can't move any farther because of the heat of the fire behind her. "If you could start with reading Matthew's letter? Then Jing's."

"Um . . . Yes. Of course."

As Betty tears open the envelope, Matthew glares at her like he wants her to stop touching it.

"Matthew," she mutters.

"Speak up," he snaps. "I can't hear you."

"Matthew," she says again, louder.

"That's better, well done." He shoots a look at Artemis. She nods, and he smiles, pleased with himself.

"We have heard lots of things about your journey at Happy-Head," Betty goes on. "You have done so well to get to where you are. We are so proud of you for committing to this. You are part of something incredibly special." I watch him grin stupidly. "However." Betty pauses.

"Carry on," he says. "What are you waiting for?"

Betty clears her throat. "We were disappointed to hear that you have struggled with some of the challenges. We expected so much more from you. Madame Manning told us that your leaders, Ares and Artemis, reported back that you have shown a lack of maturity, which they say is blocking you. This is such a shame.

Matty, we have talked about this. After everything, we had so hoped for change."

His face falls. I see him struggle to hide his emotions, the weight of embarrassment and shame too heavy.

"Should I go on?" Betty says tentatively. I notice the smallest wave of pleasure ripple through her.

"Yes, continue, Number One," Artemis says.

"We hope that you keep pushing yourself because this is what you must do. Strengthen yourself. Show HappyHead how strong you are. Show them you are not weak. Show them, Matty." Betty stops, the paper shaking in her hand. "A-and . . . ," she stammers. "And we hope to see that growth when you return. Mum and Dad."

"That's it?" he says. "There's no more?"

Betty shakes her head.

"What?" He looks at her in a way that says *This is all your fucking fault.*

She folds the letter back up and is about to put it in her pocket when he stands. "Give me that." He steps forward and snatches it from her, then wipes it on his cloak. "It's mine."

She stares at him for a moment. "Prick," she murmurs.

Um . . . OK, Betty.

Someone snorts.

Matthew steps toward her. "What did you say?"

"Nothing."

"I heard you."

As they stare at each other, my skin bristles. I think he's about to smack her, but then he swallows his anger and returns to his stone.

"Jing's letter now, please, Number One," Artemis says.

One by one, we hear the Numbers read the letters. The words of our loved ones.

We watch as Lucy cries at her parents' adoration, as Jamie laughs at his brother's jokes, as Sam nods solemnly at his father's wisdom. We listen as the Numbers tell us how proud our loved ones are, the joy we are all bringing to their lives through our success here. How we will be "part of the beginning of the change that is needed." That we are "beacons of hope for the future."

"Number Five," Artemis says. "Read Eleanor's first."

Finn opens the first envelope in his hands. "Um . . . OK. So . . ."

She tenses next to me, and I see her face is bright red.

"Eleanor," he says. "We miss you. We are so proud of you, sweetheart. Because we know how tough things have been for you."

She closes her eyes.

"We know that your life changed a couple of years ago and that you needed something to really help move you forward." He pauses for a moment. "It is so lovely to hear that you are thriving. We know you feel you have a lot to prove, and we are glad you are able to do that at HappyHead. You are helping others, which is such a great thing. We are not experts, but we do know that helping others really does change people. Keep thriving. Keep excelling. Keep making us proud."

He stops.

"Thanks," Eleanor says quietly. "Thank you, Fi—" She corrects herself. "Thank you, Number Five. That was beautifully read."

He looks at her for a moment, then turns to me, a little confused.

I think maybe he is . . . aware . . . of *something*. She did save his life, after all.

He starts opening the other envelope. As he unfolds it, I can see lots of writing. My mum's handwriting. *Why is there lots of writing?*

He looks down at it and suddenly seems *nervous*. Which makes me nervous.

"Sebastian," he starts to read. "We are so happy to hear you are doing well." He clears his throat. "We have heard that not only is your relationship with Eleanor blossoming, but also you are growing in confidence and strength. Apparently, you are excelling at the physical challenges, which we never expected. Physical strength was never your thing."

Oh no.

"We have heard that you are being incredibly caring." He pauses. "We always knew that side of you existed, and we loved it whenever we saw it. We are so glad you are nurturing it. Lily says she always knew you were a caring person, ever since you got your My Little Pony when you were seven. She reminded us you used to sit and brush its hair for hours and talk to it because you were worried it was afraid of the cat." He looks up at me, and his lips part in a faint smile. I drop my eyes. I realize people are laughing.

"We always thought you would be good at helping others. We can't believe it, Seb. We are just so proud. Gloria said you are special. And we always knew it." He stops again. "That bit's underlined," he says. Something crosses his face, a warm affection, almost like he has a faint idea of who these people are. "We have told everyone how well you are doing. Your teachers, our church friends, Bob and Barbara." *Who the hell are Bob and Barbara?* "Pastor Johnny is so pleased you have found a purpose." Oh, *God.* Quite literally. "You know that when you stopped going to church it made us sad, because we thought it had a really positive influence on you, but it seems you have found another community of people who are doing just that." *Why is it so long?* "We hope that whoever it is you are helping knows how lucky they are." He stops. Looks up. I can see his eyes are glazed over. "Love and hugs, Mum and Dad."

Is that it? Please be it.

"P.S." Nope. Apparently not. "Lily was asking if she could use your bubble bath. We said it would be fine. We know you get funny about stuff like that, but she misses you, so we let her."

My face is on fire. It goes quiet. Very quiet.

"Thanks," I mumble.

"They sound really nice," Finn says, his voice soft as if he has forgotten everyone else.

As I take him in, his fingernails thick with mud, his matted hair, the wing tattoo on his neck now barely visible through the dirt—it is very apparent to me how much I care for this person. I can't wait to tell him that.

"Well," Ares booms, and Finn flinches as he's snapped back into the hell we are in. "Wasn't that just lovely, everyone?"

I hear the Ten murmur affirmatively around me.

"Madame Manning will be arriving soon." I catch Finn's eye as his face darkens. "So if you would like to rest and prepare yourselves, please do. We want everyone ready and presentable. Be back in the stone circle in an hour."

There are no clocks, dickhead.

Artemis beckons the Keepers over, and the four of them talk quietly to each other. As they turn their backs to us, for the first time I feel like we're not being watched.

"Are you OK?" I whisper to Finn.

He nods. "Yeah."

He then looks at Eleanor. "Thanks," he says. "For . . . earlier."

"It's OK," she says. "Don't worry. It'll be all right, Finn. I promise."

I see his surprise at her using his name. "What's going on?"

"It was Seb . . . ," Eleanor says. "He . . . helped me."

"I see." He smiles at her. "Fucking finally."

She scowls.

"Just kidding," he says. "But also not."

The three of us stand together in silence for a moment.

"I think we've won," I whisper.

"I fucking hope so."

"We have," Eleanor says. "There's no way we—"

"Where's Number One?" Jing suddenly shouts from her stone, eyes darting throughout the camp. "She was just here. Where is she?" She stands, frantic, then looks straight at me. I see panic flood her face. "He's got her. He's got Betty."

I don't have to look to know who she means.

Matthew.

Seb . . . , Jing mouths, lips trembling, but she's stopped by Artemis and the Keepers darting through the circle.

"Find her," Artemis snaps. "The woods. The beach. Go."

They both move off down the hill.

"What's going on?" Rachel says.

Artemis strides across the circle. As she passes Ares, she touches his hand. "Stay here. Watch the others." She then disappears into the darkness.

"Nobody move." Ares lifts up his sleeve to reveal his wristband. The Numbers hover by the fire, unsure. He looks at the Ten. "If anyone steps out of line, you know what to do."

"Where's Matthew taken her?" Finn says quietly as Ares begins to pace around the circle, watching the Numbers.

He looks at Eleanor. Eleanor looks at me.

And then her eyes widen as if she's been punched in the stomach. "Oh my God, *Seb.*" She grabs my arm so tightly it makes me wince. "What was our first ritual?"

"What?"

"What was our *first* ritual?"

"What are you talking about?"

"Just . . . *come on.*"

"The Archery . . ."

"No. It wasn't. It was the Fire. Find the Fire. And the next one was the Archery."

"Right?"

"What are you talking about?" Finn says.

But she keeps going. "And then the *Drop* . . ."

"I don't understand," I say.

"Seb." She pauses, and I realize I've never seen her look so scared.

"What is it?"

"They're doing the same trials as us."

"OK. But we've finished. It's *over.*"

"What's going on?" Finn says.

She starts counting on her fingers as she speaks. "*Find the Fire:* they burned the Trauma Boxes. *The Archery,* this afternoon on the shore. *The Drop:* this morning with Finn on the plank." She tightens her grip on my arm. "But there's one they haven't done yet."

"What do you mean?" And then I realize. Oh my God.

"*The Pen.*"

"The pigs."

"Pigs—the farm—*Ash Farm.*" Eleanor's eyes widen in horror. "That's what she wants us to do there."

I look at Finn. Oh, God. *No.*

"What?" he says, his face riddled with panic. "What the hell is Ash Farm?" Neither of us answer. Neither of us dare. "Can someone explain what the hell you're talking about? What pen? Guys? What fucking pigs?"

"Matthew must have figured out that the challenges are mirrored," I say. "He thinks that's what she wants from us. He thinks it's his chance to win."

Ended.

By us.

Eleanor nods. "Let's just—"

"Stay here," I say. "Don't follow me."

Before they can say another word, I sprint out of the circle—ignoring Ares's cries for me to stop—and into the darkness.

THIRTY-SEVEN
Little Piggy

The single bulb swings gently from the tall wooden post. The yellow plastic speaker at the top, with the HappyHead symbol stamped on its side.

But tonight the Pen is deathly quiet.

I inch forward until I'm crouched in the long grass just outside the low fence surrounding it. I peer through the wooden slats and allow my eyes to adjust to the pool of light cast by the bulb.

Two dark figures are doused in its murky golden haze. Both of them completely still. Matthew stands, hood up over his head, shoulders hunched, holding one of the dirty canvas sacks. Opposite him, exactly where the pigs were, is Betty.

I was right. *He figured it out.*

It takes me a moment to be completely sure that it *is* Matthew, because he looks so altered in the light. Like the shadows have sketched the outline of his face and there is nothing inside him. Betty stares up at him from the ground, her eyes swollen with terror. Her arms are tied behind her back, around the base of the pole, while her legs are spread out in front of her like a discarded toy. An unwanted rag doll.

The HappyHead face watches from above as Matthew takes a step toward her.

"I'm so sorry. Please, Matthew." Betty begins to strain against the rope, trying to free her wrists.

"Shut up!" Matthew pulls the sack down over her head.

She squirms. "No—please!" she cries, her voice muffled.

"Stop talking. It won't help you now."

"Please! I'll do anythi—"

He lifts his sleeve, and her ankle flashes red.

zzzzz

Her body shudders. She cries out, and it's so shrill, so piercing, that it cuts through the air, shocking my body into action. Before I can think, I stand.

"Stop it!" I dart toward them, scrambling over the fence. "Matthew, *stop*!"

A flash of dark anger, *annoyance,* crosses his sketched features beneath his hood. "Well, if it isn't the golden boy."

"Leave her alone, Matthew."

He smirks. "Don't you have somewhere to be? Ares's ass isn't going to lick itself."

Then he turns back to Betty and stamps on her leg. Hard. I hear the thud of his weight on her shin. She yelps.

I edge toward him. "Matthew, don't . . ."

"Stay back," he says, his finger hovering over his wristband. "Or I'll press it again."

"Matthew . . ." I take another step.

"What did I just say?" He pushes his finger down.

Betty's body pulsates. She makes a gurgling noise.

No.

I throw myself at him.

"Whoa!" He steps back, dodging me. "Is little Sebby finally deciding to show some *spunk*?" He jabs the wristband again.

zzzzz

"Leave her alone!" I make a grab for him, but he ducks.

"No," he says. "I won't. And you can't stop me."

His eyes flash and he grins wickedly, *playfully*. He begins to skip around the pole. "This. Is. For. Her. Own. Good," he says, each word punctuated with a press of his finger. Betty convulses, spasming with each pulse released. "This. Is. What. She. Deserves."

I leap toward him, powered by an intense loathing. When he is right in front of me, I punch.

Thunk. It collides with his shoulder.

He laughs. "Oh, Sebby. You're such a pussy. You're weak. *Literally* weak. I hardly felt that." He puts his face in mine. "It'd be such a *joke* if you won this thing. Everyone knows it would only be because you're Eleanor's little bitch." Flecks of his spit cover me.

"You're disgusting," I say.

He lifts his elbow and lands it straight into my nose.

My head jolts backward. A ringing explodes in my ears.

Holy shit. I clutch my face, steadying myself. *My nose.*

When I regain my vision, I see his eyes are wide with frantic energy. He turns back to Betty and puts his finger on the button. This time, he keeps it pressed down. "This is what Manning wants, Sebby. You're just too pathetic to see it!"

Betty's body twitches violently. She whimpers.

I stagger toward him. There's blood on my hoodie. "Stop it. . . ."

But he laughs and laughs and laughs.

Come on, Seb.

"Get off her!"

I ball my fist up again. Before I can hit him, someone else's hand appears, smacking him straight across the face and sending him tumbling to the floor.

As he hits the ground, he squeals. Just like the pigs.

I look up. Eleanor.

Eleanor.

"Stay away from her!" she yells as he sprawls on his back, his mouth hanging open in shock, his pale complexion making him look like a private-school vampire. He stares at her in disbelief.

"You. You fu—"

Smack. Her hand meets his face again.

Eleanor leans down next to him, putting her face right into his. "Look at me, Matthew," she says. "Look at me!" He looks up. "Good boy. Now, if you ever touch Betty again, I'll make sure you leave this island in a body bag. Do you hear me?" She then speaks very quietly, but very clearly. "I am a *cruel* person when I want to be, so believe me, you do *not* want to mess with me." I watch as his terrified face registers her words. "Do you understand me?" He nods slowly. "Good. You fucking weasel."

OK. Wow.

She then goes over to Betty and kneels beside her. "Hey," she whispers, pulling the sack off her head to reveal her face. Her bloodshot eyes, the drool trickling down her chin. "Betty? It's Eleanor." She turns. "Seb, quick, help me."

I drop to my knees. "Hey, Betty, it's OK," I say. She begins coughing, spluttering up phlegm. I wipe her chin with my sleeve, but more drool keeps coming, slobbering down over her hoodie.

This isn't good.

"We need to untie her," Eleanor says.

We scramble on all fours around the pole and dig our nails into the rope. As we pull and twist, Betty groans, mumbling incoherently, the veins in her wrists bulging.

"It's OK, Betty, just hold still . . ."

She struggles, making garbled noises. "Look . . . *look.*"

I hear Eleanor gasp.

I look up.

Matthew is standing on the other side of the pole, pointing a knife directly at Betty. The knife we used to kill the pigs with.

There is a moment of complete silence, except the low buzz of the light bulb above us. No one moves. No one dares.

I realize how calm he seems. How controlled.

"How did you get that?" I say.

He smirks. "You think you're the only one who has special secret conversations with those two?" Which one has he spoken to? "Step away from her," he says. "Both of you. Step away from her. *Now.*"

"Matthew . . . ," Eleanor murmurs. "You don't want to do—"

"Step back." He flashes the knife in Eleanor's direction. I feel her flinch. She starts to stand. "Take a few steps back," he says. "That's it." He turns to me. "And you. Move."

I put my hand up toward him, as if it might calm him. But he already seems so calm. "Matthew, let's talk about this," I say, mirroring Eleanor's tone. I try to keep his eyes on mine as I slowly stand and move back around the pole toward him.

"What are you doing?" he says.

I continue until I'm directly between him and Betty. "Just take a second. Think about what you're doing. This is—"

"Get out of my way."

I keep my hand held out between us, just in front of the blade. His grip is firm. I can see no shaking. No fear. "This isn't what you want, Matthew."

"You're wrong. You are so wrong."

"No."

His lip curls. "I figured it out," he says.

I know you did. "What do you mean?"

Easy, Seb. Keep him talking.

"Manning said she wants to see us take initiative. To be strong. To use our minds. She praised *you* for it. And I thought, if *he* can do it, so can I. And I did. I figured it out." He cocks his head. "You don't know, do you? You really don't get it?" He smiles smugly. "You're both too weak to see it." He then speaks very slowly, like I'm stupid. "Now, please move out of my way so that I can win."

He steps forward so the tip of the blade is inches from my chest. I stay rooted to the spot. I hold his gaze. His face flares with anger again. And then I see something move in the darkness behind him.

A flash of color. Green.

A hoodie.

Then.

Blue. Ice blue.

Finn.

He puts his finger to his lips.

I don't move my eyes from Matthew. *Stay with me, Matthew.* "Tell me what you figured out. I want to know."

"I'm not telling you."

"Why not, Matthew?"

"Because you don't deserve to know." In the shadows, I see Finn take a small step toward him.

Not yet. Steady. "But I want to."

"Are you jealous, Sebby?"

"Yes," I say. "I am. I'm jealous."

He smiles. "And you thought you had it, didn't you? You thought you'd done enough."

"I did." Finn slowly lifts his arm. *Steady.* "I was wrong."

"Perfect little Sebby was *wrong*," Matthew sneers. "Say you're a *pathetic loser* and I'll think about telling you."

"I'm a pathetic loser," I say.

Finn's eyes flash. *Not yet. Nearly.*

"Say it again."

"I'm a pathetic loser," I repeat.

And then I feel something tickle above my top lip, just beneath my nose.

Blood. From where he hit me.

Matthew glances down at it. He falters, lowering the knife for a split second.

I flick my eyes to Finn. *Now.*

Finn clenches his fist, pulls it back, and is about to swing. But as he does, Matthew turns. And he ducks.

The weight of Finn's punch throws him forward. He topples sideways, losing his footing.

Matthew grabs him by his hood and yanks him up so he chokes, pulling him backward. I begin to run toward them, fueled by the adrenaline searing through me.

But then I stumble to a stop.

Because Matthew is now standing completely still, holding

Finn in front of him with the blade to his neck. The edge of it just on top of his wing tattoo.

"Matthew!" Eleanor cries. "Please . . ."

He tightens his arm around Finn's chest, squeezing. "Don't move," he says. "Or I'll do it."

"Please, Matthew."

"Shut up!" he screams.

"Just put the knife down," I say, trying to keep my voice level. "Let's talk about it."

He narrows his eyes. Measured. *Determined.* "Actually," he says, "maybe *this* way is better. I'll show them I can do what you would never *dare.* And when I tell them I did it, there's no way you'll win." He smiles and then puts his mouth right next to Finn's ear and whispers, "Little piggy."

I stop myself from launching at him.

I need to calm him down. *But how?*

Appeal to his ego.

"Matthew. I need to tell you something."

"What?"

"I need to thank you."

He frowns. "Huh?"

"I need to thank you because you're right. You've shown me what they really want from us."

I can see Finn breathing rapidly, the thrumming pulse in his neck visible below the blade.

Steady. Easy, Finn.

"Oh, yeah?" Matthew says. "And what is it they *really* want?"

"The Numbers' trials were a mirror of ours." I take a small step forward. "You saw that the only way to remove unhappiness is to end it once and for all. This is the final act of benevolence. Rid the

345

world of it and start again." Finn's eyes flick to me. *Stay calm.* "You deserve to win for understanding that. I was too narrow-minded. Too locked into the thinking of the old world. Too scared. You should win, Matthew." I take another step forward so I'm no more than three feet away. "But Number Five is mine to kill."

Matthew sniffs sharply. "Well, you're too late."

"Please, let me do it."

"Do you think I'm an idiot?"

"No, I don't," I say. "I don't think you're an idiot. You're much cleverer than me. But Manning gave you Betty for a reason. Don't you think she'll be more impressed if you complete the program with the Number she assigned to you?"

I hear Betty whimper.

"Number One," he says sharply. "Don't use her name."

I nod. "I don't want to fight with you. We want the same thing. Why don't we each take the person she wants us to?"

I'm now right in front of them.

But then I hear something above us. A low, pulsing hum.

zumzumzumzum

The air begins to move. The ground shakes. A stark white light cuts down from the sky.

"Seb!" Eleanor shouts. "It's seen us!"

Matthew's eyes glimmer in the light. "She's coming."

Finn desperately tries to wriggle free, but Matthew's arm tightens around him again. As the noise grows, as the helicopter hovers above us, I try to think of some way to stop this. But I'm running out of time.

Fuck it.

I make a grab for the knife.

"Whoa! Easy there, Sebby!" Matthew steps back, pulling Finn

with him, their clothes and hair now billowing in the force of the wind.

"Matthew, just—"

He tilts the blade so its point pushes right into the skin under Finn's chin. "Let's wait for the guest of honor!"

Finn's eyes plead with me, and his whole body begins to tremble. In my periphery I see the helicopter lowering onto the grass, just outside the fence.

"It's time," Matthew says, his eyes wide. Manic. "She's going to see for herself." His face fills with pleasure. He laughs. "She is going to award *so many bloodstones for this.*"

And I suddenly remember.

Bloodstones.

I take a step back. "You know what?" I shout. "You take Number Five." Matthew raises his eyebrows, watching as I shove my hands into the pockets of my pants and shrug. "I should learn. I need to."

The helicopter is on the ground now.

I feel it in my fingers. The bloodstone Ares gave me.

Got you.

Matthew smiles. "Accepting defeat already?"

I shrug again. "Yeah, I am. You should win."

The air begins to still.

"Pathetic," he says. "You hardly tried." The muscles in his hand flicker.

"Matthew?" I say.

"What?"

"I just wanted to say congratulations. You deserve this."

And then, in one movement, I clench my hand around the bloodstone and launch it forward with all my strength.

It smashes right into his skull.

He drops the knife and staggers backward, clutching his face. Then his knees buckle and he hits the floor with a heavy thud, a thick line of blood pooling out of the center of his forehead.

Eleanor gasps.

Finn steps away.

We both stare down at his limp body.

Oh my God.

"Shit, Seb," Finn whispers. "I think you knocked him out." We look to the helicopter, the door not yet open. "We have time," he says. "We get Betty, Eleanor, and we run. To the boatho—"

There's a noise behind us.

Whip.

Rustle.

Thrum.

Click.

I turn. No. *No.*

Artemis steps out from the shadows, pointing the crossbow directly at him. "Move and I shoot."

In the moment that follows, something courses through me like an uncontrollable fire. It burns within my core. As it consumes me, I see Eleanor at the foot of the pole cradling Betty in her arms.

I see Betty's head lolling to the side, eyes rolled back, white.

I see the knife on the ground next to Matthew's unconscious body, right where we slaughtered the pigs.

I see him. Finn. Paralyzed, *shattered* by terror.

I see the door of the helicopter swing open and a shaft of light spill out of it, illuminating a shadowy figure. I see the figure begin to descend the steps.

Then the fire inside me suddenly burns out. But it leaves an ember of complete clarity.

And I know. I know exactly what must happen.

The gate to the Pen creaks opens.

"Seb . . . ," Finn says.

"It's OK," I say quietly.

I watch her step into the golden haze. Rain boots, fur coat, leather gloves. When she reaches Artemis, she stops.

"Sebastian?" Manning says, confused. Almost . . . *sad*. "What is this?"

"I'm done." I say.

"But—"

"I said *I'm fucking done*." She flinches. "No more. I'm not doing this anymore." My voice is loud but calm. Direct. Certain.

Because the ember of clarity remains, glowing softly inside me. And I know there is only one option. The one I have been most afraid of. For so long.

"It's time for the truth," I say. I take Finn's hand in mine and hold it. "No more lies. No more pretending. No more *bullshit*." Finn flinches, but I don't let go. I won't. Not anymore. "So do you want to go first, or should I?"

It's all we have left.

THIRTY-EIGHT
A Breath

For a moment, Manning doesn't speak. She stands completely still in the golden haze.

The creases in her forehead deepen as her eyes move around the Pen like she's trying to draw a line between each thing she sees and connect them together. To Artemis, next to her, crossbow raised, still pointed at us. To Eleanor and Betty at the post behind us. To Matthew on the ground at our feet, then next to him, the knife, the bloodstone. When her eyes reach my hand holding Finn's, they stop. But she doesn't react.

She shifts her gaze to Matthew lying unconscious at our feet. She points her leather-gloved finger at him. "Who did this?"

Finn opens his mouth, about to speak.

"I did," I cut in. "Matthew was going to kill Betty. He was going to kill Finn."

Manning turns to Artemis. "Is this true?"

"No," Artemis says. "That is not correct."

I glare at her. "I just said no more—"

I fall silent as she turns the crossbow from Finn, pointing it right at my head.

"When I arrived," Artemis continues, "Matthew was controlling the Numbers. And Sebastian was trying to stop him."

"That's a lie." I look at Manning. "Don't listen to her."

She keeps her finger pointed at Matthew. "Is he . . . ?"

"He's breathing," Artemis says.

"He's a fucking nutter," Finn spits. "And you made him one."

At this, Manning snaps her head up, her eyes darkening. She points at Finn. But she doesn't look at him. She looks straight at me. "Did *he* make you do this?"

"What?"

"He is clearly still very unwell. . . ."

"No, he didn't make me do it," I say, feeling the ember catch light again, sparking that anger, that *rage*. "And no, he is not *unwell*."

She frowns. "I'm confused," she says slowly. Calmly. "It seems incredibly out of character for you to prevent your Number from receiving the help he needs, Sebastian. And to do *this* to Matthew."

"I just said—"

"I had thought," she continues over me, "that I was coming here to celebrate. I had been told you were achieving so much. Doing so *well*. So, as you can see, I'm a little shocked. This is not what I was expecting. Not at all."

"They have the most bloodstones, Madame," Artemis says. "They were going to win."

"They *were*?" Manning makes a sudden inhalation of breath, expressing a combination of emotions. Excitement. Disappointment.

Regret. Like I have let her down. Like I have *offended* her. "This is . . . This is very—"

"We don't want to *win*," I say. "No way."

She turns to Eleanor. "Eleanor?" she says quietly. "Is this true?"

Eleanor doesn't answer. Her head is down, and her hair hangs loose over her face as she continues to cradle Betty, wiping her mouth with her sleeve.

"Eleanor?" Manning repeats.

Eleanor keeps wiping Betty's mouth.

Manning's lips part, a shadow of pain, *hurt,* infusing her. "Oh . . . I see."

And then something switches inside her. She abruptly nods, drawing herself upright. She looks at her watch. "Come with me, both of you."

"We're not leaving them."

"Sebastian, stop wasting my time." Her voice is stronger now, regaining its authority. "We need to go back to camp and declare the winner, even if it is not the couple I had imagined it would be. I have a panel of important guests waiting to greet them back at the facility."

The press interview. The opportunity.

The ember grows. The *rage.*

"There's no prize," I say.

She frowns. "What did you say?"

"I said there's no prize. *It's not real.*"

She pauses. Her eyes flicker. "It is time to go, Sebastian."

"No."

"Sebastian . . ."

"No!" I shout.

She stiffens. "I am becoming concerned—"

"Good," I say. "You should be. Matthew was going to *kill* Finn. For *you*."

"Sebastian, stop this."

"He figured out exactly what you want. The Pen. The pigs. All the fucking trials. Beating the Numbers into submission." I feel Finn's body tense as my voice rises. "That's why we're here, isn't it? *The most benevolent thing?*"

"What has *happened* to you, Sebastian?" She remains calm. "Nobody wants to *kill* anybody. Quite the contrary. Where has this suddenly come from?"

"Stop doing that. Don't . . . *do* that."

"Who has been feeding you these lies?"

"They're not lies. It's the truth."

"We are *helping* them. You appear to be very con—"

"I'm not *confused*," I cut her off. "In fact, this is the *least* confused I've ever been. Right now, things are very clear to me. You've had us demoralizing them. Demonizing them. *Electrocuting* them. Pushing and pushing them, tearing them apart, removing any sense of humanity so it would be easier for *us* to destroy them." I point at Betty, my finger trembling. "Look at her. Look what you've done to her. *Look at her!*"

She stares at me, cold.

"You can't, can you?"

"I won't be ordered around by you, Sebastian."

"Because you're scared. You're scared that you're wrong."

"You are so far from the truth. . . ."

"The truth?" I laugh, the absurdity of her denial intensifying my anger. "The truth doesn't exist here. You created this. All of this. Look what you've created. *Open your eyes.*" I see Artemis bristle, her crossbow still trained on me. "Where's Dr. Stone?"

"Sebastian, I will not answer while you—"

"Where is she? She should be here."

"We don't have time for this."

"Tell me. *Tell me now.*"

Manning folds her arms and sighs. Like she's annoyed. Like I am annoying her. Like I'm being silly. Crazy. "Fine," she says. "I was going to announce this to everyone at the camp, but since you seem so agitated, I will tell you. Dr. Stone is back at the facility. Last night she had a bad turn in her health again. She is sad that she cannot be here, but she sends her wishes."

"Bullshit. What have you done to her?"

"Excuse me?"

"You were poisoning her."

Her eyes widen a fraction. "No."

"You were drugging her."

"You've gone too far now, Sebastian."

"*I've* gone too far? That's rich. . . ."

"You know nothing. *I was helping her!*" she suddenly bellows, her voice cutting through the Pen. "Dr. Stone has been incredibly unwell for a long time. Her mind has not been strong, and recently she has been refusing her medication. When she is like this, she is not aware she needs it. Covert medication is an important part of getting her to a place where she will take care of herself.

"So do not stand there and act like you know what you're talking about. You know nothing about Eileen. About her mind. About the kind of help it needs. You know nothing about any of this. I am the *one* person who does. I care about her, more than you would ever know."

Lies. All lies.

"You don't want to help her," I say. "You want her to keep her mouth shut."

"The Never Plan," Finn says quietly.

For a split second, I see Manning panic.

Artemis turns the point of the bolt back to him.

"What's the farm?" he says.

"Stop this."

"What is the farm? Ash Farm. What happens there?"

Manning stares at him, narrowing her eyes. "Sebastian, you need to control Number Five. He is very sick. Use your wristband. It's time this ended."

"You like that word, don't you?" he says.

"I beg your pardon?"

"Ended." Her body stiffens. "Yeah. That's right." He lets go of my hand and takes a small step toward her. "I've seen it."

He takes another step.

Artemis tracks him with the bow.

Careful, Finn.

I move to join him, standing at his side.

"I've seen my name in the Never Plan," he says slowly. "Right next to that word. So tell me the truth. Why do you want me dead?"

"Sebastian . . . ," Manning repeats. *"Now."*

"Answer him," I say.

"Why do you hate me so much?" Finn says. "Tell me."

"Control him, Eleanor," Manning shouts. *"Eleanor."*

"Eugenics," he says. "That's your plan. Start a new breed of happy people and kill off the unwell. At the farm." He is calm. Clear. "The sick. The afflicted. The diseased."

"Like the lamb," I say.

Manning shakes her head, and I see she is *smiling*. Like we are *stupid*. "You are so wrong."

"Stop ly—"

"Enough," she snaps. "I am not *lying*. The Never Plan is not what you think it is. It was never meant to be seen. And I am sorry if Dr. Stone has been feeding you these untruths, but I thought you of all people, Sebastian, were strong enough to know better." She flicks her eyes to Finn. "You are better than this."

Fuck this.

I take Finn's hand in mine again and hold it, firm. "But I'm not," I say. "I'm not who you think I am. I don't love who you want me to."

She stares blankly, as if she can't compute my words. As if they're so obscene to her that they make no sense. "You don't know the meaning of the word."

"Maybe not. But I'm figuring it out."

"Oh? You're *figuring it out,* are you? That you love *this person*?" She points to Finn.

"Yeah," I say. "I am. I do."

She laughs. "*Him?* Don't be ridiculous, Sebastian."

"I'm not."

"This boy is *deeply* unwell. Do not let him make you think you are alike, because *that* is the greatest lie of all."

"He doesn't make me think that," I say. "It's true."

Manning turns to Eleanor. "Did you know about this?"

Eleanor looks up. "I . . ." Her eyes dart around the Pen like she's calculating something, drawing a line between us, just like her aunt did.

She clears her throat. "No," she says. "I had no idea. About any of this."

What?

Finn drops his head.

"Eleanor—" I say.

"No, Seb. Don't." She begins to stand.

"That's it." I hear the relief in Manning's voice. "Good."

I watch as Eleanor leaves Betty on the ground and begins to cross the Pen, head up, eyes straight ahead, toward her aunt. She doesn't look at me. Not once.

"Come and stand over here with me, darling," Manning says. "Where you are safe."

Darling. I should have known. This fucking family.

"Eleanor, please," I whisper as she passes. But she keeps going, until she is next to Manning, with Artemis on the other side.

"Fuck you, Eleanor," Finn spits.

When she looks back at him, I realize it's not her anymore. Not *her*, the person I have just met. Just found. She is gone again. Buried.

"You've corrupted Seb, Number Five," she says flatly.

"You have." Manning nods. "Sebastian is clearly not strong enough. You have taken advantage of his vulnerabilities and infected him." *Infected?* "His mind. You have poisoned him"—*poisoned?*— "with the very thing we are trying to eliminate. The very thing that was so rife in the old—"

"The old world is *this* world," I shout over her. "It's the *real* world. This whole place—this pen, this island—is a *lie*. It's *fake*. Everything here is fake. It's a distraction. And no one is admitting it because none of us can face it. None of us can face just how painful it was back there—in the *real world*—so we're all just going along with this.

"But we're just the same. Nothing's changed. The old world

still exists because we brought it with us. I was about to win, wasn't I? And I've been lying the whole time. I'm still unhappy. I'm still angry. I'm still *sad*."

"Yes," Manning says softly. "You are. You're unwell."

"No, I'm not. Everyone is pretending. Except them." I point to Finn, then to Betty. "None of us can be what you want us to be because it *doesn't exist*. I can't. The Ten can't. Artemis and Ares sure as shit can't either."

Artemis aims her crossbow at me, but I don't care. I don't care anymore. "You're both giving it a good go, aren't you? But you aren't happy, Artemis. Not underneath it all. Ares doesn't love you. He's terrified, just like the rest of us." She keeps her aim steady. "None of us are winning here. We're all just losing our minds."

I turn back to Manning, my eyes burning. "Freddie couldn't do it either, could he?"

Her jaw clenches. The muscles in her neck strain.

Eleanor stares at the ground.

"He wouldn't have wanted this," I say quietly. "This would never have changed him. He didn't need changing. The world did. He didn't need to die, and I'm sorry that he did. But it wasn't his fault."

Her lips part, trembling.

Her face softens. Opens. Tears begin to glisten.

Just fucking . . . let it out.

"Please . . . ," I say. "Try and see it from his eyes. From *their* eyes. And you'll know that this is not the answer."

For a split second, I think Manning is going to let it all out. But then she swallows it.

"What do you think you're doing? Both of you?" She steps toward us. "I am making it my life's work to save the future of our youth from this cancer of unhappiness." She stares at me, quivering. "You have the audacity to act like you know me. What I want. Well, you do not. And you know nothing about my son, so do not lecture me about how he felt, or what it was like for him. You are *ignorant* and you are *childish*. You're both just *silly little boys.*

"The truth, since you seem so keen to know it, is this: The Never Plan was something that Dr. Stone created when she was in the depths of her madness. It was a product of her illness. I was keeping it locked in my office so no one would ever see it. To protect *her*. To protect *you*. And yesterday she became so unwell that . . ." She stops. "The truth is, Dr. Stone died last night."

Her words smash into me, knocking me off balance.

"No," I say. "No."

"Liar," Finn says. "You're lying."

Eleanor's hand goes to her mouth.

"I am so sorry," Manning says. "I wish I was. But the world was too much for her and it has sadly taken her from us. She could not cope. That is why I am here. To stop it happening to others."

I feel a tickle on my upper lip, just below my nose, where Matthew hit me. I put my finger to it. Blood again.

I look down.

I see the dagger on the ground, next to him.

Before I can stop myself, I let go of Finn's hand and snatch it up. And then I'm pointing it straight at her. "You killed her, didn't you? How could you do that? How could you? *What is wrong with you?*" I feel the heat of tears cutting down my face. "She was trying to stop you, so you weakened her and now you've silenced her. I know you have!" I'm screaming. Shaking. My whole body alight. "You're sick. Dangerous. You're fucking evil!"

My words ricochet around us.

Manning takes a step back. "Sebastian, it appears the only person who is dangerous is you. Put the knife down."

"No! This needs to stop!"

"Indeed it does." Her eyes flick to Artemis. "Silence him."

Artemis nods. Her finger moves over the trigger.

Eleanor gasps.

But then I realize something.

Finn is no longer next to me.

He is running.

Toward her.

Toward Artemis.

He throws himself at her. Crashing into her so the crossbow flies from her hands. Then he's on top of her. Clawing, yelling.

"Don't you dare! Don't fucking touch him!"

She scrambles out from under him and staggers to her feet. And then she is hitting him. Throwing her fists into his body. His chest. His face.

I'm about to go to him when I feel someone grab my hand from behind and shove me to the ground. As I scramble to my feet, I realize my hand is now empty. The knife is no longer in it. Matthew is no longer on the ground.

When I look back up, I realize why. He is now standing right between Finn and Artemis, and he is holding the knife.

But he's doing something that I can't quite make sense of.

He's pulling it out of Finn's stomach. And it is covered in blood.

Finn staggers sideways. As he collapses, as he hits the ground, the entire world shifts.

Tilts. Shatters. Fragments.

In an instant. A breath.

Everything blurs.

Then somehow I am next to him. I'm kneeling on the ground, pulling up his top, frantically trying to find the wound as Finn twists on his back in the mud, screaming, clutching his stomach.

Where is it where is it where is it?

There.

Oh, God.

I push my hands over the hole, and he wails.

"It's OK, it's OK, it's OK," I repeat because I can't find any other words.

But it's not. *It's not OK.*

"Seb . . ." His voice through shallow breaths. "Fuck . . . Seb . . ."

He strains his body, twisting in agony. My hands slip, and blood oozes everywhere. Oh my God, it's everywhere. Then someone is next to me. Pushing their hands over the hole.

I look up.

"I'll hold it!" Betty shouts. "Help him stay still!"

I take his hand in mine. "Try and keep still." But he isn't looking at me. He's staring at the sky. Mouth open. "Finn? Listen to me. . . . Squeeze my hand, it'll help . . ."

"Seb . . . ," he says again.

His eyes find mine. *He is so scared.*

"Just squeeze my hand." I feel a faint pressure as he does. "That's it. Well done. We're going to get you help."

Why is no one helping?

"Seb, I—"

"It's OK. It is." I see the tears falling from my face down onto his. "Keep squeezing, Finn."

I hear noises. Voices.

When I look up, I see dark shapes moving into the Pen.

"Help us!" I cry. "Help!"

As they come into focus, I see the rest of the Ten. Staring. Wide-eyed. Frozen.

Someone steps in front of me. *Ares.* "What happened, Sebastian?"

"Please help us!"

But he just looks at me, and I can see he is completely terrified.

"Sebastian has lost his mind," Manning says.

And then someone is dragging me, pulling me away from Finn, tearing our hands apart.

"No!" I scream. "Get off me! Fucking help him! He's going to die!"

I see their black boots.

They keep pulling me, covered in his blood. Warm on my hands.

Away from Finn. And toward the sound of helicopter blades.

I claw. Scratch. Bite.

"Get off me! Somebody help h—"

Something heavy meets the side of my head. A pain radiates through my skull.

A darkness emerges at the edges of my vision.

I fight against it.

But it is so strong. I can't make it stop.

It pulls me under.

It wins.

The darkness wins.

THIRTY-NINE
Small Circles

I'm in a white room.

I have cried. I have screamed.

I've screamed his name. So many times.

I've hit the walls. Over and over. Padded and dense.

I've screamed into them. But they swallow my voice. Steal it from me.

My clothes are white.

My thoughts are white.

White noise.

Everything is white.

The door creaks open. A man in white appears, holding a tray out in front of him.

On it, a small white plate. In the middle of the plate, a pill.

"Your medication," he says.

"I don't want it."

"You need it."

"I'm not taking it." He turns. "Wait. *Wait*—"

But he leaves without a word.

More trays. Food and water. More pills on plates.

All left untouched.

I can't cry anymore. I'm not able to.

The door opens again. Figures in white coats. More than one.

"Sit up."

I can't.

"Sebastian, sit up. We don't want to hurt you."

I *can't.*

Hands grab me. Pull me up. Hold my arms behind my back.

Fingers in front of my face. Holding a white pill.

"Take it."

"No."

"You need to. You are unwell."

My mouth is forced open. I try to bite at the fingers as they push it into my mouth. But I'm too weak.

Its metallic taste spreads across my tongue. I want to spit it out, but the hands keep my mouth closed until it dissolves.

When they let go, I scream.

The door shuts.

And I'm left with only the bitter aftertaste.

It makes me feel slow.

The pill.

Weak. Tired. Fuzzy. Like I'm in a trance.

But it takes the pain away.

It makes me feel numb. Empty.

Finn.

I'm so sorry.

I can't think about you.

I'm sorry.

"Why are you on the floor, Mr. Seaton? Can you sit up, please? We need you to start talking if you want to get better."

I lift my head from the white tiles to see a man I don't know. In a white coat. He has a badge on. A smiling face.

"Can I go outside?" My voice rips at my throat.

"Absolutely not. You are currently very unwell. You have exhibited dangerous behaviors that we need to monitor."

"I want to talk to my parents. Is there a phone I can use?"

"They are aware of the situation."

"Let me talk to them."

"That would be unwise."

Gradually I sit up, leaning against the padded wall behind me. I bring my knees up to my chest. "Where am I?"

"You are at the HappyHead facility."

No.

"This is the safest place for you at the moment."

No.

"You are experiencing something we call an intense depressive episode with psychotic features, specifically delusional ideation. Would you agree with that?"

"No."

He sighs. "You need to start cooperating. A lot has happened."

I put my head between my knees.

Go away.

Go away go away go away.

"Perhaps I will come back when you are feeling less distressed."

He moves to the door.

"Wait." I lift my head. "I want to speak to Dr. Stone."

He stops. "She has sadly passed away. You know this, Sebastian."

"I don't believe you."

"I work with Professor Manning now, here at the facility, as a replacement for her. My name is Dr. Hunt. But you can call me Tim, if you would like?"

No, I would not like that.

He smiles. "I want to help you get healthy. It might take time, but we will get there. I hear you have hardly eaten. That you are saying some concerning things. When they brought you here, you were aggressive toward the staff."

He turns to leave.

"Wait," I say again. Fuck. It hurts. *It hurts so much.* "Finn . . . ," I say. "Is he . . . ?"

"I am under strict instructions not to discuss this with you. Not yet. We do not want to add to your agitation or exacerbate your deterioration."

My *deterioration.*

"And Eleanor?"

"Eleanor Banks?"

"Yes. Eleanor Banks."

"Eleanor does not want to speak to you."

"Who can I speak to then?"

He pauses. "Professor Manning said there is someone who might be able to help you."

Two figures stand in front of me. I stare at their shoes.

One pair black. One white.

"Hey, mate." I'm dreaming. I must be. "It's me."

I know that voice. I know it well. From somewhere a long time ago. When everything was different.

She steps toward me. Her face comes into focus.

"What's going on, mate?"

Shelly.

She sits on the bed next to me.

My cheeks burn with hot tears. "Oh my God. Shelly . . ."

I grab her arms in my hands. Push my head onto her shoulder.

"Help me, Shelly. Help me . . . Please . . ." I sob.

I sob into her.

"Hey, Seb. Hey." I feel her palm between my shoulder blades making slow circles, small and gentle. "It's OK, mate. It's going to be OK. It is." I lift my head. "That's exactly why I'm here. To help you."

Oh, thank God.

She turns to the man at the door. "It's OK. I can do this alone. I think it might be better."

"I have to stay," he says. "For your own safety."

She nods.

"Madame Manning asked me to come and see you, Seb. She said you've been having a difficult time since—"

"Manning?"

"Yeah, Manning."

"She's a fucking *maniac,* Shelly." Spray flies from my mouth and onto the sleeve of her green hoodie. She doesn't seem to notice. "*This place is sick.* The whole thing." She stares at me. "What, Shelly?"

She frowns. "She told me you might say that."

"Shelly . . ."

She leans toward me. "I dunno. . . . It was all a bit nuts at first, but—I'm starting to really feel . . . I don't know. Different."

"No, Shelly."

"Less . . . negative, I suppose."

"Shelly, you can't believe her. *You can't.*"

"And . . ." She smiles innocently, like a little child. "They think I'm great."

"But—"

"She says I'm very *headstrong.*" Her smile widens. "You always said that."

"I—"

"And she loves you too, Seb." She nudges me with her elbow. "She's always going on about how amazing you are. But she's really worried—"

"Shelly, *please.*"

"Buddy . . ." She exhales. "She told me you're experiencing symptoms of . . . She said that you're *stressed,* after what happened. That your mental health has taken a really bad turn. That you're very low. I'm so sorry that you're going through this, Seb. She told me that the pills—"

"She's *lying*—"

"That you might need a stronger dose. Just to help get your brain back in order."

"You don't have long," the man at the door says. "Two minutes."

Shelly turns to him. Nods.

"I've got something to tell you." She raises her eyebrows excitedly. "I've met someone." A different kind of smile creeps across her face now. *She's happy.* "Can you believe it?"

"No, Shelly . . ."

"He's so cool, Seb. I know you'll like him. His name is Ethan. He loves Bowie too."

She takes my hand in hers. "I need you to listen to me. It's important." My head hurts. "It's good news. You don't need to be scared."

I wait as she holds my hand. I wait for the good news.

"Manning has told me to tell you something." She shuffles toward me. "Me and Ethan are one of the couples going to Elmhallow. Isn't that amazing?"

Oh, God, no.

"Shelly—Elmhallow is hell. *You can't go there.*"

"And she wants you to go back too."

It feels like the room has flipped. Like it's thrown my body upside down and smashed it back into the floor.

"What?"

"You'll be going back, Seb. To get the help you need."

"Shelly, no—"

"She said you'll be going there as something she called a Number. In just a few days' time."

This isn't real. It can't be. . . .

"And what's really cool, Seb, is she said *I* can be the one to help you. She didn't tell me what it all means, but she said you'd understand. She said you'd be so pleased to hear that me and Ethan will be your Couple while you're there. We will help you get better."

This can't—

"We'll be there *together*. She thinks it's a perfect match."

Oh, God.

I can't speak.

I can't breathe.

I'm going to be sick.

I lean forward, my head on the white sheets. Tears pouring out of me.

"It's OK, Seb." Her hand begins to rub my back again. Small circles. "We're going to help you get better. We're going to get you out of this."

"No . . . ," I croak.

Then my body moves. I feel my hands squeeze her arms.

She winces. "Ow, Seb! You're hurting me." She leans back, away from me.

I squeeze harder. I can't control it. My nails are digging in.

"Get off me, Seb!"

I start screaming. I scream and scream as I pull her toward me.

"Stop! You're going to hurt me!"

The man in white is there, tearing me off her.

The door opens. More men.

Dragging me away. Throwing me into the corner of the room.

Shelly stands in the doorway. "I'll see you there, Seb. At Elmhallow. It won't be like this forever, I promise."

And then she is gone.

My Shelly is gone.

More medication. More fighting. More losing.

Say you're a pathetic loser and I'll think about telling you.

I'm a pathetic loser.

Say it again.

I'm a pathetic loser.

A man in white enters my white room.

"Madame Manning has a message for you."

I open my mouth. Dry. Sticky. "I don't want to hear it."

His black eyes stare back at me. "She would like you to watch the interview."

"What interview?"

"The winners' press interview."

I sit up. "I'll be leaving this room?"

"No. It will be televised. Live. You will watch it in here. Madame Manning would like you to see what you have chosen to remove yourself from." He turns. "I'll be back soon."

FORTY

Her

When I lift my head again, the man is back. Standing against the wall.

I can hear voices. "It's about to begin," the man says. He then hands me something. A tablet.

I pull myself up and sit cross-legged on the bed, taking it in my hands. I look at the screen. On it, what appears to be a live feed.

I see a small table with a microphone, like something you might see on the news, and three chairs. A yellow tablecloth. A big smiling face across it. In the background, little mounds of grass. Daffodils. Spelling a word. Is that . . . *Serenity*? The pods. I can see the pods. Where we got matched.

Behind the table, there's a row of chairs. I recognize the two adults at either end. Professor Lindström and Professor Fernsby, the therapy leads from the facility.

And between them sit ten teenagers in green tracksuits. Chatting excitedly. *The next Ten.*

One of them is Shelly. Sitting next to a boy. Holding his hand.

Tall and strong, with glasses. *Ethan.* She smiles up at him, wrinkling her nose.

I can hear cameras clicking, somewhere that I can't see. Somewhere behind the camera.

And then a woman walks into the frame.

Perfect hair. Perfect suit. Perfect nails.

The ten teenagers, Lindström, Fernsby, they all stand. They all begin to clap.

She sits down behind the table with the yellow cloth, two chairs remaining empty on either side of her. She smiles, looking just to the side of the camera lens, out at her audience. She then moves the microphone toward her.

"Good morning, everyone," she says. It squeaks, the sharp noise of the feedback making her wince. "Oops!" She laughs. "Well, that was a good start."

The next Ten laugh. Fernsby and Lindström laugh. I hear other people laughing too. Behind the camera.

She leans forward. "Let's start again. Hello, everyone."

Voices say hello back.

"As you know, I am Professor Gloria Manning, and I am so glad that you could join us today in Serenity. Welcome to the future of happiness." More clapping. "We know how long you have waited, due to the unforeseen circumstances of Dr. Stone's health, and we are grateful for your patience." She stops, bowing her head. "She is doing just fine, but she wants us to continue without her. And so here we are."

She is doing fine? Is she alive? Or is Manning fucking lying?

Her eyes glimmer in the way they always do. When she is so proud of herself.

It makes me feel sick.

"We wanted to invite a select group of people to join us, and you are the lucky few. Press, health-care professionals, and members of government who have helped fund this wonderful opportunity. Some of the participants' parents are with us too." She smiles and waves. "As you all know, the world is currently a very bleak place. We have needed to keep our light shining brightly, away from the darkness. Until the world is ready to have us."

"Thank you for the privilege, Professor Manning," I hear someone call out.

Her eyes move to where the voice comes from. "Ah! John. Thank you. It is so nice to see you here. You are most welcome."

She pulls at her shirtsleeve, straightening it out. "We know many people are desperate to hear what is going on behind the scenes. To have a *closer* look at what we are accomplishing here. So you will now meet some of the young people themselves. Some of the best. The strongest. The most committed to change. I want you to see with your own eyes what we have managed to achieve here at HappyHead."

A flicker of a memory enters my brain.

It is her ego that may, in the end, help us.

Who said that? Someone said that to me. No, it was in a letter.

"Now without further ado . . ." Manning's eyes widen, filling with anticipation. "I would like to introduce you to Eleanor and her partner, Matthew."

I feel a weight drop into me.

Matthew.

It can't be him. *It can't be.*

I move the screen closer, as two people step forward.

Her: hair scraped back. Pink clips.

Him: hair neatly combed to the side.

Both wearing brand-new yellow hoodies. Yellow pants.

They wave and smile as everyone applauds. And the two of them look . . . happy. Really happy.

"Mum!" Matthew calls out as they sit in the chairs on either side of Manning.

"If you would like a photograph," Manning says into the microphone. "Which I know you all would—this is your chance."

She puts her arms around them. Eleanor shuffles into her. Matthew pushes his hand through his hair. And they all smile. Their faces flicker in the light of the camera flashes.

"Enough," Manning says, waving her hand. "I will now take questions."

She points at someone behind the screen.

"Hello, Paul Thompson, from the *Telegraph*."

"Ah, hello, Paul."

"Wonderful to be here."

"Thank you for coming." She smiles. She loves it. *She is loving it.*

"Let's start by asking how you came to the difficult decision to take young people away from their homes in order to embark on this treatment regime?"

I hear murmuring.

"Well, Paul, that is a brilliant question. However, I must correct you." She is strong. Commanding. "I think it's important we are really honest with ourselves here. Our young people are *not* safe at home. We knew they needed to be taken away from the world that is, to put it frankly, killing them. Suicide rates are skyrocketing, and the NHS is not coping with the demands placed on its mental health facilities. It is broken. It cannot deal with the pressure and the staff is exhausted.

"We knew we needed to do something radical. To start again. Reset. Sick people cannot get well where sickness thrives. We *needed* to bring them to a place they could feel safe. And that is here."

She's in control. Total control.

"Next," she says.

"Marissa Palfrey, Department of Health."

"Ah, Marissa, what a pleasure."

"And you, Professor. It is an honor to see someone really taking action."

Manning bows her head modestly. "Thank you."

"Let us talk about the theory behind the assessments."

"Ah! The theory. The most important part." Manning nods. "The theory is based on years of work we have done, looking at external factors that are negatively impacting teenagers. Technology being the first and most obvious. We did countless studies, peer-reviewed research papers, gathering qualitative and quantitative data that highlighted the various ways in which young people relate to not only others, but to themselves, via social media.

"We also looked at how it affects brain function. Social media changes the levels of dopamine and serotonin in our brains. That is a fact. The reward pathways of our children are beginning to rely wholly on external validation. That is not natural. It is not who we were created to be, as humans. It is destructive. We needed to go somewhere isolated, phone-free, internet-free, and, yes, contact-free. Without distractions or any opportunity to be brought back into that toxicity. Because at home, it is just a finger tap away. It is truly terrifying."

She is truly terrifying.

And as she carries on, she remains in control. In command. She nods, listening to their questions. Answering them thoughtfully. Cleverly. Confidently. And she sounds so *honest*. At times, I nearly believe her. *Understand* her. Because she is so good.

She is a brilliant liar. Just like her niece.

Eleanor listens to her aunt's responses. Laughing with her. Nodding in agreement. Smiling. Always smiling.

And then there's Matthew. I nearly forgot. *Nearly.*

Matthew, the boy who—

Blood on my hands, thick and black—

Block it out.

He is sitting there, on the other side of Manning. Winning.

The perfect participants. The perfect happy people.

After a while, I just can't watch anymore. I put the tablet on the floor, and I stare at the tiles next to it, allowing their whiteness to consume me.

But then I hear something.

A man's voice. Posh. Clipped.

"My name is Tom Jarrow. Member of the civil service."

I look back at the screen.

Manning's eyebrows momentarily raise, a little flustered.

Tom Jarrow? Where have I heard that name before?

And then I remember. Tom Jarrow. *Stone's friend.*

She told us about him in the hut by the lighthouse. The man she wanted us to give the pager to. The one I lost in the sea.

"I would first like to say that I was saddened to hear that Dr. Stone has been unwell. She is a good friend and has been difficult to get hold of these past few months, which is unlike her."

I can see Manning's mouth twitch, her smile faltering for a split second. "I don't think—"

"She has the strongest mind I know. Her ability to know what is good and right in this world is admirable. It is a shame she cannot be here." I remember what Manning said in the Pen. *Her mind has not been strong for a very long time.* Liar. "And I know that she would want us to have the opportunity to hear from the participants themselves, not just the people in charge."

I see Eleanor's eyes narrow.

Manning shuffles in her seat. She pulls the microphone toward her. "We really don't have time for any more questions, Mr. . . . Jarrow, is it? Yes, sorry." She starts to stand.

"Just one for the participants," his voice cuts in. "What has it been like for you two?" Manning stops, her mouth half open. "How do *you* feel about it all?"

Eleanor remains calm. Focused. Poised.

"I'll answer," Matthew says eagerly.

Eleanor looks across to him. "I'd like to answer, if that's OK?" She turns to her aunt. "I'll be quick, I promise," she says. "I won't ramble on like usual." She laughs.

The people behind the camera laugh too. Excited to hear her.

For a moment, Manning's face doesn't move. But then I see it relax. "OK, just . . . a quick one," she says.

She hands Eleanor the microphone. As she does, she beams at her.

Proud. Proud of her niece. Of her creation.

Eleanor takes the microphone. Matthew watches, chewing his lip.

She looks out at the audience and holds it up in front of her mouth. But then she pauses. "One moment."

She reaches her other hand up to her head. Then she moves it around, fiddling with her hair. When she takes it away, she places something on the table in front of her.

I pick up the tablet again and squint at it.

Two pink clips.

"That's better," she says. "I didn't feel like myself. And someone clever once told me it's important that I always do." She turns and looks directly into the camera.

Right at me.

My heart jolts. Because she changes. Her face drops. Her smile disappears.

And I see her, staring back at me.

Her. In all her fucking glory.

Eleanor.

And then she opens her mouth and she begins to speak.

FORTY-ONE
Therapy

When I'd just turned fifteen, I went to my first and only therapy session. It was not long after the PlayStation broke. Because after the PlayStation broke, I changed.

That's what Mum and Dad said. That's what everyone said. They all agreed that I had become withdrawn. Preoccupied. Agitated. *Low.* Those were the words that were used.

Dad found the lady online. He told me he had spent days scrolling through the profiles on the *Psychology Today* website so he could be sure that the person would be the *right fit.* He presented his phone to me like he'd discovered the holy grail of therapists.

"See." He pointed to the lengthy biography under the picture of her face. "She works with young people who struggle with low self-esteem, isolation, stress, bullying—"

"Oh, and look, Seb," Mum chipped in, glancing over my shoulder. "Look at this bit. *We will work toward happiness together. It is my belief that it can only be achieved through connecting with others.* Sounds positive."

I looked at the therapist's mug shot. Tight curly hair and glasses. Her smile was wide enough to say *warm,* but also *don't worry, parents, I am stern.* Stern-warm.

The session was to be an hour long. A whole hour of talking.

I looked at the name above her face. Prudence Bamford-Cargill.

"Prudence means 'wisdom,'" Dad said.

In the car on the way to her house, I googled "prudence." "It means caution, Dad," I said.

"Hmm?" I could tell he wasn't listening. He was too busy looking at the house numbers, trying to find the right one.

"Ah, here it is!" He slammed on the brakes.

It was a big house, with neatly pruned bushes and flowers in the garden.

"Is she rich?"

"I assume so, son. Your mum and I are practically re-mortgaging the house for these six sessions."

I knew he was trying to make a joke, but neither of us laughed.

"Right, in you go," he said. "I'll wait out here in the car. Just . . . be honest, son."

When I got inside, she said I could call her Pru. Then she showed me into her living room.

I sat down on the faded orange couch opposite her. I looked at her potted plants. Her big armchair. Her cat sleeping on the window ledge behind her. Her huge mug on the coffee table with a cartoon zebra on it.

She said that I seemed distracted. I said I felt it. She asked me if I had always been that way. And I said yes, probably.

She said my parents were worried because I was isolating myself and I wasn't talking to anyone. That I wasn't looking after myself. Not washing or eating. That I had made some comments that had frightened them.

She then asked me if I felt that was a correct interpretation of things. I said no.

She waited.

I hated the silence, so I shrugged and said, "Well, maybe. It's maybe *their* interpretation of things."

She then said that, for some people, reality is hard to be in. She said that for those people who are looking to escape it, it can be a very lonely place to be. That seeking to escape the "present moment" is a difficult thing to do because, ultimately, we won't find what we need outside of it.

She then asked me if I understood that.

I crossed my arms in front of me and dropped my head, hoping she might just forget I was there. But the silence was so heavy that I started to construct a reply in my head to fill it. Something along the lines of how I was just not a very sociable person, which was all fine and normal for a teenager. But instead of answering, I suddenly began to cry. And once I started I couldn't stop.

She passed me a box of tissues, and I wiped my face with one until it disintegrated in my fingers.

And then I said yes, I did understand. I had not been able to be in the "present moment" because for some reason I did not like it. It was not a nice place to be. And yes, I wanted to be somewhere else.

She asked me where that place was. That destination.

I said that I didn't really know but I was trying to find it.

She then said that it wasn't my fault. That I didn't need to blame myself, because it was clear to her I was doing that.

And she kept talking, then waited while I tried to answer her questions. To begin with I hated every word that left my mouth. I felt like I didn't make sense, or I sounded weird or pathetic. But then, over the course of that one hour, it began to get easier. And I found myself talking, *really* talking, saying things I'd never told anyone before.

About my life. My family. About my love of David Bowie. I even told her about Pastor Johnny. I told her how I thought that so much of what he said was total rubbish, but I felt bad for thinking that because no one else seemed to. I told her, very quietly, that I knew I fancied boys, but it was probably not a great idea, considering.

Then I told her that I thought I might be a bad person. That was the word that kept coming to mind. Or boring or bland or annoying. Or all of them.

I said I was so tired of being in my own head, stuck with myself all the time. Because it was suffocating. It terrified me, being with myself, because I knew that it was going to be *endless*. That it was going to be forever.

I told her that I thought I might have this thing inside me that was bad. Maybe it was evil, I wasn't sure. I hadn't figured it out yet. But if it was, maybe that meant *I* was evil. So I just wanted to cut it out, or push it down, or try and get away from it. I said that I was worried if people really saw it, whatever that thing was, they'd hate it, or be scared of it too. And that was the worst part. I didn't want anyone else to see it.

I told her how I'd always been scared. Of myself. Of life, or the present moment, or whatever the hell she wanted to call it.

I'm just fucking scared all the time. I just want it to . . . stop.

I then apologized for swearing.

But she just nodded. Made me feel like what I was saying was OK.

And it was as if something had lifted off me. That desire to run. That need to escape.

"Well," she then said. "Thank you for sharing that, Seb." She looked at me for what felt like an eternity. "I don't think you're a bad person. Quite the opposite. I think you're bright and funny and insightful and wonderfully sensitive."

I said I hated that word. Sensitive.

She suggested that I should try not to. That being sensitive was a great thing and it was a shame that I wanted to change that. It had just led me to be very honest with her, which not many people are willing to do, apparently.

She then picked up her zebra mug of now-cold coffee and sipped it. "And who knows, Seb," she said, not seeming to notice or mind, "maybe one day you will meet people who will see you, the *real* you—this person you are so afraid of. And they won't think you are bad or evil. They won't hate you. They won't try and change you. They will, in fact, love you. They will love you because you managed to hold on to all those special and unique things that make you who you are, in the face of a world that wants you to be something else. Because you showed them that reality *is* painful, but you kept going. Because you are honest and it will make them want to be honest themselves. It is, after all, the one thing we are all really searching for."

"What is?" I said.

"Ourselves." She leaned forward in her armchair so it creaked. "And the most amazing thing of all is that when you find it, your destination, *yourself,* you will realize that you are able to give that love back to other people. And whoever is fortunate enough to receive it from you will be very lucky. Because it is rare, Seb. It is rare that someone is willing to say 'I'm just fucking scared all the time.' But when you hear someone else say it, don't you agree that it's just a lovely thing? Doesn't it make you feel safer? A lot less lonely?" She smiled. "I know I do."

She then took another sip of her cold coffee. And I didn't know what to do first: answer her question or ask if therapists are allowed to say the word "fuck."

And then the session was over.

She asked me if I would like to have another one, at the same time the following week. I said yes. So she said I should tell my dad to give her a call and they would arrange it. But when I got back in the car and he asked me how it went, I panicked. I panicked that she would tell him what I said. All the bad things I had said. All the bad things I was. So I told him she was weird and that she'd said the word "fuck."

"Well, that's concerning." He looked at me, eyes wide. "We'll cancel the rest of them. Not to worry, son."

And that was it. I never went back.

But now I sometimes wonder what it would have been like, if I hadn't panicked. If I had gone back. I wonder what *I* would have been like. If I would have been stronger. Better. Happier. More honest with myself, and others.

I wonder if things would have been different.

Or if they had to happen exactly the way they did.

THE PRESENT MOMENT

I fiddle with my napkin. Pick at it, while I watch the other cus-
tomers.

On their laptops. Their phones.

Making baby noises into strollers.

Sipping their hot drinks.

Eating biscotti. Lemon drizzle.

I listen to the hiss of the coffee machine. The clink of crockery.

A lady with an apron on walks over to me. She smiles.

"Hiya, love, you all right?"

"Yeah, thanks, I'm good. Are you?"

"Not too bad, ta. Can I get you anything?"

"I'm just waiting for someone. Can I order when they get here?"

"Course you can, love."

She looks down at my forearm, at the inside of it, just below
my rolled-up sleeve. "I *love* that. I've always wanted one." She
looks up at me. "Did it hurt?"

"Not really."

"Looks new?"

"Two days ago."

"Oh. Fresh!"

"Yeah."

"I've heard the pain can be kind of . . . *nice*." She smiles again, a little sheepishly now. "Did you find that?"

"Um . . . No, I didn't. But I can understand why people might."

She nods. "What is it?"

"A flower."

"Well, I can see that, love. What kind?"

"It's called a gladiolus."

"It's really beautiful. Does it have a special meaning?"

I pause.

"Oh, it's a *personal* one."

"No, it's not that. I just—"

"Say no more, love. I'll stop prying. Come up to the counter when you're ready."

"Cheers."

She smiles at me one more time, so her nose scrunches up, then makes her way around the empty tables, gathering up dirty cups.

As I look back down at my napkin, I can hear something from the TV up on the wall behind me. The news.

"*The unhappiness epidemic continues—the growing spike in the rate of suicides in young people has caused major concerns for the World Health Organization, who has expressed that they are still working tirelessly to find a solution. . . .*"

I turn to look at it.

I see a woman talking, sitting behind a desk. She is wearing a purple blouse with blow-dried hair, and I can see her eyes flicker slightly as she reads the autocue in front of her. I notice her nail polish is bright yellow.

"HappyHead—a recent experimental program designed to tackle the crisis—has been suspended for the foreseeable future. The government has responded to the facility's closure and encourages any concerned parents or guardians not to speculate. The mother of Eleanor Banks, the seventeen-year-old girl who made a series of shocking allegations at a press interview five months ago, reports that she is struggling with the fallout and is asking for privacy at this time."

The news reader's face disappears as a silent clip of the interview starts to play. I see Eleanor speaking passionately into the camera as Professor Fernsby tries to pull the microphone out of her hand.

"The health secretary, John Wentworth, has made a statement to say that an independent review will determine the true nature of the allegations. . . ."

I've only seen it once. Once was enough.

I should look away. *Just look away.* But I can't.

". . . and that much of what was said cannot be verified yet. The review will correlate findings to see if HappyHead was at fault—and if the death of Dr. Eileen Stone was in any way suspicious, as suggested. Mark Shore, an employee of HappyHead, has been missing since the facility's closure.

"Allegations were also made about two of Manning's 'well-being instructors'—James Barton and Mia Sefton—and the methods they allegedly used to help the teenagers acquire happiness. However, they have a growing number of vocal supporters, who praise the idea of robust techniques, calling them 'necessary' in our 'snowflake society'—"

Their faces appear on the screen. Two passport photos. They look so . . . *different*. So . . . *normal*.

Artemis, *Mia,* with cropped hair, shaved at the side, eyeliner, and black ear studs.

And Ares. *James.* Trimmed stubble; wavy, shoulder-length hair. Tanned. Smiling.

I hardly recognize them.

"All the evidence of abuse is currently only circumstantial, and disputed. The reputable professor Gloria Manning has spoken passionately about the allegations coming from a place of unwellness itself, only further highlighting the insidious nature of the epidemic—"

A clip of Manning talking to some press appears, sending a shock through my body like a jolt of electricity.

zzzz

OK. Time to go back to the napkin. I start picking it apart, fingers trembling, until it's in bits all over the table.

"Hey."

I look up. "Oh, hey!"

"Sorry, the queue in the corner shop took ages."

"Don't worry. I was having a chat with the nice coffee lady."

He holds up a pack of Jolly Ranchers. "Got them." He takes off his coat and puts it over the back of the chair opposite me. "Right, you want anything? I'm getting a coffee. And some munch. I'm dead hungry."

"Me too, I'm starving."

"What have they got?"

"Cakes, I think."

"Perfect. You want a drink?"

"Just a can of pop, please."

"Pop. Great."

He begins to walk away, then stops. "Almost forgot." He leans down and kisses me quickly on my lips. Then I see him wince.

"You OK?"

"Yeah, it's just . . . twinging." He puts his hand on his stomach, then flicks his eyes to the TV and frowns. "They need to turn that shit off. I'll ask them."

"I'll do it. You need to watch yourself."

"Nah, I'm fine," he says. "I can't just sit down forever. I'll be one sec."

I watch the back of him as he makes his way over to the counter—his black jeans, his black T-shirt, his freshly cut hair. He speaks quietly with the nice lady behind it.

She blushes and looks over at me. *So sorry,* she mouths.

I hold my hand up and smile. *It's fine.*

She grabs for the remote and points it at the screen. Manning's face suddenly turns into Beyoncé dancing on top of a car. Yeah. Maybe that is better.

"Here you go," Finn says when he returns. He holds out a plate to me. "Cookies."

"Those look *amazing.*"

He looks at my forearm. "Is it still sore?"

"No."

"A little bit?"

"Um . . . Maybe a little bit."

He smiles. "Let me see."

I lift it up to him.

He leans forward and stares at it, his tongue between his teeth. "It's fucking cool, Seb. If I do say so myself."

I look down at the delicate twisted lines of black ink seared into my skin, creating shapes of petals that weave up the inside of my arm. "I love it," I say.

"Well, that's good. I mean, my drawing is now going to be on you *forever,* so I'm glad about that."

I pull my sleeve over it as he sits down opposite me. "Ow."

"Watch it! You'll get it infected."

"Soz."

He laughs.

I yank my chair in a bit. "So what are we doing today?"

"Good question. Day three of Manchester. The city is your oyster."

"We've done a lot."

"Oh, there's plenty more. . . ." He pauses. "Your train back is tomorrow afternoon, right?"

"Yeah . . ."

He looks at me in a way that makes my skin prickle. "You want to stay longer, don't you?"

"Yeah. I do."

He grins. "I knew it."

"Are your folks OK with that?"

"Um . . . Yeah. *Course.* They fucking love you, Seb."

"They love *you.*"

He picks up his coffee and sips it, thinking. "Right. I have an idea."

"Go on."

"Today we shall just . . . do nothing."

"*Yes.* That sounds mint. We could just go to the park? Get some Bowie on the speakers?"

"Perfect," he says.

I look out the window. "It's raining."

"Ah, it'll clear up."

"Will it?"

"Probably not. But it's all part of the charm, don't you think?"

"It definitely is."

He watches the rain as it begins to drum on the glass, his eyes flickering over the redbrick buildings lining the street.

"Thanks," he then says quietly.

"What for?"

"Getting me back here."

"I didn't—"

"You did," he says, still gazing out the window. "You got us all back."

"It was you who saved my life, Finn."

He turns to me and lowers his voice. "You know, when I was lying on the ground in the Pen, when they pulled you away from me, I thought I was a goner. I thought you were too, to be honest, Seb. I thought I'd never see this place again. I thought I'd never see you again." He stops. "But then . . ."

"Here we are."

A flicker of a smile. "Here we are."

"It's all thanks to Eleanor."

"Hmm," he says, chewing his lip. "You always say that." I watch him thinking for a moment. "Seb, do you ever wonder . . . ?"

"What?"

"I dunno. It doesn't really matter."

"No. Go on. . . ."

He looks up. "Do you ever wonder *why*?"

"Why Manning brought you back to the facility?"

He nods.

"I think . . . I think you're right. It doesn't really matter."

"Yeah," he says, looking back out the window. "It doesn't."

But the truth is I have wondered why. Many times. Many things.

I've wondered if she brought him back because she changed her mind. That she realized in that moment what she had done, what she had created, *who* she had created, and it scared her. It woke her up. The sight of Finn, on the ground, dying in front of her.

But then she let Matthew win. So I don't really buy that one.

I've wondered if she brought him back because she wanted to do it. Because she actually wanted to take Finn to the farm, with Eleanor and Matthew, as she had always intended.

I've wondered if she saw Freddie when she looked at Finn and felt some kind of connection or empathy.

I've wondered if she was still undecided. If she wasn't sure what she wanted.

I have sometimes wondered if Ares had something to do with it. James. If when he turned up at the Pen, he had a moment of compassion and convinced her to save him.

Part of me would like to believe that.

And sometimes, very rarely—because it scares me when I do—I have wondered if she didn't want them dead at all. If Matthew was wrong. If we all were. And, if that was the case, what Ash Farm would have looked like.

But I try not to think about it. I try not to think too much nowadays. I've decided it's not helpful.

I can hear Finn humming quietly under his breath as he watches the rain. I think it's a song called "Disorder" by a band called Joy

Division. He's been playing me his music. They were from Manchester. I really like it.

"It's so weird that you were actually in the helicopter with me," I say. "I had no idea."

"Feels like a long time ago now."

"Yeah . . ."

"Was all so fucking mad, wasn't it? Like, *Eleanor.* I mean, *proper* dark horse, that one. I thought we'd lost her, in the Pen. But she put on a good little show, didn't she? Jesus. Knowing we'd only gone and fucked it, so starting her own one-woman mission. Giving that award-winning performance." He smiles. "Hats off to her. Best liar I ever met."

"She always was," I say. "But she was better at the truth. Much more convincing."

Finn puts his elbows on the table and leans toward me, narrowing his eyes. "I dunno, Seb," he says quietly. "I think she must have learned it from someone." As he brushes my hair out of my eyes with his fingers, it makes my stomach do a little flip. "What she said at the press interview. It was all you." I shrug. "At the end of it, when they were trying to get her to stop . . . and she was shouting about a *Truth Train*? Come on, Seb. That *definitely* came from you."

"Maybe." I smile. *"Choo-choo."*

He laughs, shaking his head at me. *"Choo-*fucking-*choo."* Then he puts his hand on mine, linking our fingers together. "I knew it. You nutter."

We sit in silence for a while, and I watch the rain hitting the street.

"Oh," he then says. "I meant to tell you. I got a text from Betty."

"Oh, yeah?"

"She wants to have a get-together."

"Put it in the group chat," I say. "The others will probably want to join."

"Yeah, good idea."

He picks up his phone. As he starts scrolling, I look at the black polish on his nails, chipped just at the top where he bites them. "Where are you . . . ? Come on . . . Come on . . . Ah! *Bottom Percentile*. Got you."

He starts to type.

"Here you are, boys," the nice lady says, appearing with a tray.

"Oh, thanks," I say as she places a glass with ice and a Fanta lemon in front of me.

She places a cappuccino in front of Finn. "Thank you," he says, a little absently, still typing.

When he presses send, I feel my pocket buzz.

I pick up one of the cookies and take a bite. "Holy shit," I say. "This is so good. Wow." I close my eyes. "It actually feels like it's doing something to my *soul*." When I open them, he's still staring at his screen. "Are you all right, Finn?"

"Yeah, I am," he says. But I can see something has changed. A familiar darkness clouds his features.

I put the cookie back on its plate. "You sure? You can tell me, you know. It's OK."

He lifts his phone and turns it.

On the screen is a photograph of an old lady with two gray plaits, smiling.

Eyes crinkled. Amber. Alive.

My stomach suddenly aches.

I look at the gold lettering beneath the picture.

In loving memory of Dr. Eileen Stone

It is the order of her funeral service.

"Eleanor just sent it in the group chat. Said it's the last time we all saw each other."

He clicks the phone so the screen turns a reflective black.

A moment passes between us. It is very quick, but in it is something so huge that it makes me feel like I'm about to be dragged down into the bottom of a well and swallowed up.

But it doesn't. It doesn't swallow me up. Because I know that he is here, experiencing it with me. I know that we are in it together.

"Hey, come here." I lean toward him across the table and put my fingers in the back of his hair. Then I move his head toward mine so our noses are inches apart.

He speaks very quietly. "I just—"

"It's OK."

"I just wish—"

"I know."

"I'm still angry."

"I am too."

"I'm still fucking *sad.*"

"Me too, Finn."

"I thought it might go by now. I thought it might finally just *go,* after everything. I'm trying, Seb, but . . . Fucking hell . . ."

"Stop."

He goes still. "Sorry."

"No, I mean . . . stop trying to feel different," I say. "I've spent my whole life trying. Trust me. It doesn't work, Finn. It's all right. You're all right."

Out of the corner of my eye I can see a bloke staring at us, smirking. But I don't care. *I do not care.*

I keep Finn right in front of me. And then I remember something Stone said to me in her hut. *We have it all within us already.*

"Let's not try and change anything, Finn."

"What do you mean?"

"We should just . . . let it be here with us. All the pain, the anger, the sadness. We should keep it. All of it. It's ours. We earned it. And no matter what people say, I don't think that's such a bad thing. I met you because of it. It got us out of that place. It got us here, didn't it? That's all we have. *This. Here. Right now.*"

I suddenly have a flash of a memory. Matthew pulling the knife out of Finn's stomach. It often happens. It just comes to me. A reminder of what people will do to be seen. To be approved. To be liked.

"You know, I've been thinking. And I've decided we have a choice, Finn. I've decided we can choose to believe it's OK that we aren't what people want us to be. I've decided we can choose not to let it make us feel bad about ourselves anymore. That we can choose not to let it make us dislike ourselves. And it doesn't mean we are wrong. Or unwell. We have the power, our own power, to be able to choose to say every day, 'I'm not what you want, and I won't keep trying to bend and twist to whatever that is, because ultimately, if I keep trying, it will destroy me.' I've decided that we can be free, if we allow ourselves. So let's just try and . . . block out the noise. Think about now. Because, really, that's all that exists and nothing else matters."

I watch as he exhales, a little shakily. He leans back on his chair and closes his eyelids. They begin to flutter. Like he is expelling the past, the future, the noise—everything but *this*—right out of him. When he opens them again, his eyes blaze back at me.

It warms me.

The color. The vibrancy.

Ice blue.

Ice Eyes.

There you are.

"That was cool, Seb," he says, the corners of his mouth turning up. "Cool little speech." And then he winks. Just a small one. I love it when he does that.

"Thanks," I say. "I try."

"Right now, I feel dead happy, Seb."

"Good. That's good, Finn." I smile. "Me too. I feel dead happy too."

Because everything in this moment is enough.

And whatever the next one is, whatever they all are—all the moments after it—we will be ready.

And some might not feel great.

Some might not feel happy.

Some might not be with him.

They might, but we don't need to think about that now.

They will happen.

And we'll meet them as they come.

And when we do, we'll try the best we can.

We will get through them.

We will keep going.

Because of everything that has come before.

"I'm here," I say.

"I know," he says. "I know you are."

You are here, Finn, and so am I, and that's it.

That's all there is.

NOTE FROM THE AUTHOR

If you have been struggling with your mental health, there are people you can talk to. For people from all walks of life, take a look at Crisis Text Line, Teen Lifeline, NAMI, and The Trevor Project.

Others include, CALM, No Panic, PAPYRUS, and SANE.

For people who identify as LGBTQ+, like Seb, Rainbow Mind is a brilliant charity that offers a place to feel safe, talk, and learn useful coping skills.

You can find them on Instagram, @rainbowminduk, and on Twitter.

I have struggled with my mental health throughout my life, and still can. Finding people who I can connect with, who can be trusted and understand, has kept me here.

However isolated you may feel, you are not alone, and it shall pass. All your best days are ahead of you. Stay present, the future will take care of itself.

With love, Josh

ACKNOWLEDGMENTS

Firstly, to the incredible team at Delacorte Press and Penguin Random House. Your energy and passion for this has been a joy to be a part of. Thank you. Particularly my wonderful editor, Kelsey Horton, for your guidance and support.

My agent, Becky Bagnell, for believing in this from the beginning.

My UK editor, Katie Jennings, for your patience, rigor, and impressive skills.

Thanks to Hayley for the fantastic cover art. Leah Middleton for your levelheadedness and diligence. Alex Devlin, Amy Threadgold, and Claudia Galluzzi from the team at the Right's People.

Special thanks to Molly Scull: I knew we'd stay in touch.

Kinx for your early notes and motivation. Christian Coulson for your thoughtfulness with this story and ongoing support. My friends: Jessie, Nomes, James, Jordan, and Chris, Alex and Ross, Chris, Jen, Vicky, Lisa, Jess, Brandon, Matt, Millie and Eliza. I am grateful to know you all.

Taron for your enthusiasm and encouragement. Oli, Noah, Coop, and Mick too. Thank you.

All the young people at Collingham, Simmons House, and Phoenix Ward. The inspiring nurses and health care assistants I have worked with.

My family. Mum and Dad. Tom, Ben and Dan. Will, Julia, Danni, Franklin, Emmeline, and Valentine.

Dodger.

The Lake District.

The Sale/Chorlton water park running loop for sorting my brain.

Social Refuge in Ancoats for being so welcoming.

Manchester.

And lastly Seb, Finn, and Eleanor. It's been a blast. I'm glad to have done this with you.

ABOUT THE AUTHOR

Josh Silver is the author of *HappyHead,* which was shortlisted for the YA Book Prize and nominated for the Carnegie Medal, and its sequel, *Dead Happy.* His experience working with teenagers as a mental health nurse inspired the critically acclaimed duology.